RAVES FOR GEORGE DAWES GREEN AND *THE JUROR*

"A heart-pounding, blood-chilling, page-turning tour de force... with a villain so perfectly evil, he makes Hannibal the Cannibal look like a vegetarian."
—Scott Turow, author of *Presumed Innocent* and *Pleading Guilty*

"Swift...entertaining...will leave you feeling jangly and vindicated." —*Boston Herald*

"A classy, romantic horror tale...The author knows how to simultaneously seduce and petrify an adult reader." —*Glamour*

"Marvelous...stylish and literate. It is set apart from a very crowded field of thrillers by the high quality of Green's descriptive prose, his dead-on dialogue, and his character development...Well-drawn characters will remain in your mind long after the book is finished...Green has proven himself a master storyteller with an enormous talent for inventing compelling plots filled with interesting and unusual characters." —*Seattle Times*

"Timely and fun." —*San Francisco Chronicle*

"A remarkable stylist." —*New York Times*

"A powerful writer." —Katherine Dunn

"The tension is nearly unbearable...a gem of deft plotting, given added luster through its rich characterizations. Annie is an especially fine creation...The plot, jittering from one brutal, clever twist to the next, will keep readers in a cold sweat. Green pushes buttons without remorse." —*Publishers Weekly* (starred review)

Please turn this page for more reviews and turn to the back of this book for a preview of George Dawes Green's new novel, *Ravens*.

"If you're looking for a taut, well-crafted thriller, deliberate no further: pick up a copy of THE JUROR."

—West Coast Review of Books

"I'm impressed...Green takes what is essentially a familiar theme and, with a few distinctive touches, turns it into something more."

—San Jose Mercury News

"An ingenious, scary, and captivating novel brimming with psychological terror that captivates from start to finish...Green keeps the suspense burner turned on high right to the novel's denouement."

—Fort Lauderdale Sun-Sentinel

"A smashing read that grips the reader like an ever-tightening vise. With a flair for provocative plotting and stylish prose, Green shows himself to be a hot young writer to watch." *—Flint Journal*

"A titanium version of the thriller, highly polished, hard-edged, coolly efficient, designed for speed...Stylistic brevity serves to intensify the story's tense, staccato pace."

—Seattle Post-Intelligencer

"Ruthless to the core, plausible to the last gunshot—and a whole lot of fun...The beauty of the story is that everyone has brains. Everyone's one step ahead of everyone else. The reader just has to sit back and let it unfold. None of the usual second-guessing applies."

—Dayton Daily News

"Sparkling...deliciously original...The story rushes to its inevitable and thrilling conclusion, conveyed through a host of brilliantly sketched characters. Dawes brings his poet's ear for dead-on dialogue and an artist's eye for deftly drawn scenes...A compelling view of the passions and compulsions that rule us, wrapped in a page-flipping story." *—Lexington Herald-Leader*

"Fast-moving, violent, and totally unpredictable...shows readers there's more to scrutinize in a courtroom than the theatrics of dapper attorneys in their expensive threads."

—Greensboro News & Record

GEORGE DAWES GREEN

THE JUROR

GRAND CENTRAL
PUBLISHING

NEW YORK   BOSTON

Grateful acknowledgment is made for permission to quote from "The Gulf" from *The Gulf* by Derek Walcott. Copyright © 1970 by Derek Walcott. Reprinted by permission of Farrar, Straus & Giroux, Inc. Grateful acknowledgment is also made to Faber and Faber Ltd. for permission to quote from "The Gulf" from *Collected Poems 1948–1984* by Derek Walcott.

Publisher's Note: This novel is a work of fiction. Names, characters, places, and incidents either are the product of the author's imagination or are used fictitiously, and any resemblance to actual persons, living or dead, events, or locales is entirely coincidental.

Grand Central Publishing
Hachette Book Group
237 Park Avenue
New York, NY 10017

Visit our Web site at www.HachetteBookGroup.com.

Printed in the United States of America

First Trade Edition: June 2009
10 9 8 7 6 5 4 3 2 1

Grand Central Publishing is a division of Hachette Book Group, Inc.
The Grand Central Publishing name and logo is a trademark of Hachette Book Group, Inc.

The Library of Congress has cataloged the hardcover edition as follows:
Green, George Dawes.
    The juror / George Dawes Green.
       p.   cm.
    ISBN 978-0-446-51885-7
    1. Trials (Murder)—New York (State)—Westchester—Fiction.
2. Women jurors—New York (State)—Westchester—Fiction.
3. Mafia—New York (State)—Westchester—Fiction.
4. Westchester (N.Y.)—Fiction.   I. Title.
    PS3557.R3717J87   1995
    813'.54—dc20
                                                                          94-18831
                                                                          CIP

ISBN 978-0-446-55015-4 (pbk.)

Book design by L. McRee

For my father,
always wandering the oak grove,
playing pibrochs on his bagpipes

For my mother,
always radiating love

And for my beloved brother and sisters—
Rob, Om, Burch, and Alyce,
always pickin on me

Acknowledgments

A legion of kindly guides ...

Glenn Brazil, at the Federal Law Enforcement Training Center in Brunswick, Georgia, counseled me in surveillance and eavesdropping techniques. Jim Koster reviewed the arsenal. Bob Stapleton, retired Senior Investigator for the New York State Troopers, helped me to stalk the Teacher.

Among those who advised me in aspects of criminal court procedure were my old friend Tony Maccarini; Jim Rooney, Chief Assistant District Attorney for Putnam County, New York; Judge John Sweeney, Jr., Putnam County Court Judge; Stephen Saracco, Manhattan Assistant District Attorney; George Buchhert of the Orange County Sheriff's Department; and Judge Ronald Adams of Glynn County, Georgia.

Medical advice came from Dr. Amy Gelfand, Dr. Kirk Hochstetler, and Marland Dulaney, the Sage of Pharmacology.

My choice of birds and moths and operas was influenced by the uncanny erudition of Julio de la Torre. Tim Groover and Rick Hood tended the orchids, Susann Craig the costumes. Angela Tribelli helped me with the Italian, Leo Iterregui the Spanish, and Margo Danne-

ACKNOWLEDGMENTS

miller the Mam. Alex Mason provided the dragons. Other abettors include Timothy Horan, Ann Clark, Joel Ettinger, Thalia Broudy, Julia Carson, and Crystal Chamberlain.

Finally, a few of the Most Exalted Seraphs of Divinity in this writer's addled brain. My agent Molly Friedrich and her colleague Sheri Holman, who were not afraid of the Caveman. My editor Jamie Raab, who brought us in from the Y-ray wilderness. And all those who provided sustaining love: Drew and Ellen and Paula and Daniel and Larry and Nancy and Keith, and the crew at Wanda's, and the hard-rockin, breathtaking Kellie Parr.

Words don't work here.

1

Varnish, putty, char, clay, moss

Fur, wax, turpentine, ink, cedar

EDDIE, in the spectators' gallery, leans forward. Prospective Juror 224 has just said something that he couldn't hear. That in fact nobody in this courtroom could hear. Judge Wietzel asks her to move the mike closer.

Juror 224 takes the neck of the mike and pulls it up to her. Then gives it a quick choke. Strong rough scratched-up farmwife hands she's got—they don't match the rest of her. They don't match her gentle gray eyes, which now sweep softly across the courtroom, and light upon the defendant, Louie Boffano.

She says, "I don't think so. No:"

"Are you sure?" says Judge Wietzel. "You've *never* seen Mr. Boffano? In the newspapers? On TV?"

"No sir."

Wietzel casts her a withering look. "Do you *read* newspapers, ma'am?"

This gets him a chuckle from his toadies up front. Fuckin Wietzel, thinks Eddie. Shit on toast he thinks he is. That look he's giving the juror. The arrogant way he flicks his gavel to quiet the laughter.

But Juror 224 doesn't rattle. She says softly, "I read the paper when I have the time."

"How often is that?"

"Never."

Eddie likes this woman. Kind of weary-looking, but she takes no

3

crap from Wietzel, and Eddie likes the way those big gray eyes slide along sort of slow and then suddenly pounce on something—as though there were lots of wonderful things to catch sight of in this courtroom. Though as far as Eddie can see it's just the usual floating courtroom sewage.

She tells the court, "I'm a single mother, Your Honor. And I'm trying to be a sculptor? I have, well, just a job in the day, and when I get home I take care of my son. Then at night, at night with whatever time I've got left I work on my pieces. I mean it's tough to find any free time. I feel ignorant saying I don't keep up with the news, but that's how it is, I don't. I don't have time."

She must come from some other planet, thinks Eddie. From some place where they've all got eyes like that, and they all work hard and take care of their little boys and make art at night, take out their chisels and make *sculptures* for Christ sake—until one day one of them gets in her rocketship and comes halfway across the universe and lands here in this pit of shit and doesn't even know enough to be *scared*.

I mean here she is, Eddie thinks, surrounded by all these vipers in three-piece silk suits, by barracuda whose hearts run on grease, who would tear her apart with their *teeth* if someone gave them the word—and she just blinks those big gray eyes at them and that's it—that's her whole defense, take it or leave it.

But Wietzel frowns at her. "Ma'am, you're saying you've heard *nothing* about this case?"

224 turns and lifts her eyes to him.

"Well, no. I have heard . . . something."

"And would you share that with us?"

"Yesterday I told my son I was going to be on jury duty today. So I might not be able to pick him up. I mean when I usually do. And he said, 'Hey, Mom, maybe you'll get on that big Mafia case.' And I said, 'What big Mafia case?' And he said, 'You know, Louie Boffano—they're gonna try him for *popping* these guys.' "

Rising swell of greasy laughter from the gallery.

Eddie checks on his boss. Louie Boffano's back is to the gallery. All Eddie can see of him is a sliver of cheek. But that sliver fattens out some, and Eddie figures that Louie's flashing one of his famous devil-damn-me grins at the prospective juror.

But she doesn't seem to notice. She plows right on. She says:

"My son told me that *popping* was, when you pop somebody,

4

that's the same as killing them. And I said, 'OK, I got that, but who's Louie Boffano?' And he said I was really dumb not to know. I said, 'OK, I'm really dumb. Who is he?' He said, 'Mom, come *on*—he's the big Spaghetti-O.' "

Wietzel gets his gavel going pretty quick, but it sounds like a drummer's rimshots after a comic has landed a stinger. The laughter resounds. The lawyers, the media assholes, the gawkers—all that scum is in bliss. Wietzel himself is having a wrestling match with his lips, trying to pin them down. And at the defendant's table, Eddie's boss is roaring. He's got his head thrown back so far you can see his face upside down. He wants us all to see what a good time he's having. To see the sumptuous pleasure Louie Boffano draws from being called the Big Spaghetti-O.

The only one not laughing is Juror 224 herself. Her gray gaze is still drifting around the room, and drinking up the scene, and what plays on her face now, Eddie thinks, is not amusement, it's pride. She's simply proud of her kid's cleverness. Sort of the way Eddie himself felt that time last year when his daughter won Honorable Mention in Domestic Science at Mamaroneck High.

Wietzel pounds down the uproar. "If we have any more of these outbursts," he says, "I'm giving you all fair warning, I will not hesitate to clear this court."

Oh Wietzel, thinks Eddie. You'll *never* clear this court. You crave an audience every bit as much as Louie Boffano does. I mean if we were having a *food fight* in here, if we were all *mooning* each other, still it would break your heart to clear the court. So stick your bullshit back up your ass where it belongs.

When at last the judge gets the gloomy pindrop silence he's waiting for, he asks, "Do you think that what your son told you will influence your verdict in this case?"

"No."

"No prejudice for or against the defendant?"

"My son is twelve years old, Your Honor."

Eddie glances at the prosecutor's table. Michael Tallow, the DA for Westchester County, is whispering to one of his pawns.

Eddie sees him lift one shoulder just a notch.

Sort of a shrug.

It means he'll take her. Christ.

Nine murder trials out of ten, a white single mother from Westchester, that'd spell *acquittal*. And an artist? That'd put it in caps. And

5

that goofy South American handbag she's carrying? Ah, Jesus, that'd put it in whimpering yellow on a big white flag of surrender: PLEASE, YOUR HONOR, OH PLEASE LET THE POOR OPPRESSED MR. SPAGHETTI-O GO *FREE*.

Nine cases out of ten, the DA wouldn't go anywhere near the bleeding heart of a babe like this.

But this is a *mob* trial.

This is one time Tallow will be *looking* for weepers. For anybody old-fashioned enough to think a syndicate hit is still *murder*, and not just an unpleasantness among hoodlums. For anybody who might actually bemoan the passing of that gutter-rat Salvadore Riggio and his spoiled grandson, anyone sucker enough to shed a tear when the guy's widow takes the stand and the gnashing of teeth begins.

Tallow's assistant nods back at him—the slightest nod.

It's done then: they'll take 224.

Which pisses Eddie off. He likes this alien. Stupid, but there it is. He doesn't see why *she* should have to swim in this slime. So what if there was once a little bad blood between Louie Boffano and Salvadore Riggio, what the hell does that have to do with her? Why not let her go home to her kid and her art and her own little workaday worries?

Why should those great gray eyes be obliged to absorb this pollution?

Let her go.

And by God Wietzel seems to hear Eddie's silent plea. For once in his life Wietzel does something fair and just and good. He looks down upon 224 from his high altar and he says, "You may be excused, ma'am. If you like."

A silly grin starts to go up on Eddie's face.

The judge goes on, "I'll try to keep this trial short, but I'm sure it will last several weeks at the least. And during deliberations, you will be sequestered. This court is well aware that a trial of this nature can present unreasonable hardships for some jurors. You've told us that you're a single mother, that your economic situation is somewhat strained. That's enough for me. If you say it would present a grave hardship for you to serve on this jury—I'll excuse you."

Why, Wietzel! You know, Wietzel, I was looking forward to erasing your ugly bucket face someday—but now maybe I won't. On account of this little rag of mercy you've extended to my sweet 224.

But 224 isn't getting up and going. She's still sitting there. She has her eyes lowered, and clearly she's thinking this over. Thinking hard.

Oh Christ. *Get out of here now.*

She looks up and asks the judge, "If I did serve, would I, um, would I be safe?"

Wietzel frowns. Seems surprised himself that she isn't scurrying on her way, but he collects himself and says, "Of course. You'll be perfectly safe. In fact, let me say again that *no* juror has *ever* been harmed in a trial in Westchester County. That doesn't mean that we won't take precautions. For example, although I don't think it's necessary to sequester you throughout the trial, I have instructed that all the jurors are to be driven to and from this courthouse daily from some location known only to yourselves and your driver. Your anonymity will be *treasured* here. No one will know your name. *I* won't even know your name. But I will always be available to you. And in the event that anyone *does* try to influence your verdict on this case, you have only to say a word to me, in private, in my chambers, and those persons will be dealt with to the fullest extent of the law. So in this regard you can feel perfectly secure."

Oh, bite me, Eddie thinks.

Wietzel, you son of a stinking turd, *bite me.*

Juror 224 is thoughtfully pursing her lips, and her alien gray eyes are glimmering and she says, "Well, then, then I think I could get someone to take care of my son. For when I'm sequestered."

"And you *would* like to serve?"

"Um. Yes. I would. Yes."

It dawns on Eddie that here we've got the dumbest woman ever to walk the face of the earth.

Says Wietzel, "I commend you for your good citizenship, and I ask that you return tomorrow for further examination by the prosecution and by counsel for the defense. Thank you, you're excused for now."

Juror 224 rises. She seems exhausted. It hasn't been easy for her, arriving at that noble bonehead resolution. She's confused and doesn't know which way to go. The bailiff beckons her, and she follows him. She's a small woman. Her walk is plain but with a wisp of a wobble. A holdover maybe from when she was a kid trying to act like a starlet. Or maybe she's just unsteady from sitting around all day waiting to be called.

Whichever, that walk gets to Eddie.

He watches her go, watches the nice flip side of that wobble.

And then he sees Louie Boffano turn. Just for an instant, to glance at someone sitting way over on the other side of the spectators' gallery.

Louie Boffano has his lower lip tucked under his teeth. It's as thoughtful a look as you'll ever get out of the guy. He wants someone back there to see that look.

Then he looks away again. And no one knows that Louie has flashed a sign with that glance.

It's OK by me if that's the one you want. She's yours.

Eddie swivels his head.

The man Louie was signaling to is all the way back near the corner of the gallery. Surrounded by trial freaks, a nobody. He wears a bland turtleneck and moony tinted glasses and a furry fake blond mustache. He has no presence at all. He's gazing at nothing. At vapors. He looks to be lost in what you'd guess—if you didn't know Vincent the way Eddie knows him—were the most trivial and commonplace of thoughts.

Suddenly he gets up.

Eddie glares at his own fist in his lap and he thinks, OK then you brain-dead bitch, this is what you wanted? OK you got it. Who's going to help you now?

When he looks back, the space where Vincent was sitting is now empty.

Eddie silently counts to twenty. Then he rises and pushes his way down the row of spectators out to the aisle. He keeps his head low, and he nods to the guard and pushes open the huge door, and he leaves the courtroom. He passes quickly through the ugly jagged-edge Buck-Rogers lobby.

He goes to do what he's paid to do.

ANNIE sits in the old Subaru and waits on her son Oliver, who's studying the buckle of his seat belt. He's always studying things. He stares too long at even the simplest tasks before he gets down to work. Sometimes he'll stare so long he forgets what he's supposed to be doing.

Dreamland. He drives her crazy.

"Oliver. Let's go."

He gets the belt snapped in.

She backs out of Mrs. Kolodny's driveway and turns onto Ratner Avenue.

"Hey guess what," she says. "You were a star today."

"Bull. I was the *zero* kid today. You know where Jesse is on DragonRider? *Fifth* Dome—he did it last night. I can't get into the Second Dome without some Troll-Slave clobbering my ass. Jesse and Larry say I'm a retard 'cause I can't find the Invisible Potion."

"Maybe the Invisible Potion is in the Fallen Keep?"

"Wrong again," says Oliver. "Larry says it's in the Western Shire. The freakin Western Shire."

"Maybe Nintendo's not your forte and you should concentrate on something else."

"It's not Nintendo, Mom. It's Sega."

"Maybe you should take up some other specialty. Like school-work."

"Yeah, right," he says. "No *doubt*."

"Or maybe Jesse's trying to throw you off the track. Maybe there isn't any Invisible Potion."

"The kid's a lying weasel all right."

"You shouldn't say that about your friends."

"No doubt."

They come to the lake and take a left on Old Willow Avenue. They pass the town library, which used to be a chapel. Autumn's starting to take hold. Jolts of rust and ruby in the sycamores along the lake.

Oliver pulls from his pocket a piece of Booger Bubblegum. He stares at the wrapper. Unwraps it. Studies the wad. Pops it in his mouth.

"Anyway," she tells him, "you *were* the star today. Star of the county court. They asked me if I'd ever heard of Louie Boffano and I told them my son had called him the big Spaghetti-O and that got a big laugh."

"Wow. You're really on that case?"

"If they take me."

They pass Cardi's Funeral Home.

"And you're going to do it? You're gonna be a juror on *that* case? Are you nuts, Mom?"

Good question.

There was that moment, on the stand, when she was on the verge of asking the judge if she might be excused, considering she's got a son to raise and a boss who's threatening to lynch her if she doesn't get out of jury duty. Plus a show going on at Inez's gallery for her sculpture.

Then, when she said she'd do it, everyone must have figured her for a lunatic. That's how she figures it herself. What other conclusion can she draw?

"I don't know," she says. "Well, you know it wasn't just the old godfather who got killed. They got his grandson too. Fourteen years old. I guess I was thinking about you. I guess I thought it was my duty. I'm always telling *you* about being responsible and all. Right?"

"Sure."

"You see what I'm saying?"

"Sure."

"Well OK, you want the truth? Maybe I thought it'd be exciting.

I think I'm getting a little worn out with the grind. I mean . . . it really wasn't such a bright idea, was it?"

"Mom, is this for real? You're on the *Louie Boffano* trial? Wait'll Jesse hears this."

"No. Jesse's not hearing nothing. Neither is anyone else. I mean I shouldn't have told *you*. Listen, Oliver, it's a *secret* that I'm a juror on this case. Nobody knows my name. Not even the judge. They call me by a number. I'm completely anonymous—you know what that means?"

"Sure, it means they won't put your picture in the *Weekly World News*. That won't stop Louie Boffano. If he wants to find you—"

"Oh quit it. He wouldn't dare. They've got a word for that, you know, it's called tampering. You know what would happen to him if he were caught tampering with a juror?"

"What?"

"He'd go to jail."

"But he's already *in* jail. Probably for the rest of his life. So what's he got to lose?"

"Oliver. This is serious. This isn't a game. The reason I'm a lunatic to do this isn't because it's dangerous—it's not. It's just that it's such a nuisance. Mr. Slivey's going to kill me for taking the time from work. And when the TV's on I'll have to be careful that I don't see anything about the trial. And anything in the *Reporter Dispatch*? You'll have to cut it out so I don't see it."

"But you never read the paper anyway, Mom."

"I know, but still."

"You just wrap things in it."

"I just want to be sure. You know? And when the trial's over and we start to deliberate, I'll be sequestered. Means I'll have to stay in a motel for a while. You'll have to stay with Mrs. Kolodny."

Oliver nearly chokes on his gum. "Mrs. Kolodny? You mean *overnight*? Mom, tell me you're kidding."

"I tell you I'm *not* kidding. Yes, overnight. More than one night."

"How long?"

"Don't know. However long it takes to reach a verdict. Maybe a week. Or, I don't know."

"A week? Why? You go out, you come back in, you say 'Guilty.' You say, 'Fry the sucker.' How long can that take?"

"I don't know."

"Six seconds?"

"Maybe. Or maybe a week."

"A *week* with Mrs. Kolodny? Momba, why are you doing this to me?"

Annie shrugs.

The road forks and she takes Seminary Lane up the hill away from the lake. A pair of big three-story Queen Anne elephants to the right, with a view to the water. On the left are homelier cottages. She slows and turns at their own small bungalow. She tells Oliver, "OK, you got two minutes to change your clothes, then I'm taking you to work with me."

"Mom!" Panicky whine. "I'm supposed to meet Jesse at the church-yard—"

"Can't help you. I promised Mr. Slivey. Got to post some orders, that's all. Only an hour or so—"

"Mom, in an hour it'll be *dark*. Jeez, I trashed the whole freakin afternoon at Mrs. Kolodny's and now you tell me—"

"Two minutes, you miserable little snot. Hustle."

THE TEACHER waits in the red Lotus S4. He's got Vivaldi's Concerto Grosso in A Minor coming over the Magnus. He's parked on a side street, which runs into Seminary Lane two hundred yards ahead of him. His car sits under a linden tree, under a razor-blue sky. He has the speaker turned up on the cellular phone, and his friend at DMV is telling him:

"License JXA-385 is registered to an Annie Laird. Address: 48 Seminary Lane, Pharaoh, New York. Anything else?"

The Teacher speaks above the violins. "This woman has a son. He's twelve years old, I presume he's in elementary school or middle school somewhere around here. Could you find out something about him?"

"I can try."

"Don't push, don't force it. Drop it if you can't finesse it."

Skirl of wind. Leaf-shadow trembling on the red hood before him. A girl sails past on her bike. Liquid-limbed, maybe sixteen. Her near haunch is piston-straight as she coasts past. She seems to admire his red car. Am I too conspicuous, he wonders, in such a vivid red Lotus on such a plain street? Am I taking unnecessary risks?

I am, yes.

He whistles along with the flute.

The cellular phone buzzes, and he touches the panel.

"Yes."

Eddie's voice: "Vincent. She's coming out of her house now."

"With her child?"

"Yeah. With."

"They don't see you?"

"No. I'm parked way down. OK, they're getting in her car."

"Careful. I think she sounded somewhat frightened in court today. She might be looking for a tail. If she comes your way—"

"She's not gonna. She's going up *your* way, Vincent—and she's in a fuckin hurry."

"*Up* the hill?"

"Yeah."

"Get on her, Eddie."

"Yeah."

"But give her plenty of room. If you lose her, that's no tragedy, we'll pick her up some other time—but *don't let her spot you.*"

Then the Teacher waits.

A moment later, he sees Annie Laird's car blur by, on Seminary Lane. Only one glimpse of her. Her worn-at-the-edges loveliness.

Next, Eddie's car passes by.

The Teacher pulls out, but he doesn't follow them. He drives the other way, back down the hill. To his right a few houses, then a long stand of woods, and then he comes to her rusted mailbox. He eases up, his eyes prowling.

Across the road is another stand of trees, sloping down toward some big houses and the lake. Must be a stunning view in the pitch of winter, with the trees bare, but for now there's still some feeling of seclusion. On Annie's side of the street the next bungalow is a hundred yards down, and there's a prim wood fence in between.

He pulls into her drive. Takes his car all the way to the back, to the space between the bungalow and the old wood barn behind it.

Quiet back here.

He attaches the phone to his belt. Takes his Heckler & Koch P7 from the glove compartment and slips it into the shoulder holster under his jacket. He reaches under the seat and draws out his doctor's bag.

As he walks up to the bungalow a male mockingbird opens up in the big Indian bean tree above him. *Mimus polyglottos,* the Teacher's favorite.

Two cracked-concrete steps up to the back porch. The screen door whimpers as he opens it. Wasps' nests over the lintel—that clay-pot smell of old wasps' nests. Then the clutter of the porch. An old sofa, eruptions of stuffing. Carcass of a freezer, tires, lacrosse stick and lacrosse mask. Two bikes in fair condition. One with the masculine crossbar, the other without. Therefore they take bike rides together, mother and child. OK. Maybe we'll ride with them someday.

It takes him less than half a minute to pick the lock with his lock-gun.

He steps into the big airy kitchen. Sets his bag on the enamel-top kitchen table and withdraws from it a Mustek page scanner and a Toshiba notebook computer.

He scans into memory the list of numbers by the telephone. He rummages in the tall desk and finds some letters, some bills, invitations to gallery openings. These he also scans.

But he simply purloins the loose, scattered pages of an old telephone bill. She'll never miss them.

He uses his Phillips to remove the cover on the wall phone. Behind the printed circuit board he sets a small black device with two pairs of wires coming out of it: an "infinity bug." For monitoring both the phone *and* the kitchen. One pair of wires is already hooked to the supersensitive Lartel microphone. Using wire nuts, he parallel-connects the other pair to the telephone wires.

While he's working, Eddie calls him on the cellular.

"She stopped up at the top of the hill, Vincent. Couple of miles from you. Big old building, got a sign out front says 'Devotional Services, Inc.' Parking lot's empty. I guess everybody's gone home by now. She went in with the kid. Used a key."

"Where are you?"

"Up the road from her. Turned around. I'm ready."

"What do you suppose she's doing?"

Says Eddie, "I dunno. Must be some kind of church. Maybe she's praying. Maybe she's some kind a religious freak. You know?"

The Teacher grins. "She's at work, Eddie."

"Yeah, right. Working for some guru who dicks her every Tuesday afternoon. Vincent, you ought to let this one go. You can't read fuckin religious bozos. They get weird on you, they don't think straight—"

Then I'll tame her, the Teacher thinks, *with the simplicity of the Nameless.*

Says Eddie, "I'm telling you, she's bad news, I smell trouble."

"Eddie, I think what you're smelling is your own fear."

The Teacher disconnects.

In the homey, sloppy TV room, he shoves aside a pile of old newspapers and *Art in America*s and finds a wall socket. He unscrews the cover and installs a Hastings 3600 mike linked to a parasitic transmitter.

He notices a photograph on the wall. Some hound-eyed guy looking soulfully toward the camera. Behind him is a thatch cottage and goats and a cornfield. He's wearing a shirt with a Guatemalan ikat design.

Her brother? Her lover?

The Teacher recalls that Annie carried a Guatemalan handbag into court with her.

He soaks up the photograph with the scanner.

Then he takes his bag and goes upstairs, to the bungalow's broad-shouldered garret, to where Annie and her child have their bedrooms.

ANNIE has a mantra for times like these:

If I'm a data processor now, a data processor and nothing but a data processor, I can be an artist two hours from now.

She thinks it again. She shuts her eyes. She concentrates.

If I'm a pure and immaculate vessel for data processing . . .

She laces her fingers together and stretches them. Then she opens her eyes and goes to work.

She becomes a fiend, a speed-trance demon, and she enters one order in one minute thirty-seven seconds, and the next in fifty-six seconds.

Mostly the orders are for *Knockin' the Devil WAYYYY Back!*—the new dual-cassette album featuring the hyperenthused Reverend Calvin Ming.

Other orders ask for the Rev.'s golden oldies:

You Need a POWER-Scrub for Those Sins!

Say Yes! Yes! Yes! Yes! YES! To Jesus!

One scoop of the wrist to slice the envelope open, a quick jerk to slip the order out. Some of the handwriting is atrocious, and only by reading the addresses with her gut and not letting her brain get involved can she decipher them. Her fingers skim over the keys like a horde of gnats.

Eighteen more orders and I'm gone, I'm the wind blowing out of here.

She doesn't pause to consider how much she loathes this job. Knowing that if she stopped to reflect on that for even an instant, she'd be obliged to get up and pace around and fume and pound the desk and shriek *Say No! No! No! No! NO! To This Shitwork*! And scare the hell out of Oliver, who's sitting peacefully in the corner pondering his math homework.

And what good would it do? She's never going to get out of here. She needs the flexibility of this job. Slivey may be an asshole, but he lets her set her own hours, and because she's come to know the business better than he does himself, he grudgingly tolerates her many zone-out screw-ups.

So she types, she rides those keys, she gathers momentum. When bored Oliver asks her an odd kid question, she furnishes her odd adult reply without any thought at all. Without slowing a beat. When Oliver gets up and starts playing some game that involves taking three one-footed hops then turning and launching a wadded-up sheet of notebook paper at the benign image of our most Reverend Calvin Ming, she only murmurs, "Oliver. Sit. Math."

She loses no time, and soon she has only four orders left.

Then the phone rings.

"Damn."

Slivey.

He starts, "I left you a stack—"

"I'm doing them now, Mr. Slivey. I'll leave them on your desk."

"All right. And what time will you be rolling in tomorrow?"

"I won't be rolling in at all. You know that. I've got jury duty."

"Oh, you're kidding. I thought I told you to get out of that."

"You did. But I didn't. It's my civic responsibility, Mr. Slivey."

"Your ci-vic re-spons-ibili-ty?" He sniffs. Big disdainful snort of air. "Uh-huh. And have you forgotten your responsibility to the Lord?"

"I never forget the Lord, Mr. Slivey." *He pays my wages.*

"Who's going to get out the orders? Who's going to figure out your filing system—"

"Corinna can—"

"Corinna? Corinna's a fucking idiot."

"Mr. *Slivey*."

"Claim hardship. I mean it. Tell the judge about the Lord's work here. Tell—"

"I've got to go."

"Annie—"

"Praise the Lord, Mr. Slivey."

She hangs up on him.

She blazes into those last orders.

And when at last she has keyed in and printed out, she carries the whole mess over to Corinna's desk and dumps it there.

I'm free. Sort of. For a little while.

She steps over quietly to where Oliver is sitting and writing intently. She looks over his shoulder. First-Shield Auxbar and his faithful lizard-steed Rog are racing through the Tunnel of the Accursed.

Oliver looks up at her. Blinks. "What?"

"Math."

"This is, this is for English. English homework."

"Yeah, a likely story. Let's go."

"So soon, Mom? You sure you don't want to stay longer? I mean this place is such a Blast-O-Rama. . . ."

THE TEACHER opens the door to Annie's barn-studio. As he feels for the light switch he gets a whiff of her materials. Varnish, putty, char, clay, moss. Fur, wax, turpentine, ink, cedar: he picks out the scents one by one. Breathing, quietly, in the dark. Then at last he finds the light.

The place is bedlam. Works-in-progress everywhere. Tools running wild.

His gaze roams randomly till he sees the sculptures on the far wall.

They don't look much like sculptures. They're simply a row of crates, like orange crates perhaps, except that the spaces between the slats have been sealed, and the wood has been stained and lacquered all over. And beneath each crate is a brief coquettish skirt.

As the Teacher approaches, he sees that above one of the crates, taped to the wall, is a newspaper headline:

CARDINAL O'CONNOR ASSERTS: GOD IS MALE.

He puts his hand under the skirt of this crate. He reaches up into the darkness until his fingers encounter something heavy and globular and furry. As big as a grapefruit, hanging there in the dark. He feels along the fur and comes to another great globe, in the same sac as the first.

Two huge hairy testicles.

God's balls?

He laughs out loud. He squeezes one of them. Our juror, he thinks, has a sense of humor.

Then Eddie calls and tells him, "Vincent, she's out the door. With the kid."

"All right."

The Teacher gives God's balls a last playful squeeze, and he moves on to the next crate. He asks Eddie, "If she comes this way, how much time will I have?"

"Two, three minutes."

Above the next crate is a piece of sketch paper that says, "Alzheimer's. For Mom." The Teacher reaches under the skirt. His hand finds a chamber shaped like the inside of a skull.

Says Eddie, "OK, now she's pulling out of the lot. She don't see me. She's coming your way."

There's some sort of testiness in his voice.

"Eddie?"

"What?"

"What do you think of her?"

Moment of silence.

"What do you mean, what do I *think* of her? I don't think nothing of her."

"You seem protective of her."

"Protective? I just think she's bad news. I think she's a fuckin nun."

"But she couldn't be an absolute nun, could she? She has a child. She's had some kind of sex life. Don't you think she's sort of sexy, Eddie?"

"Come on. She's a fuckin *mommy*."

"Those eyes? You don't find them sexy?"

"Vincent, you getting out of there? She's coming pretty fast."

The Teacher's fingers are running along the cracked delft tiling of that skull-chamber. Something grows in the cracks. It feels like moss. And shreds of gossamer netting tickle the hair on the back of his wrist. Alzheimer's. Falling into dereliction, falling apart.

He tells Eddie, "I think she's sexy and I think she's also brilliant."

"Yeah? Hot shit."

"She makes sculptures that you can't see. That you can only feel."

"Hot steaming shit," says Eddie.

There's another box called *The Dream of Giving Notice,* and this title piques him, but there's no time to give the box a grope. Another visit then. Something to look forward to. He steps away.

It takes him less than a minute to set an "infinity bug" into the phone extension.

When he goes out he shuts the door softly behind him.

He backs the S4 out of the driveway and heads down Seminary Lane. Down, and then up a little rise, and then before he dips again he checks his rearview mirror and gets a glimpse of Annie Laird and her child in their old Subaru, on their way home.

ANNIE and Oliver, that evening after supper, are up in Oliver's room in the aquarium glow of his computer monitor. Oliver is working on his bowl of ice cream. Annie's at the game controls.

"What is this place?" she asks.

"Castle Keep."

"Right, I know that. But what's a keep?"

"I don't know, Mom. It's in a castle. It's the keep. You know."

"Oh God, who are *they*?"

"Don't panic. They're Troll-Slaves. No sweat."

"I have the impression these gentlemen want to hurt me."

"They're retards, Mom. They're real slow. Use your sword, they won't hurt you. No! Don't go that way!"

"Help! What's *that*?"

"It's a trap door! Don't!"

"What? Where do I go? . . . Oliver!"

"Just chill, Momba. They come to you? You waste em."

"Where? Where? What do I, they're coming!"

"This button. Here, hit this button! . . . Yes! Now get the other one! Nail the fucker!"

"Oliver."

"I mean sucker, *hit him*! Mom! Where are you going?"

"I don't know! Help! How do I turn around?"

"Here! This! Get him! Yes! Yes!"

"Yes!"

"All right, Momba!"

"They're dead?"

"They're dead."

"I did it?"

"You're OK. How do you feel?"

"I feel good."

"You should feel good."

"I'm not thinking about the widows of these Troll-Slaves here. I know that little Troll-Slave children will be crying for their fathers tonight, but I feel good. Very clear-headed. HOLY CHRIST! What's that!"

"It's a spider, Mom. Just chill. It's only a Death-Spider."

THE TEACHER crouches and studies the lights of her house.

Then he hears that mocker again, slightly hoarse, a quick knifeplay of notes. He looks up. The bird's song seems to come from a nearby beech tree. Here at the edge of the woods, at the edge of Annie Laird's lawn. He looks up. Studies the dark branches of that tree.

He judges it to be a good climbing tree.

So he starts to climb.

The bird's shadow flits away.

He ascends, spiraling around the trunk nimbly—though he has two heavy boxes strapped to his back. Two olive-drab 50 caliber ammo boxes, each of them fitted into a bed of twigs and clay and leaves, so they look something like squirrel's nests.

He climbs till he's twenty feet up with a clear view of the bungalow. Then he shinnies onto a limb and hangs one of the nests. This nest holds a battery pack. He runs the power cord from this battery farther out along the limb, and then he hangs the other ammo box.

As he works, the mocker sings again. It's a better tune now than the one it sang this afternoon. More ethereal, more pulse under the melody line. Night always brings out the mocker's highest art.

He opens the lid on the second box. Inside are five ICOM 7000 receivers, tuned to pick up the three "infinity bugs" in Annie's three telephones and the parasitic transmitters in the TV room and the child's bedroom. He feeds the five pliable antennas through a hole in the ammo box, and runs them out along the branch he's clinging to, securing them with bungees.

The four receivers are tied into a Motorola multiplexer. He fits an earplug in his left ear and jacks the cord into the multiplexer, and on the digital tuner he summons up channel one: 143.925 megahertz. The kitchen.

He listens. He hears a soft occasional *ping*ing. Leaky faucet.

He touches the channel selector. The boy's room.

The right place.

He hears the mosquito whine of a video-game theme song, and Annie's voice:

"Kill it? How am I going to kill it! It's bigger than I am!"

Then the kid, laughing: "Death-Spiders, you got to cut off *all* their legs."

Annie: "What!"

Then the *snick-snick* of some video-game weapon.

Peals of laughter in the Teacher's left ear. Meanwhile his right ear picks up a little of the real thing, the kid's actual laugh, coming directly, faintly, from the house.

"Die!" shrieks Annie. "Why don't you *die*?"

"All its legs, Mom!"

"I can't!"

"Watch out! Troll-Slaves!"

"Oh, for God's, help!"

Snick-snick. Snick-snick.

Annie crying out, "Aaaaiiiieeeeee . . ."

The music plays a slow dismal dirge.

Oliver says, "You clown."

Still, he begs her to stay and play another game.

She will not, though. She says she has to work. The Teacher sees movement at the bungalow's upstairs window. The flash of her maroon shirt, and then he hears her clopping down the stairs.

He adjusts the channel selector and picks up the kitchen. He hears her humming that video-game tune. He sees her in the yellow light of the kitchen window. She pauses at the fridge. Three leaves go tumbling past the windowframe, the frame of light. She takes a long pull from some bottle. She stands there, not moving. She looks out the window into the absorbing dark. He hears her sigh. Even from this far, he can see a wooziness in the way she's standing—she's utterly worn out.

Then she collects herself. And with her weight on her toes, forced jauntiness, she steps outside. Letting the screen door slam behind her, she moves into the darkness of the driveway. The light comes on in her barn-studio. She goes in and shuts the door.

A minute later a Joan Armatrading song comes pouring from her boom box.

The Teacher pulls the earplug from his ear, and from its jack.

In the ammo box beside the multiplexer is an industrial cellular phone. He lifts the receiver, punches in a number.

His lover, Sari, answers on the first ring. "Yeah?"

"Sari. How are you?"

"Horny," she says. He hears a slight rustle over the phone, and he pictures Sari lying back against the pillows. She asks, "How about you?"

In almost a whisper he tells her, "The same. But since you're always in my thoughts, I'm *always* horny. So this isn't news. The news, the real news . . . the news isn't good."

He's straddling the limb, breathing this cool loamy air, watching the single slender window of Annie's studio. He can't see Annie, though. Only flickers of her shadow as she works.

Sari asks him, "What is it?"

Her voice is drooping. She's guessed what it is.

He says, "I can't come tonight. I have an immense presentation tomorrow, and tonight I have to research a client."

"Where are you?"

"I miss you," he says.

"Where are you?"

"On the road. Near the village of Pharaoh, I think."

"It sounds quiet."

"Well, I've pulled over. I'm sitting outside. I'm sitting here with trees all around me, and there's a light on in somebody's window and it's making me a little lonely. I'm thinking about you lying in bed and I know your eyes are getting narrow now and I know you're pissed as hell and listen, I'm really sorry. You're absolutely the most stunning woman in the world and if anyone hears me talking out here they're going to think it's a burglar and they'll come out with a shotgun and the line will go dead suddenly and I'll never get to meet your mother—"

She tries to laugh.

"And I'm sorry," he says.

27

He waits a moment, to give his voice time to sink into her, then he asks, "Is it, Sari, is it OK?"

"Not really. I shouldn't let you do this to me, Eben. You just work all the time."

"I do . . . love . . . this work," he says slowly and softly. Just then Annie Laird, pacing, thinking about her own work, passes her studio window. Repasses. "But Sari, I miss you. What we need to do is figure out a way that I can stay inside you and meet with clients at the same time."

This time she does laugh some. Some of the tension lifts.

"We'll try Thursday?" he says.

"How about tomorrow?" But she bites off the tail end of "tomorrow." Maybe she hears the clingingness in her voice.

"Tomorrow? I'm sorry. Tomorrow I'll be having dinner with this same client."

The light from Annie's window, rippling. He does love this work. This night, that thrush, the sharp spicebush, the fine-tuned power of his own pulse, all the leaves stirring around him . . .

2

You must keep showing her

you love her.

ANNIE can't find parking anywhere in SoHo. Now and then there's a gap in the cars but the space is always guarded by a jealous hydrant. Finally she gives up and leaves the old Subaru with its butt nudging a crosswalk. Take a chance. How often do I get off like this, I'm going to waste the whole sunny day cruising for a place to park?

The gallery is over on West Broadway. She walks east by way of Spring. Clocking along. She peers into the bric-a-brac boutiques, the chichi pet shops. She checks out the latest sidewalk stencil-graffiti. She slows when she passes a bakery, and again at a shop for exotic coffee.

Now that she no longer lives here she loves this city.

A pair of lovers at a sidewalk cafe. Sitting side by side, reading. Their novels tipped toward the raking sunlight, the man absently stroking the woman's forearm with the tips of his fingers. Annie checks herself for signs of envy. For any nostalgic pining.

Perhaps she does sense a small subterranean shift or shudder.

And later she gets another tremor when she's coming up West Broadway and some beautiful city guy with gothic cheekbones passes her and gives her the eye, and she finds herself giving it right back. After he passes she drags her feet and even considers taking a quick look behind her—just to see if *he*'s looking back.

But tremors like these fly quickly.

The real ache hits her when she goes by a toy store for rich kids

31

and gets a glimpse of a complex mechanical dragon. A blast of smoke from its blue-green nostrils. To possess such a creature, Oliver would sign over his soul. She almost veers to go inside to ask the price. Almost goes *seeking* that chastisement.

If you have to ask, lady, we don't mind humiliating you.

But she averts her eyes and picks up her stride, and by the time she gets to Prince Street she's forgotten the toy, she's forgotten the lovers and the looker, she's carefree and playing hooky again. She crosses the street, then turns into a big iron loft building. She breezes up to the third floor, to Inez Gazzaraga's gallery. Where Annie has three pieces on one wall of the front room, part of a group show called *Hermetic Visions*.

She nods to Lainie, the intern, at the desk, and heads for Inez's office in the back.

But a flutter of red troubles the edge of her vision. She stops.

Over by her pieces, her Grope Boxes on the wall, a smattering of red spots. Her heart takes a bound. She shuts her eyes.

No. Can't be. Didn't see what I thought I saw.

She opens her eyes again. Beside each of the boxes is a small red disk. Her eyes move from one to the other. Three disks in all. Not equivocal half disks, not *this piece is perhaps spoken for*. But full flaming red suns.

Sold.

Follow the bouncing red ball and sing along: *"Sold! Sold! Sold!"*

The song clanging sweetly in her head in time to the rushing of her blood till she hears Lainie laughing behind her, and then Inez comes lumbering out of her office and says into her other ear, "So you made a fuckin sale. About time, too. Come."

She leads Annie into her office.

"His name is Zach Lyde." Inez lights a cigarette, wheezes into a hanky and wipes her chin. She leans back in her chair. She was once a *Vogue* model. She was the *belle dame sans merci* of beat poets and abstract expressionists. Now she's two hundred eighty pounds and tough-skinned and nasty when she needs to be. In her shaggy quack of a voice, she tells Annie, "I've seen him around, I've heard stories. He's respected. He's a bit, I don't know, he's very polite but he intimidates people, know what I mean? He *knows* his shit. He's sweet on some of the minimalists. Marden. Some Neo-Geo. Alice Aycock. Lately he's done some Christy Rupp. He does *not* care for the big-dick marble cowboys. They say he's got a fairly brilliant collection for himself, but mostly he buys for friends. I mean for big collectors, honey. Big big big shits."

"Like?"

"People you wouldn't have heard of."

"But if they're such big collectors—"

Inez frowns. She looks down at the yellow notebook on her desk. "Satō Yusūke? Heard of *him*?"

"No."

"Yoshida Yasei?"

Annie shakes her head.

Says Inez, "Well, OK, how about the ever-popular Morī Shoichi?"

"I'm getting the drift," says Annie. "My stuff's going to Japan?"

Inez shrugs. "I can't say for sure. These are just names he mentioned."

"You didn't find out where my—"

"I asked him, he gave me *vague*. You know? Like, 'Well, I have to do some exploring. Find the right home.' That sort of runaround—"

"And that was OK?" Annie asks. "That was good enough for you?"

"Well, that and a check for twenty-four thousand dollars—of which twelve is yours. Yes. That was plenty."

Inez grins. Annie tries to grin back, but the worry is still on her brow.

Says Inez, "Look, kid, maybe you're not getting this. You've just sold three of your boxes to a *power*. You ought to be squealing like a pig. You ought to be creaming your jeans."

"I'm, I'm ecstatic," says Annie. "It's just, I want to know where my pieces are going. I don't understand who this guy is. Is he a collector? A dealer? Is he, what is he? What does he do for a living?"

Inez shrugs. "I understand he manages a commodities fund. He has an office on Maiden Lane—but I gather he's not a slave to it. I know he does *this*. Collecting. That's all I know. Oh, and he takes trips sometimes. He saw my prayer wheel up on the wall there and he talked to me about Nepal and I mean, Annie, when this man talks . . ."

"What?"

"Well, you forget your questions. You wind up just . . . watching him." Inez laughs. "You'll see. You'll meet him. He told me he wants to *work* with you."

"What does that mean?"

33

"Beats me. *He* said it. Just do me a favor, OK? You'll be dealing with him directly, that's OK. But don't screw me."

Annie is astonished. "Inez, I love you."

"Oh, that's so touching I don't know what the fuck to say. But maybe when you're on your way to your opening at the Louvre, maybe eternal devotion will slip your mind—"

"Inez."

"*Everything* through me."

"Yes. Inez."

"Or I mean I will run you over. I will flatten you."

She makes a face. She pushes her lips out, which pulls taut her slabby cheeks. She rises up in her seat and puts her fists on the desk and leans forward, and Annie is put in mind of the prow of a John Deere tractor. Flattening is conceivable.

Then Inez laughs and hands her the check for twelve thousand dollars.

And Annie's unmoored. Afloat. She talks with Inez for a few more minutes, but she hardly knows what she's saying. She's got twelve thousand in her purse. She's got more money coming. She's got a career. She's kissing Inez goodbye and then Lainie, and she finds herself in the elevator and then the lobby, and amid swirls of fresh air she steps out onto the street. Sunlight jumps up off the sidewalks. She's got twelve thousand dollars in her purse and her head is stuffed with cotton, the utter incomparable bliss of success—

"Annie Laird?"

She turns.

It's the man with the gothic cheekbones.

He says, "I passed you a while ago—"

"I remember."

"But by the time I decided it was you, I was all the way to Broome Street. And then I had to stop at Paula Cooper. But as soon as I could, I ran back here."

He also has brown irises flecked with yellow. He also has a charming lopsided smile.

He says, "I'm glad I caught you."

She regards him quizzically. He tells her, "I'm Zach Lyde."

My patron?

This babe is my patron?

He says, "I bought a few of your things."

"Yeah," she mumbles. "I have a, um, a check in my purse."

She feels like the youngest, simplest sister in a fairy tale. At the happy windup, with her pockets full of gold.

He says, "I know I didn't pay what they're worth, not nearly, I know that. But then *I* didn't set the price. I might like to buy others, though, and I'm prepared to offer much more—"

Annie asks him, "How do you know me? We haven't met, have we?"

"Inez showed me your picture. In the catalog."

"Oh."

"It does not do you justice."

She forgets to say thank you. She simply nods and lowers her eyes. Awkward silence. On the sidewalk, next to his soft Italian loafers, there's one of those senseless "running beans" that some street-artist keeps stenciling all over SoHo. Annie squints at it. How can *any* of this make sense? Twelve *thousand* dollars. A patron who's a work of art himself. Her boxes flying all over the world—

Which reminds her.

"Japan?" she asks him. She lifts her eyes again and asks, "Are you really sending my pieces—"

"Likely."

"So will I ever see them again?"

"Oh, of course." That skewed, reassuring smile. "Would you like to talk about it? Would you have time for lunch?"

"Now?"

He keeps looking at her. She checks her watch. "It's eleven-thirty," she says. "I have to be upstate by two. I have jury duty."

He groans sympathetically. Then grins. "I wouldn't want to make you late for *that*."

"But just a bite of something? Why not? Sure."

So he takes her for some simple Pacific fare at a hidden vine-trellised courtyard off Sullivan Street. They sit under an ornamental maple with crimson leaves. The waiter seems to know Zach Lyde well. Is there anything that can be done, he asks, about his poor ailing phalaenopsis at home?

Zach looks concerned. "What's the matter with it?"

"The leaves getting kind of yellow?" says the waiter. "At the edges?"

"Sounds like you're drowning it," says Zach Lyde. "I suggest you relax. Neglect it a little, let it alone, leave it to its own devices, watch what happens."

The waiter nods solemnly and slips away.

Then it's just the two of them in that courtyard. The breeze doesn't get down here but the sunlight does. It blazes on the bricks behind him.

She tastes the *ahi poki* on *crostini* with chili pepper *aioli*. It's probably magnificent but how can she give it her full attention? Zach Lyde is telling her:

"OK. You want to know where your art's going. Inez must have told you about my Japanese friends. They're businessmen—of a sort. I often buy for them. Nine times out of ten, they like what I buy."

Annie asks, "They buy—what, for their homes? Their offices, what?"

"Sometimes they buy for their warehouses. Or sometimes, sometimes I simply send them pictures and they leave the art here."

This baffles her. "They don't even see it?"

"I want you to understand. You should clearly understand the nature of this sport. These men are not what you'd call art lovers. They have good eyes, they're canny, they're shrewd. But they're businessmen. Do you know Japan at all?"

"No."

"Contemporary art is a form of specie there now. Because its value is not fixed, because its value is so inconstant, so attractively pliant, it's become a form of currency."

"I don't, I'm, I'm lost."

"Then let me make a sketch for you."

He brings his face a little closer to hers.

He says, "Suppose a Mr. Kawamoto becomes indebted to a Mr. Okita. Kawamoto is a wealthy industrialist, Okita is a businessman of another kind. A *yakuza*. What we might call a gangster. But by no means a thug. Not a violent churl. No. He's a graceful man, he's cultivated, he's esteemed in his community. Now how can Kawamoto discharge his debt to this man? Not with cash of course—that would draw the attention of the authorities in Tokyo. So instead he gives Okita a work of art. Perhaps a small simple sculpture by a young New York artist. Not valued too dearly. Maybe half a million yen. Five thousand dollars. But who cares about price tags? It's the *thoughtfulness* of the gift that touches Okita so deeply. And as luck would have it, the value of the piece *blossoms* over the next year.

"One day a vice president from Kawamoto's company calls on Okita, and offers him twenty million yen for the sculpture. This is a lot of scratch, Lord knows, but the company can write it off as a business expense. Okita, of course, is loath to part with his sentimental treasure, but he reluctantly accepts the offer. The debt is paid—with the help of the Japanese taxpayer. Everyone's happy. Not least the artist, who now has a record of a six-figure international sale. You like the curried *lumpia?*"

"And what about the sculpture?" says Annie. "What do they do with the sculpture? Throw it out?"

"Why should they do that? It's worth two hundred thousand dollars."

"But not really."

"But it *is.* Really. It's important that you understand this. What I send over there is the best art in the world. The most daring, the most moving, the most original. By artists who have everything going for them except an inkling of how to create a career. That's the part I handle. The right review in *Artforum,* in *Flash Art,* the right humble little cottage in the Hamptons, the right niche in the Basel Artfair and Dokumenta. And as for the churning in Japan? That merely solidifies natural values. But anyway this is, well, this is *my* job. Leave this to me. Your job is to stay in your studio and make your boxes."

Sparks flash from Annie's eyes. "*My* job? Oh great, it's nice to know I'm still involved. Hey, listen to me, Mr. Lyde—"

"Call me Zach."

"Listen—"

"And may I call you Annie?"

"You can call me whatever the hell you want. But I don't want to have anything to do with these, these—"

"Sleazy patrons? Does the notion of that offend you? 'Sorry, Duke,' says Raphael, 'but you're corrupt and sleazy and you boil your enemies in oil, so I don't want your help—I'll just slip quietly into obscurity—' "

"What I'm saying—"

He stops her. "Annie, what do you think I get out of this? Money? I don't make money on this. I don't need to. What I do for a living, I do well."

The waiter appears. Glides soundlessly onto the terrace, but Zach Lyde raises his hand slightly, and without taking his eyes off Annie he says, "David, not now? Please?"

The waiter retreats.

Zach Lyde leans in even closer to her. "I do this so an artist like you can go into your studio and make your boxes and not worry about whether or not your kid gets fed. OK? So your thoughts can be as chaotic as you need them to be. And your life won't have to suffer. So all those idiots in the art world, those gnats, they won't bother you. So you can *work*."

Abruptly he looks away from her. Blows out a breath of air. Shakes his head. "But look, it's your career. Keep your boxes. Keep your check too, consider it a grant . . . my compliments. I wish you luck."

He turns, looks for the waiter.

"Mr. Lyde?" she says quietly.

"Zach."

"Zach. You know, you know you *are* very persuasive." She tries to smile. "It's just that this is . . . this is. Oh God. *Sudden*. It'll take some getting used to, I guess. That's all. That's all I meant. I guess." She looks down at her smoked-salmon summer rolls. She laughs. "Did I tell you how delicious this was? Though I, I'm not sure I can eat any more."

"That's OK. Anyway, you have to go. You have that jury duty, right?"

"Oh yeah. Right. Forgot. Real life." She shakes her head. "I wish I didn't have to go, though. I feel like, there's really a lot we could talk about, I mean I'm sorry, I wish I didn't—"

"Be other opportunities."

"Yes."

"For example dinner."

"What?"

"Will you have dinner with me tonight, Annie?"

OLIVER coasts on his bike. With his chin in the air he looks straight up into the great sugar maples along Church Street, the shuddering leaf-caverns, until his mother, riding behind him, cries sharply, "Oliver!" Then he drops his eyes, and in truth the bike *had* been sort of straying off to one side of the street. . . .

Side by side they coast down toward the lake. To the corner with the old stone library, where Church Street meets Old Willow Avenue.

Oliver slows not with the hand brake but by wobbling the wheels.

They wait for a few cars to go by on Old Willow. Then they cross the road and bounce over hummocky yellow grass to the bike trail that runs alongside the lake.

He calls back to his mom, "So will I get a new bike?"

"Oliver," she says.

"No, I mean a new Mongoose, Mom, why not?"

"I'm serious. Shut up."

"Who's listening to us, Momba?"

"I don't care. You do not say one word."

They pass the bronze statue of Hannah Stoneleigh, the Revolutionary War heroine of Pharaoh, clinging to her bronze horse and shouting a bronze shout.

Says Oliver, "How about a PowerBook?"

"What?"

"A PowerBook. It's a computer with a built-in Trac-ball."

"I know what it is."

"Will I get one?"

"No. And if you breathe a word of this to anyone—you hear me?—you'll get a Trac-ball built in to your little throat."

"Momba."

"What?"

"That wasn't funny."

"Wasn't supposed to be."

"It was kind of stupid."

"Good."

"Ha ha ha!" he mocks. "A Trac-ball built in to my little throat! Ho! Ha ha!"

He rises up and pushes down on the pedals. The lake breeze whips up around him. "Ha ha *ha!*" he shouts as he speeds away from her. Think of Momba famous. We'll buy the Dills' house up on Horsepound Ridge, and Mom's friend Juliet can come over to use the pool.

He calls back, "*Move* it, Mom!"

Soon they're cruising together up Seminary Lane. They pass Shawn Cardi, who gives them a nod and a quick cool fartlike honk from his bike's electronic horn. Makes Oliver feel a little sheepish to be seen hanging around with his mother. However Shawn Cardi has his own problems. He's a buzzbrain, for one thing. And *his* mother is the funeral director in town. So Oliver returns his nod sort of curtly and leans way back on his bike like he's riding a Harley, and he thinks pretty soon it *will* be a Harley he's riding. I mean we could buy a lot of land, right? And I wouldn't need a driver's license on my own property, would I?

Theoretically, he thinks, I could be riding a Harley tomorrow.

And once I get good at it, by say sometime next week, I can start letting Juliet ride behind me.

Home stretch now. Past the snippety lawn of Mr. and Mrs. Zoeller and their lawn troll (all three of whom Oliver despises). Then their own wild yard. He banks to the right, arcing into the driveway just ahead of Mom. Rides around to the back, by the Indian bean tree, and jumps off. He walks the bike to the back stoop, and he's about to reach up to open the screen door when he sees the skull.

"Holy shit," he says. "What is *that*?"

Stupid question, though—it's plain what it is. It's a human skull, hanging in front of the screen door.

Mom comes up behind him. She gasps.

A tag, like a laboratory ID tag, hangs from the skull. It reads OLIVER LAIRD.

Then Oliver feels something drilling against his temple and into his ear and slashing down his neck, and he wheels. Another burst of water hits him between the eyes. His assassin is up in the Indian bean tree. Juliet.

"You're dead."

She's peering around the trunk, with a Super Soaker submachine gun held against her shoulder. Green-eyed, red-haired Juliet, Mom's best friend. Squinting down the sights.

"Down, you're dead."

"Not fair!" Oliver cries.

"Fair? Death is not fair."

"I'm not armed!" He opens his mouth to raise further objection but she blasts it.

"It's time to die, Oliver."

He shrugs, and lets his bike fall, and drops to his knees, and slowly pitches forward. Winds up in a sort of kowtow. Looking up at her sideways. She jumps out of the tree. She's 6'2". She has sort of a boyish body but with a few soft confusing female turns. When she's gossiping with Oliver's mom, or when she's horsing around with Oliver, she slouches a little, she relaxes. But he's seen her flirting with men at a restaurant and once at a barbecue, and once in a parking lot with another resident at her hospital, and on those occasions she rose up to her full height and even leaned back a little, and swayed slightly as she talked, swayed like a snake, and Oliver wishes she would stand this way around *him* once in a while.

From his dead-man's kowtow he asks her, "Whose skull is that?"

Juliet gives his mother a hug, but she keeps her rifle pointed at Oliver. "Yours, loser. Can't read your own name?" Then she asks Oliver's Mom: "So what's this earthshaking news?"

Says Oliver, "Hey, is it *real*? Where'd you get it?" He jumps up and unhooks it from the screen.

"Neurosurgery resident gave it to me."

"A boyfriend?"

"None of your business. He *wants* to be my boyfriend. And the skull wasn't a bad idea. Better than flowers anyway."

"So do you like him?"

"You're an incredibly nosy creep."

"Yeah. I am." He works the hinge of the skull's jaw and makes the sound of a creaking door. "Yah—ah—ahh. So do you like him or not?"

"How can I like him? He's a neurosurgery resident. Do you know how incredibly boring neurosurgery residents are?"

"Uh-uh."

"If you have two hours to live, spend it with a neurosurgery resident, it'll seem like two years. You can keep the skull, if you promise not to take it to school or anything. I don't think it's legal to own them."

"Wow. Thanks."

Juliet steps around to the corner of the house and fetches her bike from where she's hidden it. She says, "Yeah, well, I thought your warped little brain would enjoy that." Again she asks Mom, "So what's this news?"

Oliver jumps in. "She got three red spots."

Juliet doesn't get it.

"That's it, that's true," says Mom. "Three red spots."

"And she's got more coming," says Oliver.

Juliet, palms upward: "You have measles?"

Both Oliver and Mom grinning. The skull also enjoying this. Then Mom makes her announcement. "I sold three pieces."

Juliet's jaw drops. *Annie.*

"To a very influential collector. Who has visions of . . ." She waggles her fingers. She can't find the word. "God, *superstardom* for me."

Juliet, her mouth wide open, lets fly a shriek. *"Eeeeeeeeeeee-eeeeeeeeeeeeeeeee!"*

"Ssshhhh!" says Mom.

"Annie!"

Mom's got one hand on her hip, and she sashays that hip. "Twelve thousand dollars *in my pocket.*"

"ANNIE!"

Juliet jumps up and down in place. Hops close to Mom and grabs her cheeks in her big hands and smushes them together so Mom's lips push out like a fish.

"ANNIE! THAT IS SO . . . FUCKING . . . UNBELIEVABLY . . ."

"Shh!" says Mom.

Mom puts both her hands up for a high-ten slap. Juliet pounds at them with her fists. So excited she doesn't know what she's doing.

Mom, laughing, grabs her wrists to restrain her, but Juliet pulls her arms free and then scoops Mom into an embrace. Pummels her back. So much taller than Mom, she's draped over her, banging away at her back and then quitting that and squeezing her. She winks at Oliver and stretches out her long long arm like a tentacle, and takes his neck and starts strangling him, forgetting that she's already killed him today.

THE TEACHER sits half-lotus in his old one-room schoolhouse. He fixes on the representation of *salagramas* that he's painted on the shining wood floor.

The pyramid of red disks.

He draws a breath. *Puraka.*

His breath runs down the spiral corridor of his spine, down along the road that Black Elk called the red road, down to the dark pond and the spreading white cypress tree.

Rechaka. The breath is released.

He draws another breath. *Puraka.*

One of the red disks begins to float in front of him. A crimson globe, as light and small as a thistle, and inside of this globe is his father. His father is drunk. He's sprawled on the rug in what they called the "wreck-room," in the basement of the house in Bay Ridge. He's singing the "Cinta di Fiori" by Bellini. In his lyric baritone, with white spittle at the corners of his lips.

The Teacher breathes out. *Rechaka.* The globe wobbles, floats off.

Another globe comes floating by. He looks in.

He sees himself in the kitchen of that Bay Ridge house. Havoc of heaped plates, moldy food. He spreads mustard on a slice of Sunbeam Round Bread. In the fridge he finds some old salami. He tears away the edge that's going bad—the warped rind. When he turns, he notices that a roach has crawled onto the bread and is hip-deep in mustard. He moves his hand slowly till it hovers above the roach. Then he snaps his wrist and snatches it, and holds it up between thumb and forefinger, delicately. All its mustard-yellow insect legs running like hell, but it's not getting anywhere.

Rechaka. He dismisses this vision.

He breathes in. Another globe floats up.

His mother, shrieking at the bathroom door, kicking it. The door flies open. His father is taking a shit, and he's got an open volume of Thomas Aquinas on his knee. Says his mother, "So *now* what, Princessa?" His father gets up. A teardrop-shaped turd falls from his ass as he rises, and drops onto the toilet seat. With his pants wrapped around his ankles he steps forward. He tries to spit in her face, but he misses. He smiles at his son, and shuts the door.

The Teacher, with his breath, arranges all three disks into a pyramid, two low and one high. He fusses with their alignment until the geometry seems immaculate, unassailable.

Then he inhales them.

He rises.

He plays his messages. Sari. Sari again. Sari a third time.

He goes to the console and summons up channel one, Annie's kitchen. He listens. Her visitor, the doctor woman, is still there with her; they're chatting away, and the Teacher's schoolhouse is filled with their laughter. It's good to be with them. *The Master travels all day without ever leaving his house,* says Lao Tsu.

Annie and her doctor friend are talking about Zach Lyde.

ANNIE's appalled. "The shirred? No. Not the shirred."

"Why not?" says Juliet. She's still laughing. "That's such a sexy number. You look so sexy—"

"Juliet, will you stop it? I don't want to look sexy. This man is my potential patron. He is *not* a potential . . ."

"What?"

"Boyfriend. Whatever."

"Oh no. No of course not, Annie. He's only gorgeous, thoughtful, rich as Croesus. Doesn't approach your standards. Though it is sweet of you to consent to this mercy-date with the poor—"

"This is not a date! *Not. A. Date.* And besides you left out self-confident and funny and you didn't say anything about his cheekbones."

"All right! That's the way! You're *wearing* that shirred thing, girl. And don't be shy with him—"

"I'm not shy."

"You are."

"I'm private."

"You clam up."

"I don't babble to men, that's all."

Juliet laughs. "Babble? You call it babbling?" She slurs the word *babble*. It's evident to Annie that her friend is far past exhausted.

She sits in the kitchen rocking chair, chattering and pushing Oliver's Lorna Doones into her mouth—taking ratchety little rapid-fire bites. She's overrevving. When she reaches for her cup of tea she lunges.

"It's not *babble*, Annie, it's an *art*. First you say something to puff up his ego. Then you say something alluring, something to draw him close to you. Then with a sly little subtle stab you *puncture* his balloon. Then you stroke his silly ego again, then you push him back, pull push pull push pull push till you've got him, by this method, spinning in circles and dizzy and staggering and falling at your feet."

"And then what?"

"Then tell him you're sorry, you do admire him but he can never be more to you than your *patron*—and Annie, you have to let me listen in when you do this or I'll kill you, my darling," and Juliet breaks out into more gales of laughter.

"Hey Jul?"

"What?"

"When's the last time you slept?"

This is a poser for Juliet. "You mean *sleep* sleep? Not just closing your eyes for a minute while you're doing a tracheotomy? Well, I don't know. What's today?"

"Wednesday."

"It is? No."

"Yeah."

"You sure?"

"I'm sure."

"Well then, I know I slept for a few hours Monday night. Not so long ago."

"Jesus, what are you doing here? You've got to get to bed—"

"No I had to come. When I got your message. I mean, Annie, what's incredible is that you never stopped dreaming, you wanted to make art and you did it and you struggled, you kept at it and now finally—"

"I kept at it because I'm insane, Juliet."

"You call Slivey yet? You quit your job?"

"I can't quit my job."

"You can!"

"This could go up in a puff of smoke."

"It won't! You can be making your boxes tomorrow."

Annie laughs. "Not tomorrow anyway. I've got jury duty."

"Oh God, I forgot. How'd that go?"

"Fine, boring. The lawyers asked me a ton of questions. They picked me."

"For what?"

"Some trial. I thought it'd be something different for me to do, you know? But now, I mean after this, I mean, now it's just a total pain."

"Get *out* of it."

"Too late now."

"Get *out* of it."

"Juliet, you got to get some sleep, honey."

"Naw, I'm going to the movies with Henri."

"You're crazy."

"I'll take your bratty kid if he wants to come."

"Depends on who's driving."

"OK. Henri'll drive. But listen, Annie, I want to tell you what happened last night."

"What?"

"You're not the only one with adventures."

"What happened?"

Juliet has this expression, which precedes all conversations about sex—her lips thinning out and then a mischievous flutter of her eyes. She lowers her voice. "Where is he?"

"Oliver? In his room. He can't hear us." Annie leans close. "What?"

"Last night. About two o'clock last night, got called down to the trauma bay. Gunshot wound. Supposed to be a fourth-year resident there but he never showed, I think he was sound asleep somewhere, so I was in charge. Unless I wanted to wake the attending, which I *never* want to do. So anyway, they wheel this kid in, this black kid, he's about twenty I guess. He's wide awake. He's feisty. He's gorgeous."

She pounces on a swallow of tea. Then she says, "Guess what nurse was working with me?"

"Henri?"

"Sometimes they let him rotate with me now. They're scared of what I'm like without him. So it's him and another male nurse. I cut the kid's pants off with the trauma scissors. He's not wearing any underwear. The wound's in his thigh. Entrance *here* and the exit *here*—pretty clean, simple, kind of dull really, except who's looking

48

at his thigh? Annie, he had the most beautiful cock you've ever seen in your life. Not so big really but it was like . . . like what's that smooth black stone, what do they call that?"

"Onyx?"

"Is that it? OK. But I mean it had these two gnarly veins, like, like vines . . . and it's lying there against his thigh pointing down at the wound, and it's throbbing a little? And it's like, like it's flared out near the head like a cobra, like a sleeping *cobra*—"

Both of them blush and tilt their faces and laugh wildly, but Juliet's still worried that Oliver might overhear, and she puts her finger to her lips. "Shhhhhhh."

This draws another fit of laughter.

"And Henri, he didn't know whether to look at that cock and drool, or watch me to see if I was gonna screw up. But I was damned if I was gonna screw up. I went around to put the IV in this kid. The kid says, 'Shit. That's for when you're too old to *eat*, right? When you don't got no *teeth*.' And he says, '*I* got teeth. *I* can eat. Eat you right up. What's your name? My name's *Richard*.'

"And he's got these *incredible* white teeth and I'm a little weak there and I say, 'Let me get this in, Richard.' He says, 'Get the doctor.' I say, 'I am the doctor.' He says, 'Oh shit. You? Oh shit! I'm a *dead* man.' So then I started cleaning the wound, and he says, 'What do you think of that sucker?'" And I say, 'Looks like you got in trouble doing something stupid, Richard.' And he says, 'When I get ahold of the motherfucker did this to me? Gonna wheel him in here in a *bag*. And you gonna unzip it, Doc, and you gonna just *pour* him out.'

"But I'm only half-listening to him, because the thigh seems a little swollen and I'm starting to think about an expanding hematoma, which means there's a block and the blood is pooling up in there somewhere. I put my hands on his thighs, because sometimes you can feel the tension. And there *is* all this tension under my fingers but, Annie, this guy is really muscular, rock hard, so I don't know, maybe it's just muscle. I have to compare the tension with the tension in the other thigh. So then I'm holding both of his thighs and he's looking down at me and he's saying, 'You know what, Doc? You got a nice touch, Doc.'

"But I already knew that, Annie. Because while I was holding him? His cock was starting to—"

"No!" hisses Annie.

"It was! I mean it was, it was, it was just rising up as I watched, and it was so beautiful—that cobra thing . . . that, that *wingspread*, you know?"

For a while they wheeze with laughter.

"And I, I was watching it and it was watching me back, and I looked up and Henri was watching too, and Richard had this big grin and he had his hands behind his head like, like, like this—"

She leans back and laughs straight up at the ceiling for a moment. Then she says, "But I was hell-bent I was going to finish this examination. So I kept my hands on his thigh, I kept examining him, and that cock kept bobbing, bobbing up, and I was blushing, you know how I blush? I think I was probably, like purple, and Annie, *I was so excited*, I just wanted to gobble that thing up. And then he reached down and put his hand right on top of mine. And I let him do it. He says, 'What's your name, Doc?' And I looked up at him and I said, 'Hematoma.' He says, 'What? That's your name? Hema Toma? What's *that* mean?' I say, 'It means you're going to surgery, Richard. Goodbye, Richard.'

"And I shipped him off to surgery, and they did a fasciotomy and I'll never see him again."

OLIVER now wishes he hadn't listened. Hadn't lain there in his Mom's bedroom on the cool wood floor with his ear to the wood, eavesdropping on Juliet's story. It's got his head all twisted up. He's at his desk now trying to do his math but the thoughts keep slithering away.

Of the ballerinas in the Marina City Ballet, four are older than 16, 35% are 10–16, three are 7–9, and one is a black, weaving-and-bobbing cobra with one eye, and all the ballerinas gather around it and try to gobble it up. . . .

And he's thinking again of what Juliet said about that guy's cock, about its *wingspread*, how beautiful it was—and his ribs ache.

She's too old for me. She goes out with really mature older guys, *wingspread* guys, what would she want with a kid like me?

But maybe the money will help. If Mom gets really rich I can buy a house next to Juliet's place on North Kent Road, a whole house just for parties, and everyone will come because I'll be the son of Annie Laird and I'll have a Harley and a private lacrosse field out back, and even Laurel Paglinino will come, but I'll make her go away, I'll make them all clear out so I can be alone with Juliet. . . .

Jesus. It's stupid and immature, this line of thought, but it's run-away, it doesn't care how dumb it is, it goes where it pleases. . . .

"Oliver!"

"Uh?"

"Come on, get ready." Mom comes up the stairs to fetch him. "You can finish at Mrs. Kolodny's."

That wakes him up. "Wait! You said I could spend the night at Jesse's!"

"Yeah, well, I'm sorry. Jesse's mother doesn't want you. You're too much of a brat. Mrs. Kolodny's it is."

"Mom! No!"

She leans close to him and cups her hands over her mouth and drops her voice to the register of a ball-and-chain phantom. She intones, "Mrs. Kol-od-neeeee's."

"Mom. You're messing with my head here, right?"

She gives him a quick drumroll of little slaps on the top of his head (she always gets in this big-sister mode when she's been hanging around Juliet). She says, "You swallowed it, though, didn't you? In fact Juliet's going to take you and Jesse out to the movies and then you spend the night at Jesse's. All right? A date with Juliet? Your true love? Now get your ass in gear. I've got my own date."

"Thought you said it was a *business* meeting."

"Oh, right. Yes. Business. *Strictly*. Hurry."

ANNIE gets twelve yellow red-throated cattleyas. Annie gets dinner at L'Auberge Conques. The wine is a Domaine des Comtes Lafon Chardonnay, but it's the chocolate ganache that does her in. Also the sharp tangy wind on the way out to the car after dinner, the moon hurtling through clouds, Zach Lyde's easy elegant laugh as he fumbles through twenty keys on his key chain. Also the smell of his linen jacket as he holds the car door open for her.

They drive, and Zach Lyde's elegant car fills up with Vivaldi.

At a corner near Katonah, Annie sees in the headlights a goat resting its chin on the uppermost rail of a wood fence. It glowers at her with its subtraction pupils. It seems to tilt its head to the passion of Vivaldi's two violins. A sudden wind-hoop of leaves rolls before the fence, wobbles, scatters. The world is filled with such unexpected shivers of beauty, how did it ever seem drab to her?

She asks Zach how he started collecting art, and he tells her:

"Down near where I work, on Maiden Lane? There was an old crumbling cinderblock wall, and I used to walk by it every day and then one day something caught my eye. I went over and checked it out. It was a *city*. Built into a hollow space on the wall. This, it was like a tiny acropolis built out of clay, with tiny clay columns. And tympanums? And flights of clay steps running up and down? Sitting in that wall. With city graffiti all around it, and posters for rock bands, My Sister's Dead Cock or whatever, and garbage, you know, beer cans shoved in the chinks of that wall—and then that perfect city.

"So I went and found out who'd built it. A homeless man who hung out on the steps of a church. I found him a home, I found him some patrons, I found him a gallery. He's insane, he's still insane but now he doesn't have to hustle for meals or a bed. He can just build his cities. Most of which nobody will ever get to see.

"Anyway, after that I was hooked."

Into the headlights come mailboxes, horse-chestnut trees, burgundy-colored barns. The scenes dance in, they dance out. All in rhythm to the Vivaldi. She's never much liked Vivaldi before, but he's certainly brilliant tonight. An andante movement, a violin and a cello swaying side by side. Makes her feel a bit sleepy. She gets an impulse to slump over and rest her head on this man's shoulder.

Stop it. You idiot, do you think this is fun? Get all swoony and tender, you think that's what we need tonight? Oh yes, get the chemicals simmering. Get yourself immersed. Get a deluge going here and let this chance at a career get swept away because *you just can't help yourself*. Because you love those cheekbones. Because you're wild for his car and his off-center smile and off-center religion and his deep brown eyes, oh Christ.

Sit *up*, you sack of shit.

She straightens herself.

She has an impulse to tell him that she just had an impulse to nestle on his shoulder.

STOP IT YOU SACK OF SHIT.

Says Zach, "You know what I really love about that artist? It's that reaching back, reaching out of the city to a *prior* city. It's that, that, that reaching down to the structure that underlies all this chaos—that's what excites me about the best art. Annie, that's why I love your Grope Boxes. Groping in the darkness, in that womb, what is that but reaching back? Lao Tsu says that returning is the movement of the Tao. Returning! I have a sense, I have a sense that what we call wisdom—"

He catches himself. He grins. "Christ, I'm on a roll *now*."

"But no, I like it," she says. "I don't talk to many people with . . . so many ideas."

"You mean so much clutter in the head?"

"That name. Lao Tsu? He started some religion, didn't he?"

"Taoism. Though really the man himself—he was perhaps mythical."

"Are you a Taoist?"

He laughs. "I don't know. Lao Tsu says when the foolish man hears of the Tao, he laughs out loud. And that, that sounds like me. But I find him compelling too. Become a valley, he says, stop struggling against that . . . structure, fate, whatever . . . and everything will flow to you."

They come to a crossroads and she tells him, "Take a left here." He glances over at her.

He asks no questions. He goes where she tells him. But he must know perfectly well that she's taking him home.

At her studio she says, "I hate this light. Wait, just wait a minute, I'll light a candle."

He looks at the row of finished Grope Boxes on the far wall. He says, "But then I won't be able to see . . . Oh, but I guess I don't need to."

She digs in a drawer for matches and lights a beeswax candle. "OK." She grabs the cord, snaps off the overhead. Lights another candle and sets it in the window. There's quite a wind outside, and the studio is drafty, and the candle flickers.

He's standing by the boxes now. He looks back at her and asks, "Which?"

She lights the third candle. "Doesn't matter. Any one."

"They're like the ones in the gallery? I just reach under and . . . ?"

"Cop a feel. Yep."

He chooses *The Dream of Giving Notice*.

Simply by watching his wrist as it disappears, by noting the frowns of intent concentration that alternate with quick revelatory smiles, she knows what his hand has got hold of. The tin birdcage first. Then he reaches through the hole in the bottom till he's got his hand inside the cage, and he finds the computer keyboard. He makes that awkward twist of the wrist so he can put his fingers on the keys.

All the keys are fitted with sandpaper caps.

Watch him.

He slides his arm farther up and he touches the bars of the cage. And then the tiny open door. Then the broken padlock. He stretches farther, stretches to get his fingers out the door of that cage. He can feel the breeze coming off the little fan, but he can't squeeze his whole hand through the door.

By now he has sunk to one knee. His eyes, which had been focused on nothing, come to focus on her, and he says, "It's wonderful. And listen, listen to me, it's not a dream. You *can* give notice. You *can* escape that hell. You can do nothing but make art from now on."

She blushes.

But he's also blushing. He says, "This is . . . this is a little embarrassing."

"What?"

"Well, I mean reaching under this skirt and feeling"—he starts laughing—"your private stuff."

Annie's face is laced up into a tipsy grin. She wants to unlace it, but she can't. Look at him, it's so much fun to look at him. Dizzily she moves over to the big rocker with its fat sweet cushions. She sits. She sprawls a little. She starts to laugh. She tells him, "Feel that one."

"Which one?"

"That one!" She points to "*Cardinal O'Connor Asserts: God Is Male.*"

"I've already felt it," he says.

"No, *that* one."

"I've felt it," he says again.

"No, no. I just finished it. I mean—"

"I felt it yesterday."

He grins. But her own smile has started to fade, because she's bewildered. "Yesterday? I didn't know you yesterday."

"But I was here," he says.

Joke? Of some kind? Maybe some kind of joke or pun that she can't quite fathom. She's wrestling with it. But he's not grinning anymore, he's coming her way, and the atmosphere has changed, his face is different, cold, wrong. The world starts to curdle at the edges and she's thinking, in her panic, *Oliver*. Till she remembers he's not home tonight, by now Jesse's mother's got him. So all right, Oliver's safe, but this stranger is still between her and the door and she's got to get out of here but where can she run? But it doesn't matter where. She's got to get out of this chair and she better grab something for a weapon, and she starts to rise—

"Stay there, Annie."

He yanks the cord for the overhead light. It snaps on. Stings her eyes. He takes a stool and moves it in front of her. He perches on it.

"Listen to me now." He speaks gently. "You're in danger. And your son is in danger."

"Oliver? What? Where's my son—"

"He's at Jesse's house, right?"

"Please," she says.

Zach Lyde's voice is so soft it's nearly a whisper. "He's an extraordinary child, isn't he? You know, when you were playing that video game last night? You remember? DragonRider? And the spider came at you and you started to panic, and Oliver said, 'Just *chill*, Momba.' You remember that?"

Her mouth is open and her eyes are filling with tears. When she tries to speak her voice seizes up. "How—" She tries again. "How do you know—"

"When I heard you two laughing I swore I'd do everything I could to get him through this. Annie. Do you hear what I'm saying? This is a dangerous time for him. He could stray, he could become confused, make some childish error. We could lose him." He snaps his fingers. "That quick."

She watches the afterimage of that snap.

He tells her, "He needs to overcome that hesitation of his. The dreaminess is fine but he also needs to learn how to *act*. I think he will, though. Give him time, I think he'll be a success. I think he'll be happy, and creative, and good-looking, I think someday you'll have grandkids running all over the place. And your friend Juliet, she'll be safe too. You've got a cousin in Titusville, Florida, right? She'll be fine. Everyone you care about, they'll all be safe as churches. Do you understand me? Nod your head. Now. Do as I say."

She nods.

"And you—all you have to do is wait. All right? Wait, wait some more, be very patient and wait some more, and then at some point you'll be asked to say two words. Two, precisely. Do you know what they are?"

She can only stare.

He says, "Yes? No? What? Have you guessed these words?"

She shakes her head, slowly.

He narrows his eyes. He leans in close to her and tells her softly, casually, *"Not guilty."*

THE TEACHER remembers what he heard Annie telling Juliet today: "I'm not shy, I'm *private*."

She keeps her own counsel. She keeps her struggles to herself.

"I don't babble to men," she said.

A woman so private that she even keeps her art in the dark—in these discreet black boxes. She wants you to feel nosy and awkward when you grope around in one of her crates. She wants you to know you're intruding.

She'd just as soon not give you *anything*.

And yet this is the woman he's calling on to carry the argument in the jury room. To cajole, persuade, fulminate and never let up on the pressure for an instant till all the other jurors give in.

He walks over to the studio's casement window. Looks out on the windy night. No rush. Take it easy. Give her a little time now.

But he's thinking, This is the one I've chosen? I've got to be out of my mind.

Out of my mind to pick on Annie Laird, he thinks, and he smiles.

ANNIE can't understand why there's no light in here. Where's the light? The studio is dismal, dim, gray. She hears her own strained breathing. She looks around and sees that the overhead light is on. But the light is so weak. There are also candles. Three candles. One of them is guttering, the flame leaping and thudding. Where did these candles come from? Why the hell did she ever light candles, and why don't they give off any light so she can see?

"Annie." That soft voice, dry as a katydid, lulling. Now he's somewhere behind her. "Annie, are you listening?"

She shuts her eyes.

"You have to listen to me."

She can't answer, her voice isn't there. She draws another breath, and finally she's able to whisper, "I'm listening."

"Because, Annie, there *is* another choice for you. If you like you can wait till I leave, then call the police. Or even the FBI. They'll have an agent here inside of an hour. They're dedicated honest people and I assure you they'll do everything they can to defend you. You and your child."

He pauses a moment. He's in no hurry.

"But, Annie, do you know what they'll have to do to you?"

He waits, until she shakes her head.

"First they'll put you and Oliver in a safe house. Then as soon as the trial's over you'll both go into Witness Protection. You know what that is, don't you? That's where they give you a new life. Somewhere far off. New names. Maybe even new faces—plastic surgery. Also a nice job in your chosen career. Which is . . . data processing, right?

"But forget about your art.

"Because I promise you, if you ever show your sculptures at any gallery anywhere, I don't care what name you use or what kind of work you're doing, we'll know it's you. And we'll come and we'll find you. No, on second thought, go ahead and put your work in the Whitney Biennial. Have an opening at MOMA. Because we're going to find you anyway. Anywhere. End of the earth, we'll find you."

He reaches into his breast pocket and takes out a small notebook and passes it to her.

"Open this."

She looks at it. She doesn't move.

"Please don't make me repeat everything," he says. "We have to work together. There's no other way."

She opens the notebook, which has been made into a little scrapbook. Glued to the first page is a newspaper clipping. A mug shot—some wan droopy-eyed man—and under it the caption:

ALLEGED MAFIA CAPO TO TESTIFY FOR PROSECUTION

The article itself has been snipped away.

She doesn't know the face. She doesn't know why she should be looking at it. He tells her to turn the page, and she does, and finds another clipping—an obit. It says that the deceased, Harold Brown, was the owner of a video rental outlet in Lincoln, Nebraska. That he "apparently took his own life." There's also a color Polaroid of someone in a coffin.

"It's the same man," he says. "Our 'alleged Mafia capo.' Of course he went into Witness Protection. Of course it didn't protect. Are you wondering how his enemies found him? Any guesses? My theory is, someone must have bugged his sister's telephone. Someone must have shown a great deal of patience and perseverance. Now turn the page."

But her fingers are shaking, and she can't get this page separated from the next. Till he reaches from behind her and turns it for her.

MAN KILLED IN MACHINERY AT SAVANNAH PULP MILL

"Well, this one now," he says, "the thing about this one is that he shouldn't have been working with machinery in the first place. He was a street mule. What did he know about machines? Why did Witness Protection make him a machinist?" His voice is close to her now. "And why did they think they could leave him unguarded for even an instant?"

He turns the page.

"Study this one."

A grainy photograph of the front steps of some federal-looking building. A woman is descending those steps alone.

"Linda Benelli. She ought not to have testified. It's my fault, because I think I could have dissuaded her but I didn't try. I didn't realize how angry my colleagues would be, and I let it go. But now look what happened. Turn the page."

Again he has to help her.

She's confronted by the photograph of a smiling elderly couple. A Christmas-card kind of photo, and it's been reprinted in this newspaper article under the heading:

THOMPSONVILLE COUPLE MISSING

"Her parents," he says.

After the first rush of dizziness, of swirling, there's a slight clearing in Annie's head. "Wait," she says. "Wait a minute, how do I—"

"How do you know these pictures are real? I guess you don't know," he says. "You can't."

He takes the book from her lap.

He says, "You're right, this is foolish, isn't it? This is like a child's game of show and tell. It doesn't prove a thing."

He slips the book back into his breast pocket. "I want to persuade you, Annie. That's all. If I could have brought you someone's *head*, someone's head in a box, I'd have done it. All I want is to persuade you. Because if I don't? If I can't convince you that we mean what we say, if you decide to go to the police—then Louie Boffano goes down and I go down with him, and someone close to you will be hurt beyond repair and to what purpose? For nothing. For the sake of stupid vengeance, so much pointless suffering. Then if they execute me it'll be too good for me. So please, Annie, please. *Believe me.*"

When she looks up he's squatting on his haunches in front of her. His face is huge, it's the only thing in her vision.

"Will you believe me?" he says. "Will you help me?"

She hears her breath getting ragged, breaking up. "I *can't*. I wouldn't be, I'll just, I'll cry. I'm a crybaby. I won't be able to stop crying, they'll take me off the jury, they'll—"

"You think if the judge sees you crying he'll excuse you from the jury?"

"He, he'll *have* to."

He shakes his head. "But if he did excuse you, then we'd suspect some kind of betrayal on your part—"

"Oh, God, *no*, I wouldn't say a word, never, I swear—"

"Annie, I know you wouldn't *mean* any harm but still, there would be that smidgen of doubt in our minds. And in turn? I know that some tragedy would befall someone you care for—"

"No, please! I, please, I only meant—"

He gives her a small dismissive wave. He rises and crosses to the bench in the middle of the studio, and sits.

"That's not a way out. I wish it were. But there's only one way out. *We need you.*"

"But I *can't*. If he's guilty I can't. Please! You don't know me, I can't lie. People always know. If I said I thought he didn't do it, but I really thought he did? They'd know I was lying. And he *did* kill them, didn't he? He killed that old man, and that boy, he killed both of them! Didn't he?"

He smiles. "This is perhaps too philosophical for my taste."

"I'm just asking you! He's guilty! Isn't he? He killed lots of people. He—"

"He's in the mob, Annie. He's been blamed for some murders, yes. But his so-called victims, they were vermin themselves."

"Not that *child*."

"The boy was an accident. Even Louie Boffano wouldn't deliberately kill a child. As for the old man, you want to weep for *him*? You want to weep for a stone killer like Salvadore Riggio? Because, Annie, I assure you, Salvadore Riggio never wept for—"

The telephone goes off. It sends a shock of panic up her spine.

"What, what do I do?"

He hands her a handkerchief.

"Wipe your tears. Answer it. It's probably your child."

"What do I say?"

"Whatever you like. Say that you're upset. Say that your date turned out to be a creep."

He offers his hand to help her up. She waves him away, stands on her own. She stumbles to the corner of the studio and picks up the phone.

"Yeah."

"Mom?"

"Yeah."

"You all right?"

"Yes."

"Mom, what's the matter?"

She sniffs. "Nothing. I didn't have a good time. With this guy. I'm all right."

"What'd he do, Mom?"

She draws a breath and says, "He didn't do anything, he just— How are *you* doing, Oliver?"

"You said you'd call."

"I'm sorry. So, so are you being polite to Jesse's mom?"

"Yeah."

"So. OK."

"Mom, you sound really weird. Is the guy still gonna buy your boxes?"

"It doesn't matter. Get a good sleep, OK? See you tomorrow. See you after school. OK?" She hangs up.

After a moment he tells her, "By the way, I *am* going to buy your boxes. The three at the gallery, of course. And these also—if we can work out a fair price."

"Forget it," she says. "I don't, I'd rather—"

"I insist. I want to do something for you. I realize that placed beside the fear you're feeling now, this can't amount to much, but still."

He rises. "Annie, I'm sorry about the fear. If I had any choice, any choice . . . I know this is going to be a scary time for you. And lonely. But please don't breathe a word of this. To *anyone*. Because anyone you tell, you're putting their lives at risk. Do you follow that?"

She gazes at nothing. Finally she sniffs, and he takes it for assent.

"When I need to see you I'll send for you. Someone will say to you, 'I met you at the bakery.' Do what he tells you. Now what will he say to you?"

"I met you at the bakery."

"Annie, this will all be over before you know it. And after that our paths will never cross."

He goes to the door. When he opens it, the air that eddies in is sharp, cold. The three candle flames dip and then crane their necks and dip again.

He shuts the door behind him.

The candles steady themselves and she hears his car start. She hears the Vivaldi start up midstrain, instantly exultant. Proud, willful, dominant by virtue of its design. Not a note that hasn't been called for, prepared for, not a note out of place, those towering scales of discipline, and then the music and the engine-purr fade and leave her to this room full of silence, to her own raw crude weak and shadowy sculptures, the beating of her heart, and not a single thought in her head that's of any use to her.

SLAVKO CZERNYK hunkers down tonight in this old clawfoot bathtub because his tightass landlord still hasn't turned on the heat and this is the only way to get warm. He lifts his foot out of the water and gets a toe-grip on the H knob. Twists it.

Treats the tub to a nice scalding pick-me-up.

He's chewing a Nicorette and smoking a Lucky Strike at the same time. A cupful of Jim Beam (with a drop of honey) rests on the tub sill. He's holding a book above the waterline. The book is called *The Essential Derek Walcott.* He owns this book because once a woman told him that Derek Walcott was the *greatest poet ever, oh my god.* He was in love with this woman. He still is. So he keeps the book at all times in this bathroom across from his office, and whenever he takes a crap or a bath he opens *The Essential Derek Walcott* and makes a stab at civilizing himself.

He glares at a poem.

The poem taunts him.

The poem says things like

> . . . and read until the lamplit page revolves
> to a white stasis whose detachment shines
> like a propeller's rainbowed radiance.
> Circling like us, no comfort for their loves! . . .

He squints. He tries that part again. He still doesn't get it. He turns the book upside down and reads:

· · · Circling like us, no comfort for their loves!
like a propeller's rainbowed radiance.
to a white stasis whose detachment shines
and read until the lamplit page revolves · · ·

This is never going to work. He takes a long pull from the Jim Beam, a long pull from the Lucky, and turns the page.

In his office across the hall, the phone rings.

Who have we got here? he wonders. Who'd be calling the Czernyk Detective Agency at this hour?

Probably Grassman Security. They're on a stakeout and no relief, and Slavko, could you please hustle your ass down here? So you can make eight bucks an hour sitting with Bill Farmer in a colder-than-shit Mercury Zephyr and keep tabs on a murky motel door across a murky street and listen all night to Bill Farmer's two-part snore-and-fart harmony, OK, Slavko?

All the god damn livelong night, how about *that*, Slavko?

No thanks.

Thanks but I'd rather stay here and read, read until the lamplit page revolves to a white stasis whose detachment shines like a propeller's rainbowed radiance, you know what I mean?

Second ring.

He lets himself sink down to his chin in the water.

Or maybe the Caruso Hotel needs me to babysit a postal carrier's convention. Like that bunch last week. Stuck in the hall all night on a folding metal chair. Keeping a sharp eye on the Coke machine, in case maybe it was one of those mass-murdering postal workers in disguise.

By four in the morning he'd sort of hoped it was.

Third ring.

Forget it, guys. I don't need the money that much. I mean, I do need the money, I've lost my apartment and soon I'm going to be tossed from this rathole office, but still . . . when I get out of this tub I'm crawling right into beddy-bye.

His machine picks up.

He hears his own grungy growl on the tape: "You've reached the

Czernyk Detective Agency. We've stepped out of the office for a moment . . ."

He sounds to himself like a cross between an iguana with a hangover and a haunted cellar door.

He brings the Lucky to his lips, takes a little sip of it, then holds it there between his fingers while he slides his head under the water. But he can still hear his grunting from the machine.

And then some other voice, a liquid and whispery song of a voice, and he lurches up out of the water.

This angel-voice is leaving her name. Sari Knowles. What a beautiful name. And her number. She says:

". . . I need, um, I may need your help, with something, I mean I guess it's not an emergency and I know it's late and I don't know you, really I just got your name out of the Yellow Pages but if you can—"

"Hello."

"Hello? Mr. Sir-nik?"

"Czernyk. 'Ch' as in choo-choo. I, um—wait, I just got out of the tub, I was, I was across the hall, wait—"

"I'm sorry, I didn't think you'd be there, I mean—"

"It's OK. It's OK."

Freezing in here. He shuts the door to the hall. He lies down on the mattress on the floor and pulls the covers over him. Pulls them over his head, scrunches way down. Yesterday's newspaper, a box of Oreo cookies, and a forlorn copy of *Penthouse* are down here with him. And the telephone. "Yes, ma'am. What can I do for you?"

"I don't know."

"Are you in trouble?"

"No. Not with the law or anything, I'm, it's . . ." She fades off.

"You married?"

"Uh-uh, no."

"Boyfriend?"

She takes a breath. "Yeah."

"Problem?"

"Mm."

"You don't know where he is?"

"But he's not in any danger, it's . . ."

"You think maybe he's with someone else?"

"I don't know *what* he's doing." She's on the edge of tears. "He doesn't tell me anymore. I mean, he's, he's busy. He manages a commodities fund, and, so I don't know, I guess he's *busy*. He's says he's got this new client? This woman?"

"And you're a little jealous."

"Oh damn. This isn't like me. You know? I mean I know how late it is, I should have waited till tomorrow, but I can't, I can't think about anything else, I can't sleep. I mean I should handle this better. I'm a businesswoman, I have my own travel agency. I'm a responsible—I mean I should—"

"No, I understand. It's tough sometimes. Can I ask you something, Ms.—"

"Sari Knowles. Sari."

"Sari. This is kind of private and you don't have to answer me, but are you seeing a therapist?"

No answer.

He tells her, "It's only that, when you're going through—"

"But if he's seeing somebody else what difference would it make? You know? If I've lost him?" A rib of near panic running underneath her voice. "Then what difference would it make if I'm sane or not?"

Slavko knows this tone. When he hears this tone on the telephone he knows he's got himself a client. Do you feel the walls trembling? Do you feel your lovelife starting to cave in all around you? Does it feel as though the walls of your lovelife are rotten at the foundation and they're starting to bow and bulge and crumble, and does it feel as though loneliness is about to come rushing in?

Then dial a private investigator.

Because you've made up your mind that what's really killing you is the not knowing. And you think that all you need for what ails you is a dose of the *truth*. So you call a detective, to unearth this truth.

Of course this is a dumb move.

The *truth* is, there's nothing a detective's ever going to find out for anybody that anybody really wants to know.

The truth is, ma'am, that if the walls of your lovelife are crumbling and tumbling, how the hell is a private investigator supposed to prop them up?

And if I were an honest man, I'd tell you that right off. If I were an honest man, I'd hang up on you.

Says Slavko, "So how can I help you there, Sari? How can I be of service?"

ANNIE's sitting up in bed. It's three in the morning. Her TV is on. A *Gong Show* rerun, which is the liveliest pablum she can find. She's not watching it. She's watching a stain on the wall above the TV, an ancient water-seep stain. She only glances at the set when they hit the gong. She wishes they'd do that more often. The rest of the show doesn't reach her consciousness.

All the lights are on. Every light in the house. And she's got the radio going, an oldtime reggae station from the city, with the bass line, the underbeat, coming in furred by lousy reception.

When she turned the TV on, she forgot to turn the radio off.

She wonders if she can't go fetch Oliver. No, it's too late. She'd wake up everybody in Jesse's house. Embarrass him in front of his friend. Best to wait till morning. He's OK, he's fine. He's OK. Wait till morning.

She has the sense that the *Gong Show* has ended and something else has come on, but she doesn't have the energy to lower her eyes to the set to find out what.

The telephone rings.

You bastard, what did you forget? What? Some threat you didn't make clear enough? Some new torture you want to detail for me—

Still, it could be Oliver.

So she picks up. "Yeah?"

Crackle and snap. A little wait, then, "Hi, Annie? What's up?"

Turtle.

He says, "You working? You on some hot date, what are you—"

"Turtle! Jesus, how are you?"

"I'm good," she thinks she hears.

"Wait!" she cries, and she stretches to the radio and slaps it off and she reaches for the TV and turns that off too. Abruptly the house is cast into deep silence except for the static on the telephone. The call is coming from the mountains of Guatemala. Whenever Turtle calls he calls from the Guatel office in Huehuetenango, the nearest town of any size to the little pueblo where he runs his clinic.

"I can't hear you very well," she says.

He shouts. "Can you hear me now?"

"Yes!" she cries.

She's so glad to hear his shout she's almost weeping.

He says, "I had to bring one of the kids down to the hospital here, and I thought about you, and we haven't talked in . . . how long?"

"I don't know," she says. "Spring? In the spring."

He asks her, "How are you?"

"I'm OK," she says.

But her voice trails off.

Anyone you tell, you're putting their lives at risk.

She can't do this. She has to get rid of him before he says something that will let Zach Lyde know who he is, where he's living.

Zach Lyde could be listening this moment.

Is he? Is he here right now, is he hanging over me, is his ear pressed up against the receiver—

Of course he's listening.

So hang up.

But Turtle would call back.

Unplug the phone then.

No, she knows Turtle. If Turtle can't get through at all he'll start to worry. He'll catch the next bus to Guatemala City and then a plane up here. . . .

"Annie, weren't you supposed to be in a group show at that gallery of yours? Wasn't that supposed to open last month?"

You know what you have to do.

He says, "How'd it go? Those artworld shits, they've cottoned on yet? They know how good you are?"

Get it over with.

"Hey, Turtle? I don't want to talk to you."

70

The hissing, the slow wheeze of the connection. Sounds like desert animals, sick and thirsty, a chain of whimpering animals from here all the way to Guatemala.

Finally he says, "This isn't a good time?"

"There isn't any good time. Look, we had something between us years ago. And since then we've tried to be friends, but it doesn't work, does it? I've got somebody with me now. OK? And he doesn't like these phone calls. OK? And frankly I don't either."

Only those cracklings. They go on for so long, she starts to wonder if he's hung up—and then she hears him blow out some breath and say, "Woo. Jesus. God. I'm *sorry*, Annie."

She thinks, For Christ sake, *I'm* being the asshole and *you* say you're sorry. That's why we never made it in the first place, Turtle. You're too god damn nice.

"Hey, it's no big deal," she tells him. "Just leave me alone now. OK?"

THE TEACHER lies half-asleep in his bed in this ancient one-room schoolhouse, listening to channel four: her bedroom. He hears her cradle the phone. He waits for the sound of her crying, but no such sound can be heard.

He knows that to banish her friend couldn't have been easy for her. He's proud of her.

He hears her bed sigh and the creak of a floorboard. Then her footsteps as she walks out to the hall, descends the stairs.

Ah, Annie, he thinks, why don't you get some sleep now? I know you're troubled. But it will seem better in the morning.

All of us can use some sleep.

He switches to channel one. The kitchen. He hears something slippery. Her jacket? Yes, she's putting on her jacket. The back door. Then faintly the whining screen door. Nothing for a moment. He turns up the volume. He hears the fridge, the stutter of a clock. Then her car engine starting up.

"Annie," he murmurs. "Oh, come back, girl. Come to bed."

He puts his hand wearily on the phone and waits for Eddie to call.

Eddie's been posted near her bungalow tonight as a precaution. In case the Teacher has misread her, in case she panics and has dreams of flight. But the Teacher knows he hasn't misread her.

The phone buzzes. Eddie tells him, "She's going, Vincent, she's in her car. I don't know *where* she's going."

"I do," says the Teacher.

"Where?"

"Jesse Grabowski's house. Where her child's staying."

"She's picking up her kid? She's gonna take off?"

"I don't think so, Eddie. I think she just wants to be close to her child."

EDDIE, ten minutes later, drives through a silent hillside development and spots her car parked across the street from a mailbox that says GRABOWSKI.

He sees her silhouette. She's sitting there in the car. He sweeps past her quickly and tells the telephone, "Yeah, she's here."

But there's no answer. Vincent has fallen asleep again. Eddie has to say it again. "She's here."

"Good," says Vincent.

"Like you said."

"Uh-huh."

"I don't get it, though."

"What don't you get, Eddie?"

"I don't get what the fuck is she doing? I mean how does it do her any good to be parking across the street from where her kid is sleeping?"

Says Vincent, "It's a mystery."

"Why doesn't she go in there and get him?"

"Wake them all?"

Oh, thinks Eddie. That's reasonable.

But he also thinks, How the hell does *Vincent* know the deal here? Vincent has no kids. How does he know more about what a parent thinks than Eddie does? Eddie's got a daughter, and he's practically raised her by himself. Vincent has nothing. Vincent's got nobody, so how does he know? How does that cocksucker always know?

"Hey, Vincent."

The voice comes back sleepily. "What?"

"Let me ask your advice."

"My advice? My advice is to call it a night. She'll be fine, really. Pretty soon she'll go home on her own."

"No, you gotta help me."

"With what?"

"It's about my daughter. Roseanne."

A sigh. "OK."

"She's fourteen years old, you know?"

"Close. She's fifteen, Eddie."

"What?"

"Your daughter's fifteen. She just had her birthday. I sent her a present."

"Bite my crank, Vincent. You mean those roller blades? She loves those fuckin roller blades."

"That's good."

"Vincent, did she send you a thank-you note?"

"She did."

"Yeah? Well, OK, now get this. Got a call from the doctor the other day. He was giving Roseanne her physical exam? For school? Standard shit? And he says, get this, her *labia*, he says. Her lips. Her pussy lips, my *daughter*."

"What about her labia?"

"She had em *pierced*. And she's got rings in em. One on each side. And she's got this little padlock that goes through the rings. So nobody can get into her pussy if they don't got a key. She's fifteen fuckin years old, Vincent. You hear this? And guess what? *She* don't got a key. Only her *boyfriend*'s got a key. I come home? I says, Roseanne, tell me the boy's name. No, she says. I says, this prince among men, tell me his name. She says no. I says, Roseanne, I mean, I got ways I can find this out. She says, Oh yeah? You gonna throw me in the East River? I says, listen, Roseanne, my dear fuckin child, I ever hit you? She says no. I say, well I shoulda! You fuckin psycho, I shoulda knocked the brains outta your skull! Padlock on your pussy! And still she won't tell me the guy's name. So what do I do? Vincent, I'm losing this kid, what the hell do I do?"

Eddie drives along Pharaoh's main street. Cones of streelight. One lonely cop car, trolling. On the phone he hears Vincent say softly, "I don't know, Eddie. Find a mother for your child?"

"Yeah? Where am I gonna find a good woman? Guy as ugly as me?"

"You're not ugly."

"Fat, face all squashed-in on one side, what're you giving me here?"

"There's plenty to love about you, Eddie. Talk to one of your friends. For example D'Apolito, who has that nightclub? Let him set you up with one of the girls."

"I've had enough fuckin whores in my life! Girl's mother was a fuckin whore! Fuckin Rita, don't get me going about Rita, Vincent."

"All right. The important thing is, do you love your daughter?"

He's asking this in his whispery trance-voice that he sometimes uses.

"Yeah," says Eddie.

"Well then I think she'll muddle through. You must keep showing her you love her. Sooner or later she'll get rid of the padlock. In the meantime, at least you know she's not sleeping around. Now let me go back to bed, Eddie."

3

You're not afraid of anything when you're around this man.

ANNIE, a week later in the courtroom, turns the page of her transcript, and so does everyone else. It's like test time in school: GO ON TO THE NEXT PAGE *NOW*.

On the tape, Louie Boffano is speaking. The tape comes from a microphone that was hidden in the back room of a shoe repair shop in Queens. Mostly it sounds like those bristly bursts of CB chatter that sometimes stray into TV reception. Annie can't understand more than a few words without the help of the transcript. Even with the transcript, Louie Boffano's gassing is all but incoherent:

"So I said, you know, I said what, what, what the fuck's going on, he's coming in? He's coming to see me? You know, Paulie? He says, no he don't want to. He's not, he doesn't want to see you. I say, OK. So what the fuck is going on with Carbone Construction? He says he talked to this guy Wilton."

Then Paulie DeCicco's voice, bed of gravel, muttering something that the transcript interprets as "Who?"

Says Louie, "Or . . . Walton. What the fuck? You know? Or Walton or something, I don't know. You know this guy?"

This time the transcript gives up on Paulie DeCicco. It reads: "(INAUDIBLE)."

Louie rolls on: "I don't know. I don't know, Paulie. But if he's working for me, Wilton or Walton, I don't know. You know?"

Grunts Paulie, "He's a scumbag."

Louie says, "Who? Walton?"

"Who?" says Paulie.

"Or Wilton or I don't—you know this guy?"

"I don't (INAUDIBLE). Talking about, weren't you talking about Vito?"

"Vito," says Louie. "You know what I'm saying? And they're *all* fuckin hard-ons. And those, those, Paulie, those are the *good* ones. But that's where the shit comes in. *Minchia!*"

Paulie DeCicco makes some hawking noise.

Annie has no notion, none, not the least shred, of what Louie Boffano is talking about.

Perhaps lack of sleep has something to do with her confusion.

But she's pretty sure no one else in this courtroom knows what he's talking about either. Although nobody's going to give that away.

Everyone stares down at his script, everyone turns the page in unison—everyone except Annie and Louie Boffano.

Louie looks bored. He pays no attention to the tape. Annie watches him. He bounces his pen against his legal pad. He smirks for an instant at something he hears inside his head. He tears off the corner of a sheet from the pad and crumples it and pops it in his mouth. A spitball, he's making a spitball. Everyone else is so studious but not Louie the class cutup.

He leans back and sticks his tongue out at the ceiling—and there, up on the tip of his tongue, behold: the little yellow spitball.

But they're all so busy reading that nobody notices, nobody laughs.

So after a moment he flicks the tongue and the spitball back into his mouth. Straightens up. Looks at the jurors. Annie slaps her eyes down to the page but not quick enough: Louie Boffano has seen her watching him.

And then abruptly, through all the murky chatter on the tape, she gets one glimmer of meaning, of *intention*.

Louie Boffano is saying:

"I mean, Paulie, does the stupid fuck think he can hide from *me*? 'Cause that's what Salvadore thought, you remember? Fuckin Salvadore Riggio, fucking invincible, right? Everybody said he was invincible. Remember? He can't be killed. He won't come out of his house, and he's got twenty fuckin guards and an electric fuckin fence. The works, Paulie. But then I was talking to the Teacher, and he says to me, 'Man doesn't want to be killed? Man won't come out of his house? So what? We can dig a *tunnel*.' Remember, Paulie?"

Says Paulie, "(INAUDIBLE)."

Says Louie, "I told the Teacher, OK, you want, you want to dig a tunnel, *dig* a tunnel. Kill that motherfucker! Jesus!"

Says Paulie, "Yeah, that was funny."

Says Louie, "It wasn't so fuckin funny to Salvadore Riggio. And it's not fuckin funny if you're some scumbag you won't come in, you won't come see me, you're trying to hide from Louie Boffano. Am I right?"

"(INAUDIBLE)," says Paulie.

"(INAUDIBLE)," says Louie.

"(INAUDIBLE)," says Paulie.

Annie looks up again and Louie has his eyes shut. His lawyer Bozeman is still wincing from the blow. Must have known it was coming but he's wincing anyway. And in the corner of her eye Annie notices that the juror next to her is slowly, unconsciously, shaking his head.

Annie knows that before this trial is over she'll hear this part of the tape played over and over and over again.

You idiot, she thinks. Why not tell the world, make a formal announcement, take out an ad in the *Times*? How the hell do you think anyone can sit down in a jury room and explain that idiotic rooster-strut away?

I told the Teacher, OK, you want, you want to dig a tunnel, dig a tunnel. Kill that motherfucker! Jesus!

SLAVKO sits in a booth of the Croton Dam Diner with this astonishing seraph Sari Knowles.

"So," he says. "You just want me to find out where he's been going at night? Whether he's sleeping with this client of his?"

"Yes."

"Got any ideas?" he asks her.

"About what?"

"About where he goes."

She shakes her head.

Slavko presses. "Well, where does he *say* he goes?"

"I don't know, his work. Deals. I told you, he manages a commodities fund."

"So when he says he's busy with that, why don't you believe him?"

She thinks about it. She puts the tip of her tongue between her teeth.

She must know what a piece of work she is. That hair of hers, all that honey-white hair breaking sumptuously across her shoulders. It reflects in the mirror beside her. It reflects again in the mirror across the way. It seems to glimmer all over this noontime diner. She's got to be aware of this. The short-order cook who leers at her, the two truckers who murmur and snicker—she pays them no mind at all but she must know what effect she's having.

She's probably used to it by now.

Probably she's come to depend on it.

Slavko notes the crispness of her eyeliner, the freshness of her mascara. The DKNY business suit with the Hermès scarf—she hasn't forgotten how to look smart and casual at the same time. She may be living in the eye of an emotional hurricane but she's not going to let the short-order cook know it.

She sips her tea and shrugs and tells Slavko, "I don't know why I don't believe him. You think I should trust him?"

"Have you asked *him* that?"

"If I should trust him? If he's lying to me? No."

"Why not?"

She blinks. "*Ask* him if he's lying to me?"

"Right."

"Oh no. I can't."

"Why not?"

"You'd have to know him."

"Why would I have to know him?"

"Because if you knew him you wouldn't ask that question."

"Why not?"

"Is this how you talk to all your clients?"

"It's how I talk to my *prospective* clients. Yeah. This can be a tricky business. I want to find the firm ground here. I want to know where the solid ground stops and the, where the, where the—"

She helps him. "Where the bullshit starts?"

"Right. But if you think I'm badgering you—"

"Oh, ask away," she says, and she flashes her palms as if to show she has nothing to hide. "All right, look. I don't want Eben to know about my . . . concerns or doubts or whatever, because, well, because then he'll think I'm weak."

"And your boyfriend—you say his name is *Eben*?"

"Eben Rackland."

"You mean like short for Ebenezer?"

"Just Eben."

"Uh-huh. And this Eben, he doesn't care for *weak* people?"

"Well, nobody likes weakness, right? Jealousy and all? I don't think anybody—"

"*You* don't like weak people, Sari?"

She gives him a look: *What does this have to do with the business at hand?* Slavko's wondering the same thing. He's asking himself, What's all this, Slavko? Just because Juliet once, on that trip to

Bannerman's Island, hinted that she didn't like weak men, and you thought she was hinting about you? So now you're going to get all bent out of shape with this client?

But he leaves his question out there, and after a moment Sari takes it up.

"Well, I suppose I do find strength more attractive than weakness. Sure."

"I see. And this Eben Rackland? You think he's strong?"

She doesn't hesitate. "He's *powerful*. Yes."

"What do you mean, *powerful*?"

For Christ sake, Slavko, leave it alone. What, are you jealous of Sari's boyfriend? You have a thing for Sari? You probably do, you little worm. Like the short-order cook over there, with his drool. Very good, very professional, Slavko. I'm sure you're just her type, too. No doubt she's been searching her whole life for a nosy, balding, posturing loser.

Still, even in the teeth of his own self-mockery, he plunges on. Can't seem to help himself. "Do you mean if he was, if he was here with us, he'd just tear me up?"

This question clearly weirds her.

"Tear you up? I don't—Eben doesn't *hurt* people. Is this what you mean?"

"I mean I'm trying to figure out why you don't throw in the towel on this one. Here's this guy, he's a great guy with a great biblical name, but you don't trust him. You can't be happy with somebody you don't trust. Right? So why don't you toss him back? Find somebody else? You know?"

She looks into her tea. She seems to be fighting back tears. She says, "Have you ever been obsessed?"

But she doesn't wait for an answer. She says, "It makes me feel stupid. Like a child. I mean, look at me, I'm successful, I told you that. I own my own travel agency. I've never had problems before with self-esteem. And now I keep saying to myself, So he works a lot of nights, he's a workaholic, so what? When he's with me he loves me. And other times I say, No. He's got to be seeing someone else. I mean, I'm going out of my mind. But Eben—when you're around Eben five minutes you think, This man *understands*. You're not afraid of anything when you're around this man. I said he's powerful? He's powerful because of his *soul*. Oh, you don't get it. I think, I think I'd kill myself, I would, before I'd leave him. But you don't get it. It doesn't make any sense to you."

"Yes it does," says Slavko.

She dabs at her eyes. Her makeup comes off on her napkin. Black smears. Why does she wear so much makeup, he wonders, when she doesn't need any makeup at all? Does she think she has to wear it for *him*? Who is this man who's hurting her, who can this bastard be?

He says, "Sari, I know what you're going through. I've been there myself."

He lays his hand on hers and she flips her hand and clutches his wrist, hard. Then she lets him go.

He's thinking, *I still am there.*

OLIVER's got Jesse up in his room with their noses close to the computer screen. Oliver's sketching a dragon. Working on its fang, but it's not coming out right. Too cute, a wimpy little snaggle-tooth.

"Come on," says Jesse. "A *fang*. *Big* fang."

Oliver says, "Oh, yeah? You want a big one?"

"Yeah."

"A *big* one?" Oliver clicks the palette, then slides the mouse against its pad. From between the dragon's rear legs, a blood-red phallus emerges.

"You buttwipe," says Jesse. But he laughs as the organ keeps growing.

"Big enough?"

"Bigger!"

Oliver coils the thing like a lariat around the dragon's neck.

"Oh yeah!" says Jesse. "Now that is *phat*!"

A bloom of sharp yellow barbs.

"What are those?" says Jesse.

"Herpes," says Oliver. "Dragon herpes."

"Wait, let me!" says Jesse, and he reaches for the mouse.

"No, wait!" says Oliver. Now he's putting leaves on the dragon's member. Turning it into a tree for some reason, dozens of twigs and leaves. Jesse trying to snatch the mouse, but Oliver holds him at bay

86

with one hand and works the mouse with the other, clicking more and more green leaves onto the screen. Both of them roaring with laughter.

Then Oliver looks up, and his mom is standing in the doorway.

She's got that strange bitter look that she's had for days now, and she says, "What's he doing here?"

Oliver quits laughing. "Jesse? What do you mean—"

"You're supposed to be doing your homework."

Winter in her voice. She never sounds like this except when she's really over the edge. And even then not in front of his friends.

"Mom, it's not, it's not even *six*—I don't have to—"

"You have to do what I tell you to do. First thing you have to do is say goodbye to your friend."

The blood whooshes up into his cheeks. His voice skips half an octave. "Mom, that's not *fair*. We were just—"

"Goodbye, Jesse," she announces.

Jesse slouches down the stairs.

Oliver's eyes sting. He swallows. "Mom, I don't understand why you did that."

She says, "Who the hell's been cutting up the newspaper?"

She holds it up. The front page, with an oblong missing.

"I did," he says. Not meeting her eyes.

"Oh *really*? It was *you*? I thought Mr. Slivey had snuck in here and done it. The missing piece, what was it about?"

She speaks so sharply and with such venom that all he can do is gape at her.

She says, "It was about the trial, wasn't it? I looked through this whole newspaper, I can't find anything about the trial."

"Mom, you told me to. You told me to cut out everything about the trial."

"Oh Jesus." Rolling her eyes. "You don't do *anything* I say. You never do anything I ask you to, now why the *hell* did you do this? Where is it?"

He hesitates.

She asks again. "Where *is* it?"

"It's in, I tore, it's in little pieces."

"Why?"

"You told me to!"

"I didn't tell you to make confetti! Did I tell you to make confetti, god damn you!"

That's it—he's lost his hold. He stares down at his lap, and his tears fall straight down. "Mom, you told me—"

"What did it say?"

"Mom, you're not supposed to know. You're not, you're not supposed to read the newspaper, you're not supposed to watch the TV, you're—"

"Tell me what it said!"

"I don't know! It said—what? There was a guy they said like a police guy, there was a, they played a *tape*—"

"What was on the tape?"

"But you were *there*, Mom. Why ask me?"

"What did they say was on the tape?"

"I don't know. I think they said Louie Boffano told a guy he should dig, a tunnel, and, and kill him."

"Did they say Boffano was guilty?"

"I don't, I don't know."

"What did they say? Did they say there was *persuasive* evidence, *compelling* evidence, what?"

"What? I don't understand."

"*Persuasive.* Do you recognize the word *persuasive*? What did they say?"

"They said—they just said everybody got quiet."

"But what did they want you to *think*?" She's holding his arms now. Squeezing them, digging in with her claws. Hurting him some, but that's not so bad. What really scares him is her voice. "Do they want you to think he's guilty?"

"I don't know. Mom!"

"Who have you talked to about this?"

"About the trial? Nobody! You asked me not to."

"Yeah? Well I'm not asking you not to anymore. I'm saying, You talk to somebody about this trial, and this is what I'll do, I'll take your bike and I'll back the car over it, and I'll take your computer and throw it out the window, and then I swear to God I'll come up here and I'll kill you. I will kill you. You listening?"

"Yes."

She lets go of him. She rises. He rubs his face into the crook of his elbow and sniffs. But she gets him by a clump of his hair and pulls his face into the light. "What's *this* bullshit? You think 'cause there's no man around you can be a crybaby? This is garbage. This, no. This stops now."

4

bounced around like a dunce with

my jaw hanging open. . . .

ANNIE, a week later, watches Louie Boffano's lawyer, Bozeman, with his big amiable walrus mustache and cunning yellow teeth, as he picks gingerly at the government's star witness.

Says Bozeman, "Now Mr. DeCicco, you testified on direct that Louie Boffano was having 'a problem' with Salvadore Riggio, is that correct?"

Paulie DeCicco has an imposing hairless skull, a craggy mountain of head. This gives him an air of thoughtfulness, even sagacity—at least until he opens his mouth.

"Huh?"

Says Bozeman, "Didn't you testify that Louie Boffano had become a distributor of cocaine and heroin?"

"Yeh."

"And how do you know this?"

"I was with him when he did it."

"You were his faithful lieutenant, right?"

"Lieutenant? No."

"You weren't—"

"I was a *captain*."

"Excuse me. Captain. Now, *Captain* DeCicco, who was Louie buying the cocaine from? Could you refresh our memories?"

"From Cali."

"The Cali cartel?"

"Yeh."

"Out of Colombia, South America?"

"Yeh."

"And heroin? Who was the connection there?"

"The Ndrangheta."

"This is a group in Italy, you say?"

"In Calabria, uh-huh."

"A group that's associated with the Mafia?"

"Huh?"

"Would you say the Ndrangheta is associated with the Mafia?"

"I'd say it *is* the Mafia."

"But now Salvadore Riggio, he was the head of the Carmine family?"

"That's right."

"And the Carmine, this was *your* family?"

"Yeh."

"And Louie Boffano is also in the Carmine family?"

"Yeh."

"OK. But now Salvadore Riggio, he didn't, he didn't approve of Mr. Boffano's connection with the Cali cartel, with the Ndrangheta . . . ?"

"He had a beef."

"OK. Tell us again, Mr. DeCicco, what was his beef?"

"You weren't supposed to deal drugs. That was the law."

"You mean the unwritten law of the family?"

"Correct."

"Why was that the law, Mr. DeCicco?"

"I dunno."

Bozeman stands at the rail to the jury box. He twitches his mustache and gives the jurors a playful glance. "It seems like a somewhat strange law, doesn't it? Mr. DeCicco? For a criminal organization?"

"I dunno."

"I'm just, I think we're all trying to picture Salvadore Riggio as this, this *crusader* against drugs. . . ." Murmur of laughter in the courtroom. "Would you have called Salvadore Riggio an antidrug crusader?"

Tallow, the DA, hops up. "Objection. Salvadore Riggio's not on trial here."

Bozeman shrugs. "State is trying to portray Salvadore Riggio as an exemplary citizen, in order to create an emotional bias against my client."

The judge sustains the objection. Whereupon Louie Boffano mutters, "What the fuck?"

It's a mutter, but it's loud enough for everyone to hear.

Judge Wietzel leans forward into his microphone. "I didn't quite hear that, Mr. Boffano. Would you care to repeat that?"

Louie Boffano gives him a grin. "Not really."

Says the judge, "I warn you again to keep your opinion of these proceedings to yourself." He glowers. Then, "You may proceed with the cross, Mr. Bozeman. But please don't ask Mr. DeCicco to assess Mr. Riggio's relative morality."

Bozeman asks Paulie, "OK, then, the fact is that the unwritten code of the Carmine family prohibited large-scale drug dealing?"

"Yeh."

"Penalty for noncompliance?"

"Death."

"And you testified that Mr. Boffano had been a member of the Carmine family for as long as you had known him?"

"Yeh."

"Twenty-three years?"

"Yeh."

"A good soldier in the family?"

"I dunno. I guess."

"And yet he was willing to depart from this deeply rooted tradition of no drugs?"

"Yeh."

"Why?"

"Money."

"A lot of money?"

"Yeh."

"Somewhere in your testimony you say there was talk of making a billion dollars?"

"I mean, that was just talk."

"Well sometimes *I* talk about making money too, Mr. DeCicco. But I don't talk about making a billion dollars."

"No? Why, a billion dollars not enough for you? Oh yeh, I forgot, you're a *lawyer*."

Judge Wietzel makes a face. "Gentlemen."

But Bozeman chuckles amiably, and his yellow teeth glimmer and his walrus mustache does a little dance. He says, "That's very funny, Mr. DeCicco. You've got quite a wit there."

DeCicco shrugs.

Says Bozeman, "Very sharp. Now would you be sharp enough to recall for us who *started* all this talk?"

"Huh?"

"Who suggested to Mr. Boffano that he enter the drug business?"

"Oh, I dunno."

"I think you do know."

Tallow roars out, "Objection! Argumentative!"

Bozeman cheerfully concedes, "Ah you're right. My error, my error. Mr. DeCicco, didn't you testify yesterday that a man known to you only as the Teacher had suggested a strategy for negotiating with the Cali drug cartel?"

"Maybe, but he didn't—"

"And wasn't this the very same Teacher who had a few ideas for dealing with the Ndrangheta?"

"Yeh, but he—"

"And wasn't this the very same Teacher who suggested to Louie Boffano that he could dig a tunnel to Mr. Riggio's house and kill him?"

"Yeh."

"Who is this Teacher, Mr. DeCicco?"

"I dunno."

"Is he in this courtroom?"

"I dunno."

"What does he look like?"

"I dunno."

"You never saw him?"

"No."

"Did you ever speak to him?"

"Yeh. But he wore a mask."

"Why did he wear a mask?"

Paulie DeCicco shrugs.

Bozeman suggests, "Perhaps he didn't trust you?"

"I guess not."

"You *guess* not?"

"Yeh. Well, one time Louie told me that the Teacher didn't trust me. That he thought I'd rat out."

"And this prophecy proved true, didn't it, Mr. DeCicco?"

"I guess."

"You *did* rat out, that's why—"

"Objection!" says Tallow.

Says Bozeman, "His words, Your Honor. Not mine."

Wietzel overrules the objection.

"You turned your back on the family, Mr. DiCicco, just as the Teacher said you would, correct?"

"Yeh."

"In fact, the Teacher was *often* right, wasn't he?"

"I guess."

"These drug dealings, did the family make a lot of money?"

"Yeh."

"Just as the Teacher predicted?"

"Yeh."

"Pretty smart guy?"

"Yeh."

"And yet nobody knows who he is?"

"Louie Boffano knows."

"Anyone else?"

"I dunno."

"And one day this Teacher said he could dig a tunnel to the home of Salvadore Riggio, for the purpose of killing him?"

"Right."

"And Mr. Boffano said, 'OK, you want, you want to dig a tunnel, *dig* a tunnel.' Correct?"

"Correct."

"After all, the Teacher was the boss, he could do what he wanted, right?"

"Wait a minute—the Teacher wasn't the boss."

"Really? Do you know of any case in which the Teacher's council wasn't followed?"

"Well, yeh. Like me. I mean the Teacher didn't trust me but Louie kept me around anyway."

"Are you saying that despite his concerns, the Teacher *permitted* Mr. Boffano to retain your services?"

A feather of laughter sweeps over the courtroom.

Says Paulie DeCicco, "He didn't permit nothing! Louie was the boss! He gave the orders!"

"I think you mean Louie *spoke* the orders?"

"What does that mean?"

"Do you know what a puppet is, Mr. DeCicco?"

Tallow's on his feet instantly. "Objection!"

"I'm sorry, I'm sorry," Bozeman mumbles as he moves back to his desk. "I'll rephrase the question."

He stoops beside his desk and comes up with a paper bag. He reaches his hand into the bag. He turns to the witness. "Mr. DeCicco, do you know what this is?"

When his hand comes out of the bag it's wearing a cloth puppet. With black hair and a walrus mustache and a scowl. In the very image of its master, Mr. Bozeman.

Bozeman holds it up. He announces: "This is a puppet, isn't it?"

Gasp from the courtroom.

The puppet wheels and scowls down at Mr. Bozeman and squeaks: "No I'm *not*! I'm the boss! *You're* the puppet!"

Above the roar of laughter Wietzel tolls his gavel. He's furious. "Mr. Bozeman! Mr. Bozeman!"

Paulie DeCicco is shouting, *"Louie Boffano was no puppet!"*

The puppet nods gravely to Paulie, then turns upon its master and huffs, "That's right! So there!"

Judge Wietzel shouts, "Mr. Bozeman!"

Now Bozeman, mock-sheepish, dunks the puppet back into the paper bag. But the puppet fights its way out and shouts, "Sorry, Your Honor!"

The Judge thunders, "Mr. Bozeman, are you trying to make a circus of these proceedings? You're in contempt, and if there's one more— All right! Calm down! Order!"

Cracking the gavel again and again.

"I'm going to initiate disciplinary proceedings against you, Mr. Bozeman, for this comedic display. One more such entertainment and I will bar you from this courtroom, do you understand me?"

But Annie doesn't see why he's so upset. She thinks Bozeman put on a good show. She glances to the juror on her left and the juror on her right to see if they're as pleased as she is.

But they've only got the vaguest of smiles.

Oh, let yourself go, she thinks. Laugh a little. This bastard Bozeman just gave us something to work with, didn't he? Do you have to be so stuffy, can't you appreciate a little low humor once in a while, when it's in the service of letting an innocent man go free?

THE TEACHER sits half-lotus on the roof of the *BOFFANO* family mausoleum, in a light rain, watching them approach. Louie Boffano's brother Joseph with his bodyguard. He watches them as they wind along the path of marble seraphim.

Joseph keeps checking behind him. He's nervous. But then he's always nervous. Particularly anywhere outside his own neighborhood on Staten Island. Although in truth Staten Island is just where he's most likely to swallow a bullet someday—right in his own driveway, perhaps, or down at the corner deli, or maybe three doors down at his brother Louie's house.

Or maybe, the Teacher considers, in his very bedroom, like poor Salvadore Riggio.

The Teacher pulls his hood down over his head. It fits snugly, with openings for his eyes and mouth. He waits till his visitors come into the enclosure below him, till Joseph makes a flurried sign of the cross and approaches the steps. Then the Teacher rises and looks down upon them and says, "Hello, Joseph."

The two of them scrabble under their jackets for their pieces. Their eyes dart left and right, but neither of them think to look up. Joseph hops up the mausoleum steps for the shelter of its entranceway.

Meager shelter, though.

From a branch of the red maple that shades this roof, the Teacher plucks a samara, a double-bladed maple seed. He holds it over the shiny target of Joseph's bald spot, and lets it go. It whirs, it drops like a tiny smart bomb. But then it veers off at the last moment. Glides in front of Joseph's eyes. He jumps back and bangs his head against the mausoleum's marble.

"Fuck."

Says the Teacher, "Relax, Joseph."

Joseph wheels and throws his head back. Glares up at the Teacher with his little squirrel eyes. Points his automatic, which trembles in his grip.

The Teacher smiles down at him. He says, "Had it been my intent to kill you I'd have done so *instantly*. I'd have you locked up in this peaceful house by now. Joseph, when the time does come, would you like the bunk above or below your sainted mother?"

"Get the fuck off my fuckin family's crypt."

"I think you mean your family's fuckin crypt. Not your fuckin family's crypt. Do you see the distinction?"

The Teacher notes that Joseph's bodyguard Frankie is clamping down a grin. Good. For a goon he's an advanced specimen. Smart whippet-faced kid. Imperturbable, graceful of movement, with some sense of humor. Among Boffano's vast family of mules and goats he stands out.

Says the Teacher, "How are you, Frankie?"

Frankie shrugs. "Ah, I'm OK."

"You still dating that Irish girl?"

"Molly? Yeah. How do you—?"

"Somebody showed me a picture. She's gorgeous. Can you catch?"

The Teacher produces a long brown cardboard box. He gently tosses it down.

"Shit," says Frankie. But he catches it. And opens it, and finds an orchid inside.

Says the Teacher, "*Lycaste Virginalis skinneri*. Freshly picked. You smell that? Leave it by the pillow tonight when you make love to her. She'll tear you *up*, boy."

"Shit," says Frankie. "Thank you very much."

Joseph mutters, "Hey, it's wonderful, Frankie, now you got your own fuckin *florist*." Then, to the Teacher: "Did you hear what I said? I said get the fuck down."

The Teacher takes hold of the base of a stone angel on the corner of the entablature, and swings easily over the side. He sets his foot into the ironwork of a small window, gets a grip on a ledge and lowers himself to the ground.

Says Joseph, "What were you doing up there anyway?"

The Teacher doesn't reply.

Says Joseph, "You wanted to check if I'm being followed? Listen to me, fuckface. If I'm being followed, I'll know it."

"Joseph. Just tell me why you wanted to see me."

"Why? 'Cause I hear you fuckin with the jury."

"Ah. Well thank you for sharing that."

Joseph raises a finger. "Shut up, dirtbag. I don't want your smart shit."

"I hear you."

"And I don't want you messin with the jury. It's too risky."

"You'd prefer a sure thing, Joseph? Like, say, your brother sitting in Attica for the rest of his life? And you in charge of the family?"

"My brother's going to *walk*, asshole."

"I understand they played a tape the other day."

"Who gives a shit about that tape! When Bozeman gets done with that tape it's not gonna sound like no murder talk. It's gonna sound like the fuckin *Muppet Show*. I mean forget about this trial. These guys, Tallow, Westchester fucking County—they're all amateurs. This isn't even the FBI. This isn't even a fuckin RICO, this is just asshole locals who think they're federal cowboys. Ridin their trumped-up piece a shit murder rap."

"That's good, Joseph, that's the spirit. But I'm told that Bozeman himself says we're going to lose this piece a shit murder rap."

"He's covering his ass."

"And I'm covering your brother's ass."

Joseph draws his eyes into thin slashes. "So which juror, fuckhead?"

The Teacher grins at him.

"Hey," says Joseph. "When I ask, you better answer. When my brother's in jail, I'm the boss of this family."

"But not my boss."

"You take money from my family—"

"I take a great deal of money from your family, Joseph, yet still you're not my boss. Your brother's aware of what I'm doing."

"Yeah well you got my brother wrapped around your dick. Your little winkie-dinkie dick. Not me. I don't like you. I don't like your fuckin Hallowe'en mask. Why don't you show your fuckin face?"

" 'The best of all rulers,' says Lao Tsu, 'is he whose existence is unknown.' "

"Say what? You stupid *shit*. I don't like nothing about you. Teacher, Teacher, fuckin know-it-all. I don't like what you're doing to my family. I don't like all this shit you and my brother are getting us into. This Ndrangheta shit, this Cali shit. And you know what else I don't like? I don't like putting the screws on civilians."

"Oh Joseph, what a tender soul you have. It's a shame they can't canonize you till you're dead—"

Frankie chuckles.

Joseph snaps his eyes at the kid, and the chuckle evaporates.

Then Joseph steps close to the Teacher. "Let me just get one thing straight with you, you fuck."

"OK, Joseph. One thing. Shoot."

Joseph's fluted nostrils are quivering. His breath is foul and the stink of it gets under the Teacher's mask.

"If they send my brother north you better run like fuckin hell. You better hide in the fuckin *ocean*, you fuckin faggot."

OLIVER comes back on his bike from Wednesday afternoon lacrosse practice. As he's carrying the bike onto the porch he hears the phone ring in the kitchen. Mom answers.

"Hello? . . . Hi, Juliet . . ."

Usually when his mother hears from Juliet she starts giggling right away—but not this time. This time her voice stays as flat and as cool as glass.

"No. Tonight? No. . . .

"We did? I'm sorry, I forgot. . . ."

Oliver goes into the kitchen. She puts her hand over the phone and tells him, without a word of greeting, "Get your clothes up. We're going to the Laundromat."

He goes through the TV room to the stairs. But he lingers there. He wants to hear.

"No, Juliet, that's sweet," Mom says. "But really, tonight I've got to wash clothes. . . .

"I'm *fine*. . . .

"No, that guy turned out to be, I mean it didn't work out. . . .

"Juliet, I'm saying I just don't *feel* like it. . . .

"Well, I've got a rough schedule too. . . .

"Yeah I'm sure. I'm sure it's a great story. But you know, I don't, I really don't want to hear it. I mean frankly I don't want to hear about *another* little escapade. They sound like fun but they sound,

I mean don't you ever want to get *close* to somebody? Or just, don't you get *tired* of these little adventures?"

Oliver stands in the TV room and watches his mom's back. She's leaning against the back door looking out into the last daylight. She's saying, "No, I'm not . . .

"I'm not . . .

"I am *not*, for Christ's sake. It's just, it sounds like empty sex. Like *bodies*, like *numbers*, don't you ever want to *grow up*? . . .

"Well that's fine, Juliet, it's none of my business, then don't tell me about it. I don't want to hear about it, and frankly I don't want my son hearing about all this warped—

"No *you* have the god damn attitude. You think you can come over here any damn time you feel like it, tell me some twisted story, is this a *life* you're living? Look, I don't—"

She stands in silence a moment, then pulls the phone away from her ear. Oliver hears the aggrieved whine of the dial tone. She hangs up. Then she turns swiftly and she sees him. Her face is red, flushed. But her voice is still cool and steady when she tells him:

"Don't. Stare at me."

SLAVKO CZERNYK is staked out, sitting in his car, watching Eben Rackland's condo. Trying to stay awake. Listening to WFAN. Tonight's lively debate: Does the New York Giants' salary/bonus structure achieve an optimal line/backfield balance in the offensive alignment? It seems every bozo in the metropolitan area has been mulling this thing over for months. Guys with the IQ of shoehorns are calling in with twenty-minute disquisitions.

Slavko digs his knuckles deep into his eye sockets, trying to uproot boredom and weariness. Oh Jesus. What time is it? 8:35. That's *all*? At midnight I'm cashing out no matter what. Nothing's going to happen here.

It's Slavko's conviction that the concept of the stakeout was designed by Satan's elves to be the greatest torment possible in this mortal life.

Slavko unscrews the thermos and chugs coffee.

On the radio, some sport opines: "I see the difficulty, Jerry, as a plethora of performance-clausing in the multiyear contracts, particularly—"

Slavko jabs his knee at the off knob. Kills that fool. Sits in silence. Again he unscrews the thermos. Chugs more coffee. Checks his watch: 8:36. Oh Jesus.

This life is not working out.

Of course if I'm patient I'll eventually die and get to start all over again. Though what if they deny me a Bonus Round? Considering how bad I've screwed up on this go-through?

He takes another chug of coffee.

Some flutter of uneasiness that he can't quite account for. A shadow? Then somebody raps on the passenger-side window.

He jumps, but miraculously manages to keep hold of the thermos.

Turns out it's Sari. Smiling at him. He reaches over and unlocks the door.

"What are you doing here?" he asks as she slips into the seat beside him.

"Hey, I'm your employer," she says. Tonight she's in plain jeans and sweatshirt. Not a whit less gorgeous than last time, however. She says, "I wanted to see if you were earning your fee. Also I thought you might be hungry. Thought you might like a sandwich."

"Thanks, but Jesus—"

"Yeah, and also I was going out of my skull sitting home alone."

"Where's your car?"

"Next block. I didn't want *him* to see me. How's my boy doing? Is he being a good boy tonight?"

She glances up at Eben's lighted window. But when Slavko doesn't answer she turns back to him. "Is this OK, sitting here with you? I mean, it doesn't—"

"It's fine."

He's taking in her fragrance, and the gestures of her long spidery hands. He's thinking how ashamed he is of this car of his, this 1980 rotten-to-the-gunwales Ford Granada, which he calls the Buzzard and which is saturated with the stink of thousands of Lucky Strikes, years of backed-up exhaust. Junk mail and greaseburger wrappers and two beer bottles are kicking around at Sari's feet. At *his* feet is a gash, half a foot long, where the floor has simply rotted through. He usually keeps it covered with an old piece of linoleum, but today when he was hunting for a quarter to pay a toll he must have moved that piece of linoleum, because it's not there now, and he has to slide his shoe over to cover the hole. So that Sari won't notice the light seeping up from outside.

Though she wouldn't notice anyway. She doesn't care. The only thing she cares about is Eben Rackland's lighted window.

She says, "I know it's wrong to be spying on him. But it's kind of, it'll make me feel better. Just to be here. Hey, you want this sandwich? I brought you this sandwich. It's roast beef. I don't take you for a vegan."

"Sari."

"What?"

"I don't think your boyfriend's in there."

She looks back at his window. Then she quickly scans the parking spaces. "No, he *has* to be there," she says. "I mean there's his car." She points at the handsome red Lotus.

Says Slavko, "Well, that's been here since I got here. Which was five o'clock."

She ponders. "Well, maybe he stayed home from work today. But he's in there, Mr. Czernyk. He phoned me from there an hour ago."

"He did? Call me Slavko. What did he say?"

"Same as always. He's sorry, lots of research, this new client, won't be able to get out—"

He interrupts her. "The light in that window there came on at 6:37. Wait." He draws from his jacket pocket his little black logbook and checks it. "6:37 and twelve seconds, by my watch."

"So?"

"At 6:42 and twelve seconds, exactly five minutes later, the porch-light came on. At 6:52 and twelve seconds, that downstairs light."

"So what does—"

"It means your boyfriend didn't switch those lights on. Unless you're dating an electronic timer. All night long, not a sound from there, not a stir, not a shadow, nothing. I don't think anybody's in there."

"Then where's Eben?"

"Well, that's a good question."

Suddenly she opens her door. In the dome light he gets a clear look at her wrath. "He *better* be there," she mutters.

She gets out and shuts the door and marches across the drive and up to the condo stoop. She leans into the buzzer.

Slavko picks up the sandwich she's brought. He starts to unwrap it.

He watches her jam her finger at the buzzer.

She beats on the door with the side of her fist. She shouts for her lover.

Slavko shakes his head and thinks, No, honey, he's *not* there. Our little Ebenezer, he's playing hooky, he's playing hooky from his own life. One of those kind of guys. Bad news. Always. Those guys. I'm sure next time you talk to him he'll have a really good reason for his behavior but whatever it is? Sari? Don't listen to it.

OLIVER sits in one of the plastic scoop-chairs at the Laundromat and tries to do his homework. But it's hard on account of the racket from the washers and the dryers and that family of five pale kids over there who are playing some version of *American Gladiators*. Bouncing each other off the cinderblock walls. Soon Oliver gives up on the book and picks up a dog-eared crayoned-over *Highlights for Children*.

Then he forsakes that and tries a *People* magazine.

Then he plays with the drawstring on his parka, twisting it around his wrist. He peers into the maelstrom of a washing machine.

The mother of the kids tells them to quit roughhousing. They ignore her. What a bitch, and what a batch she's got. They're all so eerily pale they're nearly blue.

Oliver gathers his math book and notebook and crosses the room and plunks down next to his mother.

She's going through her stack of newspapers. The *Times*, the *Post*, the *News*, the *Reporter Dispatch*, the *News-Times*. In each one, she heads straight for news of the trial, ignores the rest. She reads. She says nothing, no expression on her face.

"Hey Mom."

"Yeah."

She raises her eyes and looks straight at him, but she doesn't seem to see him. Then she goes back to her article.

He says, "I was waiting till you were in a better mood."
"Uh-huh."
"But that might be a while, huh?"
"Uh-huh."
"Well, I gotta show you this."
He takes the math quiz out of his notebook and gives it to her. It's covered with lots of violent red ink.
Up at the top, the grade: 37.
She glances at the first page. The second. "OK. That's good." She holds it out to him.
"You got to sign it," he says.
"I don't have a pen."
"Here." He passes her one. She signs. She gives him back the test and the pen and returns to her reading.
"Mom, you gonna *remember* you signed it? If she calls you?"
"If who calls me?"
"My teacher."
"Right."
"You gonna remember?"
"Yes."
"Mom aren't you gonna say *anything*? I got a *thirty-seven*."
No answer.
"Thirty-seven out of a *hundred*, Mom."
"You want me to say something?" She gives him a bitter bolted-down look and she tells him, "Keep up the good work."
Then nearly a minute ticks by while she turns newspaper pages.
The mother of the blue kids starts shoveling her clothes out of a dryer. Her kids keep slapping into the wall.
Mom folds up the newspaper she's been looking at. She sets it on the scoop-chair beside her.
"What *should* I say, Oliver? Should I say, 'Oh Oliver, you're not *trying*. It's not so hard, why don't you just *apply yourself*?' Is that what you want to hear? But why should I bother? You know as well as I do, you know what you could do if you tried. But you prefer not to. You prefer to draw your dragons and to hell with all the rest. The rest is no fun, so you sit there and you gaze at that math test and dream about how you want to be an artist like your mom. How you want to get fucked over like your mom. And so what if you never have any money? So what if you feel like shit because you can't pay your electric bill and you have to work all day as a data

processor and you can't go anywhere because your car broke down and you don't have the money to get it fixed? Who cares? You're an *artist*. You can just sit there and gaze at the life that everybody else is having. Till you're *dead*."

She keeps getting louder and louder and her voice is lined with a double spiral of razors, and this is the longest speech he's ever heard her deliver. Their dryer has quit, which means that right now there's nothing going in this Laundromat. The sallow brats have left off their game to gawk like tourists at Oliver's mom. Even their mother has stopped offloading her laundry, and she watches with the same impudent stare.

Says Mom, "And so what if every important decision in your life is made by people you don't even know? Asshole curators and collectors who can't tell art from that wallpaper there. I mean if that's your attitude, Oliver, if you think *So what*—what am *I* supposed to do about it? You want to let the bastards tell you you can't pass math? What am I supposed to do? No one can stop those sons of bitches except you. *You* got to have the guts. You want to let the bastards tell you who you are, I can't help you. *I can't help you!* All I can do is show you what they've done to me."

"Mom," he says.

"What they're *doing* to me."

"Mom."

"What."

"You've got . . . to stop."

She does stop. She glares at him.

He gets up and spills his notebook and his math book onto the floor and walks past the leering washed-out family and finds his way to the door. He pushes out into the autumn dark. He heads toward the Grand Union supermarket and then holds up in front of some stupid mechanical horsey for little kids. He's crying, he can't stop it. Please don't let any of the kids from school come by. He stands there with his head down, hiccuping air, and some old guy is asking him if he's OK.

"Yeah," he says.

"You're not hurt, are you?"

"Just leave me alone, will you?" He injects some of his mom's nastiness into it and it works, it chases the guy. After a while he looks up and sees his mom walking toward the Subaru, with the laundry basket under one arm and his books in the other.

ANNIE dumps the clothes and the books in the back of the car. Shuts the hatch, and walks toward the Grand Union, passing by Oliver, who's still staring at that mechanical horse like he wants to take a ride.

She says crisply, "Oliver." Her voice echoes in the dark lot.

"What."

"Come. *Now.*"

In the Grand Union she plows the aisles, Oliver trailing. Up one aisle, down the other. Since she has only an anti-appetite, a revulsion toward food, it's an act of will every time she puts something in the cart. No fresh vegetables. She's not up to cutting veggies. But Rice-A-Roni, sure, four boxes. She hasn't had Rice-A-Roni since one summer in Pittsburgh with her aunt. A raft of Lean Cuisine frozen dinners and Stouffer's pizza. Oliver mopes along, keeps his head low. Once or twice she asks his opinion about what to get, but he doesn't give a damn. They pause before the cereals. A fat puffy-faced guy in a Day-Glo windbreaker can't get past her cart, and she jerks it aside for him. She tells Oliver, "Pick what you want."

He shrugs.

She grabs a box of Corn Chex, tosses it in the cart.

Says a voice, "Hey, I know you."

She turns. The puffy-faced guy has spoken to her. Nose crushed. One cheekbone looks like it got pushed in by some giant thumb. He gives Oliver a friendly smile. He says to Annie, "You're the artist. The box lady."

He has a merry chuckle. But how does he know her? Probably from the little show she had at the Pharaoh Library last year.

"From the library?" she says.

"From the bakery, don't you remember? I met you at the bakery."

Forcing herself to breathe. Now what does she do? What is she supposed to do, she can't remember.

The ugly man looks at Oliver and says, "This your boy?"

OK. He wants her to lose Oliver.

"Hey hon, we need some . . . What are those frozen things you like?"

He mumbles. "RoboPops?"

"Go get some."

He starts off. Sleepwalking.

When he's gone the man says, "Tomorrow. Seven A.M. You know where the Park & Ride is? In Banktree? Off 684?"

"Mm."

"You gotta *know*."

"I know."

"You wait there. I'll come, you get in my car. OK?"

"Yes."

"You OK?"

"Yes."

"You look kinda woozy."

"I'm all right."

"What did I say?"

"The Park & Ride off 684. I wait, I wait and then I . . . get in with you."

"That's right."

He looks like he's about to go but he doesn't. He says, "Listen, you gonna be just fine. He'll take care of you. He's a good guy. I mean he can be tough. Somebody crosses him, he goes crazy. But you do what he says? You'll be fine."

She stands there trying to get a grip on her breathing.

He says, "I got a kid too. I got one just a little older than him. I know what you're going through."

Then he starts pushing his cart away from her, up the aisle.

"What's your name?" she says.

He turns. "What?"

"What's your name?"

"You don't want to know my name. How can I—I can't tell you my name."

"What do I call you then?"

"Don't call me nothing. Call me what you want. Call me—" He looks around and his eyes light on a display of Johnny Appleseed granola. "Call me Johnny Appleseed, I don't give a shit."

Oliver comes back with two boxes of RoboPops.

She says, "OK. Johnny. Thank you. For what you said, thank you." She's thinking, Maybe if you can make them like you, if you can let them *know who you are*, and who Oliver is, maybe they're less likely to hurt you.

SLAVKO waits till Sari gets into the car, shuts the door and puts her head in her hands. Then he hands her a greasy napkin. It's all he has. No idea what to say so he keeps his mouth shut. He wouldn't mind holding her but that's probably not called for either.

She gets hold of herself and takes a deep breath and shakes her head sadly. Slavko thinks maybe now's the time to speak. But then the line of her mouth starts to give way again. Then the tears come spurting out of her eyes and she's bawling and banging her fists against the dash.

It takes her a long time to regain the ground she's lost.

Finally she says, "Tell me something."

"What?"

"Anything. Talk to me. Tell me a story."

"What can I tell you about?"

Long silence.

"Tell me about her," she says.

"Who's that?"

"You said you'd been through this. So who was she? Was she a pathological liar? Like this bastard of mine?"

"No. She was, she just didn't love me. She's a doctor. I mean a resident. At St. Ignatius, you know where that is? We just went out for a little while, maybe a month or two."

"How long ago was it?"

"Almost a year."

"Jesus. And you still think about her?"

"Oh no, not so much anymore. I mean nowadays sometimes five or six seconds will pass and I won't have had a single thought about her."

Sari giggles, sniffs. She asks him, "So why didn't she love you back?"

"Amazingly unbelievable, isn't it?"

He reaches past her for the glove compartment. The little door swings open and he withdraws a fifth of Jim Beam.

He says, "I don't like to drink on the job but I'm not sure this is the job anymore. You want some?"

She sort of nods. He unscrews the cap and passes it, and she takes a snort. It surprises him, how deeply she draws on the thing. As she passes the bottle back she murmurs, "Slavko, if this is hard for you to talk about—"

"No, the hard part was going through it. The talking? That's neither here nor there." He takes a swallow to match hers. "She wanted something else. I don't even know why she went out with me in the first place. Maybe she thought I was kind of funny."

"You are funny, Slavko. And you're also kind of cute."

"Oh yeah, right."

"No, you are."

"I'm not even *remotely* cute. But that's not why she dumped me. She just . . . she wanted a poet or something. You know Derek Walcott?"

"No."

"Well, I wouldn't have either except she made me read him. He's black. He's Caribbean, he's got a dancing soul, he's pure sexiness, he writes all this poetry I can't even read, he's just the kind of guy she wants, he's a poet so OK, that's fine, so why didn't she just leave me alone?"

"Well she did, didn't she?"

"Yeah. When it was too late. When she'd cracked my heart in a lot of little pieces like she did to everybody else."

He shrugs. He starts telling Sari about this heartbreak and he takes a sip of the liquor and she takes a sip, and the next time he glances at the clock on the dash it's already eleven o'clock and two hours have blown past.

And Sari is telling him about the moment she first noticed a certain remoteness in her Eben's demeanor.

She says, "But it was so subtle I thought I was just paranoid, you know?"

"Yes," he says. "Oh, Christ, I know about that. You *hope* you're being paranoid, but really you know something's wrong. You know you're losing."

She says, "It's like everything's sunny and perfect but you feel this, it's like a little tiny breath of cold wind on your face—"

"Exactly," says Slavko.

"And you know this big cold storm is coming and everything's going to change and everything's going to be lost."

"Yes," he says.

"Is there any more?" she asks him.

"Well no, after you feel that chill I think you're doomed—"

She puts her hand on his arm. "No, I mean is there any more Jim Beam?"

"Oh. There's a swallow."

"You take it then."

"No, I'm, I don't need any more."

She drains the bottle and wipes her mouth and she says, "But you're right, there is nothing you can do. Nothing. Nothing nothing nothing nothing nothing. You know? Everything's sunny, everything is wonderful. And then that, that coldness."

When next he looks at the clock it's one in the morning and both of them are hunched low in their seats and her knee is touching his knee.

And just from the presence of her, just from her breath filling this car, and her voice, which is sort of brave and cheerful, and from the pressure of her knee against his, he finds he's nursing a hard-on. Not a painful one, though, because the alcohol and the easyness of the talk combine to keep the edge off it.

She's telling him about this guy she was dating three years ago, this guy who was playing drums in a garage band and how long it took for her to realize he wasn't *affecting* a vacant expression, he truly was vacant.

Then abruptly she says: "You know I have to tell you something. Guess what?"

"What?"

"I think I'm going to live through this."

She laughs. "I mean I wasn't so sure I was going to. But the truth is, I'm OK. You know? I don't know. Maybe it's just because I'm with you, and you're nice to talk to."

"So are you, Sari."

"Why do you think you're weak?"

"What?"

"I said, Why do you think you're weak?"

"Did I say I was weak?"

"The other night when I said I didn't like weak men you got strange."

"I did?"

"I get the feeling you think you're a failure."

"Oh yeah? Really? I thought I *exuded* self-confidence."

"Oh."

"Don't you think I should, being a detective?"

"You should, yes. I'm thirsty."

"Maybe that's why I'm such a lousy detective."

She checks the bottle again. "All gone. You're not a lousy detective."

"I don't make much of a living."

"You don't?"

"Not really."

"Well, Slavko, maybe you should try something else."

"Like what?"

"Isn't there anything else you want to do?"

"I want to be Derek Walcott."

She laughs.

"I did use to be a cop," he says.

"Yeah?"

"Yeah, but I screwed that up."

"How?"

"I better not get started but there was a woman involved."

"Of course."

"Also some drinking."

"Shit," she says. "I don't know, Slavko. You want to be a poet why don't you try it?"

"I have tried. All I can write is how I feel like a pinball."

She enjoys that, she laughs.

He says, "Like they dropped me down on this bizarre planet and I'm getting knocked all over the place and I don't know what the hell I'm doing here, sometimes I think I can make sense out of this place but most of the time I'm just lost. With my jaw hanging open. You know? I can't write for shit about sunsets and the soul of me, you know, and Greek gods and all that shit 'cause I'm getting bounced around like a dunce with my jaw hanging open. No wonder Juliet broke up with me."

"That was her name? Your doctor? Juliet?"

"Yeah."

"Romantic name."

"Yeah."

"Well, I gotta go, Romeo."

"You can't go."

"I *got* to go."

"You can't drive, Sari. You had too much to drink."

"Less than you."

"Yeah but me, I'm staying right here. I'm not done with this stake-out."

She scowls. "Oh, what, you're still worried about that son of a bitch, that Eben? Forget that son of a bitch. Don't even bother. I'm through with him."

"That's what *you* think. Wait till you get my bill."

"Kiss me," she says, and he moves toward her clumsily. He holds the saddle of her back. He rasps his lips against hers and breathes in her breath and he wants for a moment to call her Juliet. But he catches himself.

"Sari," he murmurs.

They're holding each other so hard they're crushing the wind out of each other. He tries to gear his brain up to print the message that this is an infatuation, this is a quick grope of a lonely client, it's part of the job and I better forget it in the morning. But he's drunk and what he knows to be true is this: He's in love again. He's in trouble. Still in love with Juliet but additionally with this one. The shit just keeps getting deeper and deeper.

She breaks away.

"Thank you," she says.

Then she opens the car door and says, "Yeah, I'm going to be OK. This is going to be easier than I thought. OK. Soon, Slavko."

And he can't think of anything to say to hold her and so before he knows it she's gone.

ANNIE writes:

Dear Turtle,
It's the middle of the night and *he* wants to see me again tomorrow and I wish I could talk to you. I keep waiting for you to call again or write me, I go to the mailbox every day and pray I'll find a letter but I know you're too proud and I've hurt you once before, but still I keep thinking I'm going to turn around and you'll be right here. And if you were here? I know I'd break down and tell you. I have to tell somebody. Turtle. I HAVE TO TELL SOMEBODY. But I can't go to the police so don't even ask me don't, I can't. Okay you would. I know you would. You'd think he was bluffing. You'd think that once I tell the cops, why should he bother to come chasing after me and Oliver—what good would it do him then? But he made that book that scrapbook of those people he's gone after, and he knew that even if I didn't believe it still it would scare me so much I couldn't do anything.
You'd want me to take a chance. Wouldn't you Turtle? But why? I don't care about that world out there anyway, why should I sacrifice my child to that world? Tonight when I was looking in the paper for something about the trial instead I found an article about a judge in Colombia. Three of his kids have

been killed by druglords but he still *shows up for work*. He's a hero Turtle but I don't understand him at all—what does he believe in so much he believes in it more than his children? You have to explain this to me Turtle, you have to come here and take us away and explain all this to me. I love you and miss you.

Annie

She carefully tears the page out of the notebook and folds it. She rises and goes downstairs. Down in the kitchen she rifles all the drawers looking for a match, but she can't find any. Then she forgets what she's doing and stands there a while. Then she remembers. She roots around some more. She decides she's going nuts here. Her hands are rummaging too quickly, they feel loaded up with static electricity. She quits looking. She turns up the burner on the electric stove and when the coils are bright she holds the letter to them. It smokes, and she blows at it fiercely. Finally it flashes into flame, and she carries it over to the sink. When the flame starts scorching at her fingertips she drops the page. When it's all ash she douses it with water.

5

O you sick Brain of Mine,

O you desperate Glutton for Misery . . .

SLAVKO opens his eyes as far as he can, a hairline crack, wondering what in the world is *that* thing? Wing? Silver saucer? Or maybe it's *not* in the world. Maybe it's from some other world. Shimmery, and alien, and skimming along in the darkness—

It takes him half a minute to realize this is his own rearview mirror he's peering at.

Oh shit. Did I fall asleep on a stakeout?

He tries to sit up. His brain ripples like the northern lights.

I got *drunk* on a stakeout? I'm on the skids again?

He gets a grip on the steering wheel and pulls himself up. He tries to muster some notion of where he is. Still dark. He checks his watch: 5:30 A.M. Light drizzle on the windshield. One streetlight, a row of dark townhouses that look vaguely familiar.

And then he catches a faint lingering of that woman's fragrance . . . and the whole night comes spiraling back to him.

Sari.

Sweet beautiful Sari.

Immediately thereafter comes a painful thought of Juliet. But he silently hisses at it: Ha! You weren't the first thing to come into my thoughts, were you, Juliet? Not this morning. You're not queen of my thoughts *this* morning.

Headlights flash in the mirror.

Slavko instinctively sinks down in his seat.

A car, two men inside, slowly passes him and comes to a stop. Slavko's eyes are just high enough to see above the dash, and he watches as the passenger-side door of the car swings open. The dome-light comes on. The passenger gets out and flicks his hand at the driver, a quick dismissive wave. He's got strong cheekbones, and an air of prepossession, and Slavko's pretty sure that this is Sari's boy-friend Eben.

The car moves off. Dull sedan. Late-80s Camry?—something like that. Slavko has always been weak on makes and models, and it's too dark to read plates. So he lets the car go, and he keeps his eyes on Eben Rackland as the man strides up to his townhouse door, uses his key and steps in.

Slavko gets out his little black logbook.

He jots down the time, the location, his impressions of E.R. It's his impression that E.R. is fresh and alert and has had a good night's sleep. It's also Slavko's impression—though he doesn't trouble to write it—that E.R. has been sleeping somewhere else lately but would just as soon the world thought he was sleeping here. Slavko's foremost impression is that if he doesn't get his own brain coated with coffee soon, it will throb itself into a gray gruel.

But he stays where he is.

He hunches down in his seat and nails his gaze to the townhouse door. He waits.

The leaves of the trees along the sidewalk turn from black to russet, russet to rose.

He belches. He gets a taste of roast beef, Jim Beam, bile and mayonnaise.

Lights come on in the other townhouses. A woman comes out trailing her dogs. Someone else heads to work. Presently E.R. emerges from the townhouse wearing a suit and bearing a briefcase. He gets into his red Lotus. Slavko hears a snatch of baroque violins before the car slips away.

Meanwhile Slavko's own Buzzard is wheezing, not starting, bitching about the cold and the damp and the hour.

Finally the engine catches.

Running a one-man tail, it's one thing that Slavko thinks he does pretty well. You've got to *know*—got to feel in your gut because it can't be taught—when to drop back and when to muscle in. Today it helps that he's familiar with this part of Westchester. And it helps that the quarry seems to have no anxiety about any glue on his ass.

The Lotus cruises through Yorktown Heights and pulls onto the interstate, and Slavko stays on it. Heading south. Toward the city.

But the farther south they go, the less enthusiasm he feels for this pursuit. He's cold. The wind whistles through that rusted-out hole in the floor beside his left foot. He wants his bed. And after all, he already knows where this guy's headed. Wall Street. His work. And no way is Slavko going to sit parked across from some Manhattan garage, chewing Alka-Seltzers and feeding quarters into a smirking parking meter and grinding his knuckles into his eyes and reading the want ads in the *Post* and just hanging around in the car all day like a pair of fuzzy dice.

And speaking of hanging around wasting time, why is he still hanging on to this case?

After all, he thinks, Sari told me to forget the whole thing. So who's my client? What am I doing here? Who am I working for?

Look in the mirror.

Right. Exactly. And how much is the moron in the mirror paying you?

The usual.

He decides to pull off at the next exit, go right home, and get some sleep.

But at the next exit E.R. eases off the interstate ahead of him. He's not looking for gas either: there are no gas stations around here. He takes a right on Route 22, and Slavko keeps after him.

They snake north for a few miles. Horse pastures, Slavko's deadly nausea, a white church. Slavko cedes E.R. the curves and the hills, but watches for that red flash on the straightaways.

At a forest crossroads the Lotus hangs a right. So does the Buzzard. There's a dam and a pumphouse and then the road winds alongside a slate-gray reservoir. Slavko follows blindly. This is one of those times, he's thinking, when you have to trust to sheer faith that you haven't lost your man.

The road takes a sharp turn, and abruptly starts across the reservoir on a long straight causeway.

The Lotus isn't on this causeway. The Lotus isn't anywhere to be seen. Sheer faith has failed him. The Lotus is gone.

Could E.R. have gotten so far ahead so quickly? Slavko doesn't think so. But then where is he?

Could he have turned off somewhere?

Slavko thinks back. Since his last glimpse of the red car, since the crossroads, it's all been woods and reservoir. No driveways, no houses.

Although . . . there *was* that pumphouse. . . .

He steps on it. Pours it on so he can get to the end of this causeway, so he can turn the hell around. . . .

ANNIE waits where Johnny told her to wait, on the reservoir's rocky shore. She hears footsteps, and she glances back. Zach Lyde has arrived. He sits on a rock close to her.

He gives her a look of tender concern.

"How are you holding up, Annie?"

"Fine."

Struggling to keep her anger bottled. But even in the one word it spills out.

"And Oliver? Is he all right?"

She says, "I was wondering what *you* thought about Oliver. Since you listen to everything we say, maybe you have a better idea—"

"I don't enjoy invading your privacy."

"You don't *enjoy* it? You sound like an undertaker, you know that?"

He lets that go. "You're new at this," he tells her. "It's simple prudence for me to listen in. Do you think we can afford even the slightest error?"

She looks off across the water. A car is crossing the causeway over there. Coming this way and it seems to be in a great hurry.

Zach Lyde says, "Look, I know this won't be welcome, but I'm going to say it. You're being too hard on your child."

By now her anger has short-circuited half her brain, so that even if she could think of anything to snap back with, she wouldn't have the presence of mind to utter it.

He says, "I'm not trying to tell you how to raise him. But if you kept treating him so strangely, so harshly—suppose he guesses what's going on? Suppose he talks to a friend?"

She says, "He won't guess. He's just a kid."

"He's quick, though. Show caution, treat him gently. The same with your friends. I understand that you want to keep them at arm's distance. That's wise. But if you drive them off precipitously they'll start to worry. They'll come around with questions. This Turtle, who is he? A boyfriend?"

"What difference does that make?"

"Where does he live, Annie?"

"Why do you care?"

"Answer my question."

"He lives somewhere in California. Do you want to kill him? I don't remember exactly where. Some small town. I haven't talked to him in years—"

"You mentioned to him that you two had talked last spring."

"So? He's sort of a pest, he calls a lot. You want to kill him?"

"Annie."

"Go ahead, kill him."

"I don't want to kill anyone."

"It won't devastate *me*—"

"I only want to get this over with. Painlessly. Quietly. Help me with this."

"I'll do what I can! All right? You son of a bitch."

She rubs her eyes against her shirtsleeve—a quick swipe, to get the tears off her face. Then she turns to him, and this time she holds his eyes.

He says, "You have more power than you know."

Then they hear a car, driving up to the pumphouse behind them. He tells her, "I don't know who it is, but don't look. Look at the lake. My colleague will take care of it."

SLAVKO brakes beside the pumphouse. Not far from the Lotus. And here's the Camry as well—the car that let off E.R. at his condo.

In the driver's seat of this Camry sits a goon. Ugly as sin he is, with a squashed nose. He glowers at Slavko. Maybe, Slavko thinks, I ought not to be malingering here.

But he does allow himself one quick look around—and he spots them. Sitting on the rocks by the water, E.R. and a woman. He can't see much of her. The back of her head, her long brown hair. And unless he wants to waddle on over there and get up-close-and-personal about their love life, he's got about as much data as he's going to get. Time to go. The goon, Mr. Ugly-As-Sin, has opened his car door and he's getting out and getting uglier by the second. Slavko waggles his fingers affably at the man. Then he slams the Buzzard into reverse.

He backs right into a clump of weeds, with the muffler scraping out a tune against the stones.

He guns forward. He turns the wheel hard and the Buzzard twists and lurches and Ugly-As-Sin jumps back. Slavko hauls ass out of there.

ANNIE's eyes are on the water. Behind her the sound of the car's engine dies away.

Zach Lyde asks her, "Annie, at the courthouse yesterday? The cross of Paulie DeCicco? Did you understand our strategy?"

She nods.

He says, "What's our strategy, Annie?"

"That Louie Boffano didn't order the killing. He's in the mob and maybe he's a bad guy but he's, he's a figurehead. He doesn't give the orders."

"Good. That's right. But if he's not guilty, who is? Who *did* kill Salvadore Riggio and his grandson?"

She raises her eyes, narrows her eyes and says, "You did."

His smile crawls up the side of his face. "You think *I'm* the Teacher?"

"Are you?"

"I would have you believe it. The Teacher scares you, doesn't he? And if I can keep you scared, Annie, I can save your life."

Some strands of her hair have stuck to the dried tears on her cheeks. He reaches out and slides his fingers under them, lifts them, pushes them back.

He says, "When we need to talk to you again, we'll find you on the road. We'll flash our lights once, then twice more. All right?"

She nods.

"You and Oliver, I still can save you both, can't I? Annie?"

128

SLAVKO talks to the cup of coffee he picked up at the Wendy's takeout. Scorch me awake, he says silently. Harrow my tongue. Tell me what the hell I saw by that reservoir.

Was it an assignation with a mistress?

OK. Except E.R.'s not married so why would he need to skulk around? Who's he hiding her from, from Sari? But he's been dating Sari less than a year. So why would he be going to such lengths to keep another woman from her? Sounds kind of squirmy. Doesn't sound like the powerful soulful E.R. that Sari's so crazy about.

Any other bright ideas?

Slavko gets off Route 114 and onto whatever this road is that runs behind the telephone company building. He figures if he doesn't hit a lot of red lights he'll be in his bed in twenty minutes. In that crumb-infested but nevertheless golden sack.

He lifts his cup, takes another sip of black flames.

Maybe it's the *woman* who's hitched. She married rich, she's got her own personal goon guard, but then she met Eben the Powerful and now she has to sneak out and meet her darling by the pump-house. . . .

But then why wasn't she *snuggling* with her E.R.? Why was she sitting so far apart from him on the rocks, and why doesn't any of this add up to jackshit and furthermore why does Slavko feel saner this morning, why does he feel mentally and emotionally healthier—despite his hangover—than he has since . . .

Since the last time I slept with Juliet, in fact—but O you sick Brain of Mine, O you desperate Glutton for Misery, do we really need to delve into *that* just now?

6

Whoever can see through his own fear

will be delivered from fear

ANNIE in the courtroom, on a misty morning, a week after the meeting at the reservoir. You wouldn't know it was a misty morning, though, there are no windows in here. There's a sort of deconstructed skylight way up in one of the odd ceiling angles—but it's been painted black, who knows why?

She studies the woman on the witness stand. Mrs. Riggio, wisp of a woman. Widow of the murdered Salvadore, grandmother of the murdered boy. Her hair is a thin froth, her skin is the skin of an onion, but she holds her back straight and she speaks in a clear voice. She says:

"Then I go say goodnight to my grandson."

Says Tallow the prosecutor, "To Thomas?"

"Yeah. Tomasino, he stay with us for four day. I don't see him since he was eleven. Then for four day he stay with us."

"And when you went to his room, was he still awake?"

"He watch his little TV."

"His TV?"

"The little TV that Sal give him for his fourteenth birthday. And I say, 'Tomasino. So late. You gotta turn it off. You gotta go to sleep.' He says, 'OK, Nonna.' Then I kiss him. I say, 'I love you, Tomasino.' And I go to bed."

"To your bedroom."

"Yeah."

"And your husband, Salvadore Riggio, is there?"

"Yeah. And I'm crying, I say, 'Sal, let's go to Florida. Why we no go to Florida like everybody else? I want to see my daughter.' I say, 'I'm sick of, we never go out of the house. Four day I get to see my grandson.' I say, 'Not enough. Why we got to hide all the time?' "

"Did your husband answer you?"

"Yeah, he say, 'We can't go till things are OK with Louie Boffano.' "

"What did he mean by that?"

Says Bozeman, "Objection. State of mind of another."

But Tallow doesn't falter. "What did you say to him then, Mrs. Riggio?"

"I say, 'I'm scared.' He say, 'Hey, we got guards, guards all around the house, we got Aniello downstairs, nobody comes in here, everything it's OK. We just gotta wait.' I say, 'I'm scared somebody gonna kill you.' "

"And what was his response?"

"He laugh at me."

"What happened then?"

"Then the door open and a man come in. He got a hood on his head. He got a gun. Me, I'm gonna scream. The man say, 'Don't scream.' He say, 'Salvadore, don't let her scream or I kill her too.' So, Salvadore, he tells me, 'Don't say nothing, Angela.' "

"And then what happened?"

"Then Sal, he say, 'How did you get in?' And the man say, 'A tunnel. From next door, we dug a tunnel right to your basement.' And he laugh."

"And then what happened?"

"Then he say he was come from Louie Boffano and he was gonna kill Sal."

"And what did your husband say?"

"He say, 'Me, I no mind. You think my people, they gonna sell the drug? They no gonna sell the drug.' "

"Your husband told the intruder—"

"My husband, he no like the drug. Louie Boffano, he wanna sell the drug to ever one—"

Bozeman objects.

"Sustained," says the judge. "Strike her remark, the jury will disregard. Mrs. Riggio, please confine your description to what you saw and what you heard, to what was said and done—"

"But that's what was done! He sell the drug to the little kid. To my own kid, to my grandkid he want to sell—"

"Objection!"

"Sustained. The jury will disregard . . ."

But since it's more or less the truth, thinks Annie, and since it's spoken by this ancient elf, how in the world are we going to disregard it?

For God's sake, thinks Annie, why don't they shut this woman up? We know her husband was killed, we know her grandchild was killed, we already *know* that. So why don't they leave it alone and stop raking up all this pain?

But Tallow keeps bearing in. "And now the man with the mask, what did he do then?"

"He lie down on the bed."

"On the bed with you and your husband?"

"Yeah. Between us. On his stomach. He lie there."

"And then what did this intruder do, Mrs. Riggio?"

"Objection," drawls Bozeman. "Leading, leading this good lady down the garden path—"

"Enough," warns Wietzel.

Says Tallow, "Mrs. Riggio, what, *if anything*, did this intruder do then?"

"He, he—"

But this is as far as she can get. She waves her hand in front of her. She lowers her eyes.

"I'm sorry, ma'am, but I have to ask this. What did the man do then?"

Mrs. Riggio mutters something, but no one hears.

Says the judge, "Will the bailiff please adjust her microphone?"

The bailiff comes over and grasps the neck of the microphone and twists it down, down to where the old lady's head is hanging. She put her lips close to the mike and says, "He made, he made Sal open his mouth."

"He made him? How did he make him do that?"

"He say, 'If you no open you mouth, I'm gonna have to shoot you in the face. Make a mess, and your wife, she won't like that.' He say, 'Come on, Sal. We have to work *together*.' "

"And did your husband open his mouth?"

"Yeah. And the man said, 'Wider, now. A little wider.' Like a dentist. And then he put, he put the gun in my Sal's mouth."

"And then what—"

"And I turn, I try to turn away but he, he, he take my, the man he take my face, and he make me look, and I say, *'Ci vediamo.'* I gonna see you again. To my husband. Because *you* say he's a bad man. But he's no bad man. He's a good man. He, maybe OK he does *some* bad, but he don't sell no drug, he—"

"And then what happened, Mrs. Riggio?"

"And then he kill my Sal. He shoot him."

"And then what happened?"

"Then the door open and my, my, my—"

The woman weeps.

"Did someone come in then?"

"Yeah."

"Who came in?"

"My Tomasino. My little one. Not so little."

"Your grandchild?"

"My Tomasino."

"How old was Thomas?"

"Fourteen. I don't see him. Never, he's a stranger. Since he was eleven. Then for four day he stay with us. For four day."

"And when he came in did he say anything?"

"Yeah."

"What did he say?"

"He say, 'Nonna, you OK?' Then, then he see."

"What did he see?"

"My Sallie."

"Your husband, Mr. Riggio?"

She nods. "Yeah."

"And Mr. Riggio was dead?"

She nods.

"And then what happened?"

"The man, he turn around and he see my baby. Tomasino run away. And I try, I try to, I try to . . . but he don't care. He, he, he, run after him. And then I hear the shot. He shot, he . . ."

She stops.

The judge says, "Do you need some time, Mrs. Riggio? Would you like to take a break?"

She sits with her head down, shaking, sobbing.

Tallow says, "No, I tell you what, Your Honor. I have no further questions at this time." He walks back to his table. As he sits he murmurs to Bozeman, "She's all yours."

But all the jurors can see that the prosecutor is keeping a deadly squint locked on Louie Boffano.

THE TEACHER steps off the moss bank into the brook. Two gingerly steps through the ice-cold water to the edge of the rock shelf. Then he tilts forward and plunges. He slowly somersaults, and holds himself jackknifed under the water for a full minute.

Then he surfaces.

Sits on the rock shelf, with the numbing flow of the brook up to his rib cage. But his shoulders are out in the sunlight, and he leans his head back against the bank of moss and shuts his eyes.

Provoke her, he thinks, and she transforms herself.

You sound like an undertaker, you know that?

He laughs to remember it.

Provoke her, and all her quills start to quiver and she's dangerous.

She's trying to keep it under wraps, how much she detests him. But he can feel her struggle. Her struggle to survive, it brings out all her diamond spines.

Such a jewel, where did she come from?

In the last few weeks, he's learned a great deal about Annie Laird. She was raised by her mother. The father, with a record of four DUIs and two assault convictions, vanished from the picture when Annie was four. Her mother kept a beauty parlor in Allentown, Pennsylvania, and she and Annie lived above it. In fourth grade Annie took first prize in the West Allentown Elementary School Art Fair. Her grades in high school were middling. She flunked math three times.

138

But her art was daring and personal and original and the Tyler School of Art gave her a scholarship.

Then she tried New York for a while, living in a loft in the Greenpoint section of Brooklyn. She was admitted into the MFA program at Yale but she never entered. She had a child instead.

No clue as to who the child's father was.

She moved to the village of Pharaoh six years ago, when Oliver started school. When Annie's mother fell under the spell of Alzheimer's, Annie took her in and cared for her till she died last year.

Annie's career as an artist has been floundering. Too few connections in the New York art world, and Inez Gazzaraga's is a gallery on the skids. But still she's kept feverishly working, slave-typing all day and turning out those Grope Boxes at night. She seems to have a stubborn and unassailable oak-root understanding of who she is, of the value of her work.

When his cellular chimes, he half turns in the freezing water. He reaches for the phone on the mossy bank.

"Yes."

Leaves come revolving down upon him.

Says Eddie, "Remember that nosy guy that showed up at the reservoir last week? When you and her was meeting?"

"Yes."

"We got that plate traced."

"And?"

"He's a detective."

Police. The Teacher checks his reaction. Well, he *is* sitting in a mountain stream in October, which would account for his shivering, his thumping heart. But there's also a certain added clarity to these leaves that come pouring down on him out of the sky. A precision of detail that he lays to his fear.

My sweet mentor, fear.

Whoever can see through his own fear, said Lao Tsu, *will be delivered from fear.*

"State?" he asks. "Local?"

"Private."

"Private?"

He laughs so hard that Eddie on his end of the line joins in a little, saying, "What? What'd I say?"

"Nothing. I thought you meant the *po*-lice."

He gets up out of the water, takes a few steps into the grass, into pure sun, and sprawls. "What in the world would a private detective want with us?"

"With you, Vincent—he wasn't following me. I had my eye out for a tail."

"OK, what does he want with me?"

Eddie suggests, "Maybe Annie hired him?"

That's a fascinating thought. The Teacher turns it over in his mind a few times.

"No. First she's too smart, second no detective would take the case, third if he had taken the case, he never would have blundered like that. Showing himself to us."

"So what do you think, Vincent? Coincidence? What? What the fuck was he doing?"

Three brown moths, winter owlets, tangle in the black cherry tree above him.

He asks Eddie, "You know that boy Frankie? Works for Joseph Boffano?"

"Sure."

"Get him to help you. Tell him he'd be doing a personal favor for the Teacher. Tell him I admire his character. Get him to go with you, and pay a visit to this detective. Would you do that for me?"

"Sure."

"I can't imagine what the man thought he was up to. But it should be amusing to find out."

ANNIE watches the cross-examination of Mrs. Riggio.

Bozeman asks, "Ma'am, do you know this man? And let the record show that I'm pointing at the defendant."

Mrs. Riggio flicks her eyes that way. She says, "That man? That's Louie Boffano."

"Have you ever seen him before?"

"Yeah."

"Where have you seen him?"

"He come to my house for dinner. Many times."

"Did he ever argue with your husband when he came for dinner?"

"Nah."

"Did you ever see him kill anybody, Mrs. Riggio?"

"Nah."

"Ever see him hand out drugs to little children?"

"Do I see him sell the drug? I *know* he sell the drug."

"What kind of drug, Mrs. Riggio?"

"All kind."

"Heroin?"

"Yeah. Sure."

"Did you see him sell heroin?"

"Nah."

"But perhaps other people told you he did these things?"

"Sure."

"Were these *trustworthy* people, ma'am?"

Tallow is on his feet. "Objection! Witness is not remotely qualified to assess the trustworthiness of—"

"Sustained."

Says Bozeman, "Who told you that Louie Boffano sold drugs?"

"Who told me?"

"Who told you."

"Everyone."

"For example?"

She takes a moment before she speaks. Then she lifts her lip up in a sort of sneer and says to Bozeman:

"Why you work for him?"

Says Bozeman, "Excuse me?"

"You know why he keep on killing? Huh? Because nobody stand up to him, nobody."

The judge chides, "Mrs. Riggio, please—"

"Everybody scared!" she shouts. "When he please, he kill."

Tallow to his feet. And Wietzel scolding her, "Ma'am, you need to answer the question—"

"Ah, you scared too," she tells the judge. She turns to Bozeman. "You scared." She looks to the jurors. "You scared."

Says Wietzel, "Mrs. Riggio. Shut up!"

She shrugs. "So pity the kids, huh?"

Of course Wietzel gives her a long stern lecture and tells the jurors to disregard, but Annie wonders why the hell he let her say it in the first place. *You jurors are all scared, so pity the kids.* Why don't you shut up, woman? Why didn't he kill you too? You ugly old gnome, you sound like a preacher, why do we have to hear your sermons? Where do you get the right to talk about *pity the kids* when your husband was a Mafia bastard and I'm glad they killed him, and if your grandson's dead, who's to blame for that? Not me, witch. Shut up, witch.

Annie wonders, Am I going to get through this?

I don't think I'm going to get through this.

SLAVKO checks his watch: 4:40. So whoever this Mr. Flanagan is, he's late.

The guy said 4:30—"Four-thirty at your office, Mr. Sure-Knack, on the dot." But he wouldn't say what for. Well, OK, maybe the guy found another PI. Which would suit Slavko fine, since that would leave him free to focus all his thoughts on Sari.

He watches the clock tick off another minute, then he dials her number again.

He's eager to tell Sari about her boyfriend's mysterious wanderings. But again he gets her damn machine. He's already left her two messages. Still, he listens anyway, if only to fill the chambers of his ear with her voice. When he hears the beep, he hangs up.

Slavko knows that he's seriously smitten. There's no way to get around this. Another crush, another runaway train. So I'm a passionate clown. So what am I supposed to do about it?

In the meantime, this Flanagan, is he coming or what? Because I wouldn't mind calling it a day and stopping at Gillespie's and getting myself a pick-me-up. Would not mind clearing out of this smoky claustrophobic shambles of an office and taking in some fresh air.

Well, I'll wait another fifteen minutes.

He lights another cigarette.

Then he gets up abruptly and says, "To hell with it," grabs his jacket and goes for the door.

At that moment there's a knock.

He stands frozen. He hopes if he doesn't answer, they'll go away. He waits.

Second knock.

Then the door opens.

A sharp-beaked tough-looking young man peers into the dismal office. "Mister Sure-Knack?"

Slavko corrects his pronunciation. "Chur-nik."

"That's what I said. Sorry I'm late, Sure-Knack."

"Are you Mr. Flanagan?" says Slavko.

"That's right."

The young man saunters in. He wears a suit that looks a size too small for him. Maybe he likes that, though, maybe he likes the way the tight fit shows off all his muscles and his thick stovepipe neck.

Slavko heads for the swivel chair behind his desk. He gestures toward the only other chair in the room. "Have a seat. What can I help you with?"

Flanagan doesn't sit. He bats at the smoke in front of his eyes. He says, "You don't got much ventilation in here."

"That's true," says Slavko. He does not like this Mr. Flanagan. The guy's cheekiness puts him off. But even in the dementia of new love Slavko knows he can't pass up a potential client.

He mutters, "I'll try to get the window open if you want."

"This is a detective office?" says Flanagan. "What, you got no partners? You spend all day alone here in this shithole?"

Knife edge to this guy's demeanor. Trouble's coming? Or maybe not, maybe you're overreacting. Don't wait to find out, though. Get your hand on the old Smith & Wesson. It's in the drawer. Relax, take it easy, but get your hand on it now.

He reaches for the knobs on the desk drawer. "Well, let me get out an application here—"

Flanagan slams his hands down on the desktop. Then slides them forward till they hang over the edge where they can hold the drawer shut. He curls his lips back and he says:

"I got to fill out some fancy application for you to suck my cock?"

His hands come up fast into Slavko's chest. He pushes, the swivel chair rolls back a foot and the casters stick and the chair dumps Slavko. His head hits the wall. His head bounces against a filing cabinet and comes to rest on the floor.

Get up.

Of course you'd love to lose consciousness—but you can't afford to. Figure this out. Those are your knees down there, you see them? Put your weight on them. Use your arm for a brace and stand up.

Good. Now go for that S&W.

But the S&W is already in Mr. Flanagan's hands.

"So what were you going to do with *this*, Sure-Knack? You hold up your clients, is that how you operate?" He pockets the pistol. He comes around the desk. "You *dick*."

Slavko wants to back up but the fallen chair is behind his feet and there's nowhere to back to. Flanagan keeps moving in till he's right up against him. His garlic breath an inch away from Slavko's nose.

"That's what they call you, isn't it? A private dick?"

The room is illuminated by the flash of lightning coming out of Slavko's groin. The only reason he doesn't fall is that Flanagan is holding him up.

Says Flanagan, "Oh, I'm sorry, I guess I got confused. I thought maybe it was a *public* dick."

Slavko takes a quick swing at the guy. But the air in here has turned thick and syrupy and dreamlike, and his swing gets bogged down. Flanagan blocks it with a snorting laugh and grabs him by the lapels and laughs some more and hurls him against the wall. The room takes a half spin to the left. Settles. Slavko drops his chin and drools onto his shirt.

Flanagan asks him, "What were you doing at the dam?"

"The what? The dam? Oh, yeah. Wrong. Wrong turn."

"Wrong answer."

More lightning.

When Slavko comes to, there's someone else in the room.

The goon he saw at the dam. Mr. Ugly-As-Sin. He's going through Slavko's jacket pockets, and soon enough he comes up with the logbook. He starts leafing through it. Slavko blunders forward to take the thing back. Flanagan tosses him against the wall again and this collision is even more discouraging than its predecessors. And Slavko winds up back on the floor.

Mr. Ugly-As-Sin arrives at an entry in the logbook that seems to entertain him. He chuckles.

"Oh bite my crank. Look at this. Sari Knowles."

He leans over Slavko. "So you're working for Sari? Yeah? She thought her boyfriend was dickin around on her, and she paid you to sniff out the other woman's pussy? Is that the deal?"

He catches some of Slavko's thinning hair between the fingers of his fist. He pulls. Lifts Slavko up by his scalp.

"IS THAT THE DEAL?"

"Yeah."

"But, see, those two are in *love*. So what business is it of yours? Huh? Their problems? None of your business. You SHITSUCK! Can't leave two lovers alone? No, you gotta make your fuckin fee. Look at me. OPEN YOUR EYES!"

Slavko looks into Ugly-As-Sin's rheumy and bloodshot eyes and the man tells him, "Now I'm going to give you one more chance, you lucky duck. Sari ever calls you back? You get rid of her. I don't care what you tell her. Tell her one of your fleas died, you're in mourning. But I don't want to ever hear your name again. I ever hear your name again I'm gonna erase your fuckin name from this planet. Follow?"

Slavko nods.

"You can go live on some other planet. Follow me?"

Slavko nods.

"Ever heard the name Louie Boffano?"

Slavko stares, wide-eyed.

"Well, you just heard it again."

OLIVER hears the knock and goes out to the porch, to the screen door. Jesse's waiting out there. Leaning back on his bike seat. He says, "What's up, man?"

Oliver shrugs.

Jesse says, "Where you been?"

"I don't know. I haven't felt like coming out."

"You coming to lacrosse on Wednesday?"

"Yeah. I guess. If it stays clear. If it doesn't start raining again."

"Yeah," says Jesse. "Hey, so what do you think of this, man? Is this freakin fly or what?"

"What do you mean?"

"Hey. *Look.*"

Oliver opens the door. Holds on to the jamb and sort of hangs partway out the door. Jesse cocks his head, strikes a pose—and then Oliver notices the little stud earring.

"So what do you think?"

"Cool."

"You think? I wasn't gonna do it. But Chloe kept saying come on, so I did? So I like it."

"Chloe?"

"Yeah."

Oliver blinks at him. "Chloe Zichy?"

"Yeah. You don't know about me and Chloe? I'm seeing her now."

"Chloe with the knockers?"

"Those are fresh, huh?"

"You kissed her?"

"I'm *seeing* her, man. You don't know what that means?"

"You fucked her?"

"Well I mean I could if I wanted. Come on, let's ride. I gotta talk to you about it. Man to man."

"I can't. I'm fixing dinner."

"*You're* fixing dinner?"

"Microwave."

"Where's your mom?"

"Upstairs."

Up in her room, Oliver thinks, lying in bed and writing another letter she'll never send. But that's none of Jesse's business.

Jesse lowers his voice. "She won't let you out?"

"Nah, I just don't want to come out."

"What's the matter with you?"

"Nothing. What's it like, kissing Chloe?"

"She's fly, man."

"Did you touch her tits?"

"Her items? I mean if I wanted to . . ."

"Wow."

"Come on out, man."

"Nah."

"You know what Larry Hitt says? He says he thinks you're a spaceman. I told him to go screw himself. But I mean you are turning into a freaking hermit."

The microwave goes off. The three beeps.

"That's my dinner."

"Shit."

"Thanks for coming by, though."

"Hey," says Jesse. "No doubt."

Oliver goes in and takes out the two chicken pot pies. Goes to the foot of the stairs and calls Mom. She says she'll be down in a minute. No reason to believe her except that now it's time for the local news on TV. Sometimes that'll get her down here. He turns on the set. Turns it way up. Goes and sits in the kitchen, and digs through his pie assiduously, removing all the peas he can find.

If Mom wants him to eat peas, she can come down here and eat them with him.

He breaks off a chunk of the crust and smushes it around in the gravy. The crust is the only part of the pie he likes. Doesn't like it *much*, though.

He spears the chunk with his fork and lifts it and looks at it.

He hears the words *Boffano trial*, and he slides his eyes toward the set. It's in the next room and turned away from him, but he can see an angle of it. There's a sequence of artist's sketches, courtroom scenes. The reporter is saying:

". . . though small in stature, even frail looking, Angela Riggio seemed as fierce as a tiger on the witness stand today. She insisted that Louie Boffano wanted to, quote, 'sell the drug' to the kids, and that her husband had tried to stop him. Even when Louie Boffano threatened to kill him, she said, her husband refused to accept any involvement in the drug trade."

Oliver hears a creak from the floorboards above him. He hears footsteps and then his mother's door opening. Then a few more footsteps.

She wants to listen in. But she won't come down.

Says the reporter:

"When defense attorney Lawrence Bozeman challenged her knowledge of his client's activities, Mrs. Riggio seemed to flare up, demanding, 'Why do you work for him?'—then answered her own question. 'You're scared,' she said. She pointed to the jurors and said, 'They're scared too.' "

On the screen, a sketch of the jurors. Oliver goes into the parlor for a better look. In one of the sketches a woman juror has her eyes cast down, with her face propped on the splayed fingers of her hand. Looks sort of like Mom.

Says the reporter, "Several of the jurors appeared visibly moved when the old widow said, 'Pity the kids. Pity the kids.' "

Oliver hears the floorboards creak again. Mom is going back to her room.

An ad comes on.

He mulls over what that woman said.

They're scared.

And now a certain thought, which for days has been buzzing around at the fringe of his thoughts, breaks in. He draws a sharp breath. For a long time he stands staring at the TV and not seeing it, unable to move, and every time he fights that idea out of his head it comes right back. He's helpless against it. Dumb paranoia, he calls it. Stupid, he calls it. Kid's stuff. He shakes his head. He rolls his eyes and laughs at himself.

But the thought keeps finding its way back in.

Got to get some help here, he decides. Somebody to tell me what a bozo I am, I'm going bats, *this can't be true*. Got to find Juliet, he decides, let her wisecrack some sense into me.

JULIET thinks, as she thinks every time 5555 comes up on the beeper, that she's not cut out to be a doc. Particularly not an emergency room doc. She thinks that all she really wants is to be a calypso dancer in Trinidad. Or better yet, bedridden for the rest of her life with a mountain of books beside her and an endless coffle of chained, sleepy-eyed lovers that she can order up from room service.

But in the meantime, it's midnight at St. Ignatius Hospital and 5555 is on the beeper.

She claws her way up from her trance-sleep and staggers out into the corridor. Heads down to the neonatal unit, her rotation this month. No one's in here but one second-year resident and one nurse. And one newborn on the warming table. Wishing to howl like any newborn but he keeps choking.

The second-year is a fool even when he's wide awake, and at present he's sound asleep with his eyes open. But thank God the nurse is Henri, Henri from Haiti—her best friend next to Annie. As she crosses to the warming table she gives Henri a questioning glance.

Henri tells her, "Delivery was normal. But there seems to be some respiratory distress."

The infant boy is as wrinkled as a walnut. But larger than she expects. As she takes the kid's pulse she asks, "Not a preemie?"

"Full-term vaginal," says Henri. He shrugs. Full-terms are rare in this unit. "One-minute APGAR five, five-minute APGAR six."

She finds a low pulse rate.

She asks, "Where's the pediatrics resident?"

Henri shrugs. "Crash C-section? So we've been told. I'm sorry, my love."

She uses a DeLee suction trap to clear out the nose. Then she works an endotracheal tube through the child's mouth past the vocal cords into the miniature trachea. As she intubates, the tube starts to show a brown stain.

"Shit."

"What is it?" Henri asks.

"Shit. His own stool. He shit into the placenta, it got into his mouth and as soon as he was born he breathed it in. Meconium aspiration. Hey you." She calls to the second-year. The second-year doesn't stir.

"Hey. Doc." She snaps her fingers.

The second-year opens his eyes.

She tells him, "Get the ambu-bag."

"What?"

"The ambu-bag!"

She's not in a good mood.

She straps a pulse oximeter to the infant's earlobe. Reads the O_2 saturation—60. Bad news.

The second-year brings the bag, she sets it up and starts pumping. When she squeezes down with her thumb, air is forced into the baby's lungs. Then she lets up. Then squeezes again. Every two seconds. As she watches, the O_2 saturation starts to climb. From 60 to 74. Normally a baby draws thirty breaths a minute. She's pumping the bag twice that fast, once per second, turning this kid into a turbocharged breathing machine. And still it's taking a long time to pull the O_2 sat out of danger.

She says, "Who's this child, Henri? You know anything about it?"

"I met the mama."

"Any problems? Drugs?"

"I could not be sure. But young. Fourteen, fifteen? There was some man with her."

"The father?"

"Possibly. Possibly the mother's father as well."

As Juliet pumps the bag, she lifts one of the infant's legs. "It doesn't have the tail of a pig," she says.

Henri takes a look. "No."

"Which weakens your incest theory."

"Perhaps I'm mistaken."

"Well, *something* sure got fucked up."

Finally she pulls the O_2 sat up to 90. She hands the bag over to the second-year. She tells him, "That's where we want it, ninety. Keep it there. OK? I got to get this kid on a respirator."

She gets on the phone. Tracks down the attending physician at the NICU and tells him her problem. But he's got problems of his own.

"Juliet, shit, I'm sorry, we're working both our respirators now."

"So what do I do?"

"Whatever you want. I got a kid seizing here, Juliet, I'm no use to you right now. I'll get by when I can."

She calls the hospital in White Plains and begs some graveyard-shift asshole to come take this child. He tells her, "We need an attending to make this request. We need an assessment from an attending, and we need—"

Then Juliet happens to look over at the monitor. It reads 70 and falling.

She yells to the second-year: "Get it UP, god damn it! GET IT UP!"

The voice on the phone: "Doctor?"

She slams the phone down. Charges the second-year.

"Ninety!" she screams. "I want it at ninety!" She wrenches the ambu-bag from his grasp. She starts pumping it furiously.

He says, "Sixty-five is perfectly satisfactory. Sixty-five, he'll—"

"Sixty-five, he'll be a vegetable for the rest of his fucking life! 'Cause your thumb is sore!"

"Now wait, wait a minute," the second-year begins.

"Go get the attending! Tell him to call White Plains, request a transfer. You hear me? GO! GET THE FUCK OUT OF MY SIGHT! DON'T COME BACK!"

He flees.

"Henri," she says. "What are you looking at?"

"Nothing."

"You think you're looking at the witch of St. Ignatius?"

"Precisely so."

"You think I treated him like dogshit?"

"Precisely."

"He is dogshit."

Says Henri, "I seem to remember when you were a second-year

trying to put an IV into a sailor. I believe you tried fifty times. His arm was looking like a target range."

"Who says he was a sailor?"

"He had a tattoo of a sailing ship."

"Where?"

"In this very hospital."

"No, I mean where was the tattoo?"

"Oh." He shrugs, and smiles. "I don't seem to recall."

She says, "It's your fantasy that he was a sailor. He was a junkie, Henri. He didn't have any veins left."

She slowly works the O_2 sat back to 90.

Says Henri, "I recall that eventually that young man took the needle from you, and put it in himself."

"That proves it. He was a junkie."

"You were so embarrassed, you were about to die."

"Not my fault he had no veins."

"I kept a suicide watch on you all day."

"And the sailing ship, Henri, which you recall perfectly well, was tattooed across his ugly junkie butt."

She keeps pumping. When her thumb starts to ache, she switches to the other hand. After half an hour of this, when both thumbs are killing her, she begins to regret having spoken so harshly to that second-year.

She says, "You know what? Annie broke up with me the other day."

"She did what?"

"She told me to get the hell out of her life."

"Annie did?"

"She seemed—I've never seen her like that. She said I was a bad influence on Oliver. But she knows I'm in love with Oliver. I love him more than anybody in the world. Except Annie. So why did she say that, Henri?"

"*Annie* said this?"

"You know what bothers me, Henri? What bothers me is that I'm working such long fucking hours I don't even have time to feel hurt. That's what bothers me. Can you can work this thing, honey?"

"The bag? Try."

"All right, when I count to three you take it. One two three."

He takes it. The sat dips, but not too much.

She picks up the phone and calls White Plains again. The graveyard asshole tells her that help is on its way. Any minute now, they'll dispatch an ambulance.

"Yeah, right," says Juliet. "Any little minute."

She comes back and takes the bag from Henri. "You know what, darling? I have a feeling we're going to be here all goddamn night."

OLIVER eats his Apple Jacks. He sits silently across from his mom, who's working on half a slice of toast. Her cheeks are hollow, her skin is grainy. Her big eyes, when she raises them to meet his stare, are bloodshot, with milky sleep-scum caught in the corners.

He eats as quick as he can. When he's done he gets his lacrosse stick from the porch and wedges it into the loops on the back of his bike. He puts his schoolbooks in the basket and he's about to head off when Mom shows up at the screen door.

"Why aren't you taking the bus?"

"Lacrosse after school."

"I thought lacrosse was Wednesdays."

"Kind of a special practice today. We got that game with Brewster next week."

She stares. He waits for her to say something else, but she seems to have slipped into her world again. He starts up the hill.

But at Warbler Hollow Road, instead of turning left toward school, he keeps straight. He slowly climbs Onion Creek Ridge. Past the ravine of the old quarry, past the rock spring. Then he coasts for two miles. Takes the left-hand fork and at Allen's Grocery he dismounts and walks the bike down a flight of stone steps.

Juliet lives here, in the apartment beneath the grocery.

Her car's not in the drive, though.

He cups his hands to look in the window. Her bike's here, but no lights, no movement. Of course he could have expected this, since he knows she spends ninety percent of her life at work, but still. Shit.

He's wondering should he leave a note and go, or should he camp out on her lawn all day? Or maybe he should try to call her at the hospital?

Then suddenly her ancient VW bug turns into the drive.

She gets out. She's puzzled to find him here.

"Oliver?"

"Hey."

"How'd you get here? You rode your bike?"

He nods. He notices that both her thumbs are wrapped in bandages.

She says, "It's not a school day?"

He shrugs.

"You're supposed to be in school and you—"

"I had to see you."

"Well, I'm kinda, I haven't slept much. I was going to, um. Sleep all day."

Then she squints at him. She must have some clue that something's up, because her tone changes. "What's the matter?"

"I gotta talk to you."

"About what?"

"About Mom."

She leads him into the kitchen, with its low ceiling and the bay window that looks out into her garden. The faint smell of damp basement plaster. Juliet's home surprises him on every visit by how small and humble it is. Whereas in his dreams it always *looms*, immense and exotic.

"Want something?" she says. "You thirsty?"

"Water."

"Just water? No Coke or juice or anything?"

"Water."

She gives him a glass. Nods toward a chair and he takes it. She takes another chair and leans her elbows on the table. He has a swallow of water. Studies the bubbles clinging to the edges of the glass. Can't get started. He says, "So. Juliet. Did you just get off work?"

"Yeah."

"Why those bandages?"

She shrugs. "I was squeezing this, this, sort of like a lung? All night. I had a newborn with breathing troubles."

"So what happened?"

"Finally an ambulance came from White Plains and picked the kid up. About an hour ago."

"Is it gonna be all right? The kid?"

"No idea. It's out of my hands. Oliver?"

"Yeah?"

"What's going on?"

"Oh. Well, I mean. I don't know. I mean, well, you won't ever tell anybody this?"

She does a thing that he's always liked: this little rabbit twitch of her mouth—her pursed lips sliding in a bunch to the left. "I won't unless I need to. What's wrong?"

"You gotta promise."

"What's wrong, Oliver?"

"There's this guy? He gave Mom some money for her art. Then—you remember that guy? That day you came over, she had a date—"

Juliet nods. "I remember."

"And then the next day Mom was crying. She didn't say why but she wouldn't talk about that guy, she just wouldn't. At all. And she's still crying. It's like she's lost her mind."

"You think she fell for him?"

"Fell?"

"In love."

"Uh-uh."

"You think he hurt her?"

"I think, well *I* think he threatened her. Just tell me if you think this is all my imagination. OK? But I think it's true. I think that guy? He's got her. In like a trap. The way she's always snapping now—it's like she's in some kind of trap."

"What kind of trap?"

"Do you know who Louie Boffano is?"

"The Mafia don? The one on trial?"

"Yeah. OK. Well, OK, listen. She's on that jury."

7

the cold discipline of Orion,

the sweet wild confusion of the Pleiades

ANNIE's upstairs in her room, Oliver stands at the door, and she tells him he's got to be out of his skull. "Not a chance," she says. "If it's so important you should have remembered to ask me earlier."

"Mom, I didn't know this practice was going to be so late. I went right after school, but there was nobody there, so I called Coach and he told me it doesn't start till five. By the time it's over it'll be dark, I could take my bike but I know you don't want me on my bike when it's dark."

"I don't want you on that *team*," she says. "Wednesdays are one thing. If it's going to be Tuesdays too, if I have to drive you—"

"Just this once! A special practice. I mean, Mom, if I don't go they'll call me a fag."

"Stop it, Oliver."

"Don't blame me for what *they* say, Mom."

She shakes her head. But really, what difference does it make? She can sit and worry, she can simmer, as easily in the car as she can in her room.

"You'll get a ride home?"

"Yeah."

"Let's go then."

"Let me call Jesse, he's got my helmet. I got to tell him to bring my helmet."

"For Christ sake, let's go."

161

She rattles her keys impatiently. She goes downstairs and out to the car, and waits for him.

But he's so slow. Always so slow. She honks the horn and finally here he comes.

They pull out onto Seminary Lane. She glances in her rearview mirror, as she always does—ever since this started. But there's no one back there. She heads up the hill. Takes a right on Warbler Hollow, and then drives four or five miles through pastures and blazing autumn hardwoods. When they're almost to the school she checks the mirror again and this time there *is* a car.

The beat-up VW bug that belongs to Juliet.

It's something Annie's been afraid of every time she's gone out: that she might run into Juliet. She leans forward a bit so the mirror can't track her eyes.

They turn into the big parking lot beside the phys ed fields. It's almost empty at this hour. She peeks in the mirror and Juliet is pulling into the lot right behind her.

Maybe I can pretend I don't see her. Drive away the moment Oliver gets out—

"Mom, there's still nobody here."

"Huh?"

She looks, and there's not a soul on the lacrosse field. Or in the bleachers.

"Oh man," says Oliver. "What, did I get it wrong again? Wait. Maybe they're using the back field. Wait here, let me check, wait, I'll be right back."

"No, Oliver, I'm *not* going to—"

He jumps out. Doesn't seem to notice Juliet's car, he just runs off on a path through trees toward another open field.

Annie gets out and stands by her door and shouts after him, "Oliver! Get back here!"

But he's gone, and Juliet has parked her VW and she's walking toward her. Annie sees no choice but to turn her way and smile a little.

Says Juliet, "We need to talk."

"I'd love to talk, Juliet—I can't now. I'm late, I've got to run but let's—"

But Juliet has already taken Annie's arm. She gets a good grip and commands, "Walk with me."

"I really, I really can't—"

"What if I were in trouble?" Juliet asks.

"What kind of trouble?"

"What if it were really bad trouble?" Juliet asks her, and she leads Annie toward a copse of old maples at one edge of the lot.

"What, some man? Your job?"

"I don't know if I can tell you."

This outrages Annie. "What do you mean, if you can tell me? What are you saying? You're my closest friend, if you're in trouble, you've *got* to tell me."

Juliet abruptly holds up. Faces Annie. "Would you tell *me*?"

"Of course."

"Then do that."

"Do what?"

"Tell me. What's going on. I know somebody's hurting you. How can we stop him?"

"Whoa." Annie puts her hands up. She backs up a step. "What the hell is this?"

She glances around her. First toward the silent playing fields. Then to her car in the lot. Inside it, the shape of Oliver, patiently awaiting her return.

"This is a setup. Isn't it? You didn't just run into me. Did my kid put you up to this?"

"I had to find some way to talk to you."

"What about calling me on the damn phone—"

"No good if the phone's tapped," says Juliet, and Annie's spine tightens. "So what is it, Annie?"

"No."

"Tell me."

"Oh Christ." This is too sudden. She's giving it away, she's losing her grasp. "I *can't*. I can't tell you."

She turns and walks toward the car. But her friend quickly catches up with her.

"It's because you're a juror, isn't it?"

Annie keeps her head down so Juliet won't see her crying. "Leave me alone," she says. "God *damn*, leave me alone!"

"What's he doing to you?"

Annie stops, and brings one hand up to her face. "Oh Jesus," she says. She still won't look up. "Is anyone watching us?"

"No."

"Look all around. Be sure. On the road—"

"There's no one."

"Are there any cars?"

"No."

"You sure we're alone?"

"We're alone."

"OK." Annie shuts her eyes. "OK. He said if I didn't help him he'd kill Oliver. He said, Juliet, he said he'd kill my child."

JULIET and Annie sit side by side in soft-slung swings, with the huge trunk of a sugar maple shielding them from the eyes of the road. Annie tells Juliet everything, all that she knows and all that she's guessed.

When she's finished she asks her friend, "So what do you think? What do you think I should do?"

Juliet shakes her head. In a small dry voice she says, "I can't tell you what to do."

"What would *you* do?"

"I don't have a kid."

"Still, you love him. You love him almost as much as I do, don't you?"

"Annie. You want to protect him. It makes sense."

"You think I'm a coward?"

"No."

"Tell me what you'd do, Juliet. Tell me."

Juliet sits on the swing without moving. Runs the strategy through her head one more time. Finally she straightens a little. "Well. All right. Everything this guy does, he plans. Right?"

"He seems to."

"He's orderly? Meticulous?"

"Yes."

"Whatever he does, he does for a *reason*?"

"Yes."

"So if he thinks he's a reasonable man, you can beat him. You know? You make sure there's a price for hurting you, and you make sure he knows this price. And you have to make it a high price."

"I don't know what you're saying."

"You go to the judge. You tell him you want out of this trial. Tell him, tell him your kid's sick. Tell him he was just diagnosed with leukemia."

"Oh, come on, Juliet. He'll never buy that."

"He has to. Because you'll bring him a letter from his doctor. From me. He's got to dismiss you. Then we send Oliver to Long Island, to live with my folks for a while. And then, well, well then we send a message to that man. You'll meet with him somewhere. Say, by that reservoir again. And you'll say, 'Come near me again and I go to the cops with *everything*. Or if anything happens to me? Then my friends will go to the cops.' And then, I don't know, I don't know what he'll say, maybe he'll laugh, but you'll say: 'There's a few of my friends now.' And me and Henri, we'll be across the water, and we'll wave at him and, and we'll let him see that we've got a camera. And that we've been taping everything. OK? And that's, well I mean that's it, that's all."

Annie asks her in a tired voice, "That's what you think I should do?"

"You asked me what *I'd* do."

All day, while Juliet was working this out, working it over and over in between bouts of nightmare sleep, it had seemed to her a crisp and spare and cold plan. Low risk, high sanity. Outfreeze this ice-fiend. Now it all strikes her as naive and dangerous. That part about waving to the guy and showing him a camera? Weird. Sleep-deprived dementia.

She watches Annie's eyes. Annie's simply looking at her car. Juliet looks that way too, but there's nothing to see. Nothing visible of Oliver save his forearm and his hand hanging out the window.

Says Annie, "I don't know. It sounds sort of crazy."

"Yeah. You're right. The way you're handling it, it's probably a lot smarter."

"Then why would you—"

Juliet shrugs. "I don't know. Because I don't take orders very well. From monsters I don't take them at all. But that's just me. And it's not my kid."

Annie keeps looking across the lot at her car. Those big gray eyes of hers are wide open. Is she thinking? Juliet wonders. She doesn't say anything. Is she still with us? Is she thinking, or only staring?

Finally she says, "Well, I can't . . ."

Then nearly a minute rolls by. "I mean I can't keep doing *this*."

Juliet waits. Annie sways on her swing. "Oh, God. I don't, God, I don't know."

SARI KNOWLES, at home, fixes herself a salad but can't eat it. It's all she can do to nibble a single leaf of lettuce.

She only wishes Slavko would answer his phone.

Yesterday he told her machine that he'd found out something about Eben, but now she can't get hold of him. She calls and calls, but he's never there.

What about Eben? Another woman?

I should go to Slavko's office, she thinks. Tonight. Right now. Even if he's not there I can leave a note.

Something about Eben. He knows something about Eben. Eben Eben Eben. Stop saying his name, girl, or you're going to start bawling again.

She gets into the shower but no sooner has she put her head under the water than she thinks she hears the phone ringing. So she has to turn off the tap and listen. Silence. It was only a ringing in the pipes. She turns the water on again. Again she thinks she hears the phone. She *knows* it isn't the phone—but still, it might be. So off with the water. More silence. This life, damn. She stands there dripping, with no water coming down. This pain. God. Eben, this is too much pain. This dome of damn silence I'm living under, Eben, you prick, look what you've done to me.

Don't you ever ever *ever* try to come back to me, Eben, I'll spit in your face, I'll claw your eyes out, I *swear* I will.

Then she hears a car in her drive, and she thinks, Eben? Could it be Eben? No. But it might very well be Slavko, who could tell her something about Eben—so she steps out quick and grabs a towel and dips her head and dries her hair. The doorbell rings.

Jesus, this guy shouldn't come without calling but really I don't care, it'll be nice to talk to him. My new friend, my comfort. We can get drunk again. She puts a robe on and runs to the door and opens it.

It's Eben.

He's brought an orchid. He's wearing a gorgeous Brioni jacket and Converse sneakers. He's wearing his screwy smile. He says, "I'm sorry."

"Keep your flower," she says. "Get out of here."

"I'm sorry I haven't called. I've been missing you. This is the toughest deal of my life, Sari. It's going to be the sweetest when I win. But I've been missing you every minute."

She hates him. Even the sound of his voice, everything disgusts her. She says, "The other night, the last time you called me—where did you call me from?"

"From home."

"Yeah. Yeah, that's what you told me *then*."

"It's true."

"Fuck you. You called me from your townhouse?"

He squints. He looks away a moment, then meets her eyes again. "Well, no."

Exactly, you greasy liar. So now what new lie are you going to try to cover yourself with?

"I called you from another home, Sari."

"Another home? What the hell are you trying—"

"I have a cabin. Near Garrison, overlooking the river. I never take anyone there, it's just for me. It's not much more than a lean-to. But when I'm stressed, that's where I go. I've been going there every night for the last week. How did you know I wasn't at the townhouse?"

She glowers at him.

He asks her, "You don't trust me? You should trust me, Sari."

Her eyes drop. She can feel the hatred starting to break up inside her. But she doesn't want it to break. She wants to keep this solid wall of rage. She thinks, No. He's lying again. He doesn't have any secret cabin. This is all bullshit.

Then he says gently, "I've never asked anyone this before, but, well, would you like to see it?"

"See what?"

"My cabin."

"Go there?"

He nods.

"When?"

He takes her hand. He starts to draw her outside.

"Jesus, Eben, no!"

He tugs. "Come with me."

"You don't *really* have a cabin?"

"Come right now."

"But, I'd have to, I'd have to put some clothes on—"

"It's a beautiful night, Sari. I'll lend you some clothes when we get there. Just come."

She laughs.

No. Don't laugh.

Jesus, don't give in so quickly, *don't.* But she can't help but laugh. She lets him pull her out with him. In her house robe, in her bare feet. He shuts her door and leads her across cool gravel to his car, and holds the door open for her, and she laughs some more.

Where's that pain?

She has a vague memory of a lot of silly pain, which thank God is all behind her now.

OLIVER's mom gets in the car and casts him a sharp look, and when he tries to say something she puts a finger to her lips. She pulls out of the lot onto Warbler Hollow Road, and he figures he's screwed now. Grounded for at least a month, which is an unpleasant prospect all right, but even worse, she must think he's a schizo paranoid. She and Juliet both—they must think they better get him locked him up before he wigs out and hurts someone.

Mom takes the long way home. Over to Ratner Avenue and then to Old Willow Avenue. Dusk is dampening the leaf light in all the sycamores.

She pulls over beside the statue of Hannah Stoneleigh on her horse, and she asks, "What's that? Behind the statue, what's that?"

"It's a skeleton, Mom. For Hallowe'en."

"Is it? Let's check it out."

So they walk down to the statue.

They look at Hannah and the top-hatted skeleton who rides behind her. Oliver is only waiting for her to broach the subject. To say, Maybe it's time to get you a little therapy, boy.

But what she says is, "Oliver, we can't talk in the car. Ever. They might have our car bugged. I'm *sure* they have our house bugged. Do you know what a bug is?"

He nods.

It doesn't matter how powerfully he's been imagining all this—it astonishes him to hear her confirm it.

She says, "For all I know maybe they're listening now. Maybe they've bugged our shoes or something, but that's a chance I'll take. Once we're back in the car, though, you don't know anything about this. Not a word. Not a question. You make one slip and everything is ruined, you understand?"

He nods.

"Say it. Say, 'I'll never talk about this in the car.' "

"I'll never talk about this in the car."

" 'Or in the house.' "

"Or in the house."

"You were right, it's one of Louie Boffano's men. He says I have to say 'Not guilty' or he'll hurt us. I'm sorry I didn't tell you about it before. Do you understand why I couldn't tell you?"

"Yeah."

"Have you told anyone else?"

"No."

"You sure? Maybe you were, you were afraid, so you called Jesse—"

"No! Mom, I only guessed it last night."

"We can't go to the police."

"OK."

"These men? Oliver, they don't care about the police. They'd kill us anyway."

He nods.

She says, "We're going to try something. I mean *I* am, but it's Juliet's idea. I'm going to, maybe I'm going to talk to the judge, try to get out of this. Maybe our lives will change tomorrow. Maybe we'll leave Pharaoh and won't ever come back. Are you scared?"

Truly he doesn't, at this moment, feel any fear at all. In fact he feels that now that his mom and Juliet are working together on this, the big guns, everything's in capable hands.

But he doesn't want to sound childishly cocky, so he hedges. "Yeah. I'm a little scared."

"So am I," she says. "But I'm also, I'm glad I'm doing something. I can't just do whatever this bastard tells me to. I thought I could, but it was killing me. I'm glad you went to Juliet, Oliver. God, I wish, I only wish we could kill him. I wish we could kill that motherfucker."

"Motherfucker?" he says. He almost smiles. She almost smiles back.

She asks, "Are you hungry?"

"Yeah."

"Pizza?"

"Yeah. Mom, we can go to the mall?"

"We can go the mall, we can go to your arcade, you can waste countless quarters, I'll waste them with you."

THE TEACHER outside his cabin, under stars and a slight moon. He stands behind Sari, who's shaking her head, amazed by the view. He watches her taking it in. The dark gnarled orchards. The lights of villages, the far smears of neon. The starlit sails of three sloops way off on the black Hudson.

She says, *"Oh."*

The Teacher is also moved. It's been a month since he's visited this little cabin, and he always forgets how lovely it is.

He touches her and she turns. He asks her, "Are you cold?"

"Mm, a little."

Then she puts her hands on his shoulders and makes a little leap up, and wraps her legs around his waist. She's still in her house robe, and it falls open, and her bare sex presses against the metal of his belt buckle. He carries her into the cabin. She rubs her cheek against the stubble of his jaw.

He sets her down and stretches out beside her.

No lights, no candle. Only the starglow on this rough bed. The deep shadow of the rafters above them. For a long time they lie there scarcely moving, their lips touching, simply breathing in each other's breath. His fingers graze her temple, her earlobe.

Patience, he thinks, and he sets to work.

Much later, he's lightly shaping her breasts with his tongue, whisking the nipples to a peak, making her ache, driving her slowly

174

into a frenzy. She writhes. She wants more. She tries to pull his hand to her groin, but he allows her only a touch of a phantom fingertip along the lips of her sex. No pressure. Letting the petals open in their own good time.

He tells her, "Look outside."

Through the open cottage door, down on the river, a barge—a lozenge of lights as pale as the lights of fireflies—moves slowly from one jamb of the door to the other. That huge simple night out there, which by now has fully surrendered to him. Clear title. My universe. A long time passes, then he slides down and kneels before her. With the tip of his tongue he makes a circle around her clitoris—then slides it the length of her furrow. *Darkness within darkness within darkness,* said Lao Tsu, *the gate to all mystery.* He makes another circle. She moans and arches her pelvis against his mouth but he retreats. She subsides. He returns. But he gives her only this light grazing touch of his tongue.

"Oh God, Eben. Please. Let me come."

He tells her in a whisper, "Not yet."

"Oh please," she says. "I want to come *now.*"

"Don't come till I tell you."

Much later, past midnight, she's sitting on his lap, both of them facing the door, his cock is deep inside her, and he looks out the south window and he can see both Orion and the Pleiades at the same time. The iron pattern of the Hunter, and beside it the messy blur of the Pleiades. Like me and Annie, he thinks. All over the hemisphere tonight people looking into the sky are seeing Orion's discipline and the sweet wild confusion of the Pleiades, but what do these constellations stand for? They stand for us. For me and Annie. For the Teacher and the Juror. All over the world, whatever names they give to their star-myths, they're really the myth of the Teacher and the Juror. He laughs out loud.

"What?" says Sari.

Her voice reminding him that he's not with Annie, not in the flesh, not now. He's with this other woman. But it doesn't matter. He tells her, "This night!"

Much later, a bat flies into the cabin. Sari's scared but he whispers to her, "It's all right, it won't touch us, it'll be gone soon, I'm here," and he keeps fucking her, his rhythm is undisturbed. She holds her breath and they hear the odd engine of the bat's wings all around them and then the bat finds the door again.

Later, he's on top of her and he decides that the time has arrived. He begins to move more quickly. He drums himself into her, with a little hook at the end of each beat, a harsh sliding against her pelvis that brings her to the brink, and again to the brink, and again—and this time he lets her go. He lets her moans sharpen into a wail. She thrashes, she tears at his chest with her claws.

He decrees his own eruption as well, and as it boils up he opens his mouth to cry out and he looks for and finds Annie in the darkness. Annie. Laughing the way she laughed when he was in her studio touching her sculptures. That time when she laughed so hard because he was going to make her rich and happy and she was falling in love with him, and he'll never see her laugh like that again, will he? He's in pain, and he roars. Wounded, in a bitter rage, in the splendor of his conquest, he roars.

8

Who will protect you?

ANNIE finds parking in the lot of the monstrous county courthouse. It's easy. She's early, there's almost no one here.

She's never parked here before. Every morning of the trial she's left her car at a police barracks near I-684, then waited with the other jurors for a van to take them to the courthouse. The authorities seem worried that if she parked *here*, one day she might be followed home.

It's touching, their concern for her peace of mind.

She rushes up a flight of steps. Passes under the mock-ruins of an archway and comes to the atrium. Bizarre, deconstructed, concrete. Apparently this horror of a courthouse was built sometime in the late seventies, when intimations of entropy and anarchy were all the rage.

At the atrium's center grow cactus shrubs and a willow tree. And three towering chunks of glass, black glass, clustered about a great shapeless mountain of rubble.

At the door to the court offices she tells the guard that she has an appointment with Judge Wietzel. He sends her through the metal detector.

Down a dismal corridor that's been done up to simulate the feel of a cave. Ersatz flickering from ersatz wall-sconces.

At Wietzel's chambers a secretary tries to stop her, but Annie can see right into the judge's office. He's pulling on his robe. Annie murmurs to the secretary, "I'm sorry, I can't, I can't tell you why but I've got to see him."

She walks right past the startled woman. She steps into the judge's office and shuts the door behind her.

Wietzel turns. His usual look of flabby complacency is not in evidence. He's worried, and his eyes are on her hands. Checking, Annie supposes, to see if I've got a gun.

She shows him empty palms.

"Excuse me," he says as he steps back from her, takes refuge behind his desk. "I don't know what you're doing here."

"I need to see you. You know who I am?"

"Yes." Withering chill in his voice. "Yes, you're a juror. Open that door please."

"I have to talk to you alone."

"Do you have a problem?"

"I do, I'm—"

"Well, let me just explain to you, that when you come into my chambers, it's not a trivial thing. You don't come in for a chat. When a juror visits a judge, this can have serious consequences."

She stares at him.

What is he saying?

Is he saying he's in with them?

He clears his throat. "Now, if you do have a serious problem and you still want to talk about it, I'll call the defense attorney and the DA, and we can—"

"No!"

"Excuse me?"

She says, "I want to talk to you alone. I don't, I don't want them. I only want to talk to you."

"Alone?"

"Alone."

She opens her handbag and pulls out the letter from Juliet.

"You *can't* talk to me alone," he tells her. "And whatever that is, I don't want to see it. Not without all the attorneys present." He clasps his hands on the desk in front of him and leans toward her.

She pulls back.

He is. He is in with them.

Of course he is. They have all the money in the world, why shouldn't they have him in their hire? She says, "What are you telling me? You're telling me I'm making a mistake?"

"Ma'am, what I remember about you is that I gave you every opportunity to get out of serving on this panel. But you insisted. You *wanted* jury duty. You recall?"

She nods.

"So. You want to serve, you don't want to serve. You have some problem but you don't think the defendant has a right to hear about it. I think you're wrong. I think he has every right. He happens to be on trial for murder. Now shall I see if I can locate his counsel?"

He lifts his phone. He looks at her. She hears the dial tone. She puts the letter back in her purse.

"No," she says. "No, I've changed my mind."

She backs up a step, then she turns and walks out.

SLAVKO is sitting on the floor of his office at three in the afternoon. He's writing a poem, which is called "It Doth Suck," and though it's his first poem it's a goddamn good poem. He reads over what he's got. He reaches to his left for the bottle of Jim Beam. He doesn't *look* because that would involve turning his head to the left and it hurts too much to turn his head to the left. Or to the right, for that matter. So he reaches without looking, and puts his hand into a quart takeout container from Luk Dhow. Last night's supper. His hand comes back wearing the quart container like a glove. Presently he figures out that it's not a glove. He shakes it off him.

He forces himself to turn his head. Finds the bourbon and gives it a yank.

While licking his hand he rereads his poem:

It Doth Suck

Sucks, huh?
All pretty sucky? What do you say?
Fuckhead, hey fuckbrain, cat got your tongue?
It genuine sucks.
What did you think, it was going to get better?
Be glad to answer that, but I can't because of
The BEEP BEEP BEEP

From that semi outside on Main Street.
It's backing up!!
For shit's sake,
In traffic, everybody's pissed. BEEP BEEP BEEP,
It says, so loud I can't think.
It's the National Anthem
Of my life. God it sucks. Okay? And this here,
This is my poem. Juliet, I had wanted to not send
It to you, but now I've got a new girl
To not send it to.

Is there a minimum number of poems, he wonders, to qualify for the Nobel Prize? Wouldn't just one be enough if it was a real corker?

There are some corn chips around here somewhere.

He spots the bag under the desk. Two inches of corn chip mulch at the bottom of the bag, he could eat that. But there's a cockroach down there too, looking quite content, sassy actually, his little feelers quivering. Well, when you're through, my friend.

Always serve the guest first.

Daylight comes in through the grimy window. Why doesn't somebody turn down that god-awful daylight? Somebody?

Instead, somebody knocks.

Oh, what, do you think I'm going to *answer*? Are you out of your flea-fuckin mind, boy?

Today Mr. Czernyk regrets that he is not receiving any guests larger than a cockroach. No thrashings today, please. All thrashings, please come back tomorrow.

The door swings open. Of course he's forgotten to lock it.

It's Sari.

He cringes.

The office is a mess, a stinking mess. So is he. His jaw is swollen up and black and blue and shades of forest green. His nose looks like a watermelon somebody put in the back of the fridge and forgot about for two months. Also the beating has thrown his eye sockets out of balance. Furthermore he has crumbs and bourbon stains and drops of Luk Dhow's special sauce all over his shirt.

However, he believes that his fly is all zipped up. Well, well, he thinks, detail like that, should be a goddamn *wellspring* of pride.

Sari gasps when she sees him. "I'm sorry, I didn't—"

Running her eyes up and down the wreckage of him.

"What happened? My God!"

Oh she's beautiful. It ought to be a class-A felony to let something as beautiful as that meet up with carnage like this. He's so humiliated he wants to die.

This humiliation makes him angry. He snaps, "You didn't hear 'Come in,' did you?"

"What happened to you?"

"Cut myself shaving."

"God, have you been to the hospital?"

He shakes his head. "I'd love to but I've been so darn busy. Busy as a beaver, you know what I'm saying?"

Why is he doing this to her? She's not to blame here. But the way she's standing there, it gets under his skin. She's standing there taking in the catastrophe of the office. She keeps shaking her head. He sees her eyes hesitate a moment at the splotch of blood on the wall, and then at the spattering of blood on his papers, and again at the Jim Beam bottle by his side. She's appalled, yes. She pities him. But still she keeps one hand on the doorknob, she keeps her shoulders back in that brisk designer jacket of hers, nose uptilted a degree or two. She means to keep a world of distance from all this.

She asks, "Someone you were investigating or something? Did they do this?"

Again his rage gets the better of him. He mutters, "That's privileged information, Ms. Knowles. Tell me, what can I do for you?"

"I've been, been trying to call you. Did you get my messages? I wanted to tell you, well I know you did a really good job, and I wanted to thank you. And to pay you, to settle up."

"What needs settling?"

"I mean I won't be needing you anymore. Your services. Because, well, Eben, he explained to me. Everything. And we're fine. I mean a lot, I hate to say it, but a lot of our trouble was *my* fault. My impatience and all. My lack of trust. You know?"

He lowers his eyes. He can't look at her.

"So I wanted to settle up. So if you could figure out your hours and all—"

He still can't look at her but he says, "Hey, guess what? Happens I was just noodling those numbers? And this is kind of unbelievable, but the retainer covers everything. To the penny. To the tenth of the penny, in fact. You don't owe me a thing."

"Oh."

"To the mole on Abe Lincoln's nose," he says.

She gives a nervous little laugh. "Well that's good then."

"To the hair growing out of the mole," he says.

"Great." And then before he can start in on the mole-hair's individual cells, she changes the subject. "Oh, by the way, you said, didn't you say on a message that you'd found something out? Something big?"

She has to wait for his answer.

"Yeah," he finally mutters. "I thought I had. An indiscretion on the part of Ebenezer Rackland, I mean an indiscretion of epic proportions, hoo *Daddy*. But it turns out it was committed by some *other* Ebenezer Rackland."

"Oh." Again the nervous laugh.

But then her voice relents a little, she lets some of the softness back in. "Slavko, look, I wanted, I wanted to tell you, that night in the car? I won't forget that. If you hadn't been there I would have gone over the deep end. You were great."

"Just doing my job," he says.

She asks him, "Is there anything I can do for you, Slavko?"

"Yeah. You can shut that door softly. When you go out? Don't slam it. I got kind of a headache."

She murmurs goodbye. He keeps his eyes on the floorboards till he hears the door click shut.

Then he reaches and pulls the swivel chair over to him. He upends it and wedges it against the filing cabinet and uses it to help himself to rise, painfully. He limps to the window. He's in time to see her cross the street and get in her car and drive off. He presses his face against the dirty glass and watches till she's gone, and then for a long while after she's gone.

EDDIE waits on Route 22 about a mile up from the Park & Ride, and when Annie drives past he slips in behind her. Stays on her for about half a mile, then flashes his lights. Once, then twice. The signal. She slows and lets him pass. As he goes by he looks over at her.

She won't look back at him.

They'd given her no warning of this, this summons to a rendezvous. She must have been thinking that soon she'd be home, home with her kid fixing dinner or watching TV or whatever, and now all of a sudden she's got to follow Eddie wherever he wants to take her, and she must be tired and scared and upset. She's focusing straight ahead. Dark pouches under her eyes. Her hair pulled back severely from her face.

She'll shatter at a touch, Eddie thinks. At any pressure.

Ah shit, he thinks.

Woman, why did you pull that stunt? Going to the judge, how the hell did you think you were gonna get away with that?

ANNIE follows the car of the man she calls Johnny. It's a strange switchback route that he's taking her on. North by slow baffling zigs and zags, into horse-and-woods country. Then west, then perhaps south. As she drives, she starts to worry about Oliver. Today is Wednesday—his *real* lacrosse day. After practice he rides his bike home, and she's supposed to be there when he arrives.

If she's not, he'll get scared.

She frets over this. Her fretting starts to loop around in her brain, and she has to say to herself, almost out loud: Cut it out. It doesn't matter. So what if I'm a little late? He'll survive.

Concentrate on the business at hand, Annie.

Which is this: If Zach Lyde has found out that she went to the judge, how is she going to placate him?

Seems like she's got no choice but to come clean, tell him everything—except leave Juliet out of it—and beg his mercy. And after all, how much can he fault you? You went to the judge but you didn't say a word. Truth is, now he should be trusting you more than ever.

Stroke his feathers. Don't let him rile you. Stroke and stroke his feathers and he'll let you go, and maybe you can slip away tonight, drive to Juliet's and figure out your next move. There must be someone who will help us. Must be. Someone.

Johnny pulls into the lot of a restaurant called Vic's, and she follows. She knows vaguely where she is—Vic's is an Italian place in the deep woods north of Pharaoh. With a clientele that comes up mostly from the city. A traditional crowd. Drive by on a weekend evening, the parking lot will be packed with big American boats, Lincolns and Caddies.

As she pulls in, she sees Zach Lyde coming out of the restaurant. He's got someone with him, some guy who looks to be dead drunk. Zach guides him over to a big white ramshackle convertible in the parking lot. Then he looks over at Annie and gestures to her: *Come.*

She gets out of her car and walks over.

Gracious Zach Lyde makes introductions.

"Annie, I want you to meet Rodney. Rodney, this is my friend Annie."

Annie mumbles hello. Rodney looks her up and down. "Oh Jesus," he says. He turns to Zach. "What're you talking about, your *friend*? I mean I know what you two are doing. This chick's a fuckin knockout. Fucking Knock *Out*."

Rodney's got long black greasy hair. He wears owl glasses and a green golfing jacket that's too short in the arms. Zach says with a grin, "Rodney here is a gallon of sewage that's backed up from New York City."

"Hey don't gimme that shit," says Rodney. "You and your fuckin '69 Knicks. Your fuckin Earl the Pearl. You think he could play Ewing? Ewing would fuckin—"

"You ready to go home, Rodney?"

"Ewing would blow his, I mean blow, blow his fuckin *lights*—"

"I've offered to drive Rodney home in his car. I think he's had a little too much. Will you ride with us, Annie?"

"Hey, shove it up your ass!" says Rodney. "I'll drive my own fuckin car. I can drive. Drove here, right?"

Zach ignores him. He takes off his jacket and says, "Rodney, let me try on your jacket."

"Say what?"

"It's a nice jacket. Let me try it."

When Zach Lyde puts it on, the absurd jacket looks almost stylish.

"OK. Get in the car now, Rodney."

"Fuck your mother."

"In the back. I want Annie up with me."

"I bet you do," says Rodney.

Zach holds the rear door open, and Rodney crawls into the back-seat of his own car. He sprawls.

"I bet you, I bet, I bet you fuckin do."

They drive through the hemlock woods. Rodney's old bomb gasps through the lower gears, but it comes into its own once it works up a little speed.

"Rodney is not making a great success of his sojourn on Earth," says Zach. "He's drunk. He's an imbecile. He's—"

"Hey shut up!" Rodney snarls from the back. "So what are you, what are you, some kind of angel from heaven?"

"But he has a brute cleverness," Zach goes on. "He never forgets who his friends are. And his friends keep his head above water. After all his DUIs, still he's on the road. He put a pedestrian in intensive care last year, yet his license is still valid."

Rodney's head suddenly lurches between Annie and Zach. "You said you had some *Scotch*, shit-for-brains. Break it out."

"Annie," says Zach, "would you look in my bag for the bottle that's in there?"

Something like a gym bag on the seat beside her. She rummages inside it. Dimly reminded, as she does, of her own artwork—her Grope Boxes. The faint recollection that she used to be an artist. She touches something that feels like . . . a pair of glasses? Then an infant's bottle. She pulls it out. "This?"

"Give it to Rodney."

But the very idea incenses Rodney.

"What do you think, *I'm gonna stick that in my face?*"

"Good Scotch in there, Rodney. I don't want you spilling. It's easy. Suck on it. Do you think it will affect my regard for you? It won't."

"You asshole," Rodney groans, but he plucks the bottle out of Annie's hand. She sees in the corner of her vision that he's taken it into his mouth, that he's guzzling at the nipple.

"Now lie down, Rodney."

"What?"

"Lie down. Get comfortable. I put something in there to make you sleepy—so go to sleep."

Rodney murmurs some complaint. But Annie hears him settling himself.

Says Zach, "Now would you give me the eyeglasses?"

When she takes them from the bag she sees they're not really glasses. Just a frame. A black and owlish frame like the frame of Rodney's glasses.

Zach puts it on.

"So what do you think?" he asks her. That lopsided grin of his at play. "How do I look?"

She says, "What are you doing?"

"I'm doing Rodney," he says. "I want to see what life looks like from Rodney's eyes."

She hears something like the chirr of a cricket coming from the gym bag. Says Zach, "There's a phone in there—would you hand it to me?"

She passes him the phone.

"Yes?" he says.

She faintly hears the voice on the other end telling him, "The Dragon Boy's up."

He checks his watch. "OK. That's perfect."

He sets down the phone. He speeds up a little. He glances again into the rearview mirror.

"Look at Rodney *now*, Annie. Look."

She turns. Rodney has curled himself fetally around the bottle. A drool of Scotch runs down his chin. Softly snoring.

Zach asks her, "Why do you suppose he's like that?"

Try to seem agreeable. Try to go along with him. Zach Lyde is in some kind of state. Manic. Something burning in his eyes.

She asks, "You mean why is, why does Rodney drink?"

He seems not to have heard her. He says, "He likes that bottle I gave him, doesn't he? It's put him at his ease. That's all he wants, really—that nipple. Everything else scares him, and he doesn't like to be afraid. He's like the rest of us—he spends most of his time trying to keep out of fear's way. Anything not to feel fear. Anything. Give up sex, give up love, give away every rag of your self-respect, drink yourself to death—but please God, no fear."

Then silence. Say something, Annie. Think of something to keep him talking.

She tries, "Don't you ever feel fear?"

"I feel it all the time. I had a bout with it today."

He slows at a fork in the road, and takes the left-hand tine. Warbler Hollow Road. Oliver's school is down this road.

He glances over at her. In his brown eyes those gold flecks are glowing. He says, "But I bow to fear, to its necessity. It's terror that teaches me my *shape*. Do you understand?"

"Why are we going this way?" she says. "Where are you taking me?"

He speeds up. The tires drift in the turns.

He says, "I'll go in one direction till I run up against so much fear I can't take another step. One can only go so far into the dark. So far out to sea before fear turns us around. We'll say so much to our boss or our lover or our mother—and not another word. We've reached the border. We've found out the shape of our lives."

Then he laughs. "I'm sorry," he says. "Am I rambling? It's from my nightmare today. Whenever I descend from a spell of terror, I'm always full of ideas. Elated, foolish. Long-winded."

They approach the school. The classroom building, then the parking lot, the phys ed fields.

Annie slides her eyes over to check out the lacrosse field. But it's empty, except for a pair of stragglers in the bleachers changing their shoes. In the parking lot a boy hurries toward a waiting minivan. He tosses his lacrosse stick into the back and jumps in.

Zach does not slow down.

He says, "Lacrosse. They say it's the most dangerous sport in the country. Well, if it weren't dangerous the boys wouldn't play it. It wouldn't mean anything. Would it?"

He looks over at her.

She knows what he's going to say before he says it.

He says, "Your son, Oliver, he plays lacrosse, doesn't he?"

"What are we doing here?" she demands. Let him, let him hear the wobble of panic in her voice, what difference does it make? "Who's the Dragon Boy?" she asks. "Why do you want to bring me—"

"You don't know what you love, Annie. You're letting the gray suits tell you that what you love is *Justice*. Or the legal code of the state of New York. Or your honored place in the community. And I think it will take terror, the real nightmare edge of loss, to teach you that really these trifles don't concern you at all—that *all* you care about is your kid and your work and a handful of your friends—and if the gray suits can't protect these, then who needs the gray suits?

"And they can't—they can't protect you. Judge Wietzel? He's too busy looking out for his own career, how's he going to rescue *you*? You didn't realize that? You haven't had enough terror, so you went out to roust up some more? The judge, the cops—Annie, how can they shield you against someone like me? Look at me. I'm Rodney Grosso, I'm drunk, I'm a piece of human garbage and I know it. I'm driving too fast because I'm getting fat and old and that scares me but on the road I'm still a young buck, so I take this curve too fast—"

They *are* going too fast. They come around a sharp bend and nearly skid off the asphalt before he gets the wheels under control.

"Stop," she says. "*Please* . . . stop."

"Do you think you can stop me, Annie?"

"No," she says. "No please, I'm—"

"Do you think you can contend with me?"

"No. No, I didn't mean . . . I didn't *tell* the judge, I didn't, *please!*"

"If you think you can stop me, why don't you try? Right now. Jump at me, go for my eyes—I think that's your best opportunity."

"No! No I swear to you—"

"But I'm Rodney and I'm drunk and I'm cutting things close, and if you throw me off my concentration you know I could veer off the road. I could kill somebody."

"I won't! You can, you can—"

"Who will protect you, Annie?"

"*You* will."

"You mean Zach Lyde?"

"Yes!"

"Or do you mean the Teacher?"

"*Please.*"

"Say it, Annie. *The Teacher will shield me.*"

"The Teacher will shield me."

"You trust him?"

"I trust him!"

"But it takes a bolt of terror, doesn't it?"

"Yes!"

"It takes riding shotgun with Rodney Grosso, doesn't it?"

"*Yes!*"

They come out of the curve into a straightaway. A long shallow saddle, valley pasture to either side of them, picket fence.

He says, "Riding shotgun with chaos. You could have the Teacher locked up, you could sizzle Louie Boffano, you could put away every last mule in the mob—but what are you going to do about this drunk at the wheel? I come out of nowhere. I'm lost, I'm going too fast, I look down the road and it's a blur but I think I see this kid on a bicycle—"

Oliver.

Way up there, more than half a mile, it's Oliver on his bike, headed home. *Must* be Oliver: she gets a little flash of his purple shirt. And that's his lacrosse stick, standing up in back of his bike like a flagpole.

He's on the right side of the road, on their side, with no idea of what's coming behind him—

"No!"

She flings her hand out to grab Zach's arm.

"Don't you trust the Teacher, Annie?"

She forces herself to let go of his arm.

"Yes. I trust you! *Yes.*"

Oliver, turn around and look at this. Please, Oliver, can't you *hear* us? Turn around!

She puts her wrist to her mouth and she bites at it. She pushes her shoulders against the seat back. Writhing to get away from that fear, but she can't take her eyes off her son, off that purple shirt, that lacrosse stick, that wavering bicycle.

"*Please!*"

"But it's like trusting in the whim of God, isn't it? This random Rodney, he does whatever he pleases. He just drifts. . . ."

He lets the car slide out into the left lane. But that's OK with her. There's no car coming the other way, and she wants to give Oliver as wide a berth as possible. Yes, please, give him room. Go by him, go by him, give him lots of room.

"The least error, and you're plunged into hell. And who's going to protect you from that, Annie? What if Rodney should suddenly wake from his daze and see he's in the wrong lane and overcompensates—"

He turns the wheel sharply and floors the accelerator and suddenly they're aiming right at Oliver. Her hand flashes out at him and then she reins it in, she knows she must not touch him, but he's psychotic, he'll kill him, they're headed right for Oliver and she's clawing at her own face, screaming:

"OH GOD! OH GOD! PLEASE!"

They're a few hundred yards from Oliver and closing and her eyes are straining to get out of their sockets and somehow she's twisted herself up so that her feet are on the windshield—

"Who will protect you?"

"THE TEACHER!"

"The judge?"

"NO! JUST YOU! JUST YOU! MY GOD! MY GOD! PLEASE!"

The car slips toward the road's edge. On a path to kill her child.

She slams her hands against the passenger window and slams them again, and pushes her cheek against it and she's screaming, her foot kicking against the dashboard and not for a moment does she look away: her eyes are locked on that purple shirt dead ahead of them. The wheels hit the ragged shoulder, she's thrown upward and her head is jammed into the soft roof of the car and the world scrambles. She can't find Oliver in her vision. She bounces against the passenger window, her face flattens and she's shrieking and the car's wheels are shrieking with her, and then she sees him, her son, for one instant, his face right next to hers, he's turned to find the car so close and he's stunned—

But he's still on his bike.

They flash past him. The car's side mirror misses him by inches.

She whips her head around and sees him back there. He stands there frozen, holding his bike under a hickory tree, and the car's passing has kicked up a storm of leaves around him. He's staring ahead of him. He's alive, he's OK, he's alive. She wraps her arms over her head and rolls herself up on the seat and bawls, and rocks herself into a stupor. He's alive. He's alive. He's alive. He's alive. He's alive. He's alive. He's alive. He's alive. He's alive.

9

the least spit of sound

EDDIE's waiting for them, up on the height above the Onion Creek quarry. He helps Annie—shivering, feverish—out of Rodney's car.

Then he and Vincent wrestle deadweight Rodney out of the backseat and into the driver's seat.

Annie tries to say something. "You can't . . . you can't . . ."

"What?" says Vincent.

"You can't let him drive. . . ."

"That's true," says Vincent. He places Rodney's foot on the accelerator pedal, and crosses Rodney's other foot over it for the extra weight. Then he shuts the door and reaches in and turns the key. The car comes roaring to life.

Vincent murmurs, "That's true, Annie—he could kill somebody."

Vincent takes hold of the gearshift. Gives it a nudge, another nudge, then abruptly it pops into gear, and he pulls his arm free as the car starts moving. It rumbles down the dirt road. Then off the road, bouncing toward the cliff-edge. Eddie turns away. He's seen this sort of shit before, he doesn't need to watch.

They hear a crackle of saplings, a long pause, and then the splash. Then the sound of waves lapping the banks of the quarry. All done. Simple as that. Eddie opens the door of his own car for Annie, and he helps her in. Vincent is already driving away in his Lotus.

After a couple of miles of silence Eddie tells her, "When you're sequestered, when you're in the motel, you'll have a roommate. Make sure you're the one sleeping next to the telephone. OK?"

She nods.

Then she asks Eddie, in a small, tired voice: "Why did he do that?"

"Do what? You mean with Rodney? Ah, Rodney, he was a leech. He was no good. He woulda, they couldn't get him off the streets, he woulda killed somebody. Is that what you mean? What do you mean?"

But Eddie knows what she meant.

He says, "You mean, why did my friend scare you like that?"

She stares at the road.

Says Eddie, "It was, hey I know, it had to be hard—"

She speaks softly: "You said you had a child."

"Yeah. Daughter."

"*He* doesn't have children."

"No. No. But listen, it was for your own good."

"For my good."

"You were gonna fuck things up. Going to the judge. If you'd said anything, we'd a killed you for it. We'd a had to. You know that. It was for your own good."

"You've known him a long time?" she asks.

"Yeah."

"Why is he doing this?"

"Hey."

Eddie shrugs.

She says, "He's not even one of you, is he? He doesn't *have* to do this. Why does he do this?"

"You got too many questions."

"Why do you *let* him do this?"

They've come back to the parking lot at Vic's. They pull in beside her car. Again Eddie shrugs. He tells her:

"Hey look. Annie. You scared him, OK? You don't want to do that. He's a great guy, he's, he's smart as shit, but, but you don't want to scare him. Annie. I'm just telling you, OK? You don't never want to try that shit again."

THE TEACHER is tending the orchids, discipline where needed. His sterile scalpel flicks away the mushy roots on the Broughtonia. Combs the sphagnum under the *Catasetum pileatum*. The *Paph. Maudiae* has caught a cold, so he anoints the leaves using a watercolor brush laden with RD-20 and benomyl. How quickly, without nurturing, living things will lose their shape.

Their clarity. Their order.

It surprises him, this exhilaration he's feeling. He didn't like scaring her the way he did. He detested the necessity of it. Yet now he's floating. Soaring. He snips at the leaves of the Maudiae. His every movement partakes of the motion of the Tao.

How is that simply taking care of such a nasty chore as that one today can give me this surge of good feeling?

Is it simply that for facing down the darkness, for having the strength to stand up to it, my soul is rewarding me?

Then for no reason he can put his finger on, he remembers the rocket.

He was twelve or thirteen, the age Oliver is now. He was out back in the little fenced-in junked-over backyard in Brooklyn, he and Eddie. They were standing before the rocket he'd built.

He let Eddie be in charge of the countdown.

The rocket was four feet high, blue nose cone and yellow fuselage. The fuel was a slender canister full of liquid hydrogen and another slender canister full of liquid oxygen, which Eddie's cousin had stolen from Xerxes Chem.

Had there been one little flaw in the design, the rocket would have exploded and taken much of Bay Ridge with it.

But he didn't tell Eddie about that part.

"T minus fifty-six seconds," said Eddie. "And holding."

"Why 'and holding'?"

" 'Cause here comes your old man."

The old man was drunk. He stood before the rocket and said, "It's beautiful. It's a thing of beauty, huh?"

"Yeah, but Dad, it's better you go inside."

"No no, a thing of beauty, I must sing to it."

"Please Dad."

Dad sang an aria from one of his operas. The "Ferito Prigionier" from the *Germania*. He stood there serenading his son's blue-and-yellow rocket, raising his voice to the sky.

Somebody in the apartment house next door leaned out and applauded.

"My son!" cried Dad. "His rocket! This is poetry, huh!"

"Dad, come on, it's not really legal to have a rocket—"

His father started singing again.

"Stop it, Dad!"

"What? What? Franchetti you don't like? You don't *groove* him? He's not rock and roll, so you—"

"Dad."

"Fuck yourself."

Dad went in.

T minus fifteen, his mama came out.

"What are you saying to your father?"

"What do you mean, Ma—"

"Ah, you treat your own father like dirt. He comes out to sing for you, he loves you—"

The bedroom window opened and his father yelled out, "Mary! Leave him alone! Huh? He's with his friend, can't you leave the poor kid—"

"Shut up, you jerk! You greaseball fairy—"

"Leave my son alone, you dumb bitch!"

She said to her son, "Your father's a fairy, you know that? You know why—"

But that was as much as he heard, because by then he had triggered the mixture of the hydrogen and the oxygen. A great white roaring fart of smoke and flame. His mother shrieked and ran toward the house and Eddie had a big wide grin on his face and the thing took off into the cream-colored heavens. Blue-and-yellow rocket, white smoke, cinnamon skirts of flame. Up into the sky. His ears ringing, his skull, all his thoughts, scoured and scorched clean. Clean!

OLIVER's trying to get her out of the house, so he can find out what happened. But she doesn't seem to catch his hints. She pours a box of Rice-A-Roni Chicken & Broccoli into a saucepan, stirs it. Ignores him.

He says, "I thought, I thought we'd get some, maybe pizza. Or something."

Still not a word from her.

"Come on, I want to tell you what I did in school today."

She stirs the rice. She says, "Tell me, Oliver." The rancor is back in her voice. The old regime. "Tell me about your day."

"Oh. It was . . ." He shrugs. "But I mean, how was *your* day, Mom?"

No answer.

"Mom."

"What?"

"I asked you how was your day?"

"I don't remember."

She won't meet his eyes.

He suggests, "Maybe we'll go out after? Get some ice cream?"

"No," she says.

He tries a new tack: "Did you talk to Juliet today?"

She wheels on him. Puts her finger to her lips. "Sh."

Then she says, "Juliet? No."

202

He gets up and goes into the TV room and gets his school note-book and comes back and turns to the last page. He writes her a note:

> The guy knows that Juliet
> is your friend. So why can't we talk
> about her?

She writes back:

> Don't ever mention her name in the house.
> Ever.

He writes:

> What happened today?

She writes:

> It won't work.

He writes:

> Why? What happened?

She writes:

> I'll tell you later.

He writes:

> Mom we got to fight him.

She writes:

> If we fight him, he'll kill you.

He writes:

> I'll take the chance.

She glares at him. She grips the pen hard, she's in a fury. She writes:

If we fight him, he'll kill me.

She underlines me.
That stops him.
She gets up and walks around the kitchen table and kneels before his chair. She's crying, but she's quiet about it. She takes him in her arms and puts her lips close to his ear and whispers, "Oliver. No."
After a minute she rises. She tears the page from the notebook and rolls it into a cone and lights it.

THE TEACHER thinks, That's wrong. There's something wrong there.

He unfurls from his lotus. He rises and crosses to the console.

Switches to the tape. Rewinds. Hits PLAY for a moment, then rewinds some more. Hits PLAY again.

He hears Oliver say it again: "Maybe we'll go out after? Get some ice cream?"

The Teacher wonders, Why is he so eager to get out of the house?

Annie: "No."

Pause.

Oliver: "Did you talk to Juliet today?"

Silence. Then a minuscule hiss. Maybe distortion? Maybe an escape of steam from the saucepan?

He plays it again. The least spit of sound. But he thinks he knows what it is. He thinks she's hissing at Oliver to shut up.

He plays it again.

OK. Why would she have wanted him to shut up about Juliet? The question he asked, wasn't it a reasonable one?

All he asked her was, had she talked to Juliet today?

Next, he hears a faint, scratchy, whispery crackle—what is it?

Wait.

He opens a drawer and takes out a pen. And on the flyleaf of a book of Tibetan meditations he scribbles:

AnnieLairdAnnieLaird

He stops writing. He replays the tape.
He writes:

mysoulmysoulmysoul

Yes, what he heard was the sound of writing.

They were writing messages to each other.

And that crackle at the end? That was the page burning. And the sizzle as it dropped into the sink.

Of course. They thought they had to burn that page of notes or the Teacher would have rooted in their garbage and found it.

So Oliver knows about me. And about the bugs. And about everything.

And who else knows?

Juliet.

That doctor, of course. Annie must have told that fool of an arrogant doctor. It's she who would have counseled interference. Juliet, the wild adventurer.

It's she who put the boy's life at risk.

Dr. Juliet Applegate, North Kent Road, Pharaoh, NY.

It astounds him, such a paucity of prudence. For the chance to think well of herself, to think herself valiant, for such a paltry thrill, she wades headlong and splashing against the rhythm of the Tao.

How can she tolerate the grasping recklessness of her own soul? the Teacher wonders.

EDDIE, the next afternoon, is driving the Hutchinson Parkway. He's tired. It's been a busy day, and it's not over yet. First he had to help Vincent wire up Juliet Applegate's apartment for sound. This was hairy because she lives under a grocery store and the store was open while they worked.

Next he had to drive all the way down to Queens, where he had a big problem with the Jamaicans. Instead of finding the expected $28,000 in the paper towel dispenser at Luca's Texaco, he found $24,000.

Oh! What a bullshit crank-sucking low-esteem boost!

Probably the Jamaican mule made the skim. But Eddie talked the problem over with the kid's bosses. If the kid did it, Eddie's confident his bosses will worm it out of him. Then they'll kill him. No fuss no muss. Kill his family too. Kill his neighbors. Kill the entire staff of the corner liquor store, for good measure. All in plenty of time for the six o'clock news.

Eddie envies the crisp organization and the forthrightness of the Jamaicans.

But still he's got a vicious headache.

And still he's on the road. He's back on the Hutch, headed north, because he's got to stop by Frankie's and deliver a gift from Vincent. A thank-you for Frankie's help in kicking the shit out of that nosy private eye: $20,000 in cash and an orchid for his girlfriend.

This particular chore isn't so bad. Frankie'll cream his jeans to see all that money. The orchid'll give him a kick too. He already worships the ground Vincent walks on. He's never even seen his face, but he thinks Vincent is the Second Coming of the Virgin Mary. Now the guy's giving him $20,000 and an orchid? For an hour's work? He's gonna build a fuckin shrine.

Eddie knows the feeling.

Eddie himself, he's worshiped Vincent ever since he was a kid. Maybe he still does. Although for the last twenty-four hours all he's been able to think about is that question Annie asked him.

Why do you let him do this?

Lady, get the fuck out of my head with your stupid questions, OK? All I want is to deliver this gift and then go on home and find that my daughter is more or less sane. I want to fry us up a couple nice steaks. Shrimp, boiled potatoes, watch *Married with Children*. That's all I want. I don't want to think about fuckin Vincent all night.

Let him do this? What do you mean, *let* him? Vincent does what he pleases.

Always has. Since St. Xavier's. Fourth grade. Never gave a shit what the nuns told him. Had his own mind, kept his own counsel. Like the time they were studying that big computer UNIVAC. Vincent raised his hand and said that soon there would be a computer that'd do nothing except try to figure out what God was like.

This was in Sister Francesca's class.

Said Vincent, "We'll feed it everything we know, right? And it'll find the pattern."

Said Sister Francesca, "What pattern?"

"The pattern behind the Creation. The pattern of God."

Said Sister Francesca, "I think, young man, that the Bible tells us what we need to know about God."

Vincent ignored her. "But if a computer wants to understand God? It'll have to *become* God. It'll have to create its *own* universe. And maybe that one will replace ours. Sort of, part of a cycle. Don't you think, Sister Francesca?"

In the hubbub of the cafeteria, or homeroom, in the wild free-for-all of recess, Vincent was always stiff and ill at ease. You had to see him in some situation where he felt completely in control—then he'd scare the hell out of you, the way he could draw you in.

Though there was always some question, Eddie recalls, as to Vincent's sanity.

There was, for example, the time he sent a rocket up from his backyard and his mom and dad were drunk, and nobody but Vincent and Eddie knew that Vincent's cat was riding in the nose cone.

Some three or four days after the rocket and its cargo disappeared into the sky over Bay Ridge, Eddie came by and caught Vincent crying.

"What are you crying for?"

"Madame Butterfly."

"Your cat? You're sad about your cat?"

"I miss her."

"Well then why did you blast her up to the fuckin sky?"

"They stepped on her all the time. They kicked her. They never cleaned her shitbox. My dad put whiskey in her bowl. I had to do *something*."

Eddie remembers how Vincent always wanted to hear stories about Eddie's father and uncles and cousins in La Cosa Nostra. Didn't care too much about the crimes. What he got off on was what he called the hierarchy. He always wanted Eddie to introduce him to his relatives but Eddie didn't think that was such a good idea.

By the time Vincent was a senior in high school his geekiness was gone. This lovely girl, this strange brainy hippie-girl, fell for him, and at first everyone laughed at her. But then one by one other girls fell under his spell. He'd talk to them about his Eastern religions, he'd talk and you could see them getting relaxed, curling their legs up under them and saying, "Mm, omigod, it's amazing, I had a thought *exactly* like that the other day," and pretty soon you could score another one for Vincent.

He won a scholarship to Fordham. By then Eddie had dropped out and was running in the gang headed by his second cousin Louie Boffano. Lifting auto parts mostly. Liberating cartridge players, jerk-off stuff. They kept getting fucked around by this Gambino cocksucker who figured Louie was so young, still so wet from his mama's pussy that he'd be no trouble to lean on.

That summer Louie said if he knew how to make a bomb he'd put one under the Gambino's car.

Eddie said, "I got a guy I bet can make a bomb for you, Louie. Make it right."

So he got Vincent to make a bomb. The Gambino's car started out in the northbound lane of the BQE, and when it came back to earth much of it came down in the southbound lane. The chassis, the drive shaft, the radiator, and the spare tire. Also, separately, the steering wheel with the Gambino's hands holding on for dear life. But the rest of the Gambino was never recovered. The rest of the Gambino had joined Madame Butterfly in the ozone.

Louie held a barbecue to celebrate the death of the Gambino. Of course Vincent came, and Louie drank a toast to him. He said, "You know, this kid is like a young, a young, what the fuck's his name?"

"Who?" said somebody.

"I don't know. Some inventor or something. But give him, give him a round of applause."

Everybody put their paws together except cousin Tony Speza, who hadn't taken a shine to Vincent. He said to him, "Hey, you're not Sicilian, right?"

"I'm northern," said Vincent.

"You're not even that, you scumbag. Come on, you got the complexion of a ghost. Your mother's a mick, isn't she? And your father, he don't count. He's that crazy asshole who sings opera, isn't he?"

Couple of months later, Vincent had a secret meeting with Louie Boffano. Eddie set it up. At this meeting Vincent claimed that Tony Speza was pulling some shit behind Louie's back. He produced Tony Speza's telephone bill as evidence. He explained patiently the pattern of treason it revealed, how several of the calls had been made to law enforcement agencies. Louie laughed and said he was jumping to conclusions. But a few weeks later when Tony Speza vanished, Louie didn't boo-hoo much.

And from then on there was something between Vincent and Louie that nobody could get a handle on, that nobody could touch. Vincent pursued his own life—college and an MBA and work on Wall Street and his art and his women and his religions—but any time Louie was in a jam, or needed to thread his way through the eye of a needle, he'd tell Eddie, "Go find your friend. I gotta talk to him," and Vincent would always show up. With his eyes glowing. Always glad to help.

Glad to scheme out a disappearance or a frame-up, glad to assay the loyalty of an ally, glad to strategize the fancy heroin deal with the Ndrangheta and the Jamaicans.

And whatever Vincent does, he does flawlessly.

Flawlessly.

And Louie stays out of jail, or at least he did till he tripped up on his own wagging tongue.

Very few of our people get killed.

Louie gets stinking rich.

All of us get stinking rich.

And Annie, I mean you really wonder why we let him him do this?

JULIET says, "Come in before the bugs do."

But Annie doesn't budge. She stands at the door.

She says, "He showed me what he can do. You said he could be reasoned with?"

"I said—"

"No. He can't."

"Now wait a minute, Annie. I said if we were strong, we could reason with him. But first we have to get strong. We have to hide Oliver, we—"

"He'll find him. No."

"Look, why don't you sit for a while? Have some tea, OK, Annie? So we can talk?"

"Promise me you won't tell anybody."

"Wait."

"You've got to leave us alone now."

"Wait. What does Oliver think?"

"Oliver's twelve, what does it matter what he thinks? I guess he thinks we should be heroes. I just took him over to Mrs. Kolodny's. Jury's going to be sequestered tomorrow. Mrs. Kolodny's going to keep him till we get a verdict. He was upset, he was pissed at me. But he promised to keep his mouth shut, and that's all I care about. You've got to promise too, Juliet."

"Promise what? That I'll abandon you?"

"That you won't tell anyone. It's my life, Juliet. What you said, remember? He's *my* child."

So. Put it that way, what can Juliet do? A slight cocking of her head and showing of her palm, and she's surrendered.

And Annie turns to go.

Juliet calls to her. "Hey listen, girl, I'm going to Nightbone's tomorrow night, me and Henri, why don't you come with?" She means Nightbone's Poetry Cafe in the East Village, in Manhattan. She knows Annie won't come, but she asks anyway, maybe just to remind her that there's still a world outside of the one the bastard's made for her.

Or maybe it's just to keep her here for another moment.

"I mean why not?" Juliet says. "You're not his prisoner. Get out, relax a little, I swear I won't talk about the trial—"

"Juliet, you don't understand. I'm going to be sequestered, I'm going to be in some hotel somewhere. I couldn't see you if I wanted to. Which I don't, I *can't*. Which you know. Anyway. So why do you ask?"

Then she doesn't say goodbye. She simply turns and walks back to her car.

10

Conquistador, rather

ANNIE, in the jury room early the next morning, folds her yellow sheet of legal paper and passes it up.

One slice of daylight gets in through a casement window. One mottled sliver of the rainy day—that's as much as she can see.

The Forewoman uses her wrists to scoop all the votes into a pile. Then she starts reading.

"Guilty. Guilty. Guilty. *Not* guilty."

A stirring among the jurors. There I am, thinks Annie. That's mine. They think I'm nuts.

"Guilty," says the Forewoman. "Guilty. And here someone's voted 'Yes'? I'm not sure what 'Yes' means."

"It means guilty," says Maureen, a grandmother in a lilac suit.

The Forewoman keeps reading.

"Guilty. *Not* guilty."

The news stuns Annie. My God, someone else? How is that possible?

"Guilty. Guilty."

The Forewoman unfolds the last ballot.

"*Not* guilty."

Three!

Annie thinks it's a miracle.

"All right, wait a minute." This from a little wiry guy, Pete, who

217

works for OSHA. He wears a cheap suit and snake hairs grow from his ears. "I mean, I'm sorry. Can I, can I say this?"

"Sure," says the Forewoman.

"I just, I mean, how can anybody think the guy's not guilty? I just—who voted *not* guilty? Can I ask that?"

Says the Forewoman, "You can ask. But nobody has to say if they don't want. I don't think."

"Well, I voted not guilty," says an Ann Taylorish housewife from Mount Kisco.

Says OSHA Pete, "You telling me you think Boffano didn't order the killing?"

She shrugs. "Oh, I don't know. I guess maybe he did. But don't we have to discuss it? We don't want to—"

"We're gonna discuss it!" says OSHA. Raising his voice. Already. "We just, I mean, Christ. Who else? Who else voted not guilty?"

"Me." This from a retired postal clerk.

"You? Roland? *Why?*"

The Clerk shrugs. It takes him a long time to get started, and when he does he speaks slowly:

"I don't. Think the government. Made. Its case. Necessarily. That's all."

The Clerk jams his tongue into his cheek. His skin looks liverish and his eyes are bloodshot and pulpy. He peers up at the acoustic tiles, and Annie tries to read him. Is he working for the Teacher? She wishes he'd look at her. Maybe she could figure him out if he'd meet her gaze.

"Proved?" says OSHA. "It's open and shut."

"So *you* say," says the Clerk.

"I mean there's a tape, right? There's a tape! Did you hear the tape?"

"So *you* say."

"I'm not saying anything. I'm asking you."

"So *you* say."

"What do you mean, so *I* say? Stop saying that, Roland, you're driving me nuts." He looks around. He sighs and folds his arms. "Jesus."

Says the Forewoman, "Anybody else?"

Annie draws a breath. That's all it takes—all eyes swing to look at her.

Says the Forewoman, "And your, what's your reasoning, Annie?"

But Annie finds she can't speak. Her vocal cords are stitched tight.

218

"Well—" she says. Some of the eyes drop away compassionately. She tries again. "Well, I just—"

A new voice breaks in. "Maybe it's not fair to pick on the not guiltys. Maybe, maybe *we* should have to explain *our* case. You know?"

Big and slouchy, an easygoing guy. His name is Will and he's got blue jeans and a black jacket and long blond hair. He plays clarinet for a jazz combo in Briarcliff. Weddings and conventions.

He says, "Why don't we put up on the blackboard what we think the evidence is? OK? Then we'll take it point by point." He shambles over to the portable blackboard on its easel. "OK? So what do we got? How many witnesses for the prosecution were there?"

"Three," says OSHA Pete. "First that big guy, that, uh, 'captain'? What's his name?"

"DeCicco," says the Mt. Kisco matron. "Paulie DeCicco."

"Right," says Clarinet Will. He writes "DeCicco" on the blackboard. "So what do we think about him? Do we trust him?"

Says OSHA, "I wouldn't trust him to feed my pet rat. But about this? Yeah, he sounded like, I thought he was more or less—"

"But he was trying to get a lighter sentence." This from a baker, a black man from New Rochelle.

"Yeah, but that's the only way to get them to testify," says Clarinet Will. "It's the only way they ever get anyone in the Mafia. That and tapes."

"Tapes!" OSHA Pete pounces on this. "Put down 'tapes.' Write that down!"

"Well, right now we're discussing—"

"Put tapes in *red*," OSHA insists.

"Do we have red chalk?" someone asks.

Says the old Postal Clerk, "This is how we should do it. We should keep red. For important evidence. Green, for evidence that's *comme ci comme ça*—" He waggles his fingers.

Says OSHA: "*Comme ci comme ça?*"

"It's French. It's French my friend."

"Just hold it," says OSHA. "Just wait, just listen."

He looks directly at Annie. "Suppose," he says, "suppose they were all lying. DeCicco, that 'mule,' that cop. Suppose they don't know Louie Boffano from Adam. But we still got that *tape*. Right?"

Says Clarinet Will, sweet and placid, "You know, we're sort of trying to do this in order."

"Forget the order!" says OSHA. Again he addresses Annie. "Lady, when you hear that tape, when you hear him say—what is it?— about the tunnel?"

Three voices at once, reciting by rote—for they've all heard these words dozens of times:

" '*I tell the Teacher, okay, you want, you want to dig a tunnel . . .*' "

Three more join in: " '*Dig a tunnel! Kill that motherfucker! Jesus!*' "

Smattering of laughter. OSHA Pete asks Annie: "So when you hear that, what in God's name do you think? You think he's talking about the Tunnel of *Love*?"

Annie knows she's blushing, and she knows they all see that.

Come on now, answer him. I can speak, I know how. What am I so scared of?

What I'm scared of is that they'll see right off what a fraud I am, that I don't believe a shred of what I'm saying.

But she has to try. "I don't . . . I don't think that tape proves anything. He could be, maybe, I don't know, it wasn't a direct order."

" '*Kill that motherfucker*'? That's not a direct order?"

"But . . . he was telling a story, right? Maybe he was boasting. He was boasting that he gave the order to kill Riggio, but he really didn't . . ."

She fades out. She's looking to Clarinet Will. He's got such a sweet face, such a friendly slouch, and she feels weak, and she might be getting ready to cry. She wants protection, she wants someone to take care of this thing for her. . . .

Says OSHA, "You kidding me, lady? You think he's really innocent? He was just *bragging* on how he sent a hit man to kill Riggio?"

There are a lot of smiles around the table.

But so what? Let them smile. It really doesn't matter, she thinks, because all she has to do is hold fast. Hold fast no matter how they come at her. Be a stone wall, that's all. Don't even listen to them. A week of this torture. Maybe ten days. Maybe two weeks, even—but they *will* give up on her, eventually they'll have to call this jury hung. . . .

SLAVKO at AA. Awaiting his turn to speak. He listens to one tale of pallid death-in-life after another, and he wonders, How in the world can this ritual help anyone? This singsong, what good is it? The lovers who dump us, the kids who disdain us, the TV that proposes and disposes, the hotshots who fuck with our heads: that the complaints are universal, how the hell does that make them any easier to bear?

Jesus he hates these meetings.

Though he thinks they might not be so bad if they'd only serve cocktails.

When his turn finally comes around, he says, "My name is Slavko and I'm an alcoholic."

"Hello Slavko," they all harmonize.

"I'm an alcoholic, and I'm also what you call a love-addict and a nicotine freak and a fuck-up in my former career of private investigator, which I never much liked anyway. My new career of poet is going OK. This is one bright spot. In fact I've just finished my first poem, but right now this new line of endeavor isn't earning me any royalties, you know what I mean? Takes a while to get established, to start making the big bucks. I've been living out of my office but today I was evicted, so now I'll be living out of my car. What else? Smoking, Jesus, smoking is just chewing up my lungs. Vague achiness in my lower back, so I guess pretty soon another kidney stone's gonna make its move. And my heart? My heart isn't just broken but shattered. I mean pulverized, I'm telling you it's sown with *salt* so nothing can ever grow there again. I'm a hopeless dawdler, I feel sorry for myself with a capital S, and I'm sick and tired of dancing the twelve-step in these fuckin honky-tonks of yours. Is that enough for one sitting or not?"

He shuts up.

He waits through a few more sob stories, a few more slowwww deaths, and then he gets the hell out of there.

He gets in the Buzzard and drives.

Soon he finds himself driving by Gillespie's Tavern in North Tarrytown. There are three cars out front. One belongs to Gillespie himself and one to an obnoxious rummy who frequents the place. The third car Slavko doesn't recognize but it must belong to someone so vile that he can stand even the company of Gillespie and that rummy.

So what's the point in lingering here, Slavko? Can't we move on now?

He has only three drinks at Gillespie's.

Then he drives some more.

He finds himself driving to Ossining. He finds himself driving by Sari's house, and slowing down. Like he did last night. Driving by and slowing and checking.

Checking what?

Don't know, who's asking?

Tonight her car is there, but all the lights are out. Too early for her to be in bed. So she must be on a hot date somewhere. Steaming hot passionate date with that bastard.

Maybe she's over at the bastard's townhouse.

He heads more or less in that direction, until he happens to glance down and note that the gas gauge has fallen to empty. Far below empty, in fact. It's somewhere down in the Pit of Vapors.

But luckily he's not far from a gas station.

One of these new moonbase gas stations. He pulls in and stops at a bright sodium-fluorescent pump island. The pump starts right up when he squeezes the trigger. They let him pump before paying. What classic green-gilled suckers!

He fills up. He goes in and the sad fellow at the register tells him, "Fifteen dollars and forty-two cents."

"Really? That much? I don't have that much."

"Excuse me?"

"You think I'm made of money?"

"You mean you can't pay?"

"Of course not."

"How much do you have?"

"You mean exactly?"

"Yeah. How much do you have?"

"I don't really have anything."

"You forget your wallet?"

"No, I have my wallet. I don't have any money in it."

"Wait a minute. Hold on."

The clerk picks up the phone, punches the A button.

Says Slavko, "Are you calling the federal authorities? You gonna send me to jail? Shivved, smacked around, raped repeatedly for six months? Because my wallet's empty? Oh well. Fair's fair."

Says the clerk, "I'm calling my boss."

The clerk has a few words with his employer, then puts Slavko on the line.

"This is Mr. Hooten. What's the problem?"

"There you have it, Mr. Hooten, you've nailed it again. What's the problem? After all, Slavko's not hopelessly stupid. Some find him witty. He's honest, he's not bad-looking. So what's hanging us up here? What's the problem? Well, I'm thinking some crucial piece must be missing."

Mr. Hooten says something irrelevant. But Slavko forges ahead.

"If only I could figure out what piece! What tiny flaw! I ought to be a neurosurgeon! Or a poet! Instead every humiliation that can be visited upon a suburban American male is visited upon me. Except! I still have my wheels. Oh yes, fuck you very much, Mr. Hooten, I may not be able to pay for it but I still have a full tank of gas in the old Jalop and I can cruise from here to—"

Mr. Hooten shouts at him: *"Put the clerk back on!"*

Slavko does. He turns to the other waiting customers and tells them, "I still have my wheels. I still have a full tank of gas. You call me a *loser?*"

The clerk hangs up the phone and tells him, "My boss says if you clear out of here in the next thirty seconds then I don't have to call the police."

JULIET's in Manhattan with Henri, at Nightbone's Poetry Cafe. It's Slam Night at half-past ten and the cafe is going full throttle. Slow cyclone of smoke, hecklers, junkies, zombied Eurozeros. A smattering of undeniable crazies (for example the man over there humming into half of a plastic bowling pin). A few celebrities (for example Paul Simon on the balcony with that woman three times his height) . . .

Bob Bozark, the MC, is up there in his trademark Fedora and loud suit, and he's profoundly, brilliantly, into his Snarling Leprechaun subself. He spews acid to his left. To his right. He dips and weaves and he's by God a cauldron of attitude, and finally he introduces the next poet and rushes offstage to down another beer. . . .

Juliet notices that someone is staring at her. A striking-looking guy in a black leather cop's coat.

Juliet stares back.

She's playing no games here. This is her only night off for the next two weeks. There's no time for shilly-shally if she wants to get laid. If she wants to get Annie's peril out of her head for a while (and if she doesn't she'll go crazy), if she wants to get closer to that man's screwy smile and fine cheekbones and forest-green eyes, she's going to have to let him know her intentions and leave nothing to chance.

So she sends him an enormous smile.

Then some blond tart sits down beside him.

His damn date. Back from powdering her nose.

224

"That bitch," says Juliet.

"Huh?" says Henri.

Juliet nods in the direction of the interloper.

Says Henri, "What did she do?"

"She stole my boyfriend. I just hope she never comes into my hospital is all."

Now stepping up to the microphone is the poet of the moment: a compact, tomboyish black dyke. When the applause dies down, she announces the title of her poem:

"I Want to Fuck You, Or, Straight Talk to that Redhaired Mama in That Table Near the Corner."

Everyone turns to look at Juliet.

The poet launches. A breathless bellowing full-tilt explicit erotic ballad, and she booms it out over gales of laughter, and she *is* kind of cute. In her poem Juliet is spread-eagled on the stony lap of Alice in Wonderland in Central Park, and the poet is looming over her and there's lightning flashing in the trees above.

Everyone loves the poet's fever lust, her bantam cockiness. Every straight woman in the joint is reconsidering her stance.

And Juliet—high as a kite, blushing a deep crimson—Juliet is having a blast here. Jesus, she only wishes Annie were here to enjoy this with her. The poem explodes into a shrieking orgasm. The cafe rocks with cheers. The poet leaps down and weaves through the tables, and Juliet stands and opens her arms and the poet rushes into them. Juliet shuts her eyes for the kiss. A little tongue fluking around in there. What the hell—she flukes back. Why not, why the hell not? It's like kissing a man really, except that she has to lean so far down, and there's a hundred pairs of eyes upon her. The place is coming apart at the seams. Shivaree of whistles and catcalls. The judges hold their scores aloft, and they're all perfect tens. Of course the poem itself stank—no one's fooled—but the show was a hoot, the kiss was great daring fun, so who cares?

Then Juliet looks up and the next poet is the devastating man in the black cop's jacket.

What he reads is sort of a real poem. This embarrasses everyone here. Not a party poem, not another paean to decadence, but this moving villanelle about a winter spent on a volcano in Iceland. With a crow perched in a rowan tree.

The rough wind of his voice is so compelling it quiets even these drunks and dregs and scene-clingers. They don't follow the poem but they give him a respectable score anyway. When Bob Bozark returns to the mike, sarcasm drips from his fangs—he must have been truly impressed.

Then the round is over and Juliet works her way up to the crowded bar and orders beers for her and Henri.

The black-jacket poet slips into place on the other side of her.

He says, "Hello, Doctor."

"How do you know I'm a doctor?"

"I brought a friend into your hospital once. Up at St. Ignatius? Car accident. Nothing serious. You took good care of him."

"Is that so?"

Oh, *good*. Christ, Juliet thinks, how clever can I be? *Is that so?*

"We didn't speak," he tells her. "But it'd be hard to forget you. My name's Ian Slate."

"I'm Juliet. Did you really live in Iceland?"

"Long time ago I did. I was reporting, covering the summit in Reykjavík. When it was over I took a few months off."

He flashes his crooked grin. Already she's hooked on his green eyes.

"Do you have more poetry?" she says.

"Sure. You'd like me to bore you sometime?"

"I'd love it."

"I'm with someone tonight. But could I get your number?"

She shrugs.

He produces a pen. She writes her name and number on a napkin. But as she's handing it over, damn! Here comes the girlfriend. Appearing out of nowhere, with a bitter frozen grin.

Ian Slate is very smooth, though.

"Sari," he says, "this is Juliet Applegate. She's a doctor at St. Ignatius. Next time I read my poetry in Westchester she wants me to tell her, so she can watch me make a fool of myself."

The girlfriend says firmly, "Eben, we need to go. But it was so nice to meet you, Juliet."

And she offers Juliet her comely claw.

ANNIE is lying in bed in her hotel room. Her roommate, the Mt. Kisco matron, has been asleep for hours, but Annie is still wide awake, thinking about Turtle. She's trying not to think about what she has to do in that jury room. So instead she thinks about Turtle and Drew, and those days in Brooklyn that have always been so painful to remember—but now they seem mild and piquant. Now they're the good old days.

That first winter after art school. Living in that warehouse in Greenpoint, on Franklin Street right by the East River. You could get up on the roof at night and look to the lights of midtown Manhattan. The ice-sculpture of the Chrysler Building, cold Citicorp. And closer by, the black cylinder of the shit vat, where all the city's frozen shit was ladled out onto barges and carried off.

Living in that loft, shivering. She was making huge animals, sleepy mammoths, out of hydrocal and wood and tar and feathers. Trying to force herself to make political art so the galleries would notice her, but she just couldn't do it. She kept building those huge shaggy animals, and she was so lonely and sad that winter she thought she was going to die—until she met Turtle, who was the bass player in the band that practiced downstairs on Tuesday nights.

Turtle had a fuzzy beard, little pig-eyes, a small beak nose like a baby eagle's. He hated the city. He took her to Grand Central and they got on a train and went north to a random station and walked till they found a meadow and then pushed the snow off a rock wall and had a teeth-chattering picnic.

Then on the way home the train car was steamy and she curled up in Turtle's arms and went to sleep.

And suddenly the winter wasn't so bad for Annie.

Turtle was studying at NYU to be a paramedic, on the off chance that his Great Rock Career didn't soar. He wanted to take care of people. The notion of suffering disturbed him powerfully. He had a puppy-eagerness and awkwardness. Great jolts of love and tenderness kept shooting from him.

On another picnic, in another meadow, he kissed her with frozen lips. She wasn't sure that's what she wanted. She wasn't sure she wanted to make love to him. But that night she did, on her dusty mattress, and she had a pretty good time. So she slept with him twice more.

But there was something lacking in him; what did he lack? Thinking of it now, in this dark hotel room, it makes her cringe to think that he lacked some kind of power. To think that simple good-heartedness wasn't the power she was fool enough to crave.

Then his band got a new singer, Drew, who was lanky and drugged and off kilter and sometimes mean and smelled a little rank. He had a brilliant wit, though, and he had eyes and a jawline that Annie could not cure herself of, and he drove her in his old bread truck to the Brooklyn anchorage of the Manhattan Bridge and parked and they crawled into the back of the van and talked for hours and then among the tire irons she sucked his dick, which was long, spicy and unruly. He bruised her mouth. As she sucked she squeezed her thighs together and when he came, she came, and she kicked out and stubbed her toe on the van's back door.

She couldn't call it romantic—but it seemed to satisfy some thirst.

She kept taking trips with him in that van. She broke Turtle's heart. She felt guilty over this, but the guilt scarcely made a dent in her overall excitement. When she became pregnant Drew persuaded her to keep the child. He stayed with them for a year and a half and then he got restless and flew to Bali.

Last she heard he was living in Prague singing old Beatles tunes to teenage girls on the Charles Bridge.

And Turtle went to a village in the highlands of Guatemala where they think he's a doctor and they come to him night and day. He's learned to play the sort of flute they call a *chirimía*. He plays it in the festivals. Once in a blue moon some errand will send him down to the city of Huehuetenango, and he'll call Annie.

Or anyway he used to.

And tonight, in this strange bed with the Caruso Hotel's facade lights spilling in through the window and no sleep, no chance for sleep, Annie finds that Turtle, his pig-eyes, his dumb clingy unsought love for her, is the only thing in the world she can think about to take her mind off the other thing, the thing that's killing her.

SLAVKO long past midnight, nothing else to do, figures he'll drive by Sari's place one more time. Just to see if she's home yet.

She is.

And he's with her.

His Lotus in her driveway. Oh yes, the powerful-because-he's-so-soulful E.R. is here.

Slavko parks down the street. He fiddles with the radio. He waits and watches.

Sari's house is quiet. No doubt at this very moment E.R. is presenting his graceful and classical penis to her mouth. To her rosebud mouth. How nice for them both. Me, my sexual days are over, so it's really quite all right for me to sit out here in the October witch-cold listening to splats of static and the high school football scores on the radio, and to look up at that house and know that you two kids are up there all cozy and fucking your ears off and having a wonderful time.

Eat shit, Eben Rackland. Die from doing it, Eben Rackland.

Slavko allows himself another little swallow of bourbon.

Take it real slow, Ebenezer, I've got all night. Don't hurry on my account. Go ahead and fuck her again. Wouldn't want to waste any of your precious silver soulful seed.

Sari's porchlight comes on.

E.R. steps out.

Sari comes out a step herself. In her robe, wrapping it around her, wrapping it tight against the cold. E.R. turns and takes her head in his hands and pulls her lips to him. Kisses her gently, then draws away.

But still he holds her cheeks with his fingertips.

The rhythm, the command, is all his. In this transaction Sari is a porcelain doll. And Slavko in the Buzzard feels pea-green anger spraying all over his guts.

Just kiss her and blow, fuckhead.

At last E.R. steps down from Sari's porch and walks to his car. She calls something after him, but Slavko doesn't hear it. Quietly, quietly, he rolls his window down. He listens.

He hears E.R., in the crisp hollow night, saying, "Whenever I can, as soon as I can, you know that."

Sari frowns a moment. But recovers herself, and sort of smiles, and turns to go back in.

"Hey," E.R. calls to her softly.

"What?"

"Lover."

"What?"

"Show me."

Her smile broadens, though she tries to rein it in. "Come on, Eben. People, people might be—"

"What people? At two in the morning? Show me," and he tucks his lower lip under his teeth boyishly. A trick that makes Slavko feel like puking but it seems to win Sari over. Abruptly she tilts her chin up, throws her robe open and strikes a pose.

Her breasts are an uplifting sight to behold. Her pubic hair has been shaved into a narrow strip, like a teardrop, like the top part of an exclamation point. She puts her hands on her hips to hold the robe open, and even from here you can see what great pleasure she takes in offering up this vision of herself to E.R.

And as for Slavko?

You mean the loser? Oh, he's nothing. He's but a chunk of gloom out here. He's the sicko pervert she was afraid might be tom-peeping this performance. The very deviant himself.

But he's not getting anything out of it. Her beauty only hurts him. He looks away. He hears E.R. say, "You know I'm on a leash. You know I can't go very far or for very long. I love you."

Slavko hears him get into his car. He hears the satiny engine come to life. Slavko watches as E.R. backs onto the street and drives up the hill away from him. Sari, shivering, bundles the robe tight about her and watches after him.

Slavko takes out his little log book, and he writes:

2:40 E.R. leaves SK home, w Arning Road. P.

The P is for pursuit. He slips the notebook into his jacket pocket again.

Sari's still lingering. Watching the place where E.R. vanished.

Go on to bed, Sari. Get warm.

Let me go after this guy.

At last she does go in—and at the moment she shuts her door, Slavko starts up the Buzzard. He leaves the headlights dark and ascends the hill as quietly as he can in this old bomb. But as soon as he has topped the crest, he drives the pedal into the floor. The Buzzard pants. Trying to catch E.R.'s distant red glimmer.

Driving without lights is taking a big chance. Cops see me, I'm fried. No lights, DUI, reckless driving, lapsed insurance, invalid inspection sticker, resisting arrest, assault on a police officer, murder and dismemberment of same, etc.

But it's only me and E.R. on this road. And if E.R. sees headlights in his mirror, he'll be gone like a rabbit. So Slavko has to drive blind. He squints to see the center line, and leans into his meager luck.

At Eastgate Road, E.R. takes a left toward the river. Passes the seminary, passes the big stone church—and then he turns into the drive of the Caruso Hotel.

Old dowager elephant. Used to be a whipped-cream palace of luxury, but now the paint's flaking off, the grillwork on the balconies is rusting. Place has become a draw for second-rate conventions and cheesy weddings. And sometimes when one of these affairs needs extra security, the management calls Slavko.

E.R. parks and walks briskly toward the lobby. Slavko stays out on the main road until E.R. has gone in, then he pulls into the drive. He parks off to the side of the hotel's vast lot. He pauses to make a note in the black logbook. Then he follows E.R. in.

As he approaches the hotel desk, Jerome gives him a glance. "Aren't you a little late, Slavko?" he says. He turns his eyes back to his work. He's keying something into the computer. "You were supposed to be here yesterday."

A funny round head Jerome has, and a funny nasal drawl.

"Late?" Slavko says. "For what?"

Still not looking up, Jerome whines, "The Dairy Farm Equipment Manufacturers Association?" Putting a question mark after every word, as though bells and whistles should be clanging inside Slavko's head.

Dimly, Slavko does remember agreeing to come in and work security for these crazies. But that was in another era. Week and a half ago. When such commitment was still within the realm of *possibility*, for Christ sake.

"Jerome," Slavko says. He's trying to lean over the registration counter, trying to see down to the computer screen. But the counter is too high, or Slavko's too short.

He tells Jerome, "Look at me."

Jerome looks up and gasps. "Oh my God," he says.

"Happy Hallowe'en," says Slavko.

"What happened to you?"

Slavko shrugs. "Well, you know, I should have realized, Jerome. The walls were made of shit. First big storm . . ."

"What? What walls?"

"You said it, buddy. You said a mouthful. *What* walls?"

While he jabbers he puts his palms on the counter, jumps up and flops his chest onto the Formica, with his feet up in the air. Now he can see down to the computer screen. He sees the registration that Jerome was just keying in. But it's hard to read it—because for Slavko it's upside down.

"What the hell are you doing?" says Jerome.

Keep jabbering. "You ask, what walls? Ah Christ. I thought it was a mansion? I thought it was a castle? It's shit soup. And now yours truly is swimming in it."

"Slavko," says Jerome, "you shouldn't be looking at that." He gives Slavko's head a gentle shove.

Slavko gets his brain adjusted to the topsy-turvy view, and reads: Roger Boyle. STKB (standard room with a king-size bed). Address: St. Paul, Minnesota. Room 318.

Jerome hits the *Escape* key, the screen dissolves. Slavko's feet find the floor.

He asks Jerome, "This is the guy just came in?"

"Slavko, what do you want?" Starting to sound like a teakettle.

Says Slavko, "You see the car he was driving? Hoo Daddy. And was that an Armani jacket?"

"Not quite," says Jerome. "Brioni. Two thousand dollars, minimum."

"What's he doing here?"

"What are *you* doing here?"

"Room 318, that's on this side, right?"

"For someone who doesn't show up for work, you seem awfully nosy—"

"Was there a woman waiting for him?"

"At two-thirty in the morning?"

Slavko grins. "I'm sure she'll be along. She'll be expensive, too, I bet. Two thousand dollars, minimum."

"This is not my business."

"Nor mine. Just idle curiosity. The rich. They drive you crazy, no?"

"No," says Jerome. "Not really."

"Check you later, Jerome. Give the boss my regards. Give the oaf a big wet kiss for me."

He ambles out. He can feel Jerome's eyes following him. In the parking lot he walks past the dark lounge and the dark dining room and the dark racquetball court. He walks around back. There's a door beside the kitchen that the night staff uses, that they usually leave unlocked. Slavko glides through and heads for the back stairs.

Up two flights to the third floor.

Past the Coke machine.

Down the broad corridor, his steps dead quiet in the thick pile carpet. Coming up to 318. He's not planning an intrusion. No scenes, no fireworks. He doesn't know really *what* he has in mind. Maybe just pause by the door and give a listen.

But then he sees that even that's not going to work. There's a cop in the corridor.

A sheriff's deputy. Sitting on a little folding chair, his head nodding, a few steps down from 318. He opens one eye. Slavko focuses on the carpet and plows past him. Comes to the end of the corridor and takes the stairs down.

What was the deal with *that* guy?

E.R. has a deputy sheriff for a bodyguard?

Maybe E.R.'s a county commissioner or something. And he gets, he gets a round-the-clock—

No.

OK, then maybe it's a coincidence? Maybe the deputy's here for something else? For example, maybe the Dairy Farm Equipment Manufacturers Association has been receiving bomb threats from disgruntled moo-cows?

Slavko walks back to his car and sits and thinks.

What do deputy sheriffs guard?

Prisoners, right?

OK then, how about this? E.R. has a girlfriend who's also a convict. They brought her to the Caruso for an overnight conjugal visit—

While Slavko is whipping these moonbeams into a froth, he idly stares through his windshield up at the broad ornate face of the big hotel. He can see into some of the rooms. But this is not a hotel for horny young lovers and at this hour there's nothing much to look at. One or two rooms still have their TVs on. There seems to be the dregs of a party in a big suite near the office. There seems—

Then it occurs to him: Room 318, that's on this side of the hotel, right? Couldn't he see room 318 from here if he looked for it?

He pops open the glove compartment, gets out his binoculars.

Quickly calculating: 318 ought to be on the third floor, nine balconies from the central elevator shaft. He leans forward, and with his chin over the steering wheel and his nose close to the windshield, he starts counting balconies. . . .

THE TEACHER dials room 316. Then he sets the disk of his stethoscope against the wall. He waits.

The phone rings on the other side of the wall. Through the stethoscope he hears a sleepy and startled, "Oh, hell." Not from Annie—from her roommate.

But it's Annie who picks up the phone.

"Yes?"

Says the Teacher, "Is this room 106?"

"Oh. No."

"When your roommate falls asleep again, come out onto the balcony. Slide the door shut behind you."

He hangs up.

In the stethoscope he hears Annie's roommate ask, "What was it?"

"Wrong number."

"Jesus Christ."

Then one of them uses the bathroom.

Then bed-rustling. Then they settle down.

From the two breathing-rhythms, the Teacher imagines he can pick out Annie's. Coming a little short, ratchety. He can feel her fear. He shuts his eyes to listen.

The other woman's breathing starts to stretch, to roll smoothly.

He pulls the stethoscope away from the wall. He tucks it into his little black bag.

He steps out to his balcony.

Lovely evening. A bit cool and drizzly—but full of autumn fragrance. Even up here he's getting deep, late leaf-smells and earth-smells. He stands next to the partition between his balcony and hers. He waits.

At last he hears her step out onto her balcony.

He whispers, "Annie."

She comes to stand next to him, with only the partition between them. Standing in her nightgown, with a sweater pulled over it. Both of them lean out over the wrought-iron rail. He passes her a pack of cigarettes and a pack of matches. He tells her, "Light one. Pretend to be smoking."

She obeys.

He looks at her. She's backlit by one of the hotel's facade-lights and she's beautiful.

But she won't meet his gaze.

"It's risky to talk," he says. "But I wanted you to know you're never out of my thoughts."

"Thank you." She doesn't mean it, of course. But he notices there's no sardonic sting in her tone either. There's no emotion at all.

"Will we win?" he asks her.

"No," she says.

"Why not?"

"He's guilty. The others, they all know it."

"Did you fight for us today?"

"Mm."

"What did you say to them?"

"I said he didn't do it. I said the Teacher did it."

"Annie. That won't work."

"What."

"Lying to me."

"I didn't, I mean—"

"*Three* jurors voted not guilty. And when they asked you your reasons you didn't say a word. You were useless."

He knows what she's wondering. How does he know? A bug in the jury room? Or a rat, one of the other jurors? He finds himself listening, again, to her breathing. That slight raspiness, the dryness of her breath—this he loves. He wants to hold her, to comfort her. But he has to be firm now.

"Annie, if the jury hangs because you're lazy or timid or weak, how can that be forgiven? The people I work with, they'd punish you just to punish me."

"I thought—I thought it would be all right if—"

"No. We need an *acquittal*. You can win this for us. That's why I chose you. Out of all the jurors, I chose you to carry our case because I know who you are when you wake up. When your passion boils up, when you pour yourself into something, my Lord, Annie, how can you be stopped?"

She hisses, "I can't turn black into white."

"But you can set free an innocent man. Look at me."

He sees her temples pulsing. A muscle moving in her jaw.

"Look at me, Annie."

Reluctantly she turns toward him.

He says, "Louie Boffano could not have done this thing. He could have let it happen, yes, but he could not have compelled it. He has neither the courage nor the brains. Nor the will. *You* could have done this if you'd wanted to. I mean you have the mental where-withal, the spine. You and I, we're very much alike. But Louie Boffano? You know him, Annie, you've watched him. You know it's not possible—"

She raises her voice. "What does it matter what I know? *They* don't know!"

He puts a finger to his lips. "Your voice carries."

"God, what do you want me to do?" she whispers. "You want me to threaten them?"

"I want you only to get into your own passion. Just climb inside of it, and you won't have to do anything—things will flow of their own accord. Lao Tsu's Soft and Weak will overcome Hard and Strong. That jury will be jelly for you. They'll be begging your mercy."

"I can't," she says.

"You can. You have to, so you will. I think it's likely we'll never speak again. If I ever do need you, I'll call Inez and buy another piece of artwork. For twelve thousand. If I pay more, forget it, it's just because I love your work, but if I offer twelve exactly, you call Maretti's Restaurant in Larchmont, talk to Maretti. He'll have a message for you. OK? Though I'm sure I won't need to. You'll do what's necessary on your own. OK?"

"Yes."

"On your own. Still, you should know, you should never forget that I will be with you, Annie, every step of the way."

SLAVKO, watching through the binoculars from his car, sees the woman at the balcony railing turn away from the man. Then one of the hotel's facade-lights picks up her face. For the first time he sees more than her silhouette.

He sees her big eyes, her simple figure, her long straight hair. And he's certain that she's the woman from the reservoir.

He's certain of something else, too—that she's scared.

She steps away abruptly from the railing. Goes back into her room and draws her curtains closed.

Then E.R. himself, after lingering a moment on his balcony, savoring the last moments of another soulful day, no doubt, turns and goes in.

Both balconies are dark.

In his logbook Slavko writes:

> 2:50. E.R. on balcony Rm 318 talks to neighbor
> Rm 316? Same woman as at reservoir. 8 min.

They never even touched.

So what kind of lovers' rendezvous was that?

Or could it have been a drug deal? But nothing changed hands, neither money nor merchandise. And there was a sheriff's deputy waiting outside her door. Why would they, why would they . . .

Come on, Think, Slavko. Concentrate.

But the moment he tells himself to concentrate he gets an image of Juliet from that day they rented a boat and went up to Bannerman's Island on the Hudson and fucked all day on the pine needles—but later she seemed restless and said something about how always the men she was attracted to were so focused, so *concentrated*. Now what did she mean by that exactly? Did she mean Slavko was too . . . distracted? Dissipated? But that's bullshit, Juliet was always full of such bullshit—

Cut it out, you moony clod. Do some work. Do a lick of goddamn work. Figure this goddamn conundrum.

OK.

Maybe the woman met E.R. on the balcony because she didn't want that sheriff's deputy to see them. Maybe the deputy wouldn't have let her meet E.R.. But why? Why wouldn't the deputy want her to—

Could she be under some kind of quarantine? Some kind of special cloistering or . . .

A tumble in Slavko's thoughts, a single stone shifting.

Sequestered?

Like a juror?

A trial juror? Could she be a juror? The Caruso sometimes rents rooms for sequestering jurors—

The tumbling turns into a landslide of mud and sludge and revelation, and instantly Slavko is wide awake and ten years younger.

Juror.

He straightens up.

He swings open the car door and gets out and walks across the lot into the lobby. Feels like he's floating. His walk feels like the brisk purposeful walk of a young man, a young sober man.

In his vitals blood vessels are opening up that haven't been used for years.

She's a juror.

"Right?" he asks Jerome, as he reaches over the counter for the registration card file box.

"I thought you were gone!" cries Jerome. Poor put-upon Jerome. "Slavko, you can't look at those!"

Jerome grabs for the box, but Slavko has only to skitter back a bit from the counter and he's out of the whiny creep's reach.

He flips through to room 316.

"Holy holy."

Room 316 has been rented by the Westchester Superior Court. So has room 315 and room 314 and room 313 and room 312 and room 311 . . .

Jerome comes around from behind the desk and he's hopping mad, and his round face is flushed and shiny. He wants that file box. Slavko cheerfully surrenders it. He considers asking Jerome which trial these jurors are serving on, but why bother? There's no question which trial. There's only one big jury trial in the county these days.

The trial of Louie Boffano.

Slavko heads for the door. Jerome is right behind him, berating him, threatening to summon management, to call the police, to bring down the vengeance of the archangel Gabriel, who knows what this pumpkin-headed idiot is raving about? And who cares?

Slavko turns at the door and blows Jerome a kiss.

Back in his car, he pulls out his little black log. He gives it a cursory account of his latest discoveries. He underlines the word *juror*.

He wonders, What are you threatening her with, E.R.? She's lovely, how the fuck could you do something like this? And how much is Boffano paying you to do it? And how much do you think your sweet Sari is gonna like all those long drives to Attica to visit her lonesome locked-up loverboy?

Lonesome locked-up-for-a-long-time lover. Ha!

Once I get clicking, Sari & Juliet, am I not an amazing poet?

The night air is coming into the car and he loads up his lungs with it. It occurs to him that living is a simpler business than he had thought. Living—yes, living well, doing your work, rescuing some lovely scared creature from the clutches of a fiend (in fact two lovely scared creatures—Sari and that juror both), living successfully, nobly and victoriously . . . yes. It's easy.

"Yes it *is*," he says out loud.

A voice at his right ear says, "Nah. It ain't."

Slavko drops the log book. It bounces off his thigh onto the floorboards. He half turns, and comes face to face with the black unblinking gaze of a pistol barrel.

Behind the barrel is Mr. Ugly-As-Sin, E.R.'s number one flunky. Sitting calmly in the backseat and saying:

"Nah, you fucked up again, Sure-Knack. What *is* the matter with you? Eyes forward. Hands on the wheel."

The barrel tickles Slavko's scalp just behind his ear.

Says Ugly-As-Sin, "I never in my life, I never seen nobody screws up as much as you. You got a death wish? 'Cause if you got a death wish, then congratulations, I'm your fairy fuckin godmother."

Slavko hears the guy tapping out a phone number. He hears a faint buzz and a voice on the other end: "Yes?"

"I got a surprise for you," says Ugly-As-Sin into the phone.

And dimly, the reply: "What's the matter, Eddie?"

His name, good.

Or come to think of it—not good, since the more Slavko knows about these guys, the less merciful they're likely to prove.

But there can't be any margin for mercy left anyway, so why worry about it?

Says Ugly-As-Sin Eddie: "I'm sitting here with an old friend. Mr. Sure-Knack, you remember him?"

Slavko hears the voice on the other end: "Where?"

Says Eddie: "Parking lot of the Caruso."

"You're kidding."

Eddie chuckles. "Come on out and have a look."

E.R. appears on his balcony with phone in hand. His eyes search the lot.

Says Eddie, "No, we're a little more to the left. See us? Rusted-out piece-a-shit Ford Granada? Yeah, that's us. Wave to him, Sure-Knack. I said, *wave*."

Slavko waves.

But E.R. doesn't wave back.

"What do you want to do?" says Eddie.

With a gun at one's neck, Slavko learns, time passes slowly.

At last E.R. says, "I'd like to talk to him. Take him to Frankie's house. I'll meet you there."

Eddie hangs up the phone. "OK," he says. "We're going to take a drive. *You're* gonna drive. But we're going to take it real easy, yeah?"

"Yeah," says Slavko.

"No games, no kamikaze shit, nothing. You speed up, I kill you dead. All right? Where's the key?"

"Jacket pocket."

"Left or right?"

"Don't know."

Eddie reaches over the seat back, fumbles in Slavko's pockets, finds the keys.

"Take one hand off the wheel, take these keys, start your car."

Slavko does.

"Let's go."

They move out of the lot.

Says Eddie, "Slow now, cocksucker. Slow and easy."

A left. Half a mile, then another left.

But what if I don't go slow? Slavko wonders. What if I slam down on the pedal right here, where Wine Avenue drops down this long hill, just slam it and aim for that big tree down there, kill us both?

Would there be any satisfaction in that?

Slavko can't find any.

After all, E.R. would live on. E.R. would crush Sari. E.R. would crush the juror. While Slavko would be fuming and fidgeting in his coffin and wrestling with worms. Doesn't seem satisfying in the least.

"Hey," says Eddie. "Turn here."

Onto Oak Avenue. Leafy old neighborhood. A leaf-scarecrow sitting in an apple tree. What can I do? I've got to get the word out about E.R. But how am I going to do that when I'm dead?

Maybe I won't be dead? Maybe they'll let me go if I tell them I'm so so so sorry for any inconvenience I may have caused them, and actually I was working at the Caruso tonight on an *unrelated* matter—

But all they have to do is read the log book.

By the way, where is that thing?

He remembers dropping it on the floor when Eddie surprised him. Now, while driving, he tries to look for it without shifting his head. He lowers his eyes. Can't see a damn thing down there.

Moving his left foot cautiously, he gropes for it.

His heel touches something. He raises that heel, slides it over an inch and sets it down. Something underneath. He checks the thing out with his foot. It *is* the log.

So now what? Slide it under the seat? But likely when we get to Frankie's they'll tear the car up and find it.

Slavko has a better idea.

He starts to move the notebook with his toe. Nudging it toward that hole where the floor is all rusted out, where the road-wind is whooshing in.

It's a small hole. But then it's a small notebook.

Says Eddie, "You gonna fuck up again?"

"What?"

"Slow *down*, fuckhead."

Slavko does.

They pass the Methodist church. A sign for something called Alice's Wonderland. Victorian houses. Slavko manages to get the log book right up to the hole in the floor, but it won't go through. It's sticking at one corner.

He pushes it with the side of his foot. It still won't go through.

Says Eddie, "You know what, Sure-Knack? You remind me a that kid in school, whole class had to write some bullshit a hundred times 'cause one kid was a wiseguy, you remember that kid?"

Damn, thinks Slavko. Square notebook, round hole—what did you expect? Finally he lifts his heel, stamps down on it.

"What the *fuck*?" says Eddie. "What're you doin?"

Slavko feels the notebook bend—and suddenly it's gone. Left behind on Oak Avenue.

He tells Eddie, "I'm stamping my foot, that's all."

"Why are you doing that?"

"I'm stamping in frustration at my own stupidity."

Where are we? he wonders. Oak and, what's that sign say? Holly. Can you remember that, Slavko? Oak and Holly? On the off chance, the *unchance*, that you ever get out of this alive, can you remember that you left your logbook at the corner of Oak and Holly?

THE TEACHER, in Frankie's kitchen, pays close attention to Mr. Czernyk. The Teacher is mindful that ugliness and suffering are woven into the warp of our lives, and that the sage embraces these things. So he watches with equanimity as Mr. Czernyk is restrained with cuffs. He watches with equanimity as Frankie and Eddie pommel the man with their fists, with their knees, with a chair leg. Behind his gag Mr. Czernyk is a portrait of pain. The Teacher watches from his chair. Despite his discomfort, he leans close and watches and hopes to learn.

But what he's learning, principally, is that these crude persuasions don't persuade. When the gag is removed, when cold water is splashed on Mr. Czernyk's face, a twinkle returns to the man's eyes. A sort of nothing-left-to-lose twinkle. He tilts his head slightly. He keeps uncannily some measure of remove from his own suffering.

The Teacher frowns and says, "OK, let me ask you again. What do you know about me?"

"What I told you."

"How did you find me at that hotel?"

"I followed you."

"Why?"

"I don't like you."

"You're not still working for Sari?"

"No. She fired me."

"Then what did you hope to accomplish?"

"Find out something about you maybe. Something I could hurt you with."

"Why?"

"No reason."

"For vengeance?"

"That's right."

"To get even?"

"That's right."

"You've got nothing better to do with your time, Mr. Czernyk?"

"Better than what?"

"Better than seeking vengeance."

"There *is* nothing better."

"Who was the woman I was talking to tonight?"

"Same woman you talked to at the reservoir."

"And what do you know about her?"

"Big eyes."

"What else?"

"Nightgown, sweater."

"What else?"

"I dunno. Brown hair."

"What else?"

"Nothing."

The Teacher squints at him. "You're lying about that."

"You think?"

"I'm certain. The art of dissembling is among the many gifts you lack. But what I'm not quite sure of is *why* you're lying."

"Yeah. That's a good question. Why would I lie to you? I'm not an imbecile."

Young Frankie chortles. "You *sure*, Sure-Knack?"

"OK, maybe I am. An imbecile. But I still wouldn't lie to you."

"Why wouldn't you lie to me?"

"You're too scary."

"No, I'm not," says the Teacher. "Not yet. But soon."

The Teacher rises and opens the door to the garage. Frankie follows him.

"What have we got here, Frankie?"

Frankie seems amazed that the Teacher has deigned to show his face to him—that he has come without his mask. Frankie seems honored. Perhaps a bit dazzled. As the Teacher's eyes sweep over the jumbled shelves of the garage, taking in the tiers of junk, Frankie *tsks* and says, "I really gotta clean this place out. I mean I been kinda busy lately—"

The Teacher is scarcely listening. He murmurs, "What have we got that we can play with?"

"Nothin," says Frankie. "This is just stuff. I gotta get rid a this shit."

The Teacher stands on tiptoe. He tugs at the lip of an old cardboard box so he can see in. "What's this? Trains? Toy trains?"

"Yeah, I don't know if none of em still work—"

"But the transformer—do you have that?"

"I guess."

"Also we'll need a car battery. And let me see. A curling iron?"

"I doubt it."

"Electric toothbrush?"

"Yeah. I think Mom left one."

Ten minutes later the Teacher has cleared out a workspace on the tool bench, and he's cobbling together an elaborate device using the car battery, the transformer, the gutted electric toothbrush and a coil of copper wiring. Frankie watches him. The Teacher muses out loud as he works.

"What we need to bear in mind is that whatever Mr. Czernyk thinks he's defending with his lies is *sacramental* to him. It lights up his eyes. Did you notice that, Frankie?"

Frankie shrugs. "He's defending his own ass."

"No."

The Teacher shakes his head. He snips at the wiring.

He says, "Our guest doesn't think his ass has any value. It's sort of a reverse enlightenment—he himself, the I of him, he imagines that's worthless. Meanwhile he values dearly the world around him. Some of the creatures in it. Its platitudes. Its jewels. Like all frightened losers, he makes too much of these things. What in Tibet they call the *lokas*—the blurred smoldering lights of temptation. He's built an altar to them, Frankie. When we threaten him, he puts his back to that altar. He'll defend that altar with his life."

Frankie asks him, "So what do we do?"

"We strip away the gilt and the jewels. We teach him what the world is really like. We crush out those lights one by one."

The Teacher holds up his new toy, proudly appraising it.

He says, "It won't be easy. It's not a matter of slapping him around a little. It takes *great* suffering and patience and persistence to change things at the soul's core. But once he learns this lesson, I believe that he'll be grateful for it. Or I hope he will. Despite his anger. Despite his bitterness."

SLAVKO won't open his mouth when E.R. asks him to.

E.R. asks him again.

But still no.

So E.R. gives the word, and Eddie snatches up a clump of Slavko's hair in his fist, and jerks his head back and holds it fast. There's not much Slavko can do about this, since his hands are cuffed behind his back.

E.R. says with a sly grin, "Lao Tsu would tell you to give up your sainthood, Slavko. Toss your wisdom out the window, and it will be ten thousand times better for everyone."

Who the hell is Lao Tsu? Slavko wonders. Sounds like some kind of goddamn *poet*.

Then the guy they call Frankie drives a broom handle into Slavko's mouth.

His teeth crumble inward. A ring of fire flares up all around his tongue. His lower lip catches on the broom handle's metal hook, so that when Frankie pulls back, the lip is nearly torn away. Slavko can feel it dangling against his chin.

After a thoughtful pause, E.R. says softly, "You might have considered simply opening your mouth when you were asked to do so."

He takes some weird jury-rigged gizmo, and gently works it through the hole in Slavko's teeth. Slavko feels the thing, oblong, huge, as it presses against his tongue. It's hooked up to a little black box with a lever on it. E.R. turns the lever. The shock rolls Slavko's eyes back into his skull. He can gaze upon his own spinal cord, which is wrapped in a vine of blue lightning-flowers.

Nothing has ever hurt so much since the beginning of time.

When his eyes finally find their way out of the darkness he discovers that he's vomiting. Yellow-and-ocher vomit streaked with blood. He's throwing up into a pan that Frankie holds under his chin. Two of his teeth fall out and clink like pennies against the metal of the pan.

But after he's made that offering, his nausea subsides, and he feels his head start to loll. He thinks, Maybe I'll take a little nap.

Eddie snaps his head back.

Again he's compelled to look up at E.R. and his gizmo. But so what, it doesn't hurt a bit to *look* at the thing.

E.R. asks him, "Now what would you like to talk about, Slavko?"

"Nozzung." He can hardly speak.

"Would you like to talk about the woman on the balcony?"

"Nn."

"Why the obstinacy? Do you think it ennobles you? Do you think Sari would be impressed? But I promise you, she'd scorn all your efforts on her behalf. Being a loser doesn't make you *heroic*, Slavko. It doesn't cloak you in a mantle of righteousness." He smiles. "It only makes you a loser."

But I'm not a loser, Slavko thinks. You're mistaken about that.

The huge prick-shaped thing comes back to rape his mouth again. Slavko's eyes take another tumble. And the lightning, and the PAIN.

When he fades back into the world, into this ugly kitchen, E.R. is talking again. Running on and on, in his quiet, rolling, lulling voice: ". . . you keep hurling yourself at the nature of the world, as though you thought you could *defeat* it. Knock it down, shove it out of your way. Then every time the world flattens you, you lie there whimpering and feeling sorry for your poor damaged illusions. As though misery were your *portion* in life. As though it were decreed that in this abundant universe, in the midst of this great feast of life, Slavko and Slavko alone has been selected to subsist on a diet of suffering and self-righteousness. Slavko Czernyk, Patron Saint of Losers."

But you're wrong, Slavko thinks. I'm not a loser. It only looks that way.

Again the electric bullcock is pressed into service.

It mouth-fucks Slavko in dead silence, in the vacancy of this great spiny desert, this PAIN, this white boneyard.

When Slavko can hear again, he hears:

". . . but suppose you *woke* to the Tao . . . ran with it and not against it. . . . With all your fever, your furor, all your desire? . . . look at you! The love you could draw to yourself . . . I swear to you if you were worthy of Sari, you'd have her. If your spirit ran *with* the Tao, I swear to you that *no* bliss could elude you. . . ."

Slavko sees E.R.'s fingers start to fiddle with the dial of the PAIN-maker. Bastard's ready to give it another goose. Slavko feels a rage that he's never felt before. Pure-boiled hyperdistilled hatred for that dial, for those long delicate fingers. He shakes his head. Just a little shake, but E.R. notices.

He asks, "Are you ready to work with us?"

A long time passes, then Slavko nods slightly.

Says E.R., "This is a surprise. I'm glad. I thought we'd be here all night." He looks to Frankie. "Take it out then."

Frankie pulls the bloody prod from Slavko's mouth.

"Now tell us about the woman on the balcony."

Slavko tries to speak. But his charred tongue won't lift. Grunts and moans, no words.

Says E.R., "What do you know about her?"

Drool only.

"Fucker can't talk," says Frankie. "Look at his fuckin tongue, man. How's he gonna talk?"

Slavko's eyes slide all over this kitchen, and he spots a ballpoint pen in a basket by the sink. He jerks his chin at it.

Says E.R., "Would you like to *write* it for me? That's OK. Frankie, give him that pen. Some paper. Put that chair in front of him for a table."

Frankie brings all these things.

"Eddie, take off his cuffs."

Eddie unlocks the cuffs and E.R. hands him the pen. Slavko grasps it in his fist as a child would.

Frankie sits to the left of him, holding a MAC 10 to his temple. Eddie sits to his right. E.R. says, "What do you know about the woman on the balcony?"

As he asks this, he walks across the kitchen to the refrigerator. He takes out a milk bottle full of water, and he sinks wearily to the floor in front of the fridge. He takes a long pull from the bottle.

"Well?" he says.

Slavko leans over the page and writes.

"What's that shit?" says Eddie. He takes the paper and brings it over to E.R. "Can you read that?"

E.R. glances at it and declares, "It says 'Juror.' Am I right?"

Slavko nods.

"Very good. Who else knows about this, Slavko?"

Eddie sets the paper before Slavko again. Slavko writes, "VIGRMFS."

Eddie brings the page over to E.R. But E.R. can't make any sense of it. He says, "Write this again, please."

Again the paper is placed before Slavko. Again he makes a fist around the pen. Again he writes "VIGRMFS."

Frankie leans forward, straining to make it out. "What the fuck is that?"

Actually it's short for *Vengeance Is Gonna Restoreth My Fucking Soul*. But Slavko doesn't say this. Instead he demonstrates: he swings his pen up hard into Frankie's face. Going for the eye, but he gets a swath of cheek instead—he can feel the flesh rip, the ballpoint sliding against bone. Slavko jerks back and slaps Frankie's MAC 10 forward, so that when Frankie fires, the bullet just misses.

It whizzes in front of Slavko's eyes.

Eddie starts howling—the shot must have hit *him*.

Slavko cracks Frankie's arm against the edge of the table, and the kid's fingers loosen. He tears the MAC 10 from his grasp. At the same moment he looks across the room and sees that E.R. has risen and that he's pulling out his own pistol. Slavko jams his ring finger into the trigger guard of Frankie's gun—it's the best he can do in this sliver of a second. He lurches to his left, to dodge E.R.'s bullet, and he squeezes off a shot.

The roar and echo of the two shots fill the kitchen.

Slavko's round slams bootless into the fridge. But E.R.'s shot finds a home in Slavko's right shoulder.

It knocks him back and it turns him to the right—which gives him a view of Eddie, who's scuttling backwards on the kitchen linoleum. Disappearing behind a counter. Slavko swings the MAC 10 and fires in that direction—too late.

He jerks his eyes back to hunt for E.R., but E.R. has sidestepped into a hallway. And Frankie has taken cover in the laundry room. There's no time even to take aim at his retreating legs, because at the edge of Slavko's vision he catches a movement, and he turns to see E.R.'s arm reaching around the hallway corner and firing blindly.

A rude braying of agony wells up from Slavko's left hip. No time to brood over this, though, he has to keep shooting. One wild shot at E.R.'s arm, and one at Eddie, who's poking his head above the counter, and one for Frankie sticking his puss out from the laundry room. Meanwhile Slavko keeps lurching backward, toward the only corner of the kitchen that doesn't harbor an enemy.

He makes it to the door leading to the garage.

Parcels out another round of bullets.

One for you and one for you and one for you.

But screw this patty-cake shit. This is not really my game. I gotta get out of here.

He opens the door, stumbles through, slams it behind him. Limps through the dark garage. They left the big sliding door open, good. But he can scarcely see, and the metal track for the door catches at his wounded shoulder. The overload of pain takes him out of who he is. He can't remember why he's leaving this party. Am I drunk? Where's my date? Who's taking her home? Jesus, look at this rain. Here's my car where I left it, but I'm not sure I can drive—

Then he feels a weight in his hand, and he looks down and there's the MAC 10 and he remembers.

He limps over to the Buzzard, and gets in. He finds the ignition key and the car coughs and starts.

A figure appears at the garage door. He shoots. He tries to shoot again, but the clip's empty.

He throws the Buzzard into reverse and backs down the long driveway, through the trees. Pitch dark. A bullet hits his windshield. The whole sheet of glass flurries into webbing as he bumps onto the street.

A pair of headlights flares up near the house he just left. Which reminds him: he switches on his own lights.

But he can't see anything in front of him: the spiderwebbed windshield is nearly opaque. As he drives, he bashes the butt of the MAC 10 into the glass. Smacks it again and again till he's made a peephole in front of him. He drops the piece and claws at the crumbling glass, ekes out a field of vision.

The wind rushes at him. He's rolling now.

He's broken out of that cage and he's still alive.

Which means that that juror has a chance. And Sari has a chance. It even means Slavko Czernyk has a ghost of a chance. Did somebody say *loser*?

But when he passes under a streetlight he gets a glimpse of his face in the rearview mirror, and it's a horror moon of knobs and blue swelling and blood valleys. Puke bubbling down his chin. His chest wound is a sucking wound. His hip wound—oh E.R. hit the jackpot with that one—pays out blood all over the seat.

But it's OK, take it easy, just keep steady, stay awake, keep driving. You're on Oak Road. You know this road. Bunch of houses coming up pretty soon, you'll be surrounded by plenty of good people. Oh Jesus, and just a few miles down, the hospital. Right? St. Ignatius! Juliet's hospital! Juliet! Juliet to heal me and comfort me and be sorry for all the unkind things she's ever said to me. God *damn*, Slavko—and you thought that things were going *bad* for you tonight? This is the night of Slavko the Hero, this is like a grade school fantasy. Is this what E.R. meant by running with the Tao? Well, E.R., I got to hand it to you, you mother fuck. Except that I'm in excruciating pain, and I'm confused, and I believe I'm bleeding to death. But if I can send you fucks to prison? If I can save that juror? If I can die in her arms—no, wait a minute, I mean Juliet's arms, don't I?—I mean I'm confused, but the main thing is that you won't be calling me a loser anymore, will you, E.R.?

Conquistador, rather.

Then those headlights show up again in his rear mirror.

EDDIE's behind the wheel, and his head is killing him. His head is still oozing blood from where Frankie's wayward bullet nicked his scalp.

He ought to be home in bed.

Instead he has to be out on the road with Vincent, chasing down this dickhead.

Sure-Knack's car is a fuckin barge, but the man's got no fear, nothing to lose, so he can do amazing things. He skids loosey-goosey through every curve, he keeps taking it within a finger of the ditch. And unless you're another psycho you'd better concede him a little ass-room.

Look at him now, driving down the wrong side of the road. A car comes the other way, but Sure-Knack doesn't even blink. Like a fuckin battleship, he keeps steaming along. The other guy has to veer into Eddie's lane, he's got no choice. And Eddie, he figures *he*'s got no choice but to slam on the brakes and get off the road and bounce along the shoulder, ah shit.

And by the time Eddie gets back up to speed? Sure-Knack is out of sight again.

Vincent doesn't seem distressed, though. He says calmly, "Eddie, do you have a knife with you?"

Eddie digs in his pocket, passes him his penknife. Vincent has removed his jacket, and he sets it on his lap and cuts holes into the back of it. Two eye-shaped holes side by side.

He asks Eddie, "What kind of tags have we got?"

"License tags? We're good there. From Maxie's chopshop. They can't be traced or nothing. Ah shit, where does this guy think he's going?"

Says Vincent, softly, "St. Ignatius."

"The hospital?"

"If you were shot, where would you go?"

"I *was* shot," says Eddie.

"I'm sorry," says Vincent. "That's my fault."

Eddie glances at him. *My fault?* Not a thing you'll hear Vincent say often.

They come around a curve and there's the maniac's taillights again.

Says Vincent, "Eddie, have you ever known me to so misjudge a man's mood or abilities?"

"Hey. It's done."

"I never should have let him out of those cuffs. I knew it was too early. I knew he wasn't ready. All I'd done was ignite his pride. I hadn't begun to redirect it. But I was impatient, I was pushing, I was proud myself, I was reckless, I wasn't thinking—"

"Hey! So *what*?" says Eddie. "So you're not thinkin so good. So you're a little stressed out. You're distracted maybe, don't sweat—"

"Do you think I'm distracted?"

"I'm trying to *drive* here, Vincent."

"Distracted by what?"

"By the fuckin trial. By this Annie woman, by—"

Vincent smiles. "Do you think I'm in love with Annie? Do you think I'm full of desire?"

Christ, thinks Eddie, I do not need this just now. I do not need Vincent's dumping his crazy head all over me.

Sitting there with that grin on his face.

Sitting there cutting those holes in his jacket and grinning and waiting for Eddie to say something like *Well, I don't know*, are *you full of desire?*

But I'm not going to ask him nothing. I'm too busy chasing this crazy Sure-Knack all over the county, for one thing. For another, I don't really want to know.

SLAVKO turns in at St. Ignatius, roars down the circular drive. His left eye is swollen shut and his right eye is only a thin slit. He's looking through his lashes. He leans forward, trying to see out through the hole he hacked in the windshield. A sign says "Emergency" and it's got an arrow. This juror, she's a doctor in the Emergency Room, isn't she?

Or, wait—that wasn't the juror, that was Juliet. Right?

You better wake up, Slavko. You're driving across the lawn and you're going too fast and you're falling asleep and you better wake up.

Well, here's a nice stone pillar, this should wake me, right?

The Buzzard smacks into it.

But the jolt isn't particularly rousing. If anything it makes Slavko more sleepy than he was before.

But I gotta, I gotta, I gotta get out of this car. Get the door open. Good. But these legs won't move. Oh shit, look at this blood, it'll gross Sari out I bet. No no, she's a doctor, don't worry about it.

Just relax. You always get so uptight before a date. This'll be fun. Just lean to your left and fall. OK? That's right, just topple.

People are coming, white-jackets. Voices, commotion.

He's got his head on the asphalt but his feet are still in the car.

Faces. Where is she? Where's the juror? Oh shit, look at them, they're hanging back, they're afraid the car's going to blow up.

258

Crawl, Slavko.

Crawl out of here. Come on, come on, move.

He gets about four feet.

A white-jacket (but it's not Juliet the Juror) says, "That's all right. Just lie there, sir. You're all right. Don't move."

They're doing things to him. Good, but where is she?

Where is she?

It comes out of his mouth as "Way-o, us, shhh?"

"That's all right, just relax."

"Shhh, way-o, Yuli?"

Four people around him now. Good. They'll carry him to Juli. Is that her name though? Doesn't matter. What matters is this deep cure he's undergoing.

Headlights coming. Fast, bearing down. Oh yes, the killers. Nearly forgot. The headlights stop and a man with a sort of hood on his head gets out of the car. Oh yes, he's a killer. Probably E.R. Some of the white-jacket people go away. They're afraid.

But one nurse lingers.

Tell her now. Tell this woman. You won't see Juliet ever again because that's the way it is but it's OK, this woman, she'll have to do.

Force your tongue to work. Lips to nearly close.

Tell her. It will save the juror's life.

"Og," he says.

He tries again. *"The.* Log. It's at. Oak. And Holly. The . . . *log."*

Then he hears E.R.'s voice. "Get out of my way, ma'am."

E.R. is wearing a hood and carrying a pistol.

The nurse doesn't want to move, though. She's frightened of what he'll do to Slavko.

Lady, there's nothing but nothing but *nothing* to be scared of. This is the best part.

E.R. scares her away, then kneels close and Slavko feels metal touching the bridge of his nose. He and the cool metal understand each other instantly, perfectly. You see? You do your work, that's all. Simple. Why was it always so tough for him to understand? You do your work. Rescue people, or kill, it doesn't matter: you do your work. While you're working, if you work hard and well? You're happy. You're winning. When your work is done? Absolute victory. You're a conquistador.

In fact, once that bullet touches my brain, E.R., I'll be even better than that, I'll be a *DEMON* CONQUISTADOR, and I'm gonna haunt you and haunt you and haunt you, and hound your hairy ass ALL THE WAY DOWN TO HELL, E.R., and there's NOTHING YOU CAN—

11

You can start scrubbing us

out of your head now?

ANNIE in the bottle-green prison of the jury room. Some of her colleagues are still hunched over their Styrofoam coffee cups, but Annie's done with her coffee. She's wide awake.

She's a tree of nerves.

She's contending with the man who works for OSHA.

She says, "But you do admit that the Teacher exists? You'll at least admit that he *exists*?"

"I dunno," says OSHA Pete.

"You don't *know*?" A little loud, but she's pissed. So dense, this guy. She'd rather be arguing with the blackboard. She says, "Two people testified about the Teacher. He's on the tape. And you don't know if he even *exists*—"

Says OSHA, "I just don't know who he is."

"You don't *have* to know who he is! You have to know how powerful he is! Can't you see that? Didn't that get through to you—"

"Annie," says Clarinet Will. "No need to raise your voice."

Annie turns on him. Sweet shaggy bear, maybe, but sort of dull-witted himself. "No need?" she says. "No need to raise my voice? Why? This isn't important enough?"

She lets her eyes linger on his for a moment—then she drops him. Turns back to OSHA. "Think of how they sounded when they said his name. 'The Teacher.' Almost whispering. That guy DeCicco, he'd say 'the Teacher,' and he'd be looking all over the courtroom. Scared to death—"

"Oh bullshit!" says OSHA.

"Hey," chides the Forewoman. "Fella."

But Annie waves her off. "No, go ahead, let him say what he feels like saying."

She rises and moves down the table till she's between the tree surgeon and the grandmother, right across from OSHA. She puts her hands flat on the table and confronts him. "Let it hatch. What?"

He won't meet her eyes. "I just, damn it, Boffano he's the boss. He's the *boss*. They work for him. They—"

Annie snaps back, "They've got that deal with the Ndrangheta. They've got those Italians. They've got the government of Curaçao, they've got Jamaican runners, they've got this whole huge web and one spider sits in the middle of it, one guy scheming out the whole thing, and you think it's *Louie Boffano*—"

She shreds the name with a laugh.

"He's got advisers," OSHA tries—but Annie is rocking and rolling now. She squats before him. Her face is a foot from his. She's never been like this before. This hot quick fury, her thoughts whipping so cleanly around corners of logic. She's starting to draw a sort of manic exhilaration out of her own performance. She scoffs:

"*Advise?* Did the Teacher *advise* Louie to build a tunnel? Or did he *instruct* him: '*I'm* going to dig a tunnel to Salvadore Riggio's house and *I'm* going to kill him—' "

"But Annie," Clarinet Will breaks in, "Boffano said OK. He said, 'Kill that motherfucker.' He gave his OK."

"Does that make him a murderer? Suppose, suppose I told you I was going to kill this guy here."

She points at OSHA Pete. Everyone laughs. Good, she thinks, get em laughing. Get em on my side. "Suppose I said, 'I'm going to poison his coffee'? And you said, 'Yeah, sure. *Kill that motherfucker. Do whatever you want.*' Would that make *you* the murderer?"

"Oh, Jesus!" OSHA throws up his hands. He stands up across the table from Annie. "I don't believe this. I do not believe you. You think we should let him go? You want us to let that greaseball go free?"

And though Annie doesn't smile, though she meekly shrugs, she figures that right there OSHA Pete just lost the old grandmother with the Italian name.

That's one, she thinks.

She thinks, One by one by one.

FRED CAREW, Senior Investigator with the New York State Troopers, sits atop the desk in Slavko Czernyk's office and studies a yellow legal pad. Two uniforms look expectantly over his shoulder.

A scrawled note in the upper left-hand corner:

> 2 k
> k 42000   primo
> $84000
> J the face   Tuesday 7:00

Carew wishes the unies would quit staring at him. It's too crowded in here, in this tiny office.

At Carew's feet his partner, Harry Beard, is sitting on decedent's mattress, going through decedent's files. Shaking his head, making faces.

"So what do you think?" says one of the unies.

"I think it's too god damn cold in here," says Carew.

Says the unie, "It's Jimmy the Face, huh?"

Carew calls out to the hall, to where the landlord is waiting patiently on a little three-legged stool. "Hey, mister."

The man appears at the door. "Yessir?"

"You always keep it this cold?"

"No sir. It seems there's some mechanical difficulty with the heating system."

"Yeah. It seems," says Carew.

Seems perfectly clear that this murder is the handiwork of Jimmy the Face.

Here's this legal pad they found in Slavko Czernyk's desk. And right here in front of Carew's nose are these quickly jotted numbers. *2k*, that must mean 2 kilos of heroin. *42000* is the wholesale price per kilo, a little high, but then it's *primo* quality. *$84000*, that's the total for the transaction.

And *J the face?* Must be Jimmy the Face of the Gambino clan.

Therefore: Czernyk was muling dope for Jimmy and something went awry.

ABC. Spelled out in bright red ink on a yellow background.

"Prints?" Carew wonders aloud.

"Nothing yet," says one of the unies.

"Anybody tried to roust up Jimmy?"

The uniformed troopers look at each other.

Ah Christ. Carew puts his tongue between his teeth. A visit to Jimmy the Face. What fun. "I guess," says Carew, "I guess I'll see if I can't find him." Then he asks Harry, "What're you looking at?"

"Nothing. These are just Czernyk's Reports of Surveillance."

"Are they interesting?" says Carew.

"Nope. This one is from two years ago. Some guy's wife was spending a lot of time at the house of some other guy."

"Oh, my goodness," says Carew. "Were they . . . was she . . . ?"

"It doesn't say. Perhaps they were sharing Bible study together." Harry yawns. "You want to look at it?"

"Nope. Are they all like that?"

"We'll see. We shall fuckin see."

Carew calls out to the landlord, "Hey, mister, can I ask you something?"

Whereupon the officious sparrow pops his tiny face in the doorway again. "Yessir?"

"When you evicted this guy, why the hell didn't you *toss* this shit?"

"I will right away. Yessir."

"Nosir," says Carew. "No you sure as shit won't. Not till we run down every last god damn name in that file cabinet. Monumental pain in the tush."

He sighs. The landlord tries to look penitent.

"Well, tell me this, then," says Carew. "You got a holly tree around here?"

"Excuse me?"

"Or an oak tree? Or a log or something? It's something the victim said before he died."

"We don't have any trees at all," says the landlord. But he keeps working at it in his head. He works on it so hard he gets a little cross-eyed.

"Ah, forget it," says Carew.

Meanwhile the unies are still staring at him. Still waiting.

One of them says, "Well?"

Says Carew, "Well, what?"

"It's *there,* isn't it? It's a drug deal gone sour. Can there be any other conclusion?"

Carew stares at the legal pad. Puffs his lips out. "Hey, that's right, open and shut, what do you know? I guess we're a pretty lucky bunch of investigators, huh?"

But he glances at Harry and Harry glances at him and both their faces are saying the same thing:

This stinks.

ANNIE puts a dull chemically crisp salad on her tray. She navigates around the long table of jurors and slips into a seat at one end. Right across from Clarinet Will.

She gets hold of him with her eyes and starts talking.

She remembers she used to have some facility for this sport.

She gets him to tell her about the jazz combo he plays with. Then about the kids he gives clarinet lessons to. Then about Benny Goodman, then Ives and Mozart. That leads to favorite movies, which takes them to the countryside of Ireland. Mostly Annie listens. Clarinet Will tells her how much he loves to kayak. He loves saltwater kayaking particularly, he loves to glide down the backsides of big waves. His eyes glitter when he talks about this, and Annie's glitter back.

She's frazzled. The food sucks, the fluorescent lights are encouraging her headache, she's aware that the other jurors are watching them. But she has set his eyes to glittering and now she's got to keep them glittering. She smiles and lets him believe that his tales of sea kayaking have carried her away. He shares a beach house on the coast of Georgia, he says. Sometimes he kayaks at night and the paddle stirs up the phosphor in the water and he feels like he's casting a net of shooting stars over the surface of the ocean.

Her face gets all dreamy when he tells her this.

When it comes time to leave she has scarcely eaten three bites.

She pushes her tray to one side and leans close and tells him, "You

269

know, that's the thing, that's what I like about you. You're not afraid to take risks. That's why I like arguing with you. I get the sense that you're willing to try different ways of looking at things. I mean, you're not rejecting Louie Boffano's innocence out of hand, just because *they* are."

She rolls her eyes when she says *they*. *They* means the other jurors. That ugly stupid world outside of their own intense communion here.

He says, "I *am* trying to understand. But I don't know. I just—I don't know."

He scratches his shaggy head.

He says, "You know, if you ever want to try kayaking on the Hudson? I'd be glad to take you with me."

"I'd *love* to," she says.

She closes her eyes slowly. When she opens them she's looking away from him. Just the way they teach you in the magazines.

While she's thinking, After you cave in to me, coward, after you vote to let a murderer walk free? I swear if you ever dare to call me up, I *swear* before you say *three words* you'll be talking to a dial tone.

CAREW tells his partner, "I don't think one way or the other. I don't think Jimmy the Face killed Czernyk. I don't think Jimmy *didn't* kill Czernyk. I don't think anything, Harry."

They're in the car on their way to visit the Caruso Hotel. Harry's driving.

"If Jimmy did do it, though," Carew goes on, "we're fucked, I tell you that. He'll have one of his cast-iron alibis. 'Saturday? Three A.M.? Oh yeah, I was on CNN, Larry King and the President were giving me the Congressional Medal of Honor. Why do you ask?' "

They leave the Taconic and turn onto Eastgate Avenue. They drive past the sprawling leafy campus of a seminary.

Says Carew, "Anyway, it's fishy, innit?"

Says Harry, "I mean what would Jimmy want with this boozehound PI?"

"Exactly. You know? Always with Jimmy it's Sicilians and Jamaicans. Always professional. Now suddenly he turns to this Polish drunk, or Czech or whatever he is, and he says, 'Here, buddy, here's a couple a keys of heroin. Now be sure to jot down the price and all—oh and be sure to put *my* name down too, in case you get killed and the cops want to know who did it. *Yep.*"

Harry says, "So what's up?"

"I don't know. Probably Jimmy *did* do it. You know?"

Harry says, "Probably we're being too damn smart for our own britches."

Carew says, " 'Cause the only other explanation is that somebody broke into that office last night and took away all incriminating evidence and planted that note for us to find. Which is . . ."

"What?"

"A little much. You know? A little rich for *my* blood."

They pull into the lot of the Caruso Hotel. Says Carew, "You know what I would like to know?"

"What?"

"What I still want to know?"

"What's that?"

Says Carew, "I'd like to know what those last words meant."

"You mean what he told the nurse? About the log?"

"Oak log, holly log. What the hell does that mean?"

"Maybe it's where he kept the dope."

"Maybe. Maybe this is another fine case from the fudge tunnel of hell."

At the Caruso Hotel, they have an appointment with the night clerk, Mr. Jerome Lex. They meet him in the office behind the registration desk. He seems willing to tell all he knows, but he doesn't know much.

He gives them a vague description of Raymond Boyle, the guest in room 318 who had so interested Czernyk. He tells them that Boyle paid cash for his room, and that no one saw him leave.

Says Carew, "And you say Czernyk never went up there? He just asked you about the guy and took off? He never went up to Boyle's room?"

Jerome Lex makes a thoughtful face. "Well, he might have gone up. He didn't go past *me*, but there are other entrances."

"When he was looking through the registration file, did he seem agitated?"

"That's putting it mildly."

"Scared?"

"No. Excited."

"Maybe he was stoned?"

"You mean booze? Oh, I think Slavko was *always* a little drunk."

"Did he ever deal heroin, Mr. Lex?"

"*Slavko?*" Jerome laughs.

"That's a no?"

"He couldn't have. He wasn't, he wasn't that type of guy. He was kind of a blunderer? Kind of awkward? Kind of had self-esteem problems? Drank too much. Always a crush on some girl. Couldn't get it together, you know? But he was all right. He annoyed me, but I liked him. He was, he was, I don't how to say it. A romantic, I guess I'll just say that. He was what you'd have to call a *romantic*."

THE TEACHER sits in his old schoolhouse, holding the iconic position called *sattvasana*, listening.

The receiver is tuned to the deliberations.

Annie isn't saying anything just now. Earlier she was ferocious. Now she's letting her acolytes do all the work.

She's keeping quiet and letting her new converts, the clarinet player and the tree surgeon, gang up on the housewife from Mt. Kisco.

The Sage rules without making the people bend beneath his weight. When his work is accomplished, the people say, "We did it. We did it all by ourselves!"

The tree surgeon is saying, "But Laura, the evidence tells us the Teacher ordered that killing. The evidence says Boffano's innocent. It doesn't matter what your *emotions* say—"

The housewife snaps back at him, "Do you have children?"

"No," he says.

"If you had children you'd understand!"

This seems to irk the clarinet player. "What does *that* have to do with making the right decision here?"

Finally Annie speaks up. "It has everything to do with it."

The others hush. They all want to hear her voice. The Teacher thinks that they're all in love with her voice.

Annie says, "I have a boy, Laura—nearly as old as the boy who was killed. And I'm terrified that something might happen to him someday. I know what you're thinking. You're thinking you've got to protect the children. There's all this chaos, and it keeps getting worse and worse and there's nowhere you can go to get away from it. There's no way to hide from it."

She pauses. Eleven others in that room with her, but nobody breaks in. They wait on her. Finally she says, "But the law is . . . I don't care how weak or uncaring the system is—can you see any other way? The law says that if they don't *prove* that Boffano committed the crime he's charged with, we have to set him free. We *have* to. And you just, I don't know, you pray you get him next time."

The Teacher doesn't want to laugh out loud.

"But if you try to twist the law," says Annie, "even just a little, for the best of reasons? Then the law loses whatever strength it has. And then my child's in more danger than before. And yours, Laura. . . ."

The Teacher doesn't want to exult.

Triumph and failure, illusions alike.

But every cell in his body is swaddled in a fat moist joyousness, it's all he can do not to cry out, to crow his victory to the sky.

She's beautiful.

She's powerful. She's a vessel of pure power.

And the Tao has delivered her to him, a gift. Magnificent—not looked for, not sought after, but simply set before him. Set before him! And like all gifts of the Tao, this one is a gift *to keep*.

CAREW riding, Harry driving, down a broad sleepy suburban avenue. They're on their way to St. Ignatius Hospital. They're going to see that nurse who was with Czernyk just before he was killed. She said she'd talk to them before she came on duty tonight.

It's nearly six o'clock. The sun's going down behind this neighborhood of steep Victorian houses, and Harry's hungry and cranky. Carew knows there'll be no more useful ruminations out of him till they get to the hospital cafeteria. Still he can't help but toss out his wild guesses.

He says, "So why do you think Czernyk went to that hotel? You think that guy in 318, that Boyle guy—you think he invited him up?"

"Nah."

"Right, because then why would he check the register? He must have been snooping out the guy's room number. I bet he followed him there. But *why?*"

Says Harry, "How about this? Czernyk was out cruising the Caruso Hotel, looking for a strong young sailor boy, and he saw Boyle drop his handkerchief from the balcony of 318, and—"

"We're losing it here, Harry."

"You wanna play with this one, Fred? Wait'll I eat. Then I'll play."

"Harry."

"What?"

"Stop."

"What?"

"Stop the car."

Harry does. "Why, what's up? You all right?"

"Back up," says Carew.

"Yeah?"

"Yeah."

The whine of reverse. On this wide avenue nobody's coming either way, and there's nothing to stop them from backing up as far as they want. But when they've gone a couple of hundred yards, they come to a corner, and Carew holds up his hand.

Harry brakes. Dead stop. "What?"

"The street sign there. Now just check that out, if you would."

Harry looks up. The street sign says OAK going one way. The other says HOLLY.

"Oh yeah," says Harry. "We *are* losing it."

Says Carew, "No, really. Czernyk might have gone this way, right? After the hotel?"

"He might have."

"So Oak and Holly, maybe this is where it happened."

"Where what happened?"

"Where he was shot."

"Yeah?" Still no spark, though. Harry only wants to eat.

Carew keeps it up. "Or he could have tossed something out of his car here."

"The dope?"

"It's possible. Or the log."

Harry looks at Carew as he'd look at a madman. "He tossed a *log* out of the car?"

"A notebook kind of log. The kind PIs keep when they're on surveillance."

"Oh. Oh yeah. You think?" says Harry. His fingers drumming restlessly on the gearshift.

Says Carew, "It won't take long, right? We don't meet the nurse till seven. So we got an hour to kill anyway."

"No, Fred, we got an hour to *eat*. The hour's not for killing. It's for eating."

"Ten minutes—a few doors. Or . . . maybe not, maybe you're right. You need your vittles. We'll come back some other time—"

He says this because he knows he's already won.

Harry takes the left side of the street, Carew the right.

Carew's first house has a flagstone walk, then a porch with a bushel basket full of Indian corn. Two old women peer at Carew's badge.

Neither of them saw anything unusual on the street today.

He walks around the boxwood hedge. Another flagstone path, another porch. This door has sidelights and a fanlight and a cutout of a black cat. Mother calls to her son, who comes clattering down many flights of stairs, arrives breathless.

No. No notebook, no nothing.

Another house. Lawyerly-looking gent. No.

Another flagstone path.

Nothing.

Another. No.

He spots Harry, looking plaintively at him from across the street. Harry whines like a hungry doggie.

"OK, OK," says Carew. "Forget it, let's go."

They get back in the car, and Harry starts the engine.

Then the little kid from the second house comes running up to the car.

When Carew unrolls the window, the kid hands him a small black leather notebook. "I would've told you right away. But I thought you'd think I stole it but I didn't, I found it in the gutter, right there, I mean I *would've*—"

The kid goes on like this, while Carew reads. He reads and turns pages, and reads some more. Harry peers over his shoulder. Both of them hold their faces close to the page, trying to make out the god-awful handwriting in this dusky light.

"Flip to the end," says Harry.

At some point the kid has shut up. At some point Harry has killed the engine so it's quiet in the car, just the sound of evening crickets and TV laughter from the houses.

Carew finds the last page. He sees the word *juror*. He sees the name BOFFANO and he sees the name *Caruso Hotel* and he makes a fist without knowing it. Lets it go, makes another.

Juror.

The court often takes rooms for jurors at the Caruso. He thinks, how could I have missed that—

It starts to branch in his head. His eyes leap all over that page and suddenly this little no-account drug-dealer hit is getting bigger and bigger, and he raises his eyes and stares out his window at the kid.

He doesn't *see* the kid, he just stares while he cogitates, but the kid doesn't know that. The kid sees this dangerous cop staring a death-stare at him, and he knows he should not have taken that notebook, and he knows he'll be spending the best years of his life in a penitentiary somewhere in the Mojave Desert, and he's trying to come to terms with this sudden plunge in his fortunes. . . .

EDDIE in back of the courtroom, watches the jurors file in. There she is. Dragging. Keeping her eyes down. She takes her seat and she shuts her eyes.

Says the court clerk, "Ladies and gentlemen of the jury, have you reached a verdict in this matter?"

Says the Forewoman, "We have."

"As to count one in the indictment, murder in the second degree, do you find the defendant guilty or not guilty?"

"Not guilty."

Instantly two hundred sets of lungs suck all the air out of this courtroom.

"And as to count two in this indictment, murder in the second degree, do you find the defendant guilty or not guilty?"

"Not guilty."

Tallow demands that the jurors be polled, but it doesn't do him any good. There's a brisk farewell address from Wietzel, the defendant is released from custody, and that's it.

That's this courtroom blown sky high.

Louie Boffano jumps up like he's ten years old and then turns around and swats everybody in sight. Big luscious open-hand swats bestowed on all his buddies and lawyers and wife and kid and cousins, and the courtroom is in an uproar. Jubilation, dismay. Wietzel pounds the gavel but the noise seems to comes from far off, like the sound of somebody pissing next to Niagara Falls, who cares?

Eddie's still watching her. She's still got her eyes closed.

Louie Boffano leaps into his lawyer's arms. Little Bozeman trying to hold him up. Everybody laughing their asses off.

She'll be all right, Eddie thinks. It's all over now, Annie Laird. You did it.

Vincent and you together, you did this nasty piece of shitwork and now both of you, you can let it go? Annie, you can start scrubbing us out of your head now?

Reporters push past Eddie to get to the aisle, to get out of here to a telephone. Old women push past to get down there where they can smother their hero Louie Boffano in kisses. Everybody pushes past Eddie. He sees only flickers of Annie through the crush.

Right, Vincent? I'll never see her again? You're going to let her go now, right, Vincent?

12

a child at play, a sentimental fool . . .

JULIET, in Annie's kitchen, slices up the large pizza and doles it out. Henri is here, and Oliver's friend Jesse with his new earring. Jesse eyes his slice warily. "What are these?"

"What are what?" says Juliet.

"These wormy things."

"Anchovies. What's the matter?"

Jesse gets a knotty chin. "What are anchovies?"

"They're fish," says Juliet. "Annie, here."

She serves a slice to her friend, who smiles and then fades back into her thoughts.

"*Fish pizza?*" says Jesse. "The concept here is fish pizza?"

"If you don't want them just pick them off," says Juliet.

"Oh, don't be a wuss," says Oliver.

Jesse asks, "What do they taste like?"

"They taste sort of like sardines," says Juliet.

Says Henri, "No. *Precisely* they taste like salt. But much saltier."

Oliver picks up a long anchovy and dangles it over his mouth. He drops it in. Then he puckers up his lips and shuts his eyes. "No, you know what they taste like *precisely*?" he says. "I mean *really* precisely?"

He brings his lips close to Jesse's ear. A splash of whispering.

Says Juliet, "You telling him what I think you're telling him?"

"Yes." Oliver opens his eyes wide and blinks innocently.

"Gross insulting schoolboy stuff?" she says.

"Yes."

Henri starts to chuckle.

"You're comparing anchovies," Juliet says, "to some part of the female anatomy that you know absolutely nothing about? Is that it?"

"But that's why I love anchovies," says Oliver. "They're all I've got."

"You're so disgusting," says Juliet.

"They're all I can *access*," says Oliver.

"Access *this*," says Juliet. She picks up an anchovy in her long fingers and flings it at him. It lands on his cheek and sticks there. Henri barks out a laugh.

Then Jesse cries out, "Food fight!" which reminds Juliet that she's dealing with a pair of adolescent boys here and this could get quickly out of hand. She says, "No no no no. Not now. Not here. Sorry."

Oliver smiles mildly. The perfect gentleman. He peels the anchovy off his cheek and eats it.

Everyone laughs, even Annie. But Annie laughs only because the others do. She's not listening to the chatter. Her eyes are focused somewhere else—at a high spot on one wall. Then they flick over to another wall. Juliet watching her, wondering what she's looking for.

Does she think that man is listening? Is she still frightened of that bastard?

"Hey you," she says sharply. "Annie."

"What?"

"This is a celebration. You're free. Up from slavery. It's over. Eat."

ANNIE at eleven the next morning, steps into her studio for the first time since the night she invited him in here, and it's like going back to some childhood place, some place she'd forgotten mattered so much.

Used to be an artist.

But her Grope Boxes look dull, dun, inert. They look like the crates they are.

She stands before the piece she'd been working on when all this started. *Second-Grade Passion for a TV Lion.* Or so it says, in her own handwriting on a note pinned to the wall. But she has no memory of calling it that. Now the name seems blithely postmodern, frivolous. Not like her at all.

Well OK, I'll find some other name.

The important thing is to get back to work, get back into rhythm.

The covering-box itself has been hoisted high to reveal the piece's innards as they rest on her worktable. Annie flips a switch to start the little motor. She passes her hand between a pair of whirring rotors and lets the hundreds of satin snakes slap at her. She reaches up farther and gets gusts of hot muggy air from the steam machine. Like the breath of a panting animal.

Right, OK. Clever.

But what else? Wasn't there supposed to be something else?

She casts her gaze around and spots the piece of soft deep-pile fur she found at a thrift shop. The mane, yes. The lion needs a mane.

She remembers that on the day she met the Teacher she had been about to attach the lion's mane.

She disengages the pawl on the winch, and lowers the covering-box carefully to the worktable. Upends it. Sets the fur inside it, finds some screws and a Phillips screwdriver, and begins to affix the fur to the inside of the box. After a few minutes of this work, after a few of the screws are in, she starts to relax a little—and then that memory comes back to her. Oliver's on his bike and she's in that car and the car is bearing down on him and she's trying to get out of her skin—

She grits her teeth. She squeezes the handle of the Phillips as hard as she can and the plastic fluting digs into her skin.

She waits, and after a minute the box comes into focus again.

This box.

What the hell is she doing?

This mane she's lining this box with? This fuzzy sweet sentimental . . . what is this?

Is this really the kind of art she used to make? Was it *all* like this? Warmhearted precious bric-a-brac?

This isn't going to work.

She shuts her eyes again.

She stands there, rocking on her heels, and then she starts pacing, back and forth in the small space with her head down, eyes on the paint-splattered wood slats, and she doesn't know what she's looking for but after a long time it finds her. An image. Of a house. A homey farmhouse with samplers and lace doilies and calico curtains and lovely burnished antique furniture.

But the walls are lined with shards of glass.

Thousands of twisted razor-sharp pieces of glass, *growing* from the inside walls like thorns. Walk carefully. If you stray to the left or to the right you'll cut yourself.

If you stumble you'll kill yourself.

And there's some churning sound, the cadence of an immense machine for *crushing*, as you pass through the rooms.

Is this a new piece?

But you could never make this, Annie.

Where in the world could you come up with a farmhouse? And all those shards of glass? Someone *will* stumble, someone will be cut.

Someone will sue. Even if you could find a way to make this piece, you could never *show* this piece.

But who gives a damn? she thinks. I'll make it for myself.

She sits on the floor. She stretches out on her back and stares up at the ceiling. A staircase? Yes, there will be a staircase up to a dark bedroom. Wait, no. No, *nothing* will be dark. Every window must be spotlessly clean so the sun can come pouring in. Everything must be neat, all organized by some finicky spirit. But a garden of glass shards will grow out of the goose-down quilt on the bed, and there will be homemade glass shards in the oven, and—

The telephone rings.

She lets it.

After four rings the machine picks up, and in a moment she hears Inez, her dealer:

"Hey babe. When are you going to call me? I've got to talk to you. Zach Lyde gave me a call. Told me he wants a piece he saw up at your studio. He says it's called, um, *Second-Grade Passion for a TV Lion*? Says he'll pay twelve for it—do we have a deal? Says he'd like to know immediately—he's having dinner with one of his Asian friends and he wants to be able to offer it. My god, did you charm the pants off him, or what? *Twelve thousand*, Jesus. Call me! Where are you? What is going *on*!"

Annie slams her screwdriver into the floor beside her.

She thinks, What if I don't answer the summons, what if I don't do anything?

But then I'd be simply waiting and waiting for his chastisement, wouldn't I? And what good would that do?

She rises. She fetches her jacket.

She gets in the Subaru and backs it out of the drive.

As she heads toward the village of Pharaoh, she looks in her rear-view mirror and notices a car pulling onto Seminary Lane behind her. A green sedan, two passengers. Two men.

But she bears down on the pedal, and it's easy to lose them, and in a minute she forgets them.

At Pharaoh Drugs she uses the pay phone. She calls Maretti's Restaurant in Larchmont. Maretti tells her about a stretch of abandoned railroad right-of-way near Mahopac. She's expected there in half an hour.

When she gets back into her car and pulls onto Ratner Avenue, the green sedan gets behind her again.

So she takes a right at Bullet Hill Road just to see what the green sedan will do.

It stays behind her.

She slows way down. Slows to a crawl. Fifteen miles an hour, what do you think, gentlemen? You want to come up close so I can see your faces?

Abruptly the car behind her turns into a driveway. Annie roars off.

Oh thank you, Teacher, I appreciate your attentiveness, but you needn't have bothered. I *am* coming to you. You called, I'm coming. In this as in all things I obey you, my beloved Teacher.

THE TEACHER stands inside the ruined relic of a boxcar and watches as Annie hurries along on the old half-buried ties to meet him. He loves to watch this: her blurry beauty coming out of the mist toward him. Her fury. She seems to be having a hard time reining in her gait to match the cadence of the ties. Even the steam she's breathing: it's on account of the bitter cold, of course, but it adds to her dragon mien.

At last she holds up and looks around her.

She sees him waiting for her in the boxcar's open door.

"Annie. Come up," he says. He reaches out his hand to help her into the car. But she stays where she is.

"Why do you want me?" she asks him.

"So I can thank you. Also so I can sing your praises."

She has no reply to that.

"I listened to you in that jury room," he says. "The way you spoke to them—your power took my breath away. And you, I think you were equally astonished. I think you've just found out what you're capable of. I think that soon you're going to be ruling the art world."

He crouches, lays his palms flat on the boxcar's wood floor, swings out and drops lightly to the ground.

She says, "What do you *want?*"

"I want you to know I believe in you. In your fierce talent. I'll stand behind you."

"Don't," she says.

"As much as I can help your career, I will."

"Don't."

"You remember when I said this would change your work, this would make you stronger? Has it done that yet, Annie?"

"Leave me alone."

"Ariel, thou shalt be as free as mountain winds."

"And get your bastards to stop following me."

He wonders what that means.

She says, "We made a deal. I did my part. Now get out of my life."

"Who's following you?"

"Your two mules or whatever you call them, why the hell are they following me?"

"Two men? What do they look like?"

He can hear the impatience surfacing in his own voice. The sudden concern—and Annie picks up on it too.

"Wait," she says. "Those two men. *Those two men.*"

"Not mine."

"They have to be."

"You're certain they were following you?"

"Well, I thought . . . I don't know."

"What happened to them?"

"I slowed down. Sort of challenged them. They pulled off."

"What make of car?"

"How would I know? Just a plain car. Green. Boxy. Are you playing with me? They're really not yours?"

"Annie, why would I have you followed *now*?" He steps up close to her and sets his hands on her shoulders. He studies her eyes. "Perhaps you only imagined—?"

"Let go of me," she says.

She can't get much threat into those huge soft eyes of hers, but he sees her trying, and he grins. "OK," he says, and he takes his hands off her.

"The police?" she asks. "You think it's the police? That's what you're thinking, isn't it? But how would they, how could they know about—"

"You tell *me*, Annie." And then when she has no answer he prompts: "Perhaps Oliver."

"No." She's firm on that. "If he had told anyone, I'd know it."

"Your friend Juliet, then?"

That one grabs her, as he had expected it would. *He knows about Juliet?* He watches her trying to regain her composure.

"Annie?"

She's still searching. "I don't, I don't— Juliet would never have put my son in danger."

"She told you to go running to the judge. That wasn't putting him in danger?"

"But I went *along* with that. And after I gave up on that idea, I made her promise to stay out of it. She said she *would*, she promised. She swore to me."

He tells her, "Right now, Annie, right now Louie Boffano is on top of the world. If we bring him down from there . . . you cannot conceive of how much that will anger him."

"Maybe they *weren't* following me. Maybe it was—"

"If you see them again, I want to know it."

"Yes."

"I want to know right away."

"Yes."

"I want to know everything."

"All right."

"If you need to find me, call Maretti. Tell him where you'll be. I'll have Eddie pick you up. OK?"

"Yes."

He reaches up and with his fingertips he touches the silky hair of her temple.

"Who will protect you?" he asks her.

"You will," she says.

"And why will I protect you?"

"I don't know."

"Because I can't possibly let anything happen to you now." He places his full palm against her cheek, and leaves it there long enough to feel her warmth. "We've come too far together."

FRANKIE takes his girlfriend Molly to Louie Boffano's Emancipation Party. They drive down to Louie's spread, which looks like a Virginia plantation on the south side of Staten Island. A long smooth driveway that curves up to the house like a question mark. Then some jockey takes the car—the new Viper—and Frankie goes sweeping up the marble steps with Molly on his arm. She looks god damn flawless. Wearing the Lacroix gown that he bought her today. Frankie himself doesn't look quite so perfect. His right cheek is bandaged and his right eye is still swollen. But the eye patch is dashing. The Oxxford tux is brand new and dazzling white, the shoes are Luciano Barbera. He's in a good mood, he's having a good time.

And he keeps having a good time right up until he's in the middle of a jitterbug with Molly and suddenly he looks up and Louie is standing right there. With his bodyguard Archangelo by his side. Of course Frankie quits dancing right away. Louie asks Molly, "Mind if we borrow your beau for a minute?"

But it isn't a question.

Louie's already got his hand on Frankie's back just below the neck, and he's steering him through the crowd. Archangelo on the other side of him.

Under the huge chandelier and through the big sculpture gallery full of naked women and angels with little wee-wees. Down some stairs and their steps echoing. The way footsteps do in prison, Frankie thinks.

Then out into the garden, into the chilly misty evening. Despite the chill, every inch of Frankie is covered with sweat. They're moving so briskly, the three of them, and they're saying nothing. Frankie wonders if maybe there isn't something he should say in his defense.

I ought to at least *try* to talk them out of it.

He says to Louie, "I mean I know how I fucked up the other night when I let that prick Sure-Knack get away, I'm really sorry, Louie, but shit, I was trying to, trying, to do the best I, I mean the best I could . . ."

He looks over. Louie's not even listening. He keeps up the pressure on Frankie's back.

Past the pool, past a row of shrubs all pruned to the shape of the Virgin Mary. Trees, a tennis court. Sort of a thicket with a path cutting through it, and here Louie makes a sign to Archangelo and he drops back.

Frankie and Louie arrive at a small clearing.

The Teacher is sitting on a wrought-iron bench.

"Hello, Frankie," says the Teacher.

Says Louie, "Frankie was just telling me about the incident from the other night. About how sorry he is for what went down."

The Teacher shakes his head, slowly.

Louie takes a seat on the bench beside the Teacher. He leans back. He takes out a cigar and lights it. "Do you have a problem with what went down?" Louie asks the Teacher. "Do you have a problem with Frankie?"

"Yes I do," says the Teacher. "My problem is that he's too quick, too sharp, far too loyal for the work he's doing."

"So what are we gonna do about it?"

"I think you'd better make him into a captain, Louie," he says, and he grins, and presently Frankie realizes that his jaw is hanging wide open like he's brain-damaged, and he shuts it.

ANNIE is just back from the Laundromat, opening the trunk of the Subaru to get her basket of laundry, when she hears a car crunch on the drive behind her.

Two doors open at once. Two official visitors, their ID cases tumbling out of their palms.

"Annie Laird? I'm Investigator Carew of the New York State Troopers. This is Investigator Beard."

She's still got the basket of laundry in her arms. She looks toward the street. Investigator Beard sees her doing it, and he glances that way himself.

Says Investigator Carew, "We'd like to ask you some—"

Again she cuts him off. "Not here."

She turns and puts the laundry basket back into the trunk. "You want to ask me questions, we'll go to your office. We'll go right now."

She slams the trunk shut.

"Our office is in White Plains, ma'am."

She walks right past him to the rear door on his sedan. She says it again. "Now."

That seems to suit the investigators. Carew holds the door open for her.

An hour later, she's sitting in the antiseptic windowless office of inquisition, before a square desk. Carew and Beard on the other side of it. There's a painting on the wall to her left. Hazy hillside. Below this painting is a brass-colored plastic plate that reads *"Summer Birches."* That's nice, how thoughtful of them to provide me with this happy smudge of Art.

The wall opposite has a darkened sheet of glass. Annie supposes it's a one-way mirror. But why are you hiding, whoever you are? Does the Dread Juror frighten you? Come out, come out, you weasely cowards.

Investigator Carew is grilling her. "Roger Boyle?"

"Don't know him."

"The name means *nothing* to you?"

"Nothing."

"The Caruso Hotel?"

"Where we stayed. The jurors."

"You remember the room you were in?"

"Vaguely."

"You recall it had a balcony?"

"Hmm-hm." Get *to* it, she thinks.

"On Friday night you stood on that balcony and had a conversation with someone on the balcony of the next room. You remember that?"

"No."

He sighs. "Ms. Laird. It's not the sort of thing that happens every day, is it?"

"I guess not."

"An eyewitness saw you."

"Maybe saw my roommate."

"No, Ms. Laird. The witness says he saw the same woman that he saw at the Mapougue Reservoir."

"What's that?"

"October 17. You were sitting on the rocks by the reservoir, you were talking to a man. Remember?"

"Not really."

"The same man you were talking to on the balcony."

"Oh?"

"The man who called himself Roger Boyle."

"Oh?"

"You recall?"

"Not really."

"Not really? You weren't there?"

"I wasn't there."

"But we know that you were. So now we've got this conflict, don't we? How would you explain it?"

"Explain what?"

"This conflict."

"I wouldn't."

"Oh, give it a stab. What do you think?"

"Mushrooms?"

"What does that mean?"

"You, you investigators, maybe you take a lot of mushrooms and you see things that aren't there."

Now the other one, Investigator Beard, speaks up. "Ms. Laird."

"What."

"What do you do for a living?"

"I used to process orders for a company called Devotional Services. But this trial went on a while, I suppose by now my boss has found somebody else."

"Ms. Laird, your bank account took a real friendly little bounce this month—"

"Yes."

"How come?"

"I sold some artwork."

Says Carew, "You did? Good for you. But you know what? We don't really care how you got it. Because we don't think you did this for the money. We think these guys scared you. They're still scaring you. But now it's time to quit being scared. Let us get you out of this mess."

"How would you do that?" she asks.

"If you open up to us, help us, testify for us, we'll put you somewhere safe. You and your boy. Then we'll put Mr. Boyle and his friends in jail. We'll put them away for a long time."

"And then what?"

"Then whatever you want. You could relocate for good if you liked. Or come back here—"

"You mean to Pharaoh?"

"If you want."

"To my house? After I testify—"

"The mob's not what it used to be, Ms. Laird. Their bark is worse than their bite. They don't often kill civilians."

"Often? Not *often*? You're sweet. Now can I go?"

Investigator Carew glares at her. She glares back.

"Not yet," he says.

"Well, make it quick then. I've got to get home before my kid gets out of school."

Says Investigator Beard, "We could send someone over to pick your son up. Take him wherever—"

She erupts. "No! Stay away from my house! You put me in danger when you come around my house! Don't you stupid bastards understand that?"

Carew looks over at Beard. Then he makes a steeple of his fingers in front of his face, and asks, "In danger, Ms. Laird? In danger from what?"

"From the Man in the Moon. Let me out of here."

"I'm afraid we're not finished."

"I'm finished."

"Ms. Laird, we're trying to help you. But you have to cooperate."

"Well, I can't."

She pushes her chair back. Ready to get up, but Carew shakes his head and says, "All right. Listen. Suppose the press got hold of some bad information. All sorts of crazy things happen—suppose there was a leak to the effect that you *were* cooperating. That'd make a great story, wouldn't it? State to Bring Tampering Charges Against Boffano, Juror Will Testify—something like that. Your friend, your visitor at the hotel, he'd be glad to see himself in print, wouldn't he?"

"You do that," she says, "and they'll . . ."

"What?"

She feels the skin tightening around her cheekbones. The hell with it, she thinks. They know anyway. So she says it. "They'll kill my child."

He's ready for that. "No, they won't. If you help us they won't."

"Oh fuck you! You don't know them! You don't—"

"Ms. Laird, I've spent the last twenty-five years of my life locking these punks away. They always threaten. Always. But they don't do squat. They're not going to hurt you. Or anyone close to you. They know we'd consider that an act of war, we'd use that to wipe them off the face of the earth. They're dumb but they're not *that* dumb."

"But you can't be *certain*—"

"I'm certain you're in danger without us. If you play by their rules you'll lose—I'm certain of *that*. Let us protect you. That's what we're here for. Who else will protect you?"

He looks at her for a little while, then he drops his eyes to his clipboard. When Investigator Beard starts to say something, Carew clears his throat and shakes his head slightly to silence him.

For two minutes Carew works methodically at a doodle of chained triangles.

Then Annie says, "Look, I'm not saying no, but I'll need to think about it."

"OK."

"But not now. Now I've got to pick up my son from school. Give me time."

"How much time?"

"Just, just a day or two. But keep your goons away from my house. You want to watch me, OK. But don't let anyone know you're watching. You hear?"

"A day or two?"

"Forty-eight hours. Just give me that long."

JULIET in Ian Slate's Stiletto. Skimming down the Hudson past Riverdale, past the mansions preening themselves in the last light.

Ian lets her take the helm. The boat is a twin-hulled catamaran and maniacally quick. She keeps the throttle open. They skate between a fishing trawler and a coal barge. They whip around a far slower speedboat. She imagines she flicks her tail at them as she passes. Let them eat wake.

"Am I going too fast?" She laughs.

"Yes," he says. He puts his hand over hers and gives the throttle another nudge.

She finds to her surprise that his touch is welcome to her.

She's been telling herself she doesn't really like him. She's been thinking he's much too self-possessed and controlling for her. For example the way he has choreographed this evening to such a fare-thee-well. Picking her up in his Range Rover, with the music all dreamy Irish ballads (harp, strings, soprano). Taking her to the dock in Peekskill where he had a man waiting with two dry martinis and his boat. And an extra jacket for Juliet, to ward off the river-chill.

The delight he takes in all his glimmering, confident, liquid-green gauges.

The way he so crisply points out landmarks. That palisade way over *there*, under that blazing sunset, where Aaron Burr shot down Alexander Hamilton. This cave here on the Manhattan side where the crazy Caveman once lived. She's been telling herself that such a self-assured *helmsman* simply isn't her type—and then he touches her and his touch gives her that little jolt. She looks up at him, into his green eyes. Flicker of mischief there. Reminds her of that look he gave her in Nightbone's Poetry Cafe. And now here comes his screwy smile.

It occurs to her that she's having a blast with this guy.

She surrenders the tiller.

He takes them under the George Washington Bridge and down the long neck of Manhattan. When they come abreast of the old westside piers, he spots what he's looking for. A yacht bobbing on the velvet water. He steers a graceful J, and as he approaches the yacht he cuts back the engine.

He flings his bowline to a man in a white tuxedo, some sort of steward or majordomo.

The man unfurls a ladder for them.

Juliet tosses the man her left shoe and then her right. Then she climbs aboard, and Ian follows.

Floating nightclub? Restaurant? She's not sure, and she never asks. There are half a dozen other couples already in the dining room, and a guitarist. The repast is coquilles St. Jacques with sautéed asparagus. Ian's eyes hold hers. They talk about ten thousand things. He tells her about the orchids of Easter Island. He tells her about a family of Basque shepherds he knew in Idaho. She spins one of her hospital war stories, and then another, and another. He has a trick of listening that loosens her tongue, and she finds it easy to tell him all about the drudge-rounds and the sleeplessness and the fluorescent wound-up hell of St. Ignatius Hospital.

Always his gaze is steady, curious, cool.

He gives her the story of the Croat cellist who played for him all one scorching summer night in a Mostar garden, and then left the cello in Ian's care while he went to join his brothers up in the Dinari foothills.

At some point she asks him what he does for a living.

He says, "Reporter, didn't I mention—"

"But this isn't, all this seems a little extravagant for a reporter's salary, doesn't it? I mean the boat and the car and all?"

He simply laughs.

"Well of course the poetry brings in quite a bit," he says, and laughs some more.

She leaves it alone.

The waiter brings them Stilton cheese and port wine, and then coffee. Finally, nothing so gauche as the presentation of a bill. Simply a warm handshake between Ian and the waiter—that suffices.

They step out onto the yacht's stern. Gusts of the guitar music follow them. It's a cool moist night, but it's not as cold as it has been. The yacht has come around to the East River, to the lights of City Hall and the Brooklyn Bridge. Ian and Juliet lean against the taffrail, lean into the breeze.

She tells him, "A man was shot to death at my hospital last week. Right outside the emergency room. You read about that?"

He nods. "I read something. Were you there?"

"No, but I knew him. I used to date him."

"You're kidding."

"Slavko Czernyk. I have an idea he was looking for me when they killed him."

Ian Slate smiles at her. "I thought he was wounded and he was looking for a hospital."

"Well. All right. Maybe just that then."

"But your gut tells you he was looking for you?"

"Mm."

"Why did he want you?"

"I don't know."

"That must have been hard for you, Juliet."

She shakes her head. "What's hard is that it was so *easy*. I came in late the next day and I heard about it and I went over to the hospital morgue. I wanted to see him. Freddie let me look at him. Big GWH. Gunshot wound to the head. We get them often, but this one was fascinating. I'd never seen one like that. The bone of the skull was blown away. The cortex was exposed. The gray matter? And the blood had drained from it perfectly, so you could see all the wrinkles—it looked like it's supposed to look, like a head of cauliflower."

"What did you feel?"

She shrugs. "Nothing really. Something like pity, I don't know. But then something like contempt because this, this cadaver, this head of cauliflower? I'd made love to this guy, and now he was, he was just the object of my pity. And then, I mean I guess I felt guilty because, because I was thinking those things."

"But you'd never loved him?"

"No. But still, we *made* love. That should count, shouldn't it? So I shouldn't have been looking at his brains with *contempt*, should I?"

At the pier, a car is waiting for them. A limo, but not stretched. Nothing ostentatious, nothing tawdry.

Ian tells the driver, "Coliseum Books." He prepares two more dry martinis. This time the music is the Cowboy Junkies: *The Black-eyed Man.*

They lean back with their drinks. Tenth Avenue goes by in the mist.

He touches her hand. He says, "Juliet, every day you see all this suffering—so you have to switch your compassion off. Now you want to instantly switch it on again? You can't do it. Don't beat yourself up. The grief will come to you—"

"I mean it's not that I'm not *capable* of tenderness."

"I'm sure of that—"

"I mean there are people that I *love*," she says, but the way she blurts it—she recognizes that she's a little drunk.

"Who do you love?" he asks.

"I love my friend Henri. I have a friend Annie, I love her. I love her child—God do I love him. He's twelve years old and Annie thinks he's got a crush on me, but I think I'm the one with the crush." She laughs. "But there's all these annoying laws against statutory rape."

He asks her, "So if it had been this Oliver who had been hurt? Instead of your old boyfriend?"

"Don't—" She raises her hand. "Yes. If Oliver had—? That I would have felt."

At Coliseum Books he asks her to wait for him and he steps in and a minute later comes back with a gift for her, some books.

He murmurs to the driver, "Take us to Belly Mortar?"

While he pours another martini she looks over the strange selection of books he's brought her. A historical romance, *Love's Warrior*, by Sarah Rebecca Nightsmith. A thriller called *The Delta Triad*, by Dean Locket. *Sister Hearth*, by Dannika Jackson, which the jacket describes as a reverie of a Deep South African American girlhood.

She laughs. "Why, why *these*?"

"You wanted to know how I earned my living."

He smiles. Takes out his pen and writes on the flyleaf of *Sister Hearth*:

> To Juliet, on this night . . .

He signs it Dannika Jackson.
Then he opens *Love's Warrior*, and on the flyleaf he writes:

> . . . of surprises . . . and intoxications . . .

And he signs it Sarah Rebecca Nightsmith.
In *The Delta Triad* he writes:

> . . . and rare passion—Ian.

She's gaping at him. He shrugs and laughs and tells her, "If I were just *one* writer, I'd get restless."

The limo takes them to Belly Mortar.
Dark street in the meatpacking district. A crowd waiting on the cobblestones by a loading dock. Ian and Juliet push through. A phalanx of bouncers parts for them, they step onto a milk crate and then onto the loading platform, and then they click down a long bare-bulb passageway. The music starting to pulse. They spiral down two flights of water-smooth steps to the factory's immense basement.
Hundreds are churning and raving.
A huge hip-hopper, nearly round, serene and still as an idol, chants the crowd into delirium.
Ian and Juliet are swept out into that surge. They dance for hours. But all the time he keeps his green eyes locked on to her green eyes. And every now and then he touches her—quick guiding fingers on her elbow, her shoulders—and when he touches her she shuts her eyes so the sensation will linger a little longer.
She's letting this tide tumble her, letting that touch lead her.
She's certain that what she's feeling now she has never felt before in her life.
She tells herself, Oh yeah, it's called *getting drunk*.
But if that's it, then she damn sure has never been this drunk before.
Swirled out of her mind, out of her name and her character, floating

now into this man's arms and letting him rock her into a corner of the club where suddenly she pulls his head down to kiss him. To devour his mouth. Hitching up her skirt so he can boost her up against the cinderblock wall with his hands cupping her ass, with her legs wide open like a bird's wings. He's crushing her, smothering her against this wall. Feeding on her mouth, and she feels the heat of his cock throbbing against her panties. Her ankles lock behind his back. Witnesses everywhere if anyone cares, but the amp-blast and the boil and murk erases them all, and all she can feel is his lips, and that stone ridge of his cock grinding against her, and the pain where the rough cinderblock scrapes her shoulders. She arches her pelvis forward into that ridge and she pushes her shoulders back into that roughness. And she breathes into his ear: "OK." As though he'd asked her, but really he hasn't said a word.

She tells him, "It's OK, if you've got a condom."

She thinks she hears him laugh. She thinks she hears him say, "Well, it so happens . . ."

She reaches down and unzips his pants. She wonders if they'll be arrested. His cock in hand. That ropy vein under her thumb. Her eyelids flutter open, just long enough to see the flash of the condom packet between his teeth as he tears it open. She laughs and tries to kiss him again but the curled edge of the packet is still between his lips. He turns and sputters it away. Then kisses her harshly and she feels him unfurling the condom down his cock. She pulls her panties aside to make room for him.

It's dark. They're all stoned out there. Nobody's watching. But even if they are watching I don't care, I don't care, I only, *Oh my God*. She's got her arms flat against the cinderblock, her palms flat and he's sliding into her. Too slowly. She's *hungry*. She jams herself down on him, then jams down again. Again. Ugly damn squat and a *brook* of her juices pouring from her and can these ravers see this, see his cock? Oh Jesus, his cock slide into me? She's never had an orgasm during intercourse and she's not going to have one now, but yes, this thing, this is close. This is *farther* than orgasm, what is this thing? This is, this crushed-out lost-my-mind gone-to-hell, Jesus, this. This *man*. This *man*. Ian. Ian. No handhold. No purchase on anything. Riding him like a child. Arms wrapping now around his neck—anything to hold on to. *Ian*.

THE TEACHER, hours later in Juliet's bed, holding close to her as she drifts off to sleep, murmurs her name. "Juliet?"

"Mm?"

"Sweet Juliet?"

"Mm?"

"Would you do a favor?"

He can feel her smile.

"For you?" she says. She arches her back, pushes her bottom into his groin. Yawns.

"No. For your friend, for Oliver."

"For Oliver?"

"A huge favor."

"I don't understand, what?"

"Wait," he says. "Let me show you."

He rises. From his night-bag he withdraws three blister packs of 200 mg Tuinal, and a bottle of Ron Botran. He asks her, "Will you take these?"

She turns over sleepily to see what he's talking about. "What." She blinks. "What are they?"

"Secobarbital, amobarbital, and rum. If you take them now, take them quickly, you can save Oliver's life."

She rouses a bit. Sits up in bed. Stares. "What are you talking about?"

Now he takes his HKP7 automatic from the bag. He places it on the little dressing table catty-corner across the room from the bed.

She switches on the lamp.

He can feel her stare as he takes his shirt from the chair back and puts it on and buttons it.

"Who are you?" she says.

"You haven't figured that out? I'm Annie's friend."

He listens a moment to her wide-open hoarse breathing. As he tucks in his pants, zips up, buckles.

"You . . . you bastard, you—"

"When you were putting Oliver at risk," he says, "the boy you love so much, then you had ice in your veins. You felt like such a heroine. Now I ask you if you can be a *real* heroine."

He takes out his vivid green contact lenses, puts them in their case.

She tries to speak. "Why—"

"Because now after what you've done, after you've interfered, it's Oliver's only chance. Unless we do something, he's going to die. You don't believe it. You think I'm lying. You think I'm an opportunist, a rationalist. But you don't understand me at all. I'm a child at play, Juliet. I'm a sentimental fool. And I will have him killed. Like *that*."

He leans over the bed and snaps his fingers in her face.

"Even though no good will come of it. Even though it will cause immeasurable pain. Even though I love him as much as you do, Juliet—still. I'll kill him. I told Annie, I told her what we'd do if she betrayed us. And I'm a man of my word. *The Way of Power is an unvarying way.* What, do you still think we're playing? You don't believe me?"

She stares at him.

"Annie doesn't believe me either. Not really, not in her gut, not since *you* were so persuasive. And now the police are with her. Babysitting her, waiting for her to break. There's a choice that she has to make, and there's no one to help her, no one with her interests in mind. No one but the police. All day and all night. Which way do you think she's going to go? I think she's going with her new friends. Unless she gets some kind of signal, something clear, something to convince her that I mean what I say. We have to wake her up. Give her a little taste of grief, an inoculation, does that make sense? Just enough to make her afraid. So she'll believe me."

Juliet says nothing.

"It'll be easy for you. Enough Tuinals, enough rum, get your GABA system hopping, flood your neurons with chloride ions—it'll be simple and sweet and painless. And forgiving, Juliet. Will you help me? Will you help me to save Oliver?"

She doesn't answer. She's no doubt scared out of her wits. The pupils of her eyes are tiny pinpricks. But he's sure she hears what he's telling her.

He says, "Or you can try to fight me. In which case I'll kill you now. I'll leave a suicide note for you anyway but I'm not sure the cops will buy it. I'll have to vanish for a few years. Someone else will have to kill Oliver. I'll have to go down to my place in Curaçao. Snorkeling, sailfishing, waste of time. No good for me, no good for you. No good for Oliver. No good for anybody. But it's your choice, Juliet. Is that the way you want to do this? What do you think?"

For a long time she doesn't move. Then her left eye twitches—and then there's something resistant, something he finds ugly and primitive and mulish that passes across her features. He braces himself. He wonders if she's going to try to rush him.

But that look passes. She blinks, and her eyes slip shut.

He says, "Juliet? Oh, Juliet. Do you want Oliver to die before he's lived?"

He whispers, "We can save him."

He whispers, "Juliet?"

13

Does it seem depraved—

my fascination for that man?

ANNIE the next morning is in her studio, on the phone to Inez.

Inez complains, "A *house?* Are you crazy? Do you know how much a house costs in Westchester?"

Says Annie, "But I'm talking about an abandoned house. Get me a falling-down house anywhere. Nobody's going to live in this house, Inez. It's going to be a sculpture."

"What kind of sculpture?"

"I don't want to say any more."

"You want me to get you a fuckin grant to buy a house but you don't wanna tell what it's for? What are you, nuts?"

Says Annie, "I just don't know the details yet. I need to see the house first."

"So who you think's gonna spring for this house?"

"I don't know. Find somebody for me. If you love me, find me this house because this is going to be a work like nothing anyone's ever done or will do—"

"OK. I'll call Zach Lyde."

"*No.*"

"No? What're you talking about? He's got the bucks, he worships the ground you walk on, he might even be crazy enough to do something like this—"

"Not Zach Lyde. Not for this one."

"But he's the *only* one, Annie."

"*Not that son of a bitch! You hear me?*"

"Hey girl—"

"NOT *YOU!* ARE YOU LISTENING TO THIS? STAY OUT! THIS IS *MY* WORK!"

"Who the hell you think you're talking to, girl?"

"Inez, I don't, I don't mean you."

"What's going on?"

"I'm sorry."

"What the hell's the matter with you? You in trouble? Are you depressed about something, Annie?"

"No no, I'm soaring. Really. I'm going to do my house, Inez, I know it. Somehow or other."

After the call, Annie paces in her studio. Thinking about the house. She hasn't been this wild for her own work since she was in school. Back and forth she walks, with sudden inspired spurts. The phone rings and she grabs it just to shut it up. It's Henri, Juliet's friend from the hospital.

He says, "Annie? Annie?"

"Yeah?"

"Juliet is dead."

"Juliet is dead," she says back to him.

"They say she killed herself."

"Wait."

"She's dead."

"Wait."

"She took sleeping pills. There was a note, she left a note. Said she was tired of the hospital, tired of the pressure, tired of no way to escape, tired of her life. Tired of pretending that she was strong enough. Annie. But I don't believe it, she, Annie, why didn't she fight? Annie, what is this? What is this?"

Desperate to dampen the pain, Annie finds herself in the tool corner of her studio and she has her hands on the long-handled garden shovel, and she brings it up and swings it against the glass panes of the studio door. Shatters the glass. Then she swings it against the casement window. Her heart's raw wish being that in the thousands of glass tidbits, in the sheer anarchy of their trajectory, there will be distraction—some measure of oblivion. But the smashing makes no dent on her grief, none at all. Her shovel changes the Grope Box called *The Dream of Giving Notice* into splinters and bits of cage-lace and flying screws, but the pain is invulnerable. There's no cure, never will be, no relief. . . .

She drops the shovel. It bounces at her feet. Her howling shrivels. She bites down on her hand. Silence. Her face is bleeding. Her cheek when she touches it feels white hot.

OLIVER and Jesse pull into the driveway on their bikes. The clouds are low and fat, it's chilly, another day of this rotten weather. Mom's car's not here. Maybe she just drove out to do a chore but Oliver feels an inkling of worry.

He and Jesse cruise around to the back. Suddenly Oliver squeezes hard on the hand brakes, nearly wipes out: what he sees. The glass has been busted out of one of the studio windows. The door hangs on one hinge. Shards and slivers everywhere.

Jesse says, "Holy shit."

Oliver's off the bike and running up to the broken door. He swings it open, scraping it over the concrete step. He looks into the studio.

Sons of bitches have trashed one of Mom's pieces. Scraps of wood and motor and wire mesh all over, and then he sees the blood, blood on the handle of the shovel and spattered on the floor.

"Mom!"

He runs out again—pushing deadweight Jesse aside. He slips on the thin gravel of the drive, crying, "Mom! Mom!" He uses his key to get into the bungalow but the bungalow is also quiet. He shouts for her again and scrambles up the stairs, but she's not there and he wonders what he's supposed to do. Does he call the cops now, does he dare call the cops, will that guy hurt Mom if he calls the cops? Why would the fucker want to hurt her, didn't she do everything he asked? *Mom!*

And then he looks out her window and he sees the Subaru pulling in. Jesse looks up and sees him in the window and calls, "Hey man, chill. She's right here."

The Subaru beeps. Cheerful little chirp.

He races down again—nearly breaks his neck on the stairs. He runs outside and she's waiting in the car and he cries out, "Mom!" He's crying. Rushing toward her side of the car. *"What happened?"*

She unrolls the window. Doesn't seem to notice his tears. Her cheek's been cut by something, and there's a slash above her eyebrow. She's dyed her hair *red*. She's got a vague smile on her face. "Get in the car," she says. "You and Jesse, I'm taking Jesse home. How was school, baby?"

"Mom, *what happened?*"

He can feel Jesse standing at his shoulder.

She looks casually over at the studio. "Oh. I got into a mood. You know? One of my moods? The hatch is open, put Jesse's bike in and let's go."

They do as they're told.

She pulls out onto Seminary Road and she offers them Life Savers.

Driving beside the lake with that odd smile. She's got the radio going, bubblegum music, and she sucks away happily at her Life Saver and doesn't say a word.

Once, Oliver looks back at Jesse, and Jesse does a mock-paranoid shifting of his eyes, as if to say *your mother is a spooky woman.*

When they get to Jesse's, Oliver gets out and helps him to unload his bike. Mom gets out too. Jesse's saying goodbye when suddenly out of nowhere she asks him, "Hey Jesse? Do you know where your passport is?"

"Excuse me?"

"Your passport. Didn't you and your parents take a trip to Wales last year? Where's your passport?"

Jesse looks over at Oliver. He says, "Um, my mother keeps the passports in, in a drawer. In the living room."

"Could I look at yours?" she asks. "I mean just for a second— I'm doing this sculpture and I want to paint Oliver's passport in it. I need a model."

"So why don't you use Oliver's passport?"

"Oliver doesn't have a passport."

"Mine is real stupid looking," says Jesse. "I mean the picture, it's dumb."

"Just for a second?"

Jesse does his shrug.

He goes to fetch the passport. Comes back in a minute and hands it over. "I look goofy, though."

Mom studies the snapshot. She opens her purse and takes out her own passport and compares that photo.

"It's a lot like mine," she says. "Not smiling—very serious."

Oliver wishes she'd get over this weirdness and let's get out of here. But she keeps looking at Jesse's picture and shaking her head. She says, "You look like your dog just died, you know?"

"Yeah?" he says.

She gives him back the passport and she and Oliver get in the car. They're driving on Old Willow and Oliver asks her, "What was all *that* for?"

But she puts a finger to her lips.

When they get home, as soon as they're out of the car she draws him to her and says in a whisper, "Let's go for a walk."

"OK," he says. "Where?"

"You remember your shortcut through the woods? Back to the old railroad right-of-way?"

"Yeah. Sure."

"Show it to me."

They walk around behind the studio. Mom keeps glancing behind her—and then she takes off running into the woods and he follows her.

She doesn't slow down till they get to the power line cut. They stop a moment to catch their breath. After that she lets him lead, lets him guide her along his secret trail through the brambles.

He says, "Mom, why did you pull that switch on Jesse?"

"You saw it?"

"Yeah."

She asks, "Do you think *he* saw it?"

"Uh-uh. He was looking at you. He just thought you were nuts. But why did you want his passport?"

"Because *you* don't have one," she says.

He holds up. "Do I need one?"

She simply steps around him, ducks under a vine and walks on. She's in a hurry.

He follows and says, "What, are we leaving the country? Mom, what's happening? What happened to your studio? What's going on?"

"Another time," she tells him.

"Mom, the trial's *over*. The Mafia guys, they won't bother you anymore. You're not flipping out, are you? I mean, you know that it's all over?"

"Almost," she says.

"We should talk about this, Mom."

"I don't want to talk about it."

"Well, OK, but maybe you could talk to Juliet? Why don't you call Juliet?"

She doesn't answer.

They emerge at the old railroad right-of-way. Just a straight trail through the woods. She asks him, "If we go this way, where would we come out?"

"Morris Road," he says.

"No, I mean farther," she says. "If we cross Morris Road, keep going?"

"I don't know. Croton Falls?"

"That's fine."

"But that's like seven or eight miles."

"So let's get a move on."

They walk. Soon a drizzle starts up. Gray drizzle and a gray junco flitting above a gray wall. Oliver's bewildered, and frustrated by her silence. But as they walk a strange contentment falls over him. Are they running away? If they run away forever, math quizzes and Laurel Paglinino will no longer be a concern. Only problem is he's going to miss Juliet. He's already missing Juliet.

They walk for hours. This long mysterious side-by-side trudge down the straight path through October trees and pastures, through the soft rain.

Once he asks her, "Couldn't we have stopped in the house to pack something? Anything?"

"What do you want, Oliver? What do you need?"

"I don't know. Nothing, I guess."

But after a while he says, "That skull that Juliet gave me. Would have been nice to have that. For good luck. Does Juliet know where we're going?"

"No."

By the time they get to Croton Falls, to where this old right-of-way connects with the active commuter line, it's past noon and he's starving. They grab sandwiches at the village deli and then cross to the station and take a train down to the city.

From Grand Central Station they take a cab to a luggage store. She buys them each a suitcase. Next a quick spree in a cheap clothing store. Then a cab to La Guardia Airport. She buys the tickets under the name Juliet Applegate. She uses Juliet's passport—she won't tell him why. She's changed a few numbers. She's changed the height from 6'2" to 5'3", she's taken thirty pounds off the weight.

At the ticket counter she pays cash. When she hands over Jesse's passport she says, "My nephew." She ruffles Oliver's hair and tells the lady, "I finally made him cut it. Don't you think it looks better?" She lies with such grace and easy polish and insouciance.

The plane to Guatemala is leaving in thirty minutes. She sets him into a plastic scoop-chair at the boarding gate, and she goes off to make a call.

CAREW turns down the sound on the Islanders game. His wife sets the phone on the coffee table in front of him and he picks it up and it's Annie Laird. He hears some kind of public jostle and bustle in the background.

She says, "I've decided I *will* work with you."

"Good."

"He killed Juliet," she says. "Did you know that? He made it look like a suicide but he killed her."

"I don't, um, who is that?"

She's silent.

He says, "They killed someone? What was the name again?"

"Juliet Applegate," she says slowly. "My friend. The doctor. You didn't know she'd died?"

"I don't know anything about her," he says.

"Why not?"

"Why not what, Ms. Laird?"

"Why don't you know? *He* knows. He knows *everything* about my life."

"Well, maybe he knows because he's looking for ways to hurt you. Me, I'm not looking to hurt you."

"But you *are* hurting me," she says.

"Now that you're working with us, we'll stop him."

"Right," she says. No irony in her voice. No enthusiasm either. Nothing he can read.

He says, "Do you want to come down to the office now?"

"Not now."

"OK. We'll start in the morning?"

"Soon," she says.

"When?"

But then his call-waiting goes off, and he says, "Could you hold on for just a second?"

It's Harry Beard on the other line, telling him, "Annie Laird has flown the coop."

"Huh?"

"There's no lights on in her house. We checked, she's gone. So's the kid. The car's there. Somebody smashed up her studio—"

"Harry, she's on the phone with me right now."

"Oh shit. Where is she?"

"Well, I don't know," says Carew. "Let me ask."

But of course by now the other line is a dial tone.

ANNIE and Oliver ride in the back of a bus that threads through the sprawls of Guatemala City. They're headed north to the mountains, to Huehuetenango, where they'll look for a ride to Turtle's village. They have to share their seat with two stout Mayan women. Oliver sits nearest to the window. Next comes Annie, then the two women in their bright complex *huipiles*.

All four of them shoehorned into this one school bus seat.

Annie's trying to sleep. Her head droops forward.

An antsy hen leaves its basket in the seat up ahead. It tries to perch on the seat-back in front of Annie. The bus lurches and the hen opens its wings and flutters them against Annie's face. She starts. The hen ogles her with one eye. Annie has never strangled a chicken and she wonders what it would feel like. But the hen seems to read her look, and it hops back into its basket.

Annie prays for sleep. Anything. Even just a little drifting around the fringes of this rage would do her good.

She and Oliver spent all night in the bus station, waiting for this bus. Afraid to rent a car. She didn't have any of Juliet's credit cards, and she didn't want to use one of her own—because then the investigators might find out she was down here.

They'd know, and then *he*'d know.

Salsa music blares on the bus driver's radio. The windows are open, and the fragrance that rushes in is a mix of exhaust and cedary woodsmoke and rancid garbage and some kind of tropical nightbloom.

He knows anyway. Because they're all working for the Teacher. The whole thing with the investigators was a ruse, a setup. Even the trial itself was a trick. They want an excuse to kill my child, so they set up the trial and Juliet's murder and they're waiting for me to make a slip.

Oliver barks, with a laugh, "All right, who laid it?"

No one back here knows English but they all understand Oliver's disgusted sniff. The women laugh and the owners of the hen laugh. The word is passed around. Finally a drunk, with breadcrumbs and flecks of perhaps butter clinging to the stubble on his chin, rises and bows to Oliver. He seems to be confessing to the crime.

The others laugh at him, and Oliver laughs as hard as anyone. Plainly he's having a good time down here. She's seldom seen him so excited, so cheerful. He hasn't complained once since they boarded the plane. Get him away from that video screen, get him out on a renegade jaunt like this, he thrives. Right now he's laughing so hard he has to clutch his stomach.

But Annie thinks that the Teacher is watching him.

She thinks that the Teacher knows precisely where they are. She thinks that somehow he's found a way to listen in on Oliver's laughter. This fear is so vivid that she puts her hand on his shoulder and tells him, "Not so loud."

"Why not?" he says.

She shrugs. "I don't know. Because these people don't know what you're laughing at."

"We're all laughing at the same thing. At the guy who farted."

"OK."

The bus pauses, to squeeze a few more passengers aboard. Out the window a horde of orphans gathers. Wheedling, whimpering, hawking peanuts. One of these kids has no legs and he rides a sort of low-slung soapbox cart, propelling himself with his hands. As the bus pulls away he races alongside it, digging his knuckles into the asphalt, staring up at Oliver and Annie, saying nothing, just keeping up.

"Jesus, Mom," says Oliver. Horrified and rapt. "This city, it's like a nightmare, isn't it?"

She hadn't noticed.

THE TEACHER gets gas and then parks and goes into the all-night coffee shop of this rest area. He uses the men's room. When he comes out, he goes out the rear door. Back to where all the trucks are. The vast lot is lit up like a ballfield. He crosses to the edge of it, to a copse of dark beech trees and a picnic table.

Eddie's waiting there.

He says, "Vincent, she's gone."

The Teacher takes note of how the skin tightens at the back of his neck just below the hairline.

Says Eddie, "I didn't want to tell you on the phone. Can't use the phones no more, Vincent. They gotta be on to us. Shit's gonna come over the dam. I mean it's gonna come over the fuckin dam."

The Teacher says evenly, "She disappeared?"

Eddie nods.

"When?"

"This morning. I think the fuckin feds got her in a safe house somewhere. Or the state, she's working for the state. She's working for *somebody* now."

The Teacher weighs the possibility. Then he shakes his head. "No. She's been learning too quickly, and she needs some air. But she won't betray us."

"You fuckin crazy? They got *to* her, Vincent. Time for us to say goodbye. Go down to Curaçao, they'll never find us. What the hell, we did our best for Louie. Let's go. Right now. Leave your car here. Get my daughter, we'll take the early bird to Miami."

The Teacher asks, "Where's Frankie?"

Eddie shrugs. "Now? Four in the morning? He's asleep for shit's sake."

"I need him to check out the woman who owns that gallery. Annie's close to her, she might be hiding with her. Or maybe with the man she called Turtle. In that picture of him it looked like he was somewhere in Guatemala. We need to find out if—"

"We need to get the fuck outta here!"

"No. Flight's not called for. What we need now is to maintain the pressure. Annie's stunned, that's all. She's in a vulnerable state. A friend of hers died last night."

"What friend?"

"That doctor."

"*Died?*"

"According to the papers she took her own life."

"You killed the doc? Oh Jesus, Vincent, what did you do that for?"

"There's no suspicion of foul play."

Eddie glowers at him.

Thruway headlights ooze up and down the trunks of the beech trees.

"Eddie."

"What."

"*The Sage is impartial. The Sage sees the people as straw dogs.* So don't stare at me. If there are things you don't understand, I'll try to explain them."

"I don't want your fuckin explanations, Vincent. All I want's this shit to be over. If they clip you? They gonna clip me too. You know what I'm saying? I'm saying you're being a fuckhead. I'm saying I love you, but it's time for you to take a break."

The Teacher looks at Eddie's dark-socketed eyes, and at all the flesh-baggage beneath them. "You're not sleeping these days, Eddie?"

"Who gives a shit?"

"Are your dreams keeping you awake?"

"Like what dreams?"

"Do you ever dream about Annie?"

"Fuck you. She did what we asked her to, OK? Now let her the fuck go."

"I'd like to. I can't. It's as though we were married, Annie and I. How can I let her go?"

OLIVER and his mom ride in the back of a pickup with fifteen people from T'ui Cuch, on a precarious dirt road that switchbacks higher and higher into the mountains above Huehuetenango.

Oliver has made a friend, Juan Calmo Cruz, a kid about his age or maybe a few years older. Oliver is teaching Juan Calmo a little English, and Juan Calmo is teaching Oliver a little Mam—the local Mayan language.

Oliver points and says, "Cigar."

Juan Calmo points and says, "*Sich*." He flicks imaginary Groucho-ashes.

Oliver points and says, "Woman."

Juan Calmo practices getting his mouth around the globe of that word: "WO-mun. WO-mun."

Oliver shivers and says, "It's cold."

Juan Calmo doesn't understand.

"Mom, what's cold in Spanish?"

"I forget. *Fría?*"

"*Sí, frío*," says Juan Calmo. He regards their thin shirts. He turns and leans over the cab of the pickup, toward the driver's window, and shouts something.

After a while they pull up at a little thatch-roofed store on the side of the road. Juan Calmo takes Oliver and Mom inside. He helps Mom to bargain, and she buys Oliver a heavy cotton shirt with red and white stripes like Juan Calmo's—like the shirts of all the T'ui Cuch men. Also a woolen jacket embroidered with the figure of a bat.

She buys herself a heavy wool coat lined with rabbit's fur.

When they get back into the pickup everyone applauds.

These T'ui Cuchians look nothing like the moon-faced lowlanders on last night's bus. These people are tall, with carved cheekbones, emphatic chins, a cocky grace to their stance. They sit steady, even on this jolting ride, with their shoulders thrown back.

The road climbs up to the top of the mountain, then dips again. Into the belly of a cloud. Oliver and Juan Calmo stand side by side behind the cab and look forward, the white wind in their faces. They stand silently, bouncing along for nearly an hour.

Then the mist lifts, and they can see down this long valley of Oz-green acres to a hillock girdled by mountains. And there, amid cornfields and potato fields and dwarf apple trees, is the village of T'ui Cuch. Merely a cluster of thatched roofs. And way up on a slope above them, the stone ruins of a church. And smoke. And waterfalls tumbling down the steep sides of the mountains.

Oliver turns. "Mom?"

"Yeah?"

"We're here."

She raises her eyes. Her expression doesn't change. She asks Juan Calmo, "*Conoce, conoces . . . un gringo . . . se llama . . . Turtle?*"

"*Cómo?*" says Juan Calmo.

"Or Walter Reisinger?"

"*Cómo?*" says Juan Calmo.

She shouts over the wind. "Walter Reisinger?"

Juan Calmo shakes his head.

She asks some others. Nobody knows the name.

She says, "*Es un, un médico?*"

Again they shake their heads.

Oliver takes out his little dictionary and looks up the word for turtle. "*Tortuga?*" he tries.

"*Ah! Claro!*" Several at once: "*Tortuga!*"

The driver blasts the horn and comes breakneck into the village. A furry pig runs out of its pen and grunts at them. This grunting gets pigs and dogs started up all over town.

The pickup stops at the village market and Juan Calmo and his mother volunteer to guide them down to the casa of El Tortuga.

Most of the others join the company. They walk down through cornfields, down narrow flowery lanes. Oliver's suitcase bumps against his leg. Now and then they pass a knot of T'ui Cuchians, a few words are exchanged and the company swells. Oliver hears the words *novia* and *esposa*.

"Mom."

"What?"

"They think you're Turtle's *wife*. I think."

Oliver looks around and there must be thirty or forty T'ui Cuchians with them now, grinning and laughing.

They pass a waterfall and keep descending.

They come at last to a long squat building with a tin roof and a sign that says *Clínica*. Beside it there's a little home with a garden and chickens.

Outside the door is a wooden turtle on a post.

"Tortuga!" the crowd cries. "Tortuga!"

And this guy comes out and Oliver for a moment is a little disappointed. Come all this way for this *dork*? Whose posture is even worse than Oliver's, and who's pig-eyed and balding up top and ponytailed and scraggly-bearded, and who has repaired the broken earpiece of his glasses with a bit of electrical tape? Plus when he smiles at Mom it's sort of a horsey smile.

Is this the kind of guy you travel thousands of miles to see? Well, only if you're on the run, like us, thinks Oliver. Only if you've got no other choice.

SARI's in her office at the travel agency with the door shut, and locked, and Eben pushing her against it. Out there telephones are chiming, ticket printers are clattering. But that's somewhere else. Sari's concern is this man's lips, this man's bothersome shirt buttons.

He takes her hands and lifts them up and gently kisses them. It seems a subtle way to slow her down, to deflect her ardor.

"You don't want to make love to me now?" she whispers. "You can make love to me right here, Eben, please."

He doesn't answer. He slides his fingertips along her arms, all the way up till he can stroke the undersides of her breasts with his thumbs. But there's something absent to his gaze.

"Eben?" she says. "Are you all right?"

"I just wanted to see you."

"What's the matter?"

"It's not, it's. Well. Business . . ."

"Tell me."

"I'm in trouble."

"Darling, what?"

"Today one of my friends got a contract from Pemex to build a new pipeline out of Mexico. Pete Mordacai. Billion-and-a-half-dollar contract from Pemex."

"That sounds like *good* news."

"It should be. Except yesterday this futures fund that I've been advising bought up a mess of West Texas Intermediate crude futures. *Before* the announcement. The futures took a favorable tick, and we cashed in. Looks like insider trading, and I'm taking the heat."

"*Was* it insider trading?"

"Not on my part. You ought to know by now, Sari, I've got insane scruples. But yes. I'm fairly sure that the manager of the futures fund made a secret trip to Guatemala in the last few days. Some of the Pemex people were down there for the Americas Fair. I think she had a secret meeting with them, made some payoffs and got the word."

"So why are *you* in trouble?"

"I can't prove it was she. If I, if I could even prove she went to Guatemala City, that's all I'd need to clear my name. But I can't."

"Wait. You need to find out if this woman went to Guatemala in the last few days?"

"Yes, but I don't know how I'd do that."

"Maybe I can help," says Sari. "Let me make some calls." She twists her monitor to face her. "What's her name?"

"Annie Laird."

"You know where she lives?"

"In Pharaoh. Seminary Lane."

"Didn't you call me from Pharaoh one night? You said you were on the road and—"

"Yes. That's who I was meeting, Annie Laird. I thought she was just a client. I thought I could trust her. Now because of her they're going to break me into pieces."

"No," says Sari. "No, I won't let them. But this could take a while. I'm going to have to call you."

"Sari, you're an angel."

ANNIE wakes up in the middle of the night at the crowing of a cock. At first she's terrified. But then she remembers where she is. Turtle's cottage. Guatemala, far away, safe. She gets her breath back, and her composure, and finally she's glad for the interruption.

In her dream she was a UPS driver, making pickups at hospitals, taking in cratefuls of broken glass.

This moonlight is much better than her dream.

The lace shadows of leaves. A night bird starts singing and it sounds like water pouring through rocks. She sits up a little so she can look across the room to where her child is sleeping. Not much to see. A curved ridge of lumps on that far bed. The shiny knoll is likely an elbow. She waits to see him breathe.

He does, the mound stirs a little.

Then Turtle, lying beside her, whispers, "Annie?"

He looks better like this, with his hair loose. With his lips puffy from sleep.

"I'm OK," she tells him. "Hold me."

He lifts his arm out from under the blanket and draws her to him. Her cheek on his. Smell of his hair, familiar Turtle smell. But his hand keeps moving. Slipping around on her back. Dropping down her spine, on some kind of expedition. "No, please," she says.

"OK."

He relaxes. They lie there, and finally she hears his breathing deepen again, and she thinks, This is all right, just like this. Lie here and listen. What's the point of dreading the morning? It's not morning *yet*. Listen to Oliver's breathing and Turtle's breathing and that water bird, and let this night go on and on.

But the sun comes up in a rush.

Turtle makes them huevos rancheros and a paste of black frijoles. An old woman brings them a basket of warm weighty tortillas, corn-yellow.

Juan Calmo comes by and he takes Oliver out to show him around.

Then Annie and Turtle walk on down through pear orchards and through open fields to a hidden stream-gorge, a waterfall. The sunlight is blinding, the sky is an immaculate blue and so dark it wouldn't surprise her to find stars in it, broad-day constellations.

They sit on a mossy rock by the stream and he says, "Well, now will you tell me?"

She tells him.

She tells him everything—but it's all *one* thing. It's all about the Teacher. It's everything she's managed to glean or guess about his workings. How he seduces. How he overwhelms. How he always gets there before you, how you can never know how far he'll go.

By the time she's done, it's nearly noon. The sky is no longer quite so blue. The mist is starting to flow down from the mountains.

"So no one knows you're here?" says Turtle.

"Not yet. I don't think."

He considers a moment. "Well, you've come to the right place. Get the hell out of there, that's what you should have done from the start. You're safe here, Annie. This is about as far away from Westchester as you can get. The people here are my friends."

"I know," she says.

"Most of the men have fought in the army, or against the army. Or both. They have rifles. They don't mind using them. It'd be harder than hell for anyone to get in here and hurt you."

"OK."

"You'll like it here. I'll take you up tomorrow and show you the mountaintops. There are Mayan altars on all the mountaintops."

She smiles. "I wish I had more time."

"More time? God, Annie, listen, you can stay here as long as you—"

Then he catches her drift. "Hold it. You *can't*—"

"I have to, Turtle. I have to go back. But I need you to take care of Oliver. There's no one else in the world I'd trust."

"Annie, wait a minute."

"If he comes back with me, that man will kill him. You've got to take him."

"No. Wait. You're not leaving! No way I'm letting you go back!"

"You can't stop me."

"Annie."

"That's not your choice. Your choice is, you can take care of Oliver, or you can send him home with me to be killed. I'm asking you to take care of him."

"For how long?"

"Till it's finished."

"What do you mean, till it's finished? Jesus, what are you asking me, Annie?"

"I'm asking you to raise my child. Keep him healthy, he doesn't have to be a big success or anything. Just give him whatever you can. I don't care if he's an artist, I don't care if he goes to college, I don't care if he stays here and raises sheep for the rest of his life, just tell him every night how much I love him, that's all you have to do. I know how much I'm asking. I know it's *too* much. But there's no one else, there's nobody else I can go to."

"But why do you want to go back there?"

She stares at the waterfall. "I need to."

"Is there something you don't have? Something you forgot, what? If there's anything—"

"I need to go back."

"*Why?* To see that man again?"

"Yes."

"*Why?*"

"Turtle, tell Oliver about Juliet. Tell him what happened. Tell him I'm sorry I didn't say goodbye, but I can't. If I tried to say goodbye, I wouldn't—how could I do that? Say *goodbye*? Don't ask me that. Don't ask me, don't. I'm not strong enough. He'd talk me into staying. Or you would. And then sooner or later the Teacher would find us here."

"No he won't, Annie. He'll quit looking."

"He'll never quit looking."

"How do you know that? You don't know that."

"He'll never leave us. Turtle, what we've been through together? The Teacher and I? It's like some kind of marriage."

OLIVER and Juan Calmo are up in the old ruined church. A narrow stone gallery wraps around and overlooks what used to be the nave— but now the roof is gone and the pews are gone and what's down there is a sort of ragged sun-washed courtyard. There *is* a gnarled makeshift cross. And an old man kneeling before it, chanting. A fire smoulders around the base of the cross. The old man has a live turkey in his hands, and he holds it aloft. The turkey is struggling to get away, craning its neck, its wattle shivering. Oliver and Juan Calmo watch from the gallery. They crouch behind the stone railing and peek over it. They see the old man slash the turkey's throat and shake the blood into the fire. Long rips of smoke issuing.

"Whoa," Oliver whispers.

A small whisper. But the ruins pick it up and toss it about, and the old man hears.

He raises his eyes to the boys.

They duck and giggle. Juan Calmo, still in a crouch, shuffles down the gallery and Oliver follows.

They take a left and break into a run, skimming along the top of what used to be the wall of some side building. Stunning view of T'ui Cuch and of the mountains around it. At the wall's end they come to a flight of rough white stairs. Juan Calmo holds up. He sits on the stairs. He pulls a couple of pearlike fruits from his pocket, and offers one to Oliver. Bitter—his face shrivels, and Juan Calmo grins at him. The crackling sunlight everywhere. Music coming up from the village. Oliver can look down and see a marimba band playing in the little square. Gearing up for some sort of festival they're supposed to be having soon, something about All Saints' Day. And also in the square, not far from where the band is playing, he spots that battered pickup, the one he rode in on. It's full of T'ui Cuchians, waiting for the ride down to Huehuetenango. The pickup's engine is running, little clumps of black smoke. Delicious, to sprawl back on these steps in this thick light and suck this impossible fruit and watch the day go by down there—

There's a woman and a man approaching the pickup. The woman is carrying a suitcase.

It's Mom.

She's leaving. She's leaving him here.

Oliver rises from the steps. Rises slowly. He can't believe this. He stares. He doesn't move. He watches her lug that suitcase. The driver of the pickup takes it from her and hefts it to some T'ui Cuch men in the back. Hands reach out to help her up. Oliver's watching all this unfold as though he has no presence here, no power other than the power to witness.

And then Juan Calmo says, "*Qué pasa?*" and Oliver remembers that he has a voice too. He shouts:

"*Mom!*"

But with that music and the sputtering wind and the distance no one can hear him. Nobody even glances up to these ruins.

He starts down the steps. Three steps at a time, then down the slope of the hill, taking huge risky strides. Down a narrow beanpatch lane with goats squinting and dogs yapping at his passage. He slips in the mud and almost wipes out, but he does a wild dance, his feet falling all around him, and somehow he keeps his balance, he keeps running. A knot of chickens, a donkey laden with corn shuck. Then a stretch of open road, then a sharp turn, then he blasts into the square.

Turtle. The marimba band, the crowd.

But the pickup is driving away.

One last glimpse of her.

"MOM! MOM! MOM!"

She's looking back, and though she doesn't acknowledge him, he knows that she sees him.

His breath is raw in his lungs, sandpapery. He casts one look of bewildered fury at Turtle and keeps running. Hopeless because he'll never catch the pickup now, but how could she do this, leave him here? He keeps after her. Even after the pickup vanishes he keeps running. Dogs at his heels, children staring, can't even hear the pickup's engine now, just his own gasping and the marimba. The pig that barked at them yesterday comes out and barks at him now.

ANNIE, the next morning, in the office of the New York State Troopers, refusing to answer Investigator Carew.

Does he think he can stare her down? Think again.

Eventually he makes a face and lowers his eyes to his desk. "Ms. Laird, if you won't tell us where your son is, how can we shield him?"

"I don't *want* you to shield him. I want you to do your job."

He bristles. "What's my job, Ms. Laird? Tell me my job."

"Your job is to investigate murder. Juliet Applegate's murder."

"Well, we're doing that."

"And?"

"It'll take time," he says.

"Nothing?"

"Not yet." He makes a fist with one hand and draws his finger around the knuckles. Looping up and down.

She presses. "But you do believe she was killed? That the Teacher killed her?"

"What I believe doesn't matter one way or the other without evidence."

"Then find some evidence."

"We're trying, Ms. Laird. You're going to help us?"

"Yes. What do you want, do you want me to wear one of those, those radio things?"

340

"No, that's too dangerous. If he figured out you were wired—"

"He wouldn't."

"If he decided to pat you down—"

"He wouldn't," she says. "He thinks I'm timid. He's used to me being timid. He'd never touch me if I didn't want him to. He likes to be thought of as a gentleman."

"Ms. Laird, I think a better idea, a safer idea? Is for you to get him to come to some place where we've already hidden a mike—"

She shakes her head.

He says, "We'll be right there."

"But *he* won't. He wouldn't come anywhere with me if it was my idea—he'd sense the trick. You don't know him the way I do. Listen, please, give me the wire. Please. One time, that's all I need, just once. I'll get you such juicy stuff you can put them *all* away. Boffano, rest of his life. The Teacher and his sidekick, fry them, Jesus. You wanted my help, here it is. I know the risks. They're mine. I'll take them. It's a worse risk to let him get away."

THE TEACHER hears the car in his drive. He goes to the school-house door and waits for Eddie to trudge up.

Eddie says, "Just talked to Tony Maretti. Annie called him. She's back. She came back like you said she would. She said she wants to see you tomorrow at one."

Vincent's breath comes a little quicker, with a slight push on the exhale, almost a laugh. The ghost of a crow of triumph.

"Come in," he says.

Eddie shakes his head. "Nah, I just wanted to let you know. I shouldn't have come here at all."

"No one knows where I live except you, Eddie. Come in."

"Gotta run."

"I'll need your help with this."

Eddie makes a face. "You know I'm not too wild about this fuckin deal."

"I know."

"I think we ought to shove it all."

"And I keep encouraging you to have patience."

"Shove the whole load a shit. Shove it, and clear out."

"Eddie, she came back."

"I'm outta this one. You hear me? I mean it's time to leave her the fuck alone. Her and her kid, you can't play with that no more, Vincent, it's time to shove that whole load—"

"Eddie?"

"Yeah."

"Look at me."

"Yeah."

"I know you're concerned. I also know that you're my oldest friend, and I need your help."

"Oh Jesus Christ."

"Eddie."

CAREW's colleague Sue Ranzi checks under Annie Laird's armpit. Feels the tiny Technidyne transmitter, no bigger than a pack of matches, and its humble battery. The antenna runs under the elastic of her bra to the back. The microphone's up front, between her breasts. All secure.

Sue Ranzi turns to Carew and nods.

In a quiet voice Carew says, "OK, Ms. Laird. Remember we'll be tracking your transmitter. No matter where you go, you call for help and we'll be there right away."

She says, "But you'll stay back, you promise? You won't let him see you?"

"I promise."

He turns and Murray Randall, wearing the headphones, gives him a nod—he's receiving perfectly.

"OK then," says Carew. "We're set."

Says Annie, "Can I go to the bathroom?"

"Sure."

She smiles her vague drift-away smile. She goes down the hall.

Harry Beard asks, "What do you think?"

Says Carew, "I don't know what to think. Usually a few hours before a setup like this, I start getting a hard-on for it? Antsy? This time, I don't, this time nothing. I don't really know who this woman is. I don't really know who we got there."

Beard nods. "Sometimes you think she's all there and sometimes you think she's off on Planet X."

"All I want to know is, is she on our side?"

"Well hell, she wouldn't be doing this if she weren't."

"You're sure?" Carew wonders. "She's on our side?"

"Gotta be."

"Or has she been jumping through that bastard's hoops so long she's starting to like it?"

EDDIE pulls up to the curb at the Brewster train station. Annie comes out quickly and gets into his car.

As they pull away he asks her how she is.

"Fine," she says. Scarcely opening her mouth. "Great."

They drive north for a few miles.

He tries to say it.

"I wanted, Annie, I wanted to tell you something. I mean, I want to tell you what I think about all this—"

She says, "You know what?"

"What?"

She says, "I don't really give a shit what you think about all this."

That's all she says. Not another word, and he churns inside. Hates this bitch. Also feels sorry for her. Also he's scared because the chances are not inconsiderable that she's rolling with the law now.

He keeps his mouth shut but his head keeps grinding out all this trash.

He hates this. He hates this whole fucking deal. He hates this.

They ride in silence till they get to a weedy turnaround up in North Stoneleigh. Opposite the old shut-down Mexican restaurant, with its giant sombrero creaking in the wind. He pulls over. Soon Vincent drives up.

She gets out of Eddie's car. Vincent rolls down his window and he's about to say something to her, but she puts her finger to her lips and shakes her head.

She points to her chest.

She looks up and down Route 22. No cars, nobody.

Then she unbuttons her shirt. A tiny microphone is clipped to her bra, between her breasts. She's wired. She's wearing a fucking wire.

Jesus Christ. Eddie wonders what he's said, what that wire might have picked up—but then he remembers how she shut him up, how she wouldn't let him say anything to her.

Now she hands him a note:

> Eddie, don't say a word. Drive around,
> drive anywhere, give us half an hour, pick
> me up here.

Meanwhile she tugs gently at the surgical tape under her armpit. She uproots the transmitter and disengages the antenna from her bra. Vincent watches with a small grin. She sets the wire carefully on the seat next to Eddie. Then she shuts the door, and gets into Vincent's Range Rover.

So. Fuckin Vincent, he was right about her all along.

Fuckin Vincent. What is it about him that always gets to these women?

He gives Eddie a wink and the two of them drive away and leave him sitting there watching after them.

THE TEACHER asks her, "What do you think of them?"

"Who?"

"Your guardians. The troopers."

"They're clueless," says Annie.

"They're only trying to protect you." He turns at a narrow dirt lane, and they drive up into a meadow full of autumn ghost-wild-flowers. He stops the car.

"No, they're incompetent," she says. "They're bureaucrats. They irritate me. What irritates me most is their weakness."

They take a walk through the fields of this old farm that he bought a few years ago. It's risky to bring her here, he supposes, but it's only one risk among thousands. It makes him smile. All this unseen, looming peril—as he and Annie cross a pleasant little footbridge and then amble along a bridle trail. Cottonwoods, mostly bare, lining the stream. Hierarchy of crows in that black-cherry tree over there. Risk, what is risk? Risk is a gift that teaches us what we love.

He says to her, "Still, Annie. I think you should try to forgive them. They're weak because they deny the Tao. They deny the Tao because they're afraid. But their hearts are fine, they love you, they—"

"Don't tell me that," she says.

She stops where she is. She says, "*You* tell me to forgive them? *You?* You bastard! I hate you, you know that? I'd kill you if I could!

348

You talk about anyone's heart, is that the lesson for today, Teacher? Or is it how terror is doing me so much good, how *strong* all this is making me? Or is it how your love will save my child—"

"Annie—"

"Shut up!"

They stand beneath the naked cottonwoods. It hurts him to see her in such anguish, but he loves the weave of her hair, and he loves the rich weave of the yellow grasses on the slope behind her.

She says, "Don't smile at me. Don't ever fucking think you can smile at me, I would *kill* you if I could! Do you think I even listen to your shit? Don't even *look* at me!"

With an infinitesimal shrug, he lowers his eyes. But he knows that he hasn't quite extinguished his sheepish and unconquerable grin.

"I HATE YOU!"

Then she walks on. He walks beside her, perhaps a step behind.

After a while, though, she pauses to pluck the last brown leaf off a white oak, and she says, "What I hate the most? What I hate the most is that you're right. I *am* stronger. You're right, OK? Does that make you happy?"

"Yes."

She says—and now something softer, more yielding, something like resignation has crept into her voice: "I went back into my studio again, and looked at all my old work, and it all seemed restrained. *Smothered.* No guts, no pain, no fire. That's the way my whole life was. Smother the passion. Anything that frightens me, lock it out. Eyes down, keep marching. OK? And now I don't want to live like that anymore. Does that please you, what a good student I am? Does it?"

"Yes."

"Well, it shouldn't. Because it makes me hate you even more."

He swallows. Tension in his rib cage.

"Annie."

Now when he speaks her name he finds he can't scrape together enough breath to speak above a whisper. "And is that, Annie, is that *all* you feel?"

"Stop it," she says. She won't look at him. "Please. Stop it."

But he knows what she wants to say.

In silence then they climb a long broad open slope. Loosestrife and goldenrod, going off their colors. And Queen Anne's lace. Halfway up she stops again, turns, and gazes at the view. She says, "This is

what I don't understand, though. Zach. You have all this strength.
But still you work for Louie Boffano. For that, that—"

"That goon?"

"Well. If he's a friend of yours—"

He laughs. "Louie Boffano's not anyone's friend. He's a freak.
He's a monster. But he intrigues me. Does it seem depraved—my
fascination for that man?"

"I don't know. Yes. Or no, maybe not—"

"Everything about that family fascinates me. It always has."

"Then why don't you run that family yourself?"

She casts him a quick glance.

A metallic, acquisitive glance. My God, he thinks, this is Annie?
Starving-artist Annie, *my* Annie?

He laughs again and tells her, "Maybe someday I will."

"Soon?" she says.

"Maybe. I'm in no hurry. I'm relaxing. I'm cultivating allies, bring-
ing them up through the ranks. Really, Annie, I do very little. I only
stretch my limbs. My actions are the most trivial imaginable. Yet the
power does flow toward me."

"And will you get rid of Boffano?"

Again her directness delights him. "Oh, I don't know. You think
it would make any difference? I might discard old Louie, or I might
not. Perhaps I think it's wise to have a figurehead. To take the heat
off me. Let him be the mountain, I'll be the ravine."

"But how—I mean, Zach, how do you do all this? How do you
communicate with him without the police knowing?"

He shrugs. "Messages. Couriers, go-betweens."

"You never see him?"

"Once in a while. On Sundays at five he goes to visit his family
tomb at Greenview Cemetery. The authorities never bother to follow
him in there."

"Today?" she says.

"What?"

"Today is Sunday. Will you see him today?"

"Should I?"

"I just—I don't know. It *is* exciting, Zach. It's compelling. OK?
You've shown me that. What I still haven't learned, though, what I
wish I understood is *why* it's so compelling."

He tells her, "We love temporal power because it all derives from the Unvarying Power. From the Tao. That's what draws us to it."

"I'm not sure I get that."

He grins. "I'm not either. And there are times when I think I've had my fill of it. More and more now. Enough of these lessons in power. I think maybe I'm ready to learn another kind of power. Give all this up. Go hide out in a monastery somewhere. Maybe the Ajanta caves near Hyderābād. Somewhere clean and spare and simple. Or even better . . . even better, Annie. Come look at this."

He reaches, takes her hand.

She doesn't pull away.

They walk together up the hill.

They quicken their pace, and he leads her to the top of the rise. From there they can look down to the other side and see the old sagging farmhouse under its stand of sugar maples. The windows all broken, the porch pilasters rotten. As they gaze at it, he strokes her palm with his fingertips. The lightest touch possible—but he can feel how it makes her shiver.

He tells her, "I'd like to restore this house. It'll cost me more than building from scratch. But think of it, Annie: a farmhouse with calico curtains and a rocking chair on the porch. And polished floors. And kids. A kid like Oliver. And then no more trafficking with power. Then nothing but love. Do you think I could turn myself into sheer love, Annie? Do you think I have *that* power?"

He doesn't look at her, but he can feel the warmth of her.

He says, "I want to find a lover who's creative and maybe a little chaotic, a chaos to balance my structure, does that, does that—? Annie? Let me say this, Annie. OK? I'm sorry you hate me. Because I love you."

They stand there gazing at that house. Is she as scared as he is? he wonders. He's scared, but he's devoted to his fear. He's devoted to the feel of the big clapper ringing inside his hollow chest.

He turns to look at her, and then she meets his eyes and she reaches up and lays her hands on his temples and draws his face down to her.

She weeps as his lips touch hers.

No tongue, no pressure. Just the touch of her lips against his, the taste of her tears.

Never been kissed that softly in his life.

He leans into her but she pulls back. "No," she says. "No."

She turns and hurries away from him, back down the wide-open slope.

He catches up with her at the car. She's standing at her door. "Drive me back," she says.

"When will I see you again?"

It's hard for him to have to *ask*. But it's hard for her, too. She can't speak. She seems as though she's going to shake her head, but then she's saying, "Soon. Yes. But not tomorrow. Soon. Oh, give me time, Zach. Please."

ANNIE, forty minutes later, is back in her favorite FBI cubicle, and Carew is giving her hell. He's flushed and squinty-eyed, hoarse.

"What the HELL were you doing getting out by Papa Taco?"

"Excuse me?" she says.

"On Route 22. In Stoneleigh. You were riding with the guy you call Johnny, he pulled off the road. We heard the door open, we heard the door shut. Why? What was going on?"

"He told me to get out."

"Oh yeah? How come *we* didn't hear that?"

"He *motioned* me, OK? I thought that's where I'd be meeting the Teacher. But after a minute nobody showed up, so he told—he *motioned* me to get back in the car."

"And then?"

"And then we drove around."

"Without saying a word?"

"He wouldn't talk to me."

"Maybe that's because you told him to shut up."

"Maybe. Did you *want* me to talk to Johnny? I thought you wanted me to talk to the Teacher."

"Then half an hour later you went back to the same place?"

"Yeah. Same thing happened all over again."

"That doesn't make sense to me."

"For some reason," she says, "the Teacher didn't show up. I think he must have guessed what's going on."

"How would he have guessed?"

She shrugs. "I don't know. You figure it out. Me, I'm going home."

He shakes his head. "We have a lot of things to talk about."

"Great." She grins. "We'll talk tomorrow. We'll set up another sting, huh? Oh boy. It'll be a blast. But right now I'm exhausted and I want to go home."

She rises.

"We're not done, Ms. Laird."

"I'm going home."

"Sit down. I want to know what the hell is going on in your head."

"What's going on in my head? My child. I'm thinking about my child. That's all. Nothing else. Nothing fancy. Just my child."

"Sit down."

"No." She fixes him in her gaze. "You want more out of me today, arrest me. Get me a lawyer. Otherwise I'll be in tomorrow. Tomorrow afternoon, say four o'clock?"

"Annie—"

"Don't call me Annie."

"Ms. Laird—"

"Meanwhile, get fucked."

She walks out.

She gets in her car and drives toward Greenview Cemetery.

FRANKIE and Archangelo stand guard at the Boffano mausoleum while Louie Boffano communes with his late beloved mother. Frankie's looking down the long corridor of angels when suddenly this woman appears. Wearing a black windbreaker with the hood up, walking swiftly toward them.

He barks the news to the others: "Who the fuck is that?"

Can't be a mourner. No mourners are allowed in here this late on Sunday. Except Louie Boffano.

Louie turns and sees her himself. "Wait a *minute*," he says.

Frankie knows that if anyone were of a mind to, it'd be a good time to kill Louie Boffano. After his stretch in stir, he's vulnerable. He doesn't have his land legs under him yet. This babe coming on, coming so quick out of nowhere—this babe could be bad news.

Frankie steps back to stand in front of Louie. He calls out, "Hold it!"

She keeps coming.

He reaches into his jacket and puts his hand on his Glock. "I said hold it!"

She keeps coming. "Mr. Boffano?" she says. "I need to talk to you."

Nothing in her hands. Her handbag's slung over her shoulder—no immediate problem there. Unless she's planning on strangling Louie with her bare hands, we're all right, Frankie thinks.

But Archangelo isn't feeling so relaxed. He pulls out his piece and drops into a stance and bellows: "STOP OR I'LL BLOW YOUR FUCKIN HEAD OFF!"

Just like a *police*.

Jesus.

It works, though, the woman holds up. Ten yards away. She stands there on the grass in the corridor of angels.

"Archangelo," Louie chides gently. He waves the pistol down. Then he asks the woman, "What can I do for you?"

She says, "Do you recognize me?"

"Yeah, sure. The lady juror. What do you want?"

"I have something for you."

Reaching for her handbag.

Frankie shouts, "DON'T TOUCH THE BAG!"

She shrugs. She dips one shoulder and lets the bag slump off of her. "Then you come get it."

"What is it?"

"It's a peace offering," she says. "I want to make an arrangement with you. I give you what's in my bag. And I promise I won't cooperate with the state investigators. And you leave me alone. Me and my family and my friends."

Says gracious Louie, "Of course I would never hurt your family. Nor you, nor nobody. I don't even know you, why would I—"

"Swear it, Louie, and I'll give you your gift."

"Well, I tell you the truth, I'm not interested in your fuckin gift."

"Oh, yes you are," she says, and goes for the bag again.

"DON'T!" cries Frankie.

She smiles at him. "You think I would want to kill Louie Boffano?" Contemptuous sneer when she speaks his name. "But he's nothing to me. Why would I want to kill *him*?"

Louie signals Frankie to ease up.

The woman picks up her handbag, and opens it. She brings out a minicassette recorder. She presses the PLAY button.

They hear the Teacher's laughter.

"Louie Boffano's not anyone's friend. He's a freak. He's a monster. But he intrigues me. Does it seem depraved—my fascination for that man?"

She stops the tape. "Did you enjoy that, Mr. Boffano? Would you like to hear more?"

"When did you tape this?" says Louie.

"Today."

"Who wired you?"

"I wired myself. It's an Olympus something—I bought it last night on Forty-second Street."

Louie holds out his hand. He wants her to bring the thing to him. Frankie can see that his hand is trembling.

"Louie," Frankie warns him under his breath, "this could be some kind of tricky shit. The Teacher wouldn't, he wouldn't—"

"Get that thing from her," Louie tells him.

She says, "No. Not till you swear. Swear you'll never hurt me. Not me, not my child, not my friends—"

"Just gimme the tape," he says. "I swear I'm outta your life forever."

She fixes him with her huge eyes, with the black pouches under them. Frankie thinks, Isn't she the one Eddie called a beauty? But she's no beauty. She's a scary damn witch.

She walks up to Louie, and she hands him the machine.

"Waste no time," she tells him.

She turns and walks away. As Louie finds the PLAY button and depresses it. They watch her walk down the corridor of mausoleums. On the tape they hear her asking the Teacher, *"Then why don't you run that family yourself?"*

And they hear the Teacher laugh and tell her, *"Maybe someday I will."*

They watch her disappear among the graves.

On the tape the Teacher is saying, *"I might discard old Louie, or I might not. Perhaps I think it's wise to have a figurehead. To take the heat off me. Let him be the mountain, I'll be the ravine."*

14

Struggle as hard as you like and I won't love you any less for it. . . .

THE TEACHER, bright and early on Monday morning, rides in Eddie's car down the long rutted drive of what was once St. Theresa's on the Hudson. Used to be a private school for girls, until that went belly up a few years ago. The campus is still used in the summer by the Fresh Air Fund, but the rest of the year it's deserted.

Eddie pulls up beside a cedar-and-glass cafeteria. They get out and wait. The Teacher rests his briefcase on the hood of Eddie's car, and gazes down through the chestnut oaks, through branches as dark as the lead in stained-glass windows, to a shattered view of the river. He waits calmly, saying nothing.

But Eddie keeps checking his watch and muttering, and finally he says, "Hey, Vincent, if you're worried about this, let's get out of here."

"I'm not worried."

"You're not?"

"Are you worried, Eddie?"

"Yeah. To be honest? Yeah."

The Teacher smiles. "Louie's not going to hurt me. Louie and I, we go back a long way."

"Yeah, I know that."

"He says he wants to talk about the deal with the Calabrians. Why shouldn't I believe him?"

" 'Cause why is it such a fuckin emergency? Why does he want to see you *today*?"

"Louie's been in prison. He's restless. He wants to get moving on our plans. Seems reasonable to me."

"I dunno, Vincent."

The Teacher ambles up to the cafeteria's door, to examine an alabaster Virgin in her alabaster niche. What do they find to worship, he wonders, in such a bland, expressionless totem?

Except perhaps that her eyes look a little like Annie's eyes.

He waits.

At last the black Lincoln appears. Louie Boffano and his party—his brother and Frankie and Archangelo. Frankie gets out of the backseat and stands by the open door. Louie, in the front passenger seat, asks the Teacher, "What's in the briefcase?"

"Spreadsheets. Plans for the Calabrian deal. Isn't that—?"

"Check it, Frankie."

Frankie opens the briefcase, rifles through the papers, feeling for a false bottom.

"Nah, it's just fuckin paperwork, like he says."

"Search him."

Frankie pats him down.

"He's clean."

"All right. Gotta check these things, right, Vincent? You never know, right? Come on in."

The Teacher gets in the back. But when Eddie moves toward the door Louie says, "Ah, not you. We don't need you for this one, Eddie."

Eddie peers anxiously into the car.

Says the Teacher, "I'll be fine, Eddie. I'll see you later."

Says Eddie, "Well, I'll wait for you here then."

Says Louie, "Nah, go on home. Why wait? Wait for what? You just take the day off. How's your daughter? How's Roseanne?"

"She's OK, Louie. But—"

"Spend some time with her. Give her a smooch from Uncle Louie, huh? We'll get Vincent home."

They drive off, down the narrow road.

The Teacher is squeezed between Frankie and Archangelo in the backseat. Louie sits up front. His brother Joseph is at the wheel.

"Vincent," says Louie, and he turns to give him a smile. "I'm glad you came."

The Teacher shrugs. "Command performance, what could I do?"

The lane gets rougher as they descend toward the river. A gopher-haunted soccer field opens to their left, and they start to angle across it. But in the middle of the field, they stop.

Louie turns again. "More than twenty years we've been working together, isn't that right, Vincent? Any time you had some fancy idea, well shit, I got the manpower, I got the organization, we worked it out. We both got rich. More than twenty years of this, you know?"

The Teacher has a sparkle in his eye. "An extraordinary alliance, yes."

"But you know what?" says Louie. "I don't know the first fuckin thing about what makes you tick. In all those twenty years. Didn't learn nothing."

The Teacher tells him, "It seems simple to me."

"It does?"

"It seems simple."

Says Louie, "This woman, this juror woman, yesterday at my mother's grave she comes to me, she says you was saying ugly things about me."

"Annie came to see *you*?"

"You spoke ugly about me?"

The Teacher ponders a moment. "Well, nothing really ugly, Louie. Dismissive, rather. I think I called you a fool, or a freak, or some such—"

"You called me a motherfuckin *monster*! Don't bother to fuckin deny it, shitsmear, 'cause it's on tape."

The Teacher chuckles. "I wouldn't deny it. I'd only deny that I spoke with malice. Not at all. I spoke with indifference."

"You said you'd fuckin discard me—"

"I said I *might* discard you. I might or I might not. I said it didn't matter to me. Does that offend you?"

"Offend me? You *cocksucker*."

"There are no blood ties between us, Louie. We never pretended to be soulmates. I'm sure you and your brother here have called me worse things than a freak."

Joseph breaks in. "You want to know what *I* call you? I call you a fuckin sicko pervert, like you always been. When you was a kid you was a sicko. I told Louie, I said stay away from this cunt."

Says the Teacher, "This is such a useful dialogue, Joseph. I'm so glad you're sharing these feelings."

Joseph leans over the seat and spits in his face. "Fuck you, asshole. Get him outta here. Let's get this over with."

Archangelo opens his door and steps out. "Let's go."

Frankie pushes the muzzle of his Glock into the Teacher's temple. *"Move."*

The Teacher slides across the seat and gets out.

They walk across the desolate field. Frankie on one side of the Teacher, Archangelo on the other. While Louie and his brother wait in the car.

They come to a rock wall and a belt of woods. The Teacher looks through the trees, down to the railroad tracks and the river. He says, "Hey guys? Do I get a last request?"

"What?"

"I want you to do something for me."

"What?"

"I want you to watch Louie's car."

He digs the heel of his hand into his thigh—pushes down on the trigger of the transmitter in his pocket. He doesn't get to see the blast directly. Only the flash against the trees and then the *whump* and the glass shattering, and afterwards somebody—he thinks it's Joseph Boffano—shrieking with pain.

He turns to Archangelo, who's gazing stupidly at the wreckage of the car. The Teacher takes Archangelo's Beretta 92 away from him. Then Frankie pours three shots into Archangelo's left ear.

Frankie and the Teacher hasten back to the car. The passenger door is open, and Louie has crawled out. He's missing an arm. He's covered with pieces of his brother. His face has come loose and it hangs down from his chin like a bib. The Teacher kneels and says, "I'm sorry this was so untidy. I couldn't fit much Flex-X in that briefcase. Forgive me?"

He fires into Louie Boffano's head, shielding himself from the blood-spatter with an open palm. Then he and Frankie hurry across the soccer field and up the hill.

On the way he says, "Listen, Frankie, I'm grateful to you for tipping me off, I really am."

"It was nothin."

"I value loyalty."

"No big deal."

"But I have to tell you, Frankie—as for these promises I made about taking over Louie's operation and setting *you* up as boss? On further consideration, I think those were all cloud-castles. Do we have enough sway in the organization? You and I? I think we don't. Besides, I'm preoccupied—I've got this tragedy of Annie Laird and her son thrashing around in my head."

"Wait a second," says Frankie.

He stops, under the dripping trees. "What the fuck are you *talking* about? We made *plans*, we got—"

"The truth, Frankie? I don't think I have the patience for any fancy family footwork just now. Will you excuse me?"

"What the *FUCK* ARE YOU—"

Frankie scrabbles under his jacket, gets hold of his pistol. The Teacher shoots him in the carotid artery, and Frankie's neck snaps out long whips of blood. The Teacher has to stand to one side to avoid the spray. He slams the butt of his HK into Frankie's hand and he can hear tiny bones breaking. Frankie's pistol drops and the Teacher catches it.

"God *damn*," says Frankie.

Those arcs of blood-spume, one after the other.

The Teacher heads up the path at a rapid pace. But Frankie comes running after him.

"What the fuck is the matter with you!" he still wants to know. The words come out soggy with blood, but they come. And the Teacher, as he trots up the road, turns to look at him and to smile wonderingly.

He says, "Frankie, how in the world are you still able to talk?"

"I don't trust you for shit!" says Frankie. He puts on a burst of speed and tries to grab at the Teacher.

The Teacher bats his hands away. "Frankie, you're not thinking."

"Shut up. I don't trust you no more, I don't trust you for *shit*," Frankie says, and then his eyes roll back in his head, and he pitches forward and his face drops into the mud.

SARI is driving slowly on a dirt road near Garrison. This is where Eben told her she could find him. But there seems to be no one here. Only these barren trees and the railroad tracks and the river below. Then suddenly he's in front of her car, standing in the road, and she slams on the brakes, skids on the wet mud. He gets in. He's grinning. Blood on his jacket and on his shirt. His hair is wild, his irises are plates of hammered gold, and he kisses her passionately.

He tells her, "Drive, lover."

She drives to the end of the dirt road, then turns onto a blacktop road that loops along at the foot of great estates. Glimpses of Tudor mansions.

He says, "I thought perhaps you wouldn't come."

"Of course I came. Tell me what happened." She's begging her heart to ease up on her.

"No, I really shouldn't."

"Tell me, Eben."

"Better not to involve you."

"Are they chasing you?"

"Yes."

"The police?"

"Yes."

"Are you innocent?"

"Of what?"

"Of whatever they think you did."

"What man born to woman is innocent? But I was trying to save a child's life. I struggled in the name of love."

In a patch of woods, she pulls over. Not enough room on the shoulder to get all the way off the road, but it's a lonely road—there are no cars coming anyway.

She turns to him.

"Did you fuck *her*?"

This feeling that she has for him, she can't call it love anymore. No name for it. Just lips inside of her skull, sucking at her brain, that's what you could call it. As though her brain were a rotten black lemon.

He sighs. "Why are you asking me all this?"

"Did you fuck her?"

"Have I made love to Annie? No."

"Who is she then? Don't give me any bullshit because—"

"Sari. I won't tell you any lies. But I shouldn't say who she really is."

"No? Well, that's too bad, Eben. Because you know what? If you told me the truth, I'd do something for you. I'd tell *you* something. Something about a little trip to Guatemala."

She turns to look at the gold flecks in his eyes. She sees them shimmer like struck gongs.

"Where?" he asks her.

"No." She shakes her head. "First tell me *why* you want to know."

"Because if I know I can rescue her. And her child. I can rescue them both."

"Rescue them from what?"

"Not from tragedy. They can't evade fate. But from mendacity and hypocrisy, yes. I can't tell you any more, though. You have to trust me. Don't you trust me?"

"No."

"Then simply love me, Sari."

"I think I was insane to love you."

He says, "Tell me. Where did Annie go?"

"No!" She's adamant. "First I have to understand what's happening."

"What's happening?" He laughs. "Certain constellations are burning up the sky. Scorching the heavens, destroying all in their path. Now what in this universe can shelter us from such danger? Do you know? Do you know, Sari?" He puts one finger under her chin and lifts it up, so she'll have to look at him again. He tells her, "Love. Of course. Nothing less. Love will deliver us. Where did she go, Sari? Lover? *Tell me.*"

She looks out the window. She looks at him. Maybe he's right, she thinks, maybe she ought to stop fighting this and simply follow her heart.

No! Her heart's misled. He's a liar. *He's a cancer.*

But he's the man I love. And love will deliver us.

He's grinning at her. He says, "Where did Annie Laird go in Guatemala?"

She hates him.

She looks at her lap and says, "She didn't go at all."

She can feel his eyes upon her.

She says, "I have friends in the airlines, I got them to look through every damn passenger list on every flight to Guatemala City in the last week. I made up every excuse I could think of. I was breaking the law, and I could lose my ARC number, but I wanted to do this for you, Eben, because you asked me to. Annie Laird's name never turned up."

He mutters something under his breath.

Then she says, "But guess what? There was somebody else from Pharaoh, New York, who flew to Guatemala City. A Dr. Juliet Applegate. I remembered meeting her at the poetry cafe and how you were flirting with her, so it got my curiosity going. Maybe she's Annie Laird's friend? Maybe she went for her? The agent who booked the flight, I know her a little. I called her and told her Juliet's father had died, I told her we had to find her. And she told me that Juliet Applegate had asked for a connecting flight to this village, T'ui Cuch, but there aren't any—"

Eben's glowing. "Sari," he says softly. "Sari! You're astounding!"

He takes her head in his hands and gives her such a warm sweet affectionate kiss and then laughs so heartily that her heart can't help but warm a little toward him.

"This makes you happy?" she says.

"Oh yes! It's revealing. It opens avenues that I had imagined were completely shut."

"But who are these women, Eben? Juliet Applegate and Annie Laird, if they're not your lovers—"

But by now Eben isn't listening to her. He's thinking. He stares at the dashboard.

Then his head stirs slightly, an almost imperceptible nodding. He says with sudden decision in his voice, "Sari, I need this car."

"Where do you want to go?"

"No, actually I need the car with you out of it. I need to be alone right now."

"You what? You . . . Is this a joke?"

He laughs. "It is! Yes. But it's also true that I couldn't possibly handle listening to your vapid prattle just now. Sari lover."

"You son of a *bitch*! I leave my job in the middle of the day, look what I'm doing for you, and you have the fucking nerve—"

"Please give me the keys and get out."

"Fuck you! What are you talking about? What, do you think I'm going to *walk*?"

Eben sighs. "No." He sighs again. "No, I guess that wouldn't be practical. All right, wait."

He reaches over and jerks the keys from the ignition. He gets out and goes around back and pops open the trunk. Then he comes and opens her door. She feels the pistol barrel against her neck. He tells her, "Come on. I want you to get in the trunk."

She looks sidelong at him. "Eben."

"Now. Sari. Or I *will* kill you."

"Eben!"

"Sari, I'm grateful to you for your help, and I do love you, and I don't want you to suffer, but the Tao is restless today, today all the Tao's patience is flowing in another direction."

He takes her elbow, hauls her out of the car. In a daze she lets him lead her back to the trunk. He pushes her head down. She puts her palms on the felt floor of the trunk and tries to resist. But this is a dream, she doesn't understand any of it, she doesn't know what to do. He stands behind her and lifts her legs, folds them, and she falls forward onto her elbows. He tells her, "Sari, I'm sorry about this, I ask your forgiveness. But if you'll just do this, you'll be all right. Nothing bad will happen to you."

She shouldn't trust him.

She should never have loved him.

She shouldn't be curling up into a fetal ball in this musty space, but she's scared witless, and she does.

The pistol touches her cheek. She sets her eyes on the barrel. She tries to focus on it, but it's too close.

He tells her, "I promise you, if you'll listen this once to Lao Tsu? If you'll stay in the center and embrace death with all your heart, you'll endure forever. *Forever*, OK?"

He gives her a moment to answer. When she doesn't, he answers for her. "OK," he says, and it's the last thing she ever hears.

EDDIE gets a call from Vincent.

"Touch of chaos, Eddie. I advise you to pull up roots, take your daughter south, find a more serene home."

"What the fuck you talking about?"

Vincent laughs. "It was a difficult meeting. With your cousin and his retinue. We had divergent approaches to the same problem."

"What the fuck does that mean?"

"A whittling. It was a complex situation, and it needed to be whittled. Seek shelter, Eddie."

"You coming?"

"Not right away, no. I've got something to take care of first."

"Like what?"

"I'm curious, Eddie. I wonder if Annie thinks that real love is somehow not my portion in life? Does she think that it's too simple for the Teacher? Or too common? I wonder if she thinks I'm some kind of ghost, I just wander the Earth dispensing ageless wisdom?"

"I dunno," says Eddie.

"Does she think it would be a sin to offer *me* a seat at the table?"

"I dunno," says Eddie.

"Did I tell you that I found out where she's keeping that child? A little village in Guatemala, up in the mountains. End of the earth. But didn't I warn her about that? Didn't I patiently explain to her that there was nowhere she could go? Didn't I move Heaven and Earth trying to stop this tragedy?"

"You're crazy," says Eddie.

"But no, it's pointless, trying to interfere. Because it's all under the wings of the Tao. It's set. There's nothing I can do, there's nothing Annie can do. It's set. I'll see you soon, Eddie. Give your daughter my love."

He hangs up.

Eddie says to the dial tone, "You're crazy."

He cradles the phone.

Then he says to the air:

"Kill my *family*, you cocksucker? Kill my cousins and then call me like nothing's happened? Treat me like I'm your fuckin poodle all my god damn life, and you think I'm gonna let you get away with KILLING MY OWN FAMILY? Oh, you're a stupid crazy fuck."

ANNIE is rehanging the curtains in her studio when the news comes on the radio. She's replaced all the broken windowpanes, sealed them. Now she's standing on the arm of the dog-eared recliner, reaching up, trying to fiddle the aluminum tab on the curtain rod into its slot. Trying to keep busy here. And it's almost working. For a sliver of a moment there's nothing else in her head, nothing but this curtain rod. Then a snatch of quick thumping theme music comes on the radio—the local news:

> "Car bombing near Cold Spring. Police suspect a mob hit. De-tails after this. . . ."

Annie drops the curtain rod. It clatters, bounces. She steps back off the recliner. She's pushing her knuckles together in an attitude close to prayer. She approaches the radio. She bites her lower lip, and her eyes shimmer. Oh, Jesus. They blew him up? Up? You bas-tard. Up, blew you *up*.

She's on tiptoe. The ad drones on and on. This studio of hers has a good smell, what is it? It's all the lacquer. And all this fresh cold October air from the window being broken for days. She only just now noticed how sweet it smells in here. Please, it's him. It's *got* to be him, doesn't it? Blew the bastard to little tiny bits? She tries to catch her laugh and smother it, but it jumps up out of her throat.

Don't, wait till they say his name, but she's laughing this long childish ungovernable laugh as though this were the funniest ad in the history of radio.

The newsman comes back and he says:

"Four bodies have been recovered from a car bombing at an abandoned school near Cold Spring. Police say they have evidence that the bombing was mob related. At least two of the victims have been identified. Their names are being withheld pending . . ."

Four?

Killed *four*? Why? Louie, you only had to blow up the one. Or maybe his buddy Johnny, OK *two*, but—

The phone rings.

She picks up and a voice says, "He knows where your kid is."

She says, "Who is this?"

But she's asking only to gain time, to collect her thoughts. She recognizes Johnny's voice.

"He knows your kid's in some little town in Guatemala. You gotta stop him. I can't stop him. I got my own kid. I gotta get my daughter outta here. I can't help you now. You gotta do it. You gotta stop him, Annie."

THE AGENT at the American Airlines ticket counter looks at this poor woman before her. Then she glances up at the clock, shakes her head. "I'm afraid you've just missed that one, ma'am. But the Aviateca flight leaves in a hour, that ought to be—"

"I can't wait! My child. My child is down there!"

"Ma'am, I believe the plane has already left the gate."

"My child, please! My child—I've got to get there now. He's dying."

"Your child is in Guatemala?"

"He's dying. Please. It's—there was an accident, he's hurt. He's dying. My husband called me. He's dying."

There are rules of course, strict guidelines, and the ticket agent knows them, she knows she's going to get herself in trouble. But there's also this woman before her, and this woman is the most desperate and frantic and unstrung creature she's ever set eyes on. The ticket agent tells her, "Hold on," and she reaches across the counter and takes hold of the woman's wrist and gently squeezes it, and with her free hand she reaches for the telephone.

ANNIE, three minutes later, sprints down the great wide vacant corridor until a steward steps out and signals to her, and they hustle her aboard.

"Thank you, thank you, thank you," as they show her to her seat. The plane is backing away from the gate even before she gets her belt fastened. She has the window seat. No seatmates, thank God. She's been given this simple oblong of gray window. Whorls of minute scratches on the plastic. Something meaningless for her to look at. Why did I ever challenge him? Why did I imagine I could fight him? He's huge, he could crush us both with one finger—why didn't I do what he asked? Why didn't I? Why didn't I? The plane takes off and the boroughs of the city reveal themselves beneath her. Grim brick, the streets crosshatched or whorled like the scratches on the window.

Then the Teacher takes the seat next to hers.

THE TEACHER says, "This is somewhat eerie, isn't it? That we find ourselves on the same flight today?"

He can feel her rage, he can feel the scream that's boiling up inside her. He puts his hand on top of hers—urging, with this gesture, her restraint. "Don't raise your voice," he says. He opens his jacket just enough to show her his weapon. "I have friends who let me carry this pistol aboard. I won't mind using it. I'll kill you, kill the pilot, kill the crew, kill myself. Will that help Oliver? On the contrary, it will seal his fate. A colleague of mine is on his way to T'ui Cuch right now. He's flying down from California. He'll be there in the morning. Your only chance of saving your son is to stay alive. Get to him first. If you approach this calmly, if you meditate on this, I think it will start to make sense."

But the fear keeps pouring off of her. The fear and the indecision. He knows what she's thinking: What if there is no colleague, what if the Teacher is lying to her?

In fact he is lying, which he hates to do, but this is the necessary work of the Tao—the Tao, which turns temporal lies into eternal truth.

"Believe me, Annie. This time, please listen to me. If you had listened to me before, I mean to *me* and not that foolish raggedy-ann doctor? I think we wouldn't have come to this in the first place."

He pushes the stewardess call button over his head. When she

377

appears he tells her, "I was sitting in first class? Seat 3A? But then I ran into this old friend, it's an unbelievable coincidence, and I'd like to stay with her a while? Will that be all right?"

"That'll be fine, sir. Of course."

"Could you bring us a couple of drinks?"

"What would you like?

"Gin tonic for me." He turns to Annie. "How about you?"

She expresses no preference.

So he orders two gin tonics.

After the stewardess goes he says, "I had a dream about you today. In the taxi, I fell asleep, and I had a nightmare. You were drunk, Annie. We were at a cocktail party at the house where I grew up in Bay Ridge, and you were drunk, and for some reason I went out and found your car. Oliver was in it. I locked him in and set fire to it. Then I went up and told you, but I couldn't make you understand. You kept trying to blow out the birthday candles. I yelled, "No, *Oliver* is on fire!" and you poured your drink on the cake. And I woke up in a cold sweat. In the taxi. It's incredible, how scary that was—and now you're here and everything's fine. I don't blame you, Annie. For anything."

"I didn't—Zach, I'm sorry for what I did—"

"You were scared."

"I didn't *understand* you. Now I do, Zach—"

"I know that. Still, what's destined can't be halted. True? Self-evident? The force of one rain-fed orchid will crush the universe. Oliver is *destined* to be killed in the morning. I think we both understand that now. God, we fought it, though. Didn't we? You and I, didn't we look like fools trying to interfere? And Juliet, stepping into the path of that fate, didn't she look like a clown? We were like a troupe of circus clowns—"

The stewardess brings them their drinks. He gives her a twenty-dollar tip, she gives him a flirtatious smile. When she's gone Annie asks him, "Zach, instead of, of . . ."

"Killing Oliver?"

"Yes. Why don't you just kill *me*? I mean take me somewhere and torture me and kill me in some really interesting way? Wouldn't that be satisfying?"

He gives her a look full of concern. "Annie, listen, I don't *want* to kill anyone. It's just that I know what I'm going to have to do. Do you remember that night in your studio? When I told you that if you would only trust me, then Oliver would be safe—but if you betrayed me, then no matter what the personal cost to me, then Oliver would suffer. Do you remember that? And I *begged* you to believe me, I begged you. But how could I ask you to trust me when mistrust, and betrayal, and faithlessness are rooted in who you are? Change your character? I could have as easily asked you to change the pattern of the stars. Do you understand? I know that I can't change what's going to happen. I can only witness. I can only watch, in agony, as you hold the body of your dead son in your arms."

"But Zach, Zach, *please*—"

He puts his fingers to his lips.

"Ssshhh. Relax. Cut the universe a little slack, OK Annie?"

He envelops her hand in his own, and he holds it tight. He thinks what a long strange ride it will be, just the two of them, sitting together like this, and there's much for them to talk about. So many questions he wants to ask her. Fear and sorrow and rapture at the same moment. He takes a sip of his drink. And it tastes like liquid silver.

ANNIE, four hours later, descends to the tarmac of the Guatemala airport. She pushes through the mob of passengers toward the terminal. The Teacher is twenty paces ahead of her. He looks back at her once, and winks, then weaves on through the crowd.

They enter a long broad hallway, at the end of which are the booths for customs. The Teacher moves quickly, and when the queue forms, he's near the head of it.

A customs agent, a woman, summons him to her booth.

Now, Annie thinks, *now* should I call for the police? But no, he can still see me. He could still kill me, and kill himself, and the assassin will get to Oliver.

So she has to stand there and watch as he flashes his floppy smile at the agent, as he breezes through.

He vanishes into the baggage claim hall.

Now.

In a moment he'll pick up his rental car, he'll start toward T'ui Cuch, too late to catch him.

Now.

She steps out of line. The passengers around her raise a complaint. She walks right past the woman in her booth, who shouts after her.

"Murderer!" Annie says to the air. "He's got a gun! He's a murderer!"

She points. There's someone in front of her now, in a uniform. And other uniforms are coming.

"He's got a gun!" she cries. "Stop him!"

They answer in Spanish.

"I don't *speak* Spanish. *Gun!* The man in the blue suit! Doesn't anyone speak English? Please, stop him! Stop him!"

One of them tries to hold her. She wrestles her arm away, keeps moving. She sees a glass-walled office to the right with several uniforms coming out, coming toward her. She stumbles that way, shouting.

Again she's snared.

A voice at her ear, speaking English, says, "What is the matter here?"

A small trim police officer.

She says, "There's a man with a gun! Up there! *Up there.* Blue suit, red tie, an American. Stop him! He said he'd kill someone! STOP HIM!"

"Who are you?"

"He sat next to me! Please, he's going to kill someone."

"Who is going to do this?"

"Blue suit! Red tie!"

"What color of suit?"

"Blue suit! Red tie! Handsome! Guapo! KILLER!"

The man mutters to his aides. A melee, cops coming from everywhere. "How do you know this man!"

"Killer! He's got a gun!" What's the word? *"Pistola?* PISTOLA! PISTOLA!"*

Now her shouts cause an uproar in the lines. Some woman panics and screams, and the scream catches fire and spreads. The shrieking and the echoes of the shrieking are deafening.

"How do you know that he has a pistol?" shouts the officer.

"HE SHOWED IT TO ME! FOR CHRIST SAKE! KILLER! ASSASSIN!"

THE TEACHER, standing in line at baggage check, hears the commotion, the uproar, swelling behind him. He knows what it means: Annie is struggling again.

He knows that her struggling is foolish, but he loves her foolishness. He smiles. He doesn't look back. He takes a breath.

The baggage checker walks away from his post to see what's going on.

The Teacher shuts his briefcase. He heads for the wall of glass doors.

"Señor?"

He turns. A policeman is standing there. And two security men are coming toward him. Indicating that they want him to put his hands up.

Two more cops are crossing toward him from the baggage carousel.

He pulls out his HK and takes down one of the cops. He fires at the other but misses. Instantly he's the center of an eruption, a concussive wave expanding from the muscles of his heart outward, toppling hundreds of people at all points of the compass.

He fires two more shots, and two more waves of mad panic spread outward. He runs out onto the street. He has only to raise his HK and a path is cleared for him. Ten steps across the street. Hurtling down a flight of stone stairs and over a fence and alongside a culvert and into a dense slum of tin-roofed shacks, a warren, a maze, he's perfectly safe. Annie, struggle as hard as you like and I won't love you any less for it, but there's other work as well, a work of meditation. You should be preparing yourself for the morning.

ANNIE begs this Officer Foncea to understand. "You have to find him tonight. Tonight. My child, tonight!"

"But you say that your child is in T'ui Cuch. This man, this teacher you call him? He is here in the capital."

"But he's *going* to T'ui Cuch."

"T'ui Cuch is hundreds of miles distance. The teacher of your son is on his feet. The car rental agencies are alerted, no one will rent him a car. All the police of the capital is looking for this man. There is no danger for your son tonight. In the morning we will inform the Guardia in Huehuetenango. They will visit T'ui Cuch. They will visit your son—"

"Tonight! Please!"

"Tonight?"

"Yes! They've got to go there tonight. Oh please!"

"Tonight is not possible. Tomorrow is the day of All the Saints. That is the feast day of T'ui Cuch. There is no telegrams to T'ui Cuch tonight."

"But you could call there!"

"I am certain there is no telephones in T'ui Cuch."

"OK, but you could call Huehuetenango. They could drive up there."

"Yes. Exactly. This is a good, a good . . . idea."

"You'll call them?"

"Yes, yes."

"When?"

"Soon."

"Now! Please. Oh please God. Please call them *now*."

"I cannot call them now."

"Why not?"

"I cannot make this call."

"Why not?"

"It will be made at the headquarters."

"No, *here*, please. I'll pay for it."

"I will first need to file my report."

"God damn! Damn you!"

She looks away. Looks out the office at the customs booths. Already another planeload of gringos, another line.

"Is this from California?" she says.

"This? No, this is the Aviateca. From Miami. The flight from San Diego arrived two hours ago."

"Two hours? *Two hours?*"

The policeman asks her, "Why are you no relax? The teacher of your child, we will find him soon, I am certain."

"But there's another one! Another killer! He was on that flight!"

"To kill your child?"

"Yes!"

"Why they kill your child?"

"Please! Listen, the New York, the New York State Troopers! Just call, call an Investigator Carew in New York—"

"The New York—I'm sorry?"

"The troopers. They know this man! This man is a killer! Please!"

"I will call them."

"From here? *Now?*"

"I cannot call from here."

"You bastard! Call them right now! These men are killers! If you don't do what I say, I swear I'll have you fired!"

"You will what? Are you threaten me?"

"Yes! I'm threatening you, I'll have your job!"

"If you threaten me I will arrest you. You think because you are from the United States—"

"I'm not threatening you, I'm begging you, please, just let me call Carew, I'll pay for the call, please how would it hurt you to let me call—"

"This is Guatemala. The New York policemen can do nothing in Guatemala."

Then the officer raises his eyes.

She hears a voice behind her. "Annie?"

She turns. It's Johnny.

"Where is he, Annie?"

"He got away. How did you—"

"I came on the Aviateca flight. First I had to get my daughter off to a friend in Curaçao. Where's your kid, Annie? We got to get to your kid."

Says Foncea, "Who are you?"

"I'm a friend of the lady's. You?"

"I am Officer Rogerio Foncea."

"Well, Captain Foncea, can I speak to you a moment in, uh, in private?"

Twenty minutes later, Johnny's driving and Annie's navigating the little Celica they've rented. On the winding highway that rises steeply out of the city, Johnny careering through both lanes and sometimes even sliding onto the thin right shoulder to gun past a lumbering truck. He's driving like a fiend. But still not nearly fast enough for Annie. He tells her, "Thank God a couple hundred dollars was enough to shut the creep up."

"Johnny," she says.

"My name's not Johnny. It's Eddie."

"Eddie. We have to stop. I've got to call Carew."

"Who's Carew?"

"The New York State—"

"Forget it."

"But they could, they could send a helicopter."

"They could but they won't. Not in time. Think about it. This guy Carew, he'd have to call his boss. Then his boss would have to call *his* boss. Then that guy'd have to call the fuckin FBI. The FBI'd have to call, I don't know, the fuckin State Department. Twenty more calls and six weeks later somebody'd send a helicopter to Brazil. Forget it, girl. It's just us. Holy Jesus."

A herd of cattle are crossing the road. Eddie lays into the horn and veers and the car lifts onto two wheels and they thread a needle between a pair of horned steers. But Annie scarcely notices. "Is there another killer?" she asks. "He told me there was someone from California."

"Yeah? Well that was a story for you. That was a bedtime story, to keep you quiet. Nah, there's nobody come here from California. There's nobody come here but just him. But Jesus, he's enough, isn't he?"

15

The Path of Scorched and Scoured Love

THE TEACHER drives over the crest of a hill in an old Z-car, and looks down this packed-dirt hinterlands highway, and spies another car on the road far ahead of him.

A pair of taillights, glowing through a thick membrane of dust.

It still strikes him as an absurd extravagance that he had to *kill* for this jalopy he's driving—that he had to proffer two bullets to the head of some rich Guatemalan mama's spoiled girl-child as she waited for a red light not far from the airport. It's certainly not a car worth killing for. It's out of tune. The steering feels far too plush and the tires too fat. The tachometer is palsied. The headrest is still uncomfortably sticky from the previous owner's blood.

But this is the vessel granted. The Teacher's not complaining. This Z-car is no odder, nor any less stunningly appropriate, than any vessel the Tao picks out to bear its cargo. And for all its infirmities, it's still much more agile than the car ahead. The Teacher gains quickly. And when he's close enough to see the tag of that car up ahead, he sees that it's a rental.

There's a twinge in his gut.

He speeds up. He's been missing her, he's desperate to be near her again. He comes to a curve and takes it at seventy-five, closes in.

He flicks to his high beams.

There are two people in that car. In the passenger seat, the shape of Annie's head. Faint, haloed. He's thrilled. A wire stretches from one end of the universe to the other, and it's full of juice. Where this wire happens to cross another such wire, a spark is created. A blinding throb of passion, a roaring howl in the darkness. Then the wires are fused. No matter what you do, my stubborn bride.

She turns to look back into his fierce-headlight gaze.

He can see that her face is full of animal fear and confusion. She's tender and childlike and afraid. Her image wavers and wobbles because the Teacher has tears in his eyes. She says something to her driver and then she raises a pistol. She points it back at the Teacher's car.

She fires, and her rear window shatters. The bullet wanders off into space.

The Teacher hangs back, biding his time.

He waits until he comes to a bend in the road, a long seesaw S-curve, and here he pours on the gas. The driver of Annie's car is trying to block him from getting by, and that driver is clever, but the Teacher feints once to the right and once to the left, and then as they break out of the curve he downshifts and comes burning along on Annie's side of her car. The Teacher has no music, but one high ledge of his brain plays a Vivaldi allegro motif to another. He rolls down his window and squeezes out a precise sequence of shots from the HK. Not that he wants to hurt her. He doesn't dream of hurting her. But he needs to distract her from her fantasy of stopping him. So he fires over her head, one shot after another exploding her car's windows as he comes. But even with the glass shattering all about her she doesn't cringe. She calmly draws aim. He can't believe her courage. He's so proud of her. He fires a final shot, and it sails over her head and slaps into the windshield in front of her driver.

The driver grabs her head, forces her to duck. And hits the brakes at the same moment.

And the Teacher takes the opportunity that's been handed him. He crushes the gas pedal under his foot and surges ahead of them, loses them in his dust.

But before he does he gets enough of a look into that car to see Annie's driver. To see that he's his oldest friend in the world.

ANNIE and Eddie drive on in the dark, rising higher and higher into the mountains. The cool air whistles in through the busted windows. But it doesn't whistle loud enough for Annie. She's going crazy with frustration. Why does this fool slow down at every nothing nuisance bend in the road? Sometimes he slows so much there's no wind-whistle at all, nor any sound from the tires. The tires should be screaming, because when they're not screaming they're losing, *we're* losing, we're still hours from T'ui Cuch and we'll never catch him if the tires don't scream, doesn't he realize that?

She says, for the fifth time, "*Please* let me drive."

"No," he says.

"Please! Why not?"

"You'd kill us. You want to drive so fast you'd kill us."

She sits silently for a moment. Then she says, "You're still working for him."

Eddie says, "I'm going as fast as anyone fuckin can. I think we're gonna die anyway, I'm goin so fast. But at least with me driving, we got a fuckin chance."

"You're still working for him."

"Christ."

"If you're not working for him, why didn't you let me kill him?"

"*When he was shooting at you?* He was gonna kill you, Jesus Christ, why don't you shut up?"

393

She says, "He wouldn't have killed me."

They sweep through a narrow pass, black scarps pressing in, the road twisting along and the car twisting with it.

"Yeah, well, you're right," he says. "Maybe you're right, he wouldn't have killed you. You understand him? 'Cause I known him all my life, and I don't understand shit about him."

"I could have killed him."

"All right."

"Let me drive."

"No."

They pass a cluster of mountain cottages, then another. A road sign announces some village. Lights. A stew of lights up ahead.

He comes down hard on the brakes.

"No, don't stop!" she cries. "Whatever it is, who cares what it is, just go!"

But how can he? The way is blocked. They've come to the edge of some town and there's a chain across the road and a crowd of revelers on the other side of it. Marimbas and dancers and the smallest Ferris wheel that Annie's ever seen. All right out in the middle of the road, and a string of dim cheerless yellow lightbulbs hanging over them.

And a hand-lettered sign: *Vía Cerrada.* The road is closed.

For this fool block party.

"Go through them!" she pleads.

He looks at her. "Can't go through a Ferris wheel."

"Well then go around! Let's go back, there's got to be some way around!"

He shakes his head. "If there was? He'd have taken it."

He shifts his eyes and points with his chin, and she looks in the direction indicated. The Teacher's car is parked beside the white stucco wall of a little store.

"He's here?" she says. "He's waiting for us?"

"Fuck if I know, Annie. Give me my thirty-eight. Let's go."

They get out and step over the chain, wade into the crowd of drunken celebrants. A row of three marimbas has been set up under torchlight, and each marimba is played by three stone-drunk Mayans. Nine madmen in all, all in a row. All hammering as hard and as recklessly as they can, an earwash of burning red chord. The Ferris wheel, no lights, goes round and round, nobody in the gondolas.

The dancers are dancing each to himself. Looking up at the stars and howling. Some of them carom off of Annie as she struggles down that street. "Let me through! Please!" A firelit drunk in a monkey-mask falls into her, clutches at her. Burbles into her cheek. Confusion of stinks she can't begin to sort out. Eddie peels the man off of her, tosses him back into the melee, takes her hand and bulls a path.

At the far end of that celebration, on a wooden bench under a tree of feathers, sits a gringo. Balding kind of dreamy-looking guy, swirling a pint bottle of clear liquid.

Eddie stops and stares. "Oh shit! No, *can't* be. Sure-Knack? You're dead!"

"What," says the guy, in a slow cracker drawl. "I'm dead? You sure? Anybody tell my mother?"

"Ah, forget it," says Eddie. "You look just like this asshole I used to know. You don't got a brother who's a private dick? I mean in Tarrytown? I mean used to be?"

The Cracker takes a swig out of the bottle he's holding. He says, "I got a brother in Nahunta, Georgia. I think he sells aluminum siding. Before that he worked at some place where they made baseball caps. He used to put the cardboard or whatnot in the visors? Before that he was in the—"

Annie stops him. "Listen, we're on our way to T'ui Cuch. But this—whatever *this* is . . ."

"All Saints' Eve. Hallowe'en. It's a big deal in this neck of the woods."

"Is there any way around it?"

"You mean in a car?"

"In a car."

"Oh, well sure," says the Cracker. "Go on back to the Pan-American Highway, take a right—"

She says, "The big highway?" She looks to Eddie. "Where we got gas? That was, that was an *hour* ago."

Says the Cracker, "Yeah, about. Why, you in a hurry? You in a hurry, you got the wrong country, babe."

"Can't they move for us? Just for a minute, can't they—"

"Depends on what you're driving. You driving a tank?"

Says Eddie, "What are *you* driving, friend?"

The Cracker laughs. "I don't got a car," he says.

Says Eddie, "Are there any cars in this town?"

"Was. One taxi. I expect he took it, though."

"Who's *he?*"

"Guy I just had this same silly-ass conversation with. What's all this rush to get to T'ui Cuch? Take you all night. And when you get there, what're they doin? I tell you what they doin. They gettin drunk. They bangin they damn marimbas. It's the same fuckin fiesta, children."

Annie leans close to the man. She speaks slow and loud, as though he were deaf. "Aren't there *any* other cars?"

"You all right, babe?"

"*Any?*"

"Nah. Well, one, yeah, the Chino's got one. The Chino's got an old Plymouth. He won't let you use it, and it wouldn't make it that far anyway—"

"Where is it?"

"Up the street. Take your right at the *tiendacita*. Then your first left, kind of a dogleg left? But now you got to picture kind of a *cripply* dog—"

Says Eddie, "You want to make some money?"

"No."

"A hundred dollars if you take us to the Chino's."

"You mean *walk* with you?"

"A hundred dollars."

"No."

"Why not?"

"I'd rather party. Havin a good time, don't it look it?"

"Five hundred."

"But money I don't need. I'd do it for a Big Mac, though, if you could get me one."

"Do it," says Annie, "because that man that was here before us, he wants to kill my child, and my child is in T'ui Cuch—"

Eddie stops her. "No. Annie. He's not going to help us. Let's go." He takes her elbow.

"*Please.* It's my child, he's going to kill my *child*," she pleads as Eddie pulls her away.

They start up into the shadows. Behind them, the Cracker belches. Then he says, "Hold up."

The dark street, full of cedar-smoke. Lined with drunks: black moaning heaps.

Says the Cracker, "Why does he want to kill your kid?"

396

"I don't know," says Annie.

Light from a doorway, a cantina, more hammering and howling.

Says the Cracker, "He's crazy?"

"Yes."

"But why does he want to kill your kid?"

She turns to him and says, "Faster? Can you walk faster?"

"Walk as fast as I like," says the Cracker.

"Are you old, is that it?"

"Younger than you, babe."

"But you seem old. You seem tired, it's like you're very old and—"

"*Damn* you don't let up, do you?"

He starts to trot. Leaps over a sleeping drunk. Eddie and Annie run beside him, Eddie holding his heart with one hand. He asks the Cracker, "Hey, my friend, what do you do here?"

"I give guided tours in the middle of the night. Like see that stain on the wall there? That's a piss stain. You havin fun?"

"I'm just trying to figure it," says Eddie. "You don't look Peace Corps. You don't look hippie. You don't look tourist."

"Yeah? So what do I look?" says the Cracker.

"Truth? You look poppies."

"Oh yeah? You know the Spanish for poppies?"

"No. What's the Spanish for poppies?"

"It's shut-the-fuck-up."

They take the dogleg left.

Says Eddie, "But I still can't figure what *end* of the business. Not management, you know? You're no fuckin chemist, you're not refining the stuff, so what—"

Says the Cracker, "You know the Spanish for refining?"

"Yeah," says Eddie. "OK."

"And I mean it," says the Cracker.

"OK. OK. But I was just thinkin, maybe you're in the *transportation* end—"

"Bullshit."

Eddie puts his arm on the Cracker's shoulder and stops him. He squeezes that shoulder. "I'm just thinkin, we're in a *real* hurry here, we got to get to T'ui Cuch *fast*, and maybe you can help us out. Or you know someone who can."

The Cracker shrugs. "I don't know nobody except the Chino. What are you talkin about?"

"I'm just thinkin—"

"You're dreamin," says the Cracker. "T'ui Cuch—it's a little tiny piece a nothin. There's no level place. Nothin but mountains all around. And it's the middle of the night. Can't get nothin in there but a car, I mean it. Anything else, any fancy ideas you got? You're dreamin. I *promise* you, motherfucker."

"Eddie," says Annie. "Come on, there's no *time*. Hurry!"

But Eddie keeps staring into the Cracker's eyes.

"Help us," he says, "and I'll make you fuckin rich."

"I *promise* you, you're dreaming," says the Cracker. "This is all the help I can give. Now do you want it? You want me to take you to the Chino? Or you want to talk to him yourself?"

"Ah, bite my crank," says Eddie, and he lets the Cracker go, walks on.

Halfway up the next block they come to a hole-in-the-wall restaurant. Chinese-Latino-Mayan. The old Chino rises from his table by the cooler. The Cracker addresses him in a burst of rapid Spanish, which Annie can't follow. But she does hear the Chino's reply. "Esta *noche*?"

"*Sí,*" says the Cracker. "You bet *esta noche.*"

"*Dónde?*"

"T'ui Cuch."

The Chino laughs and shakes his head, turns away.

"Thousand dollars," says Eddie.

The Chino turns back, makes a face.

Takes two minutes, and he's settled on three thousand dollars for the use of his car for one night. He hands the keys to Annie. He points with his thumb to the rear of the restaurant. They hurry through the sordid kitchen, push a dozen dogs out of their way, step into the alley that runs behind the restaurant.

There sits the ancient bomb.

Cracker lingers in the doorway. He says, "Little troll hanging under the rearview mirror there? His name is Pepe. The transmission gives you trouble, you talk to Pepe about it. Have a pleasant ride, guys. See you tomorrow night."

Annie heads for the driver's door but Eddie stops her. "Wait a minute, let me drive."

"No."

"I'm telling you, you'd kill us. If you're drivin I'm not goin."

"Then stay here. I'm better alone—"

Some movement in the dark Plymouth.

The driver's door swings open.

The Teacher slips out from the shadows.

"I'm afraid you can't go anywhere in this car. It seems the distributor cap is missing. But why don't you come with me, Annie?"

She will not look at him. She turns, and looks at Eddie.

Says the Teacher, "I have a taxi parked just around the corner. I could give you a lift all the way to T'ui Cuch, it would be my pleasure. And as for you, Eddie, oldest friend, dear Judas, why don't you take another route? Why don't you take yourself down to the realm of those smoky *lokas* that you worship, and wander awhile, and when your soul has been harrowed and cleansed and hallowed by ten thousand reincarnations, then rejoin us, OK, Eddie?"

He fires one shot into Eddie's chest.

"NO!" Annie cries.

Eddie on the ground, and she's bending over him, and all the restaurant dogs and all the dogs in this town are braying.

"But, Annie, we need to hurry," says the Teacher. "Leave him. He has his own journey to make."

Her face is down close to Eddie's. A hoarse rumbling in his chest, no other sign of life. "Eddie," she says.

Then she slips her hand under his jacket. Looking for his gun.

Behind her, the Teacher commands, "Stand up, leave Eddie's pistol alone, leave this foolishness. You know, my love, that I could kill you in a heartbeat."

But you won't, thinks Annie.

She thinks, All I have to do is turn around and kill you. I know that you won't stop me.

Hunched over Eddie, so the Teacher can't see what she's doing, Annie reaches under Eddie's jacket and slides the gun out of its holster.

Gets her finger into the trigger guard.

The Teacher's voice: "Make the right choice now, Annie. Think. Your child's life is at stake, you can't afford any flashy heroics. Isn't that evident? You have to come with me. We have to work together. What chance do you have of stopping me if I'm in T'ui Cuch and you're—"

She wheels and fires blindly.

Darkness. No one near the car. Across the alley from the car is a square stone archway, leading to a passage from which she hears the echo of his footsteps.

She runs after him. "Wait!" she cries. She stops, she listens. No more footsteps. Only the yowling dogs. Then she hears a car engine start up, and she runs toward that sound. "Wait, I'll come! Wait! *I'm sorry! Please!*" Flying down a long patio, under another arch, into another solemn dark street.

His taxi, roaring away from her.

"WAIT!"

But it's already gone.

She's trapped here.

He's gone.

Soon he'll be in T'ui Cuch, and there's nothing she can do, she was a fool, nothing—

She hears someone behind her, and she turns: it's the Cracker.

"Please," she says. "Please. I don't, I don't, I don't—"

"I saw it," he said. "Shit, I didn't believe you, but you wasn't fuckin, was you? *That fucker wants to kill your kid.*"

"Please," she says.

"We gotta get outta here."

"Where's—?"

"Your friend. He's dead. Come on."

"Where?"

"T'ui Cuch. Come on."

She shakes her head. "Does the car run?"

"The Plymouth? Forget the Plymouth. Let's go. We gotta hurry."

"But there's no *car.*"

"We don't need a car. You don't get it? Your friend, he got it. You're in luck, ma'am. Me, I'm heading into a shitstorm, but you're in real luck."

She's weeping. She's trying to understand, but it's all a swirling confusion. She says again, *"We don't have a car."*

"Yeah, yeah, but we don't need a car," says the Cracker. " 'Cause I got an airplane."

BUDDY BAUMGARTNER figures he has about as much worry in his head as his head can fit. He's worried about finding T'ui Cuch in the dark. He's worried about how he's going to land this plane, since T'ui Cuch is nestled in the mountains and there's nothing around that even approaches an airstrip. He's worried about the engine on the left wing, which has a funny sort of shudder whenever he climbs. He's worried about random patrols of the Guatemalan Air Force—the Few the Proud the Psychotic. He's worried about the story that this Annie woman just told him, he's worried about all of Louie Boffano's surviving brothers and cousins and nephews and nieces and grandnieces. And he's worried about that Teacher guy, somewhere on the road below.

And of course there's a fat load of the standard worries as well: the temper of his bloodthirsty boss, the six kilos of heroin that he ought to be taking to Biloxi this very moment, the warrants for his arrest that are still outstanding in the states of Georgia, Alabama and Rhode Island, I mean here's one sorry asshole who has to worry about Rhode fuckin *Island*.

Still and all, he feels wonderful.

Despite the stream of silent interior wisecracks that his brain keeps cranking out, he feels better than he has in years.

This woman, this Annie Laird, she brings out some kind of feeling in him. It's not love exactly, but something like love, some deep tenderness. He's even worked up some feeling for this Oliver kid. This woman tells him her story, and every time she mentions the kid Buddy thinks, But if we get there in time, I can save this kid's life. His *life*. God *damn*.

And every time he thinks this thought, it gives him a charge so deep that he forgets all about his worries and all about what a fuckup he is, and for a split second he forgets all about Miss Kellie O'Keefe from Folkston, Ga., who dumped him for some pasty-faced veterinarian who specializes in *ducks* for Christ sake, I mean the man is a goddamn *quack* of *quacks*, Kellie, is that what you really want?

But if I can find somewhere to land? If I can save the life of this Oliver kid?

Why, he thinks, that ought to wash an awful lot of crap out of these old brain-pipes. That ought to wash Kellie and her quack-man out of my head *for good*.

In the meantime, this Annie woman is done with her story and she's fallen silent, and he wishes she hadn't. It's only when the woman is talking that he can keep the worry in rein.

But she only stares down at the black folds of landscape below.

The engines snore along.

Buddy can't think of a thing to say. He's never been any good at all at talking to women.

Finally, he tries, "Annie?"

"Yes."

"So, so tell me."

"What."

"Well, tell me, tell me about your kid some more."

"Like what?" Testiness in her voice.

"Anything. I mean, so what is he like?"

"He's a child."

End of interview.

To the east, the arc of the world is starting to carry some light. Some brushed blue, some shoots of crimson. That's what we need all right, thinks Buddy—but you better hurry it up over there. I ain't landing this wreck in the dark.

Then he sees it.

A thimble-scoop of white light down on the carpet of blackness below.

He points. "You see that?"

"What."

"Right there. You see that light? It's a car. It's headlights."

She says, *"Him?"*

"At this hour? In these mountains? Ain't nobody else. Yeah, it's him."

She's suddenly nervous, excited. She says, "What are we going to do?"

He shrugs. "What do you mean? This old bird's going as fast—"

"But can't we go *down* there? Can't we stop him?"

"Stop him how?"

"Can't we, can't we—I don't know, can't we drop something on him?"

"Drop what?"

"Or I'll shoot him," she says. "You fly over him and I'll shoot him. Through the roof of his car." She picks up the pistol from her lap.

"He's in a ravine, Annie. He's halfway up one side of a ravine, that's where the road goes. I could never get down there, and if I could? You could never hit him."

"All right," she says.

"I mean, what is that, a thirty-eight? If you had a rifle. If you were a marksman. If I could get down there—"

"All *right*," she says sharply.

Then a minute later she says, "I'm sorry. I know, you're right. I can see him but I can't stop him. I know. It's clear. How long to T'ui Cuch?"

"Well, you know we can't land right in the valley. I told you that."

"I know."

"There's a ridge on the west, sort of a road there, way up above the town. I'll try to land there. If I can even find it. Then we have to walk down from there."

"To run."

"Yeah, to run, but still it's a long way."

"How long?"

"I don't know. It's all downhill, at least there's that."

For a few minutes, nothing in his ears but the engines.

Then she says, "Do you want me to talk about my child? About Oliver?"

"Oh, that's OK."

"I can't."

"I understand. It's OK."

She says, "That investigator I told you about—once he asked me what was in my head. *In my head.* I told him I was thinking about Oliver. About nothing but Oliver. But that wasn't true. That was a lie. The truth is, I haven't been thinking about Oliver at all. When I'm with him, I try not to even look at him. And when I'm not with him, every time he comes into my head I turn away. Turn my thoughts away. I think about something else. I keep everything dark in my head. Do you want me to think about him?"

"No, really, I didn't mean—"

"How can I think about my child? If I think about my child, I'll think about my child being killed. If I think about that, it'll split me open. If I love him, even if I just *love* him, that'll split me open. I don't love him. I don't keep that around. You want to know what I keep around?"

"If you—"

"Hate. That's all. That's all I think about. Those headlights down there, that little light of his down there, it's about the size of a beetle, isn't it? I think I could reach down in the dark and find it, that's all I have to do, grope around in the dark till I find it and squeeze it, crush him to death. You know what? You know what I just realized? I don't care whether he kills my child or not. You know? I don't love my child, there's nothing left of my child inside my head anyway, so what do I care?"

"Hey, Annie, stop. That's not true—"

"Shut up. What right do you have to tell me what's true? Or what's not true. What do I care what's true or not. I just want to kill him. That's all I want to do, just kill him and kill him and kill him. Please, get there, land this plane."

"Soon."

"Land us."

"We will."

"He wants to see me holding the body of my son, why should I do that? It's just a body, why should I hold it up for him? I won't, I will not. I'll hold *his* body, that fucker, I'll hold him up and I'll eat his heart, please, will you go faster, will you *get* there, will you land this thing, please! I just want to eat that man's heart! He can kill all the children he wants, that's fine with me, let him kill, kill Oliver? I

don't even *know* Oliver, let him! Let him kill, let him, if he wants
to kill let him kill but when he's done I want to eat his heart. Do
you understand? *I want to eat that man's heart!* Please! I WANT
TO EAT THAT MAN'S HEART! PLEASE! DON'T FLY ANY
MORE! GET THERE! LAND THIS!"

THE TEACHER, at the first light of dawn, sees a little store by the side of the road, and a light is on. He's tired, tired of this mud-driving, and he's hungry. He pulls over.

Dead silence when he shuts the taxi door.

He looks down the mountain road he just came up. He wishes she were here with him. He hopes she found some transportation. There won't be much time after he kills Oliver before the police come. He won't be able to wait long. She'll have to hurry. Hurry, Annie.

Find some way.

The sky is utterly clear and filling up with light the way a sail fills up with wind.

He thinks of the morning when Lao Tsu left his *Book of the Way* with the Royal Gatekeeper, and walked out of China forever.

He steps inside the store.

There's a table and three Mayans having breakfast. They make room for him. He has eggs with salsa, and mutton stew and tortillas, and sweet sweet coffee. The coffee is so sweet it makes him laugh.

He says to the men, *"Hay una fiesta hoy? En T'ui Cuch?"*

"Sí," says one. All three of them are drunk as skunks. *"La fiesta."*

"Empieza muy temprano?" the Teacher asks.

"Sí. La carrera. Temprano."

The race, the T'ui Cuch horse race, they'll start it bright and early. There will be a crowd, and Oliver will be in it, and he'll be easy to find.

ANNIE runs from the wrecked airplane, runs in the rose light of daybreak across the barren black potato field till she comes to the field's edge and looks down the steep cliffside.

Below, far, swaddled in mist, the village.

"It's too far," she says.

Buddy hobbles up beside her. "Fucked my knee up," he says. "My knee, my plane, my whole life, fucked."

"Hours. It'll take hours."

"We're just nothin but fucked," says Buddy.

Annie turns. A small crowd of Mayans have gathered in the potato field. Some of them gawk at the wrecked plane, some of them gawk at Annie.

One of them is a boy on a gray horse.

The boy is wearing a gaudy riding jacket. His hair has been braided and ornamented with long rainbow scarves.

Annie asks Buddy, "That boy? Why is he dressed like that?"

"For the fiesta. I expect he's gonna ride in the horse race today."

"What horse race?"

"In T'ui Cuch. Some kind a horse race. I don't know."

"Will you ask him something for me?" says Annie.

"Yeah," says Buddy.

"Will you ask him if his horse is a fast horse?"

THE TEACHER lingers at the little store. He buys himself a nice wool coat with the pattern of a bat on its back, and he buys himself a small wooden representation of the local black saint, San Simón.

Then he asks the three men at the table, who are just finishing their sweet coffees, *"Quieren ir conmigo? A T'ui Cuch. Tengo un auto."*

They confer among themselves.

"Sí. Gracias, señor."

They all get into the taxi.

One of the men hands him a bottle of the local white lightning. The Teacher takes a swig, and his eyes water and the men laugh. A festive atmosphere in this taxicab, and every moment is chiseled into his mind's eye and into his memory. They ride up over the mountain and down into the valley of T'ui Cuch.

When they come into town he drives carefully around the loose chickens and the sleeping drunks and the families that are heading into the market where the horse race will begin. He finds a place to park, and says farewell to his passengers. He salutes the village policeman, who is barely able to stand. He walks briskly into the market.

Cacophony of marimbas and trumpets, and the church bell is tolling. The dusty trees are crowded with boat-tailed grackles, who are all screeching at once, and children are screeching with them. A costumed dance is under way. Looks as though it's been going on all night, the dancers stumbling and shuffling. And in the soccer field the horses are gathering, and the men are dragging them by the reins and swearing at them. Oh, it's all noisy and colorful, and perhaps charming if it were some other occasion. If he were coming here as a tourist, coming with Annie and Oliver for example, a gringo family gawking at the local grotesqueries—then all this nonsense wouldn't irritate him so much. But what he wants now is silence. He wants solemn clarity. He wants a revelation of pattern. He wants the world to be as clean and simple as that sky up there.

A ragged boy approaches him with a tray of boiled peanuts. *"Maníes? No quiere maníes, joven?"*

He smiles. *"Sí, por favor."*

He buys a bag, and gives the boy a five-quetzal tip.

And while the child is still blinking at it, the Teacher asks him, *"Conoce un muchacho, un gringo, se llama Oliver?"*

"Oh-levar? Sí. El gringito? Sí, sí."

"Y dónde está?"

"Ahorita?" The boy scans the market, looking for Oliver. He raises his eyes to the steep hillside. Suddenly he points. *"Oh-levar,"* he says.

A knot of five boys, on a street overlooking the market. Looking down at the field of horses. Oliver not apparent. But two of the boys wear masks and gaudy robes. One's a horned bull, the other a long-faced deer.

One of the unmasked boys waves a shirt, and the bull paws the ground with his feet and then rushes that rag.

"Yo no puedo verlo," says the Teacher.

"Está allí," says the boy. *"El Toro."*

The boy-matador wheels, and the bull wheels with him, around and around, then dizzily cartwheels into the dust. Slowly picks himself up. Lifts up his mask. It *is* Oliver. He pushes his hair out of his eyes and laughs and replaces the mask and he's the bull again.

The peanut seller shouts, *"Oh-levar!"*

But fortunately the marimbas and the church bells and the grackles drown out his call. Oliver doesn't hear, doesn't turn.

"Por favor," says the Teacher. He puts a hand on the peanut vendor's shoulder. *"Mi visita . . . es una . . . sorpresa."*

The kid shrugs. "OK."

Now the bull and the deer separate from the other boys. They start to ascend the hillside, climbing a long earthen stairway.

410

"*A dónde van?*" the Teacher asks.

The kid shrugs again. "*No sé. Probablamente a las ruinas.*"

He points to the crumbling carcass of a stone church, high up on the hillside.

"*Gracias,*" murmurs the Teacher. "That's perfect."

He winds through the milling throng, crosses the marketplace, hurries up to the long stairway. This he climbs. Quick strides. Up through a narrow space between two thatch cottages. He looks over the palings of a whittled-sapling fence into a garden, where a woman is weaving at a backstrap loom. Her young daughter squats beside her. The woman smiles, and the Teacher smiles back. He holds up his bag of peanuts, and tosses it to the girl, and nimbly she catches it. He wishes Annie were with him. He climbs on.

The stairway meets a road that zigzags up the steep hill. When he looks up he catches another glimpse of the bull and the deer.

The mask, that's wrong. That mask is clutter. I want to see your face, Oliver. Your open clear face.

But still the Teacher is content, because he can feel the power gathering. The wild din of the market is fading, the shape of the valley is showing itself. He likes the geometric Jacob's-ladder structure of this road. He likes to think of the measured distance between himself and Oliver, the distance that grows a bit shorter with every one of his long strides. He climbs higher, passes through a huddle of thatched homes and comes to a clearing.

Again he spots Oliver.

Though it's just for a moment, as the boy trudges between dry corn fields. This time he's alone. His friend the deer must have gone home, must live in one of these houses. *There are only the two of us now. Simpler and simpler.*

Only the one child and the one man climbing dutifully to the meeting-place.

The Teacher hastens his steps. A little impatient now, eager, can't help it. He trots through the corn patches and through an orchard and out into an open field. Just above him is the ruins of the church. Oliver has paused. He's standing on an old ruined retaining wall of the church, and he's looking out at the view. The Teacher supposes that the child has noticed him, but with that mask it's hard to tell.

Anyway it doesn't matter, he's never seen my face, he won't recognize me. To him I'm just another gringo tourist in a hurry to visit the church.

411

Oliver turns and goes inside. The Teacher is sweating but he can't take off his woolen coat without exposing the HK. He stops for a moment. He looks down the hillside and sees the village and the road winding away from it. A lovely lone horse on that road. The Teacher draws a deep breath, wipes his face with his sleeve.

Then he angles across the hillside and ascends the stone steps of the church.

Under the arch into the great wide-open nave. With the roof gone, it's only a shabby stone courtyard. Silent. Weeds burgeoning in the stone cracks.

Oliver. Where are you?

Blood-encrusted cross in the middle of the courtyard.

Then he sees Oliver, his horns and his gaudy robe, down at the far end of the nave. In the old chorister's gallery, leaning against a wall, looking the other way. What's he doing? Is he taking a leak? Reading something on the wall? What is he doing?

Is he weeping? Is he weeping from homesickness?

I will comfort you.

The Teacher takes a step closer, and says in his gentlest voice, "Oliver. Your mother, your mother's sorry she left you. And she's coming back for you. Today, Oliver. She'll see you today."

The kid doesn't move.

"Oliver."

The Teacher notices that there are no hands emerging from the sleeves of that robe. Makes no sense. A breeze comes into the church, a gust of pure chaos blowing down off the mountain, and it flurries the robe's hem, and the Teacher sees there are no legs either—only sticks.

It's a scarecrow he's talking to.

He draws his pistol and wheels.

No one.

But then a man's voice, a southern drawl, comes from the wrap-around balcony above:

"Go on now. Drop your pistol."

Faces show up at the balcony's stone rail. Human faces, and masks, and cross-eyed shotguns, and rifles.

"Drop the pistol."

But the Teacher *needs* the pistol.

Monkey masks, owl masks, jaguar masks, swine masks. And the

ones without masks, they wear masks as well. The Teacher thinks he needs to kill all the animals in this zoo, before they suffer another moment of the tortures of this masked random world. This loveless havoc! When love is denied! This jumble, this ragtag riot of cross-purposes, I detest this as much as you do, poor creatures.

A shotgun goes off. The shot hits his hand. His HK and three of his fingers skitter across the stones. He flaps his hand contemptuously to dismiss the unruly jolts of pain, and spatters of his own blood fly into his eyes. Spatters. When Love is denied, Pattern shall become Spatters.

Then he sees Annie up in that balcony.

Annie?

Oh Annie, it was so fierce you could not stand to raise your eyes to it! Orion and the Pleiades, Teacher and Juror, the dam-break onslaught of the Tao roaring about our hearts and scouring us clean, scouring us of this filth and shambles, Annie, and if there has been any error, I swear if I have strayed one step from that Path of Scorched and Scoured Love . . .

She raises a pistol, a .38, and takes aim at him.

But before she can fire, Oliver comes running up beside her. With his bull mask pushed to the top of his head, he stands at the railing and looks down. Annie tells him, "Go back! You're not supposed to be here!"

"But so what?" says Oliver. "Here I am."

"Then turn around."

He doesn't, though. He's lost in studying the bleeding man in the courtyard. The Teacher with his missing fingers. The Teacher—who sinks slowly to a squat now, because he wants to gets his good hand closer to the snub-nose .22 that is strapped to his calf.

Annie says it again, much louder. "Turn *around*, Oliver."

Loud enough this time for everyone to hear. Still the boy dawdles.

The Teacher smiles up at him, and thinks, You'll need to overcome that hesitation of yours, Oliver. The dreaminess is fine but you'll also need to learn how to *act*. Before it's too late, before opportunity slips away.

The Teacher thinks, If you'd do what your mother asked you to do, she could kill me—and I know she *would* kill me too, I see it in her eyes—and then the power of the Tao would be scattered to the wind, and you'd still have that little life that you so cherish.

One of the gringos says to Annie, "Put it down now." Must be her old boyfriend, Turtle. "Just put the gun down. We got him. OK? He can't hurt you now."

Annie ignores him. She says, "Oliver, you're *not* going to see this! Turn *around*."

Says Turtle, "Annie, you can't, he's unarmed! It's murder! You can't!"

"But I have to," she says.

"Damn it, Annie, *we've got him! It's over! Put it down!*"

"He'll kill my child."

"He's going to prison!"

"But when he gets out he'll kill my child."

"GIVE ME THE GUN!"

Turtle reaches for it, she steps back.

"I *have* to," she says.

Now the Teacher, in a soft voice—but in these old ruins it carries well—calls to her. He says, "No, listen to the man. Listen to all of us, Annie, because we love you. If the Guatemalans send you to jail, who'll raise Oliver? Think of your child. Forget vengeance, we have no use for vengeance, do we? Think of, think of—"

He reaches into his thoughts for something Lao Tsu might say, a word to bring her to heel, some flash of wit to restore order. But there's so much distraction! This menagerie of animal sentinels. That distant marimba racket. The shimmer of his own hand as it approaches the cuff of his trousers, the hidden .22. That sheer sunlit mountain. The flock of grackles flying against that mountain—

Too much sunny surface-of-things. The Teacher can't quite focus. He falters a moment—and Oliver fills the pause.

Oliver says, "Mom, you're right. Kill him."

Then the boy turns his back to the Teacher.

Oh, but it's too late for you, my child, it's far too late because now Annie is mine again. I have her great gray eyes in the grasp of my own. I have her unruly spirit in thrall, overwhelmed by this voice of mine, this voice that runs so easily along the valley-channel:

"Think of Oliver," he cries. "What happens to Oliver if they send you to a Guatemalan prison?" His fingertips brush the smooth skin of the .22. "How would that serve you? Annie, for the sake of your *child*—"

Perhaps he should not have said that. He sees her arm leap from her pistol's recoil, and a bark emerges from his own throat. He seems to have lost touch with his tongue. He hears a great roaring. He seems in truth to have lost touch with one half of his body, with one half of the world. Some part of him is being flooded with blood. He wants to spit that blood out, but he's not sure if this whirlpool of blood is in his mouth or in the socket of his eye, and he's afraid he might spit out his eye. Confusion is at large. The sky-trail of the Tao grows faint. Less light, less and less. Just barely light enough to see the back of Oliver's glittering robe.

The Teacher wraps his fingers around the snub-nose revolver. He pulls it from its holster. He tries to lift it to level.

But then this church fills up with gunfire.

All this dim draggle-tail barnyard rabble making nonsense out of everything I've been trying to teach them. The owl, shooting at him. The pig, in deepening shadow, shooting at him. The churlish Zeke of a besotted farmer, shooting at him. The monkey, class clown, cutup, shooting at him. Annie, even his Annie, even his stubborn groping grim earthly bride, shooting at him. Annie, Annie, Annie, Annie, daughter of chaos, killing him.

16

a wild honky-tonk Chopsticks

ANNIE waits in the darkness. She has her eyes shut, because these ruins were suddenly much too bright for her, that blossoming of blood dazzled her.

She's waiting for the echo of the shots to fade.

Someone takes the gun from her. She lets them draw it from her fingers like a glove.

In the dark silence, the valley begins to speak up.

Some of the marimbas have quit, but there's one still going, still cranking out a wild honky-tonk Chopsticks. Above her, half a bird-call. Then to the left, a horse sneezing. Dogs barking. No rhyme or reason, no judgment or law or ordering to any of this, just odd fragments of sound, coming to her ears. She reaches. Touches Oliver. Reels him into her. Some shout from the valley and an answering shout from a voice near her. Not Spanish, but that guttural, hive-of-bees local language. Her lips against her child's hair. I *will* open my eyes soon, but first I want to remember how beautiful it was to see that man in shards, to see the whole ex-church stained with his leaping blood, and first I want to listen to the howling dogs of T'ui Cuch. I want to run my fingers along my child's eyelashes and down his temples beside his ears down to his jawline and dipping under it, slipping my fingers along the faint fuzz of Oliver's neck, lightly, so lightly that it tickles, so that he laughs. So that I can hear him laugh, and then right after that hear some more of that disorder of the T'ui Cuch dogs and the T'ui Cuch music, that pure ungovernable ruckus. More of those dogs. More of everything, before I open my eyes. More of this silent weighted sunlight, blood-red on my eyelids. More of the smell of his hair. More of that hive-of-bees shouting. More of that sneezing horse. A moment or two more.

Reading Group Guide

Discussion Questions

1. When Annie Laird agrees to become a juror, it is a decision that irrevocably changes the course of her life. Does she consider its ramifications before she makes it? What other kinds of seemingly routine decisions commonly shape the direction of a person's life? What might the consequences be if those decisions are impulsive?

2. Annie is attracted to the villain when she first sees him on the street as "some beautiful city guy with gothic cheekbones" (p. 31). How long does this attraction last? Do you think the author is commenting on the nature of evil? Can evil be seductive?

3. What do you think of Annie's art, particularly her "grope boxes"? Why do you think her art appeals to the villain?

4. Why is the villain called The Teacher?

5. Annie Laird asks Eddie about The Teacher's motivation for his involvement in the Buffano case, for scaring her, and perhaps for his twisted behavior. She asks, "Why is he doing this?" (p. 198). Why do you think he is?

6. Discuss the way Annie's behavior changes as a result of the threats against those she loves. How do you think you'd react?

7. What do you think of Annie's friend Juliet? Do you think her name was chosen for a reason?

8. One by one the major characters in the book are killed off. Did the death of any of these characters surprise you? Which one(s)? Why?

9. Why do you think boys like Annie's son, Oliver, are attracted to video games, particularly violent ones? Is there anything symbolic about Annie playing the video game with Oliver very early in the book and the life-and-death decisions she is forced to make later in the novel?

10. The page that opens the first section of the book includes the words "varnish, putty, char, clay, moss, fur, wax, turpentine, ink, cedar." What do the words refer to? What is the purpose of the heading or excerpt that accompanies each section of the book?

11. Is this book simply an entertaining thriller or are there layers that go deeper than the suspenseful story? If so, what are they?

12. What is the difference, if any, between the criminals in the story? Are some better than others? Did you like Eddie? Why or why not?

13. Do you think the novel takes a "dark" or "negative" position on romantic love? What happens to each of the couples in the book? What does this say about the various forms of love and attraction?

14. To paraphrase Edmund Burke, all that is necessary for evil to triumph is that good men do nothing. When Annie and her son are writing notes to each other to evade the listening devices, Oliver writes, "Mom we got to fight him." Annie writes back, "If we fight him, he'll kill me." Who do you think is right?

15. Discuss the final section of the book that begins with "a wild honky-tonk Chopsticks." Is the ending satisfying? Is it what you expected?

A Q & A with George Dawes Green

Q.   *What sparked the writing of this novel? Did a real-life incident
     or situation inspire you?*

A.   Thomas de Quincey's thunderous essay "The English Mail Coach"
     tells of an approaching accident that the narrator is powerless to
     avert. I wanted to re-create that atmosphere. So I dreamed up a ter-
     rifying car ride during which a protaganist realizes that the destina-
     tion is the murder of her own child. I filed that away in my head and
     years later, when I came across a small news item about a juror who
     had perhaps been threatened by some mobster, I knew that was the
     story to wrap around this core terror.

Q.   *You are a poet as well as a novelist. In* The Juror, *you create
     two characters who actually write poetry. The hotel night clerk
     describes the first fictional poet, the detective Slavko Czernyk,
     as a "romantic" (p. 273). Eddie says about the second poet, the
     villain: "There was always some question...as to Vincent's san-
     ity" (p. 209). By choosing these characters, are you commenting
     on the nature of the poet, or just poking a little fun?*

A.   Vincent creates worlds, as poets and murderers will. Slavko is a
     failed poet, and thus is deserving of our deepest compassion and
     reverence.

Q. *You also include an excerpt from the poem "The Gulf" by the Nobel Prize–winning poet Derek Walcott. Why did you choose Walcott?*

A. There I *was* poking a little fun. But Derek charged me an arm and a leg for the rights to use that one little stanza, so he had the last laugh.

Q. *It isn't common for an accomplished poet to also write genre novels, and vice versa. Yet you have done both. Are the experiences of writing in each genre the same or different? How does your use of language as a poet influence your style as a novelist?*

A. As Cheever said of novels versus short stories, they are two distinct disciplines—utterly dissimilar. One doesn't seem to help with the other.

Q. *You also associate the villain with Taoism and refer to specific aphorisms by Lao Tzu. Can you share with readers why you included the Tao?*

A. Because Lao Tzu's meaning is so difficult to plumb, he's always been beloved by charlatans. Such as Vincent.

Q. *Protagonist Annie Laird is a talented artist who has to work at data entry to support herself and her son. Is this a comment on the artist's struggles in contemporary society?*

A. Not a "comment" but it is how things work.

Q. *Like the character Turtle, you spent time in Guatemala. Are there any parallels between you and that character? When the heroine Annie escapes with her son, she goes there. How did your personal experience influence that plot twist?*

A. She wanted to get as far from her tormentor as possible—to the very end of the earth—and I recalled the Cuchumatanes Mountains, which perfectly fit that description.

Q. *There are many kinds of criminals in* The Juror, *from figures in organized crime and corrupt officials to the novel's villain Vincent/Zach/Eben/Ian. Are any of them "evil"? Is crime boss Boffano? Is Vincent? Would you talk a bit about your concept of evil?*

A. The word has no meaning to me. I suppose that should worry me.

Q. *Will you share some of your writing life with us? Do you write daily? Do you have a routine? Do have a specific place to write?*

A. I wrote most of *The Juror* in a one-room schoolhouse in the Pennsylvania Mountains, in winter, with two-foot snowdrifts all around. I was alone. At night I would slog through the snow and shine my flashlight at deer in the meadow, and pick up the slow-gliding headlights of their eyes. All of them moving away from me. Then I'd go back to the schoolhouse and work some more. Vincent got into my head and loosened the hinges. I was having an affair with a beautiful girl I'd met at a bar in town (Stroudsburg, Pa.); she was also sleeping with her father. I think if I'd stayed out there much longer I'd have lost my mind. Maybe I did anyway.

Q. *How do you go about developing a story? How carefully do you plot your novel before you write it?*

A. All the pieces of a thriller have to fit seamlessly, and should be weighed and measured scrupulously before any assembly is undertaken.

Q. *Do you base characters on real people?*

A. On myself mostly, although the characters of Vincent and Annie were informed by people close to me. But when the writing begins, all personas must say good-bye to their models and board the train and make the journey by themselves.

Q. *Discuss your choice of a female protagonist. Do you feel a man writing about a woman's emotions and mental state faces any special challenges in making them seem authentic?*

A. Creating any character is impossible. To me "authentic" always signifies really good sleight-of-hand. Woman, monster, child—I do the best I can.

Q. *How important is storytelling for a society? Would you talk about your founding of The Moth?*

A. The art of the raconteur is a beautiful thing—there's its prime importance. It may have some kind of therapeutic or societal value, but I'm mostly interested in the beauty. So far as I know, there had never in history been a public forum for the kinds of stories we celebrate at The Moth—unscripted, personal, "kitchen" stories. So I created one—with the help of a thousand friends and, in particular, Joey Xanders and Lea Thau—and now we're traveling all over the world and we're downloaded by millions and the art of the raconteur seems to be exploding. As it should. If you haven't been to a Moth, please go—the evenings can be rapturous.

Q. The Juror *was your second novel and was tremendously successful. Your first book (*The Caveman's Valentine*) won an Edgar Award. Then over a decade passed when no novels appeared. Now you have a third book,* Ravens. *Why did you take a hiatus after* The Juror *and why did you return to novel writing?*

A. The years just kind of got away from me.

Q. The Juror *became a Hollywood movie. Would you tell us something of your experience and the process through which your novel was transformed into a film?*

A. The studios were captivated by a certain strain in the novel, the core story, which they seemed to find compelling. The rest they jettisoned. And naturally, it was "the rest"—the other strains, the surrounding layers—that I most cherished. It's very tough to make novelists happy. But we're paid handsomely so no whining.

Q. *Are you currently working on another novel?*

A. I am, and I've sworn to deliver it soon, and my amazing, beautiful, patient, and gracious editor has threatened to put me in irons if I don't.

Please turn this page
for a preview of the long-awaited new novel

BY GEORGE DAWES GREEN

RAVENS

Available in hardcover

WEDNESDAY

Romeo was driving down from the Blue Ridge Mountains in the baffling twilight, going too fast, when a raccoon or possum ran in front of the car. The impact was disturbingly gentle. No thud—just a soft *unzipping*, beneath the chassis. Still, it tore at Romeo's heart. He braked and pulled over.

Shaw awoke. "What's wrong?"

"Hit something," said Romeo, and he got out and started walking back up I-77, hunting for the carcass. Shaw followed him. A tractor-trailer bore down on them with a shudder and the long plunging chord of its passing. Then the night got quiet. They could hear their own footsteps. Cicadas, and a sliver of far-off honkytonk music. "God," said Shaw. "This is it. We're really in the *South.*"

But they found no trace of the animal.

They walked quite a ways. They waited for headlights so they could scan up and down the highway. They backtracked and searched along the shoulder. Nothing—not so much as a bloodstain. Finally Romeo just stood there, watching the fireflies rise and fall.

"Hey," said Shaw, "I bet your friend got lucky."

"Uh-uh. I hit it."

"Well maybe it was like a sacrifice." Playfulness in Shaw's tone. "Maybe it just wanted us to have a propitious journey."

When they got back to the Tercel Shaw said he was wide awake and could he drive? That was fine with Romeo. He got in on the passenger side, and they descended into the North Carolina piedmont. His ears popped; the air grew humid. He tilted his seat all the way back and looked up at the moon as it shredded in the pines. Somewhere after Elkin, NC, he let his eyes slip shut for just a second—and then the highway started to curve beneath him, and he felt himself spiraling slowly downward, into a bottomless slumber.

Tara kept away from the house on Wednesday nights.

Wednesday nights were jackpot nights. Mom would start drinking early. Pour herself a g&t in a lowball glass; then fan out all her lottery tickets on the coffee table and gaze lovingly at them, and touch them one by one and wonder which was going to be *the* one. The TV would be on but Mom would disregard it. All her thoughts on the good life to come. Yachts, spas in Arizona, blazing white villages in Greece, the unquenchable envy of her friends. She'd finish her first drink and fix herself another. Her boy Jase—Tara's little brother—would put his head in her lap while he played with his Micro. She'd tousle his hair. She'd swirl the ice in her drink. At some point the colors of the dying day, and the TV colors, and all the colors of her life, would begin to seem extra-vivid, even gorgeous, and she'd tell herself she was the blessedest woman in the world, and pick up her cell phone and text her daughter:

```
I know we win tonite!!
```

Or:

```
I need u!! Tara baby!! My good luck charm!!
Where are u? Come home!!
```

They were siren calls though, Tara knew. She had to be deaf to them. Study late at the library, catch a movie, hang out with Clio at the mall—just keep clear of the house till the jackpot was done and Dad would come home to take the brunt of Mom's drunken post-drawing tirade. By midnight Mom would have worn herself out with rage and grief, and she'd have passed out, and the coast would be clear.

But on this particular Wednesday, Tara had made a blunder. She'd left her botany textbook, with all the handouts, in her bedroom. She'd done this in the morning but she didn't realize it till 7:00 p.m., after her organic chemistry class, when she checked her locker and saw that the book wasn't there.

She had a quiz tomorrow. She hadn't even *looked* at that stuff.

She thought of calling Dad. Maybe he could sneak the book out to her. But no, it was too late. He'd be on his way to church by now, his Lions of Judah meeting. Maybe Jase? No, Jase would tip Mom off; Jase was in Mom's pocket.

No. What I have to do, Tara thought, is just go back there and be really docile and *don't* let Mom draw me into a fight, whatever she says don't fight back—and first chance I get I'll slip away to my room before the drawing, before she blows up.

Tara went to the parking lot and got in her battered Geo, and left the campus of the Coastal Georgia Community College. Fourth Street to Robin Road to Redwood Road: streets she despised. She hated their dull names and their blank lawns and their rows of squat brick ranch houses. Hers was the squattest and brickest of all, on a street called Oriole Road. When she got there, she slowed the car to a crawl, and looked in through the living room window. Mom, the TV. The painting of Don Quixote tilting at windmills. The wooden shelf of Dad's # 3 Chevy models, and Mom's Hummels. Jase's feet stuck out at the end of the couch. Everything that Tara despised about her home was glowing and warm-looking like an advertisement for low mortgage rates or pest control, and such a depressing show she had to call Clio and tell her about it.

"I'm spying on my own house."

Said Clio, "*That's* kind of perverted."

"It's a really ugly house."

"I know."

"I can see my brother's little marinated pigs' feet."

"OK."

"But I have to see how drunk Mom is."

"How drunk is she?"

"That's the problem, I can't tell. I can't see her hands. I have to see how she's holding her glass. If she's swirling her glass with her pinky out, then I'm already in deep shit."

"Are you going in there?"

"I have to."

"But isn't this your Mom's freak-out night?"

"Uh-huh."

"So what are you *doing* there? Come over to Headquarters. You know who's coming? That Kings of Unsnap guy. Jonah. The one who wants to do you."

"You told me that, Clio."

"So come let him do you."

"I got a botany quiz in the morning."

"Oh God. You're such a boring geek."

"Why don't *you* do him?"

"OK," said Clio. "You talked me into it."

"You're such a whoring slut."

"I know. Hey I gotta go. If your Mom does something interesting, like touching your little brother's weewee or something, let me know."

"I'll send you the pics," said Tara. "You can post them." She hung up, and sighed, and pulled into the carport.

As soon as she stepped into the living room, Mom was at her: "Where were *you*?" Tara consulted the lowball glass and saw that the swirling was quick and syncopated, with the pinky fully extended, which presaged a grim night.

"I was in class."

"You should call me when you're gonna be this late."

Not late, Tara thought, but drop it.

Mom kept pressing. "Which class was it?"

"Um. Organic chemistry."

"Why you taking *that*?"

Leave it alone. The only goal is freedom. "I don't know, I guess it's some kind of a requirement."

"But if you're only gonna be a goddamn *whatever*—why do they make you take organic chemistry?"

Tara shrugged.

Said Mom, "They want all our money and what they teach you is worthless."

Hard to let that pass. Inasmuch as Mom contributed not a cent to her tuition—inasmuch as every penny came from Tara's job at the bank plus help from her grandmother Nell plus a small scholarship, and all she got from her parents was room and board for which she paid $450 a month so that wasn't a gift either—it was a struggle not to snap back at her. But what good would that do? Remember, all you want is to get to your room. Remember, this woman is the same birdnecked alien you were just watching through the living room window a moment ago. Pretend there's no family connection, that you're invisible and you can slip away unnoticed at any time—

"Wait. Sit for a minute. The drawing's coming up."

"Got a quiz tomorrow, Mom. So I should probably—"

"You know what it's worth this time?"

Tara shook her head.

"You're kidding me," said Mom. "You really don't know?"

"I really don't."

"Three hundred and eighteen million dollars."

"Wow."

The sum touched Tara's life in no meaningful way, but she thought if she showed sufficient awe maybe Mom would release her.

"Though if you take the lump sum," said Mom, "then after you pay your taxes, you'd only have a hundred some million."

"Oh."

"Like a hundred twenty-odd. Hardly worth bothering, right? You mind freshening this for me? So I won't disturb the Little Prince here?"

Mom swirled her glass.

On the TV was *Nip/Tuck*, which wasn't appropriate for ten-year-old Jase but then he wasn't watching it anyway. He was playing *Revenant* on his Micro. Oblivious as ever—and Tara was happy to ignore him back. She carried Mom's glass to the kitchen, filled it with ice and Bombay and tonic, cut a thin half-wheel of lime and placed it festively. Be solicitous, servile. Try to soften her. Don't resist in any way.

But when she returned, Mom was holding up a thin windowed envelope, a bill from some credit card company, and demanding: "Know how I got this? Came right to the office. *Angela* gave it to me. I didn't even know this bill existed. It's for seven hundred dollars. Your father never *mentioned* it."

What would be the least resistant reply possible? Tara tried, "That's awful, Mom."

"Awful? It's the most humiliating thing that can ever happen to *anyone. Anyone. Ever.* Of course your father isn't worried. Your father thinks we'll be fine."

"Well, won't we?"

Oh, that was dumb. That was way too cheerful. Mom pounced. "You don't get it *at all*, do you? They're gonna *foreclose*. They're gonna take our *house*. They're gonna take it out from under our feet and take the damn Liberty with it. You're gonna have to leave school. I'm sorry, cupcake. You're gonna have to start producing some *income*."

"Mom, I'm a little tired. Would you mind if I—"

"Do you think I'm *not* tired? I am so *damn* tired of being this poor and your father in total denial and you kids thinking this is some kind of bad dream we're gonna wake up from! We're gonna lose *everything*, do you not get it? This boat is *sinking*. Nobody's gonna bail *us* out. The boat is going down! I mean, baby, sugarcake, you're gonna have to start *swimming*. You're gonna—"

But then came a fanfare on the TV, and instantly Mom left off. She gave Jase a little swat and he hustled out of her way, and she leaned forward to check her flotilla of tickets.

"And now," said a somber announcer, "here's tonight's drawing for the Max-a-Million jackpot. Tonight's jackpot is worth... three hundred and eighteen *milly-on* dollars."

No one onscreen. Just the voice of that undertaker. And a hopper in the shape of a funeral urn, full of lightly waltzing plastic balls. One of them flew up suddenly on a puff of air and rolled down a serpentine ramp and posed itself before the camera.

"The first number is...tuh-*wenty*-seven."

Mom murmured, "Uh-huh. Got that here." Trying for indifference. But her eyes were full of eagerness.

Tara quietly cheated a few steps toward the hall.

"The next number is forty-two."

"Well I do have *that*," said Mom.

And Tara made her move. Melted silkily away while Mom was too dazzled by the numbers to notice.

In her room, Tara shut the door and sat at the laptop on her desk. Clio had just posted:

u still "studying" bitch? do u think jonah wrights sperm has
beneficial properties of healing? wil it help u lose pounds
from hips waist and thighs? he wasn't at headquarters tho just

creepy seth from jax. I h8 the wick. die if I dont getout of the wick.

Tara wrote back:

Havent started yet. Caught by Mom. She's watching the drawing. In 20 seconds she'l lose and go skitzo.

And right on time: Mom's hell-on-the-loose shriek from the living room. Worse even than usual. Then: "TARA! TA-*RA*!"

Tara typed brb and opened the door. "Yes?"

"*TARA!*"

Particularly anguished tonight. Tara returned to the living room to find her on her knees before the TV, with Jase cowering in the corner. Mom had utterly lost it. Her mouth was open and she was holding up one of her tickets and tears were pouring down her cheeks, and this wasn't just another drunken display of self-pity: there was true fear. "GRACE OF GOD!" she cried. As though she were beholding His face at that very moment. She clutched the ticket in her fist and rocked back and forth. "GRACE OF GOD! GRACE OF GOD! GRACE OF GOD!"

GEORGE DAWES GREEN is a highly acclaimed novelist and poet and the founder of the not-for-profit storytelling organization, The Moth. He currently divides his time between Georgia and New York.